F
L96   Ludwig, Myles Eric.
             Golem, a hero for our
       time.

DATE | ISSUED TO

F
L96   Ludwig, Myles Eric.
             Golem, a hero for our
       time.

Temple Israel Library
Minneapolis, Minn.

Please sign your full name on the above card.

Return books promptly to the Library or Temple Office.

Fines will be charged for overdue books or for damage or loss of same.

GOLEM

Myles Eric Ludwig

GOLEM

A HERO FOR OUR TIME

WEYBRIGHT AND TALLEY

NEW YORK

For my family and for the
people who have always
lived on the hill.

In the first week
           of their life
           male jews
           are crucified

Jews
      who
      go to
      no
      synagogue
      have
      faces
      which
      change
      all
      the time

from DEATH FOR THE LADIES AND OTHER DISASTERS
by Norman Mailer

THE FIRST BOOK

"For behold, the day cometh, it burneth as a furnace. . . ." *Mal. 3:19*

I

1   A figure, surrounded by himself, standing next to the post which bears a sign forbidding parking. The tips of his should-have-been-a-piano-player's fingers hanging down far below where the bottom of the C used to be on his stretched-out high school lettersweater (monogrammed for basketball, initialed for reaching higher than anyone else) which had been worn nearly every day and which was now a camphorous bundle protecting a plastic and brass trophy deep within a trunk—a trunk which had waited beneath many bottom bunks in many camp cabins and which now contained the artifacts of his adolescence—a trunk which was now tagged and shelved in some warehouse in New Jersey alongside, above, and beneath hundreds of other such containers of lives.

A figure in a very conscious pose. A figure which had always been conscious of its poses; sometimes, too conscious of its position in the mise-en-scène. A figure in the sun, your orphan with his gun, leaning against the post like a long shot of the sensitive young man, nonchalantly awaiting the death of his ideals.

3

Come on, Time. Mellow me, baby.

Inside the synagogue—though here it is called a Temple and tries hard, very hard to live up to its name—the congregation is involved in Yizkor, the memorial service. Each member, each organ standing and sitting at Rabbi Lowe's unspoken, lifted or lowered indexfinger command. Each trying, without success, to visualize the faces, never the bodies but at least the faces of those for whom, or rather because of whom, they are praying.

Outside, their children—traditionally excluded from this service for fear their presence might be mistaken as an omen or the unconscious enactment of a wish—their children, some with cigars and others with sticks, run through the small park across the street and talk of their parents in the past tense.

Thus, the unbroken generational line.

In the park, the air is filled with a kind of hesitant defiance. Conversations are mundane but they are carried on with eyes lowered so that the sight of the domed building across the street might not interrupt the flow of stomach ulcers and business problems. A few people smoke, but not many. For most, standing outside is signal enough. Their clothing is new, purchased especially for these days. So new that jacket collars stand away from freshly barbered necks and many belts of alligator conceal many size 40 labels which were unremoved by the dressers in their haste to be on time—on whatever Time they had set for their appearance. Few women are in this company; some are home from college, others are of the type that are rumored to have skeletons of Hanukkah bushes in their dark closets. The other women, those whose gray hair is now or will be a fashionable shade of television blue, remain inside—occupying, even guarding the ticketed pews against the possibility of any Wandering Jews.

To Golem (for he is the conscious figure or the figure of consciousness) the air is delicious. He opens his mouth and tastes the air; he inhales it deeply. It is not clean and yet its brand of tarnishment (hopelessness plated with a thin layer of cynicism) is familiar to him and infinitely preferable to that brand (hopelessness layered with an epoxical compound of complacency and fear) which he has been ingesting for the last few months in Georgia.

What is he doing outside?

4

For him, the Yizkor is the beginning of a journey, though he has just ended one to get to this place, and he is about to enter the synagogue to join his mother, who does not expect him, in a ritualized remembrance of his father.

He turns from the park and walks up the stone steps which he remembers once served as canvas for anti-Semitic artists, and enters the heavily, baroquely carved doorway. The shammes, recognizing him as an old Bar Mitzvah boy, hands him a sidur and directs him to a bin which contains white for the holy-day yarmulkes. He finds one which he estimates to be his size and sets it on the back of his head. He decides that it is too small and so he discards it, rummaging through the satiny hats until he finds another for which he settles. He removes a talis from a stand and carelessly throws it over his shoulders, feeling guilty and sad now as he always has because he had never memorized the blessing which is to be spoken before the fringed garment can grace one's body. He looks up and sees the shammes waiting for him. He follows the man who, after the congregation has been seated, will lead Golem to a seat beside his mother. Golem strikes what he considers to be a religious pose and is ready.

DISSOLVE TO:

II

2   "I feel like I'm in a goddamned movie," said Golem to his wife who sat crosslegged, naked and crying, on the farthest corner of the bed like a color photo out of a future *National Geographic* article on some remnant species of Western Civilization. "What am I supposed to do? You keep asking me the same questions. I keep giving you the same answers," he said, now raising his voice above the level of an on-the-bed whisper, past the normal bedroom squabble point, and dangerously close to a very definite after-supper, kitchen shout.

     And Anna, the Wife, concentrating on her crying, trying very hard to keep it going for at least another ten minutes, up to the point at which Golem would finally say Christ, I'm Sorry —It's ALL MY FAULT and take her around her not so frail shoulders, began to get concerned about the very definite possibility, the probability that this argument would, as most of the others had, penetrate the paper towel walls of the Married Students' Apartment in which they lived and join the others on that long reel of tape which the people in the next Married Students' Apartment kept as evidence. But she kept crying, knowing that, if she were to stop now, she would definitely lose. What?

"I didn't mean to yell," said Golem, bringing his voice back down to the bedroom squabble level. "But you are really exhausting my patience."

Sob, Sob, Sigh. Was the answer from the corner of the bed.

The bell rang.

All right, said Golem to himself who was the only one listening in the first place. And said it very loudly. All right. She'll keep this up for another ten minutes and then I'll apologize and we'll cuddle up and go to bed carefully, promising ourselves that we'll wake up cheerful in the morning. It's ten of one now which means we won't get to sleep till one-twenty and I've got to be up by eight, make that eight-fifteen, to make my nine o'clock. This gives me, let's see, one-twenty or one-thirty from eight-fifteen, that's roughly seven hours and fifteen minutes to sleep. To be alone. I suppose that's enough. OK, I'll let her keep it up for another ten minutes. If it was an hour earlier, I wouldn't apologize.

"We've been married for four years. Four fucking years! And we're still having the same arguments. I'm not wrong. I may be wrong other times, but I'm not wrong about this. Can't you do what I ask? Is it too much for you? It can't be, for chrissakes. I'm not asking you to do anything that any other Wife doesn't do."

Sob. Sob. "I know, but . . ."

"Yes, but. Yes, but. Shit, I don't want to play that game at one o'clock in the morning."

Or any other game, thought Golem. Mostly, he was not mad at Her. He was mad at himself and at something nebulously called the Situation (he had read that somewhere). He didn't like it at all when his defenses intersected her defenses until the conversation formed an ellipse called an Argument which seemed to go on by itself, making both of them nothing more than semi-animate objects, loudspeakers for the dialectics of the Situation. He'd been tuned into that before, but he'd never been able to articulate it to himself as well. Still, however, though he saw it coming and realized when he was into it, he didn't quite know

7

how to extricate himself. He was certain that she would regard his stopping the Argument as some rude and arbitrary act. So he continued. Taking out his anger for continuing on Her.

The ten minutes went by quickly and, precisely at one, like the mouse running down, Golem shut up and took his Wife around her not so frail shoulders. She continued to whimper for about thirty more seconds and then they made their peace.

Eventually, they both shut off the lights on either side of their bed and rested in the darkness.

What a bastard I am, thought Golem before he went, not drifted, to sleep. He did not know what She thought, but he hoped it was the same thing.

3   Over a cup of coffee and a toasted cheese danish whose center of yellow is still frozen as if in resistance to the brown 'n' serve world into which it had been thrust, nearly unprepared, after his nine o'clock seminar on Psychoanalysis and Literature, Golem assays himself. What? Twenty-eight next November? Tall and thin and pushing on toward his Ph.D. with only two more years left in which to write his thesis, the topic of which has become seasonal. Married. Married after having slept with, let's see —there comes a time in every man's life when he must, no faking now, count up the number of women with whom he has had intercourse—four or five, make that four before marriage and four afterward or, rather (don't want to be premature), during. Like candles on an Anniversary Cake, one for each year of marriage. Four Fucking Years. Yes, a good head for nuance. What else? Oh yes. There are other things. A Live Mother, a Dead Father. All the rest of that stuff.

Golem often talked to himself in this way. Is that unusual he asked himself—ambivalent about what he wanted the answer to be. Nah, everybody does it. Well (crap) that's good!

What is this, an interior dialogue or a monologue?

Interruption.

Along comes Cohen. Marvin Cohen, frustrated Psych-Prof, withering away in the labyrinthian underground of that building erected for the teaching of English (Glory be thy name) where he writes tortured little stories of Bar Mitzvah eve epiphanies to be published in tortured Little Magazines—thus earning for himself the somewhat bewildering title of Resident Jewish Writer. A title which Cohen often attenuated in Gentile (or Gentiler) company by saying, "Being Jewish is just a shtick." The nuance on that one bounces off the walls like a squash ball.

"Hello, Marv. Heard any good anti-Semitic jokes lately?" asked Golem, half expecting to be rewarded with a listen, did you hear the one about the . . .

Cohen smirked and sat down across from Golem, putting his overflowing coffee cup in front of him so as not to miss it when he wanted it. "How's Anna?"

Ever since he had read *Herzog,* Golem had been certain that Cohen had more than a how's she feeling interest in his wife. Not that it bothered him in the usual manner because he knew that Cohen had read the book and, in fact, had worshiped the book and it was not at all beyond him to attempt to pattern this period in his life after Valentine (in fact, he had been finagling for a late-nite talk show on the local radio station). However, Golem never let on that he had read the book—even steered away from conversations about it with an I don't know if I'm ready for it yet ploy—and so he was able to observe Cohen's actions with a kind of bemusement (funny word, that). He had not relayed his observations to Anna because she seemed to enjoy Cohen's company —which bothered him, he had to admit.

Golem felt he could break the whole thing open by casually calling Cohen Val at the right moment and, many times, he had a very strong urge to do just that. Once, at a large party to which Cohen had been invited as a kind of representative of the Understanding Establishment, Golem, caught in a spaced-out miasma of marijuanamphetamine, stood by a refrigerator for what seemed like thirty-six days on the inside and watched, no stared as if his eyes were attached by rubber bands to the buttons of Cohen's elbow-patched corduroy jacket (even his clothing was redundant) while the latter cornered his wife in a conversation or conversed his wife into a corner. Unable to resist any longer, Golem had said (rather quietly, he later thought and reproached himself for this small cowardice), "Hey, Val."

But no one had heard him. Or, had they?

"She's fine. Working on anything new?"

"Yeah, a story. But it's a bitch."

"Can't get hold of the Goddess, eh?"

Cohen laughed in order that Golem might know that he recognized the allusion. "Reading anything good lately?"

"Oh, I've been looking through the Talmud."

Cohen laughed again but, this time, there was an edge of uncertainty in his voice. He bided his time by taking a long drink of coffee, waiting for Golem to make a qualifying remark. But it did not come. Finally. "Listen, Osterman's having a party on Saturday night. Why don't you and Anna come over?"

"He's living in the country, isn't he?"

"Yeah, I'll give you the directions."

Cohen took a thick black fountain pen, one which Golem had seen advertised for something like thirty-three dollars and had always wondered who, besides a possible UN diplomat, might invest that much money in a fountain pen, out of his jacket pocket and carefully drew off the cover. He pulled a napkin out of the dispenser and began to create a map.

Golem watched as the black lines began to appear on the stippled surface of the napkin. Here was an arrow, there was a box which, in Cohen's mind, represented a gas station and, at the end of an arbitrarily curved road, was a larger box marked with an O. "His name's on the mailbox," said Cohen, covering up the pen and clipping it back to the inside of his jacket. "Think you'll have any trouble?"

"No. I'll find it. Thanks. I've got to split now, though. Anna's working today and I've got to take the meat out of the freezer precisely at twelve or it'll be frozen pizza for dinner. Maybe we'll see you Saturday."

"Try to make it. Everyone'll be there."

Golem picked up his books and his newspaper and walked away from the table, not looking back for fear of turning into a pillar of salt.

4   Part of their historic collection of dishes (half from his family and half from hers—married four years, they still had not been able to agree on a pattern), painted with the remains of last

night's dinner, was arranged like a bunch of jacks in the kitchen sink. Golem looked at the mess for a moment, half hearing the dishes calling out to him, begging to be washed clean and set out to dry in the rubber rack. Then he took the meat out of the freezer and unwrapped its aluminumfoil skin, setting it out on the plasticized table to thaw. He also took out a bottle of inexpensive wine ("Frankly, it's cheap," he used to say at parties, "but I find it to be an inoffensive wine") from the refrigerator and, not finding a clean glass in the house, he poured several inches into a purple plastic cup which rested in a niche in their bathroom.

Back in the kitchen.

He made himself a peanut butter and jelly sandwich on SUPREMES WHITE BREAD (there's your hip black power for you) and sat down in the livingroom to eat and watch *Supermarket Sweep* on their small television set.

Golem was addicted to this program. Here was a microcosm of American life. . . . The American Way of Life. Three perky-faced housewives, their suburban short hair all tipped and frosted like their insides, stood excitedly at three cash registers in the giant, squareblock SaFood Supermarket in Teaneck, New Jersey . . . scenic Teaneck, of course. Normally, the housewives and cash registers were natural enemies, each fighting the weekly battle for King of the Mountain. But, like those other two natural enemies, the Tiger and the Horse, when properly trained and displayed in the vibrant atmosphere of the Circus, both began to work together to provide entertainment for the paying customers. Into this strange relationship between Woman and Machine, the producers of the program (for the safety of his own ironic sense, Golem attributed an awareness to them which he was nearly certain that they did not in fact possess) had inserted the Husband, that figure who normally portrays the role of God, silently neutral in the battle, but whose unspoken demands and preferences were the terrain on which the engagement was fought. Not only had they *inserted* him, but they had *inverted* him as well. Now, God was chained to the housewife's shopping cart, at the mercy of both the mechanized receptacle and the encouraging shrieks of his Shekinnah to grab as many five-pound salamis as possible in anywhere from one to two minutes.

11

The men stood beside their women, trying to look at their toes as their bellies drooped beneath the cheap-looking golf shirts (something for the men in the audience, no doubt; Golem could remember when they were forced into the ignominy of T shirts. Wearing their underwear *on* television!) on which was emblazoned the crest of the program, placed, conveniently, just above the heart. One, on the right side of his shirt, sported a stylized crown and the word CHAMP—ah, the stuffings that dreams are made of.

At a signal from the sunlamped announcer, the men darted through the aisles, pushing their carts before them, keeping a sharp eye peeled for the Bonus Prizes strategically placed among the ordinary canned goods and vegetables—green vegetables, heading directly for the Meat Counter. One could imagine a pre-broadcast huddle between husband and wife. The Team.

He: **Let's not waste any time with the little crap. Where's the real money in the store?**
She: **It's a tossup between Meat and Gourmet Foods.**
He: **OK, honey. I'll go for the MEAT.**
She: **OK, honey. You go for the MEAT. And try to get me a good cut of veal, will you?**

Not knowing a good cut of veal from the high-priced spread, he piled his cart, or rather, Her Cart, high with anything that looked big and therefore expensive; huge salamis (their obvious phallicness attracted him first), blanched and pebbly chickens (which he hated but which looked larger than an armful of luncheon loafs), giant Canned Hams, not knowing, not caring how they were cured or whether they were, in fact, cured or if, indeed, they still carried the disease and then, his patience exhausted . . . on to Gourmet Foods, stopping at Frozen Foods to shovel in seventeen boxes of DeLite Fish Sticks and two handloads of an off-brand TV Dinner which he figured he could always feed to the dog (oh America), resting a second at the canned soup shelf, but only long enough to sweep half a shelf full of umpteen varieties into his basket of goodies, ignoring Paper Goods & Picnic Needs, plunging through Pies & Cakes for a quick stack of, can it be, yes it is, Apple Pies, yes and three Coffee Cakes, hefting two sacks of flour at the end of the line and then, exchanging a full cart for an empty one, he turns the corner and comes to a dead stop in front of Gourmet Foods.

Now wait a minute.

What the hell is this, he says to himself. What the hell do you do with these things, eat 'em or what? Hell, he says, the money's here is what the little woman said. Hell, it ought to be. All those taxes I'm payin' to keep these ferin countries alive so's they can send us this crazy stuff. Damn right the money's here, don't I know it, yessir. Screw the Federal Government. Screw Foreign Aid. Screw the Underdeveloped Nations. What them people need is a job and a little responsibility. Gourmet Foods is nothing but a commy plot.

So.

And, looking over his shoulder to tell a technician who is sweeping a cable toward him to get the fuck out of the way (a damn good thing the producers ordered no close shots of faces), he gives the Gourmet Foods a great American Bear Hug and thirty-five little boxes and cans and bottles bearing names in languages which he could not identify come cascading into the cart.

That'll teach those little bastards!

Then, a quick rush to the Checkout Counter before his Time is up and a congratulatory hug from his wife who, if her husband has been fast enough and greedy enough, will get to stand by the side of the CHAMP next week at the giant, squareblock SaFood Supermarket in Hackensack, New Jersey . . . scenic Hackensack, of course.

Golem was convulsed with laughter. He choked on his meager sandwich and washed the lumpy bread down with large gulps of wine.

After *Supermarket Sweep* came the Midday News and Golem was not interested in what the rest of the world was doing for lunch. He had enough catastrophies in his own house; he didn't need plane crashes with two survivors—though he did wonder how and what those two felt. He didn't need the bumbling of the government; he didn't need his indignation at the bumbling of the government. If so many people on the block were idiots and so many people in the town were idiots and, if one carried the line

13

far enough, it was idiotic to expect the people who ran the whole mishmash not to be idiots of a similar stripe—where did he get that line from? Golem figured that his being mad at the dry-cleaner for starching his shirts was representative of his being mad at the rest of the idiots. Why bother to find out whose shirts the President was starching?

So, having nothing more to do than to work on his thesis, Golem turned off the tube and went back into the kitchen where he slid his dishes into the kitchen sink—expecting a metaphor, maybe?—and then he went into the Library which did double duty as the bathroom and perused his five-foot shelf of dirty books. He examined the titles printed in large type on the spine of each paperback and tried to remember the sexy part of each book.

What was he looking for today? Leather-Fetish-Sado-masochism? Straight Screwing? A little animal stuff or some of the old Under the Influence of an Evil Drug routine? If a title did not immediately call forth a remembrance from that vast Dewey Decimal System in his mind, he pulled the book out a little and checked its cover. Here were the girls with forty-two inch chests that he had dreamed of as a junior high schooler. That's boobs! they used to say. Here were the girls with thighs like redwoods that wrapped themselves around your back and pulled you tight because they just couldn't get enough of you. Here they were. But only here. The real forty-two-inchers had wax faces that seemed to peel around the edges—near the hairline and the ears—or they made themselves look ugly and crossed their arms in front of their chests and talked incessantly at cocktail parties about how they wanted someone to love them for themselves instead of for their appendages.

Finally, he chose three titles; two lesbians and a high school sex club. When it came down to it, Golem's idea of sexy heaven was probably to watch two fifteen-year-old chicks give each other a bath and then maybe, just maybe, to watch some hairy but handsome thirty-seven-year-old child-molester whip the shit out of their nubile bodies. Yeah, he dug the youth. But nobody's perfect.

So he took his three books into the bedroom, flopped down on the unmade bed, pulled off his pants and his undershorts (which he noticed were torn) and began to read.

5   From an entry in a five-year diary that Golem kept for six weeks:

Dear Diary,
Masturbating is my way of getting back at the system. The act of creation is the same, metaphysically speaking, whether you are creating a child or a work of art; it all comes from fucking. By jerking off and letting my semen—I am tempted to say seed but I will forswear—spurt out indiscriminately, I am exorcizing my need to create something specific. Getting rid of my desire to be somebody, to do something. . . . I am something, a nonspecific orgasm. But it bothers me the way I look after I jerk off. My post-orgasmic appearance is crappy. Yesterday, after I jerked off in the bathroom, I jumped up and looked in the mirror, freezing my face, expecting to find an Exultant Being. Well, dear diary, what I saw—accounting for the distortion of the Woolworth's mirror—was a wide-eyed, tongue hanging out of the side of a slack-jawed, open-mouthed caricature of a drooling idiot. Wow! I am thinking of tapering off. But, then again, since I am such a good jerk-off artist, I cannot really deny the call of my Muse. It's the only one I got.
Why do we always hold our breath when we come?
Are we trying to die?
Answer this question tomorrow.

6   From another entry:

Dear Diary,
I am not garbage and I will neither be thrown away nor incinerated.

7   Anna came home and found him, eyes closed, on the bed, one hand on his groin, the other keeping his place in the book he had been using. It was not the first time she had found him this way. And she did what she had done before. She went out of the apartment and then walked back in again, slamming the door shut and calling out, "David, are you home?"

Golem, who had not been asleep, but had only been pretending as he had done several times before when Anna had come home after his afternoon nap—always testing her reflexes, always hoping that she would walk in and replace his hand with her lips —jumped up, pulled his pants up, and tiptoed to the bathroom with his reference books.

"Yes, I'm in the bathroom."

8   Shall we take a tour of Golem's medicine chest?
Forget it.

9   Golem flushed the toilet and the sound filled the house.
He walked into the bedroom and found Anna naked, between
changes of identity. "Hi, how was work?" he asked as he bent
down and planted, no, stuck, a kiss on her right buttock.

She moved away from him quickly and he was left
squatting with his lips puckered.

"The same." She enveloped herself in a kimono that
Golem had bought for her in a large Japanese department store in
New York. It had a fire-breathing dragon embroidered on its
back and Golem had been disappointed when, after taking the
garment out of its plastic bag, he did not find the words SEOUL,
KOREA, FIRST INF. like on those acetate jackets that all
sisters of Servicemen used to wear in the fifties. "Work is always
the same."

"You didn't check out any interesting books today? No
first editions? Nobody asked you for the stuff in the secret cabinet,
the stuff the library wouldn't admit to having?"

"I never look at the books. I just stamp them."

"You don't look at the titles? You don't wonder what
the guy who's checking it out is going to think of it? Or how he's
going to read it? Will he underline important, no, significant,
passages with a yellow felt pen or will he turn down the corner
of the whole page? You can tell a lot about a guy from the way
he marks significant things, you know."

"Come on, David. I just stamp them."

"You have no poetry in your soul," said Golem, who was
still squatting.

"Well, at least I don't . . ."
"What?"
"You know."
"What?"
"Do what you do."
"What do I do?"
"You know."
"Say it."

"No."

"Say it."

"Play with . . ."

"Myself?"

"Oh, David!"

"Play with myself? Play with myself? Wow! It is out in the open, now. No calling it back, now." Golem jumped up. "How do you do? I'd like you to meet my husband, David Golem. What does he do? Oh, he plays with himself a great deal. But only in the afternoons, of course . . . he has a certain sense of style, you know. Isn't that right, David? Well, say I most shamefacedly, sometimes in the evening, too. Really? Oh, yes. But not frequently. It isn't a habit. Only do it when I cannot resist my need to create. The life of an artist is not his own, you know."

Anna watched him go through this routine. She was on the verge of mixed emotions. She held her hands at her sides, waiting for a signal to laugh or cry.

"You have no poetry in your soul, my dear. I do not *play* with myself. Jerking off is very serious business."

She cried.

"But, don't worry," he said, holding his palms up before her eyes, "I have no hair on my hands. Only warts."

She hit him.

Not very hard. Anna wasn't very strong.

But hard enough to crack the smile on his face.

Golem shrugged his shoulders. "Anything interesting for dinner?"

"What?" She stopped crying. "I should make dinner for you?" (Whenever she was furious with him, she affected a Yiddish intonation which she felt would remind him of his Mother or, at least, his archetypal Mother and that would, as they say, teach him a lesson. "Go out, you bum."

"OK, but it's coming out of your allowance."

She tried to hit him again but he moved out of the way and waved as he left the bedroom. She ran after him, but he went outside, knowing that she would never let herself be seen in the kimono. Next trip, he thought, I am going to buy her a pair of wedgies. That will, as they say, teach her a lesson.

10   Golem had dinner with his one true friend, Peter Paul Mangini.

"Paulo, you're my one true friend," he used to say.

(For this year, he used to think.)

"And so are you, Golem," Peter Paul used to say.

(For this year, he used to think.)

"We understand each other," they used to say.

(Or so they thought.)

They are in the University Beer Joint which, after nine o'clock, became a kind of circus of student sin. Six rubber machines in the men's room, god knows what in the ladies' room, a psychedelic Schlitz sign, a motel-modern painting on the wall surrounded by the stenciled signias of the various Fraternities and Services of Our Country—soon to surround a hundred and fifty white males and a few assorted females—always entering to the sounds of cheers, whistles, etc.—shouting, no, grunting, encouragement to three spade GOGOGIRLS in blonde wigs who pretended to be vertically laid by every one of the customers (women included) on a platform above the bar to the tune of electronic soul music vomited out by the Mafia-owned jukebox in return for what seemed like a dime. (When a combo played, the Manager came around to your table and asked you for fifty cents saying, with an ingratiating smirk as if he knew that your sheet was at the cleaner's with his, "You've got to pay the niggers before they'll dance.")

But, before nine, it was a place for those who were breaking their study or those whose wives had refused to cook dinner for them and had dreams of getting good and drunk and sending penciled notes on the backs of crinkled Guest Checks which would be followed by quick screws in musty rooms lit only by paper Tiffany lampshades covering blue sixty-watt bulbs.

Golem had none of these dreams. Not tonight. But he had had them.

Golem had called Mangini after he left the house.

"Paulo? This is the Golem."

"Right. What's happening?"

"I'm out again."

"Aha. Dinner for two at the Ubie? By candlelight?"

"Meet you out front."

"No reservations?"

"Only attenuations."

"You know, Golem, if you stopped studying philosophy and psychology and learned how to talk like regular people, maybe you'd get along better with your wife."

"Thanks for the advice, Pop. Just tell Mom you're going bowling. She'll never suspect that I've got these two honeys lined up for us. These two showgirls."

"Cheap hussies?"

"Not even hussies are cheap nowadays, Dad. Not with lettuce going for 39¢ a head."

"Watch who you're calling a head. My phone may be tapped."

"Meet you out front?"

"Right."

11   Inside the Ubie, they were silent as they ate their Triple-Burgers; Golem not yet wanting to begin, Mangini anxious to hear but hesitant to seem anxious. Golem thought over his lines, trying to anticipate Mangini's reactions. Watching the way Mangini's mouth opened to nearly twice its apparent size, the upper lip seeming to curl over the bent nose, as he surrounded the Triple-Burger with teeth that were not Snow White or, he imagined, breath that was Spring Fresh. What words would come from that dark—shall we say saturnine, no we shall not—face which thought itself beautifully ugly in a Belmondo-esque manner? A face not unlike mine, thought Golem. But his head is just a bit large for his body and mine is not. While his kind of sticks up like that thing inside a flower, mine fits into the handy groove between my shoulders. How shall I begin, to make him listen and yet not think me graceless?

I don't know what to do.

Shit, I don't know what the hell to do.

Shit, I don't know what to do with my fucking wife.

Old lady.

No.

Wife.

Each one was different and yet none worked. They all seemed sophomoric.

I'm in a jam.

Nobody says that, not even Personnel Managers for insurance companies. Well, then. Maybe it has a ring of truth. Even that sounds like a cliché.

Do you mind me talking to myself?

How about starting with Listen, followed by four or five dots, and working it out from there?

Finally.

"Listen . . . . ."

Mangini raised his dark eyebrows as if he were begging me to describe him as saturnine, but still chewed on his Triple-Burger, not yet lowering it to the paper plate on which was imprinted a design certain to be mistaken for plastic wood, even by the most experienced eye. Like that of a catalogue order clerk at Sears Roebuck.

Come on, you bastard. Listen to me. I need your voice.

"Listen . . . shit. I'm in a goddamned jam. I don't know what to do. About my old lady. My fucking wife. What the hell should I do?"

Got it all out.

"What's the matter?"

You had to say that, didn't you. All I want is your voice and you have to ask me what's the matter. You couldn't say, oh yeah? Which would leave me twenty or thirty minutes to get it out. You have to know now. You have to make me know now.

"I don't know."

Mangini shrugged his too small shoulders. Golem thought how much they looked like Mutt and Jeff together. Then he took another bite of his TripleBurger. A large one which would keep his mouth busy for at least forty seconds. Enough time to think. Enough time to shoot the President five times, or fifteen times, depending on how you calculated the probabilities and on which network you watched, the red or the blue.

OK, cock robin. We'll start now.

"She's getting to be a drag."

Evasive action.

"Is that what's bugging you?"

Bastard caught on.

"Oh, I don't know. Maybe it's just me. I'm bored. Bored as plywood. What the hell am I doing here? Christ, I sound like a sophomore."

Mangini smiled.

"Golem, baby, what's the difference whether you're here or there? Relax, man."

Golem had heard him use that line at least seventeen times. He was certain that he had read it somewhere. One of these days, saturnine baby, I'm going to turn you in for plagiarizing somebody else's philosophy.

In which case, we would all be under arrest.

"Yeah. I know."

"Look at me."

Moralize for me, baby.

"I do my school thing when I have to. I know I've got it. When I'm ready, I'll say it."

"You'll be The Man."

They both laughed.

"Yeah, but you don't have the responsibility of a wife, man." The old Yeah But Gambit—what page was it on?—will he fall into it?

"She supports you, doesn't she?

Give him a little more line.

"Financially, only."

"Well . . ."

Come on, say it.

"I've got my chick . . ."

Yeah, that's right.

"Toni."

O Schmuck. O Schmuck. Your chick. Your Toni. Man, you don't know how much I want to tell you that you no longer own that beautiful girlchild. That girl whose face radiates a kind of innocent depravity, whose slight body is as soft as kapok. That person is no longer your exclusive property, Paulo. I have invested in her. I own stock in her soul. Two weeks ago, we made love by motorcycle light. By Motorcycle Light. You would appreciate that,

21

my one true friend. Two big chopped mothas with apehangers standing, no, leaning casually on their kickstands in the living-room, their single eyes focused on us as we made quick, nervous love, but long-awaited love, on the couch of a vacationing friend.

You have a groovy body, I said.

You have a groovy fuck, she said.

We were both trying to be cool and groovy.

But where were you then, man? Relaxing? Relaxing while I was inhaling the perfume she had applied to her belly? Doing your school thing while I was reaching inside her body? Telling it like it is while we were doing it like it ought to be?

I was inside her body; she owns a part of me and I a part of her. Maybe that's what they mean by getting a piece.

We told each other, man, that we loved each other. We didn't mention you. You didn't exist for us then; no one existed for us, then. Only us.

I want to tell you. I want to tell everyone, for that matter. If you're in love, it's good, no matter what the circumstances are. Everybody has to be in love and that is what is good in every-body. If you can't be in love or be loved, then you die.

Maybe, someday, I'll write you a letter about it.

Or do you already know?

"Yeah, you have Toni. She is a beautiful chick. Does she make you happy?"

"Most of the time. We have a really solid relationship, you should excuse the cliché. We're very open with each other. We don't ever lie. She can't lie; it's against her nature."

WoW!
ZooM!
There goes that old squash ball rattling around the court!
Do you
Know? Are you sitting here waiting
For Me
To tell You?
Is that Possible?
zOOm!
wOw!

—*a little head poem by David Alan Golem aged twenty-seven pushing forty-five and a half.*

"Never lies, huh? That is nice."

This requires another bite of the TripleBurger. Pick it up. Open your mouth. Chew it good. Swallow it. Come on, chew it good. Don't let any get down the wrong pipe, thus making you cough suspiciously. Swallow it, goddamnit. Do not move your eyes around. Just cool it. Essentially, Mangini is a schmuck. He can't top you. No one can; only yourself. You are your own enemy. You and Hamlet.

"Anna doesn't lie either. She just omits. She's not completely honest with me. And, I guess, I'm not with her."

Very, very good.

"You have to be. That's the most important thing in a relationship. Complete honesty."

"Yeah."

They both took large bites of their TripleBurgers. Devouring the end of the conversation. Washing it down with glasses of beer. Letting their respective enzymes take it apart, cleanse it, and, later, excrete it altogether.

Altogether?

"Anything good at the flicks tonight?"

"Nothing in town," answered Golem who was aware of his position as a kind of Walking What's On among his friends. "There's a new John Wayne at the Centre in Liberty. But then, there's always a new John Wayne and I'm not up for going out of town."

"Neither am I. What's on the tube?"

"Ahyes, there we have something. And I quote . . . Movie—Melodrama. 'The Manster.' Parenthesis. 1962. Using an experimental serum, a Japanese scientist turns a reporter into a manster—half-man, half-monster. Satoshu Nakamura is in it."

"I see you've been memorizing *TV Guide* again."

"In my spare time."

"Satoshu Nakamura, eh?"

"Yes, old Nakamurrrrrrra. A nova in the heavens of the Tohorama cinema. You got any grass at home? We could turn on and watch it."

"Well, I suppose that's better than playing with ourselves at the Ubie. Toni's home reading, but she won't mind."

Golem's heart did a little two-step, then dipped and

changed into a quick rhumba. All dances that nobody does any-more.

"Let's finish up and split."

12   A light snow had begun to fall. The lacy images that Golem remembered as being pasted on windows in his kinder-garten classroom were just drops of white wetness. Everything changes as you get older, he thought, as the two of them walked the five blocks to Mangini's apartment, their collars up around their heads, their hands jammed into their pockets, cigarettes hanging limply from their closed mouths. And not always for the better, either. Snow erases all the natural boundaries, like age.

"I'm fed up with this snow," said Golem, the cigarette bobbing between his lips as he spoke.

"It's the first snow of the year."

"So what? Say, Paulo. I've got it. The real reason why southerners are so uptight with the spades."

"What is it?"

"Well, it's got to do with snow. See, in the North, we take snow for granted and, consequently, whiteness for granted— so we're not bugged by somebody who's not white. Dig?"

"Yeah."

"But in the South, it doesn't snow. So they figure white-ness to be something special. It's a very important symbol. Like if it doesn't snow on Christmas, the Gentiles figure that God has let them down; they wait for snow like the Jews wait for the Messiah. Consequently, boom boom, racially tense areas, as the newspapers say."

"I don't know. I don't think that's it."

"What do you think it is?"

"I think the niggers have bigger dicks and the whites know it."

Golem laughed into his collar, not at all minding being the straightman. "Yeah, I guess that's the real cause of My Colored Problem and Yours."

13   Mangini lived in a five-room, mazelike apartment above an abandoned movie theater which sat on the line separating the white and black communities of the town. During the flourishing

of civil rights (or CR, as the Movement people referred to it in that peculiar democratic shorthand) spirit, the theater had been a favorite target for picketers. The owner, a white businessman who lived in the capital city and was, some said, being groomed for the position of Grand Kleagle or Kludd or whatever those kats kalled themselves, had klosed down the theater during a large protest march which was started in the black community and came down to the line where it was joined in front of the bulding by a march which had originated in the white community. As if the entire scene had been directed by Otto Preminger, the two groups joined hands and began to sing We Shall Overcome. The Manager, acting on telephoned orders, had come out of the theater and had, symbolically of course, padlocked its doors. The next day, people passing in front of the theater noticed that the marquee had been altered from

T RIPL THRILLER HORRA SHO

to

NO SHO TONITE
HA HA HA HA.

Eventually, the
NO SHO TONITE
had fallen off or had been stolen.
But the
HA HA HA HA
still clung to the graying Plexiglas. And that was why Mangini had chosen this place to live.

To get to the apartment, one had to climb a rusty fire escape on the side of the brick building; then, you opened a large once-green steel door which Mangini had painted fuschia and walked into the livingroom which Mangini had painted white—all white including the floor and the ceiling from which hung a globular Japanese lantern which, when lit and spun, made the entire room feel like a revolving cage. The furniture in this room was Thrift Shop Baroque and the other rooms were similar in style and in intention.

Toni, casually wrapped in a white terry happi coat, was draped over the couch, reading a paperback on Medieval Architecture. As they walked in, Golem's heart and knees did a little step that would have gladdened the heart of Arthur Murray.

"Hey, baby. We're going to turn on and watch the tube. Want some?"

Toni looked at them the way old Mother Earth must have looked at Adam and Eve when they tasted that apple—just a couple of kids. She shrugged her shoulders. Maybe yes. Maybe no. She smiled a Cheshire cat kind of smile. Raised her eyebrows.

Golem treasured each movement, inscribing it in his brain. She moved, man. This woman moved. He could barely stand to watch her move. The sight of her (and even he admitted to himself that this was a horrible cliché made barely acceptable by the substitution of a popcampy kind of image)—the sight of her turned him to My-T-Fine Pudding and Pie Filling.

"Hi," he said.

What more could he say?

Maybe, some day, I'll write you a letter.

She did not move from her position on the couch, but when Mangini went into the kitchen to get the grass out of the refrigerator ("I like my shit to be cold and fresh," he had once explained to Golem) she blew him—yes, beautiful expression that —blu blew bleu him a kiss. He received it, was stunned by its force, tingled with the luscious illicitness of it and lit a cigarette to keep his balance. She watched him as, after his first exhale, he made his mouth large with the soundless I LOVE YOU as if he were talking to deaf people, making it easier for them to read his lips, hoping that they will understand—and then stuck the cigarette back into his mouth as Mangini walked into the room carrying a Pyrex bowl half-full of grass and covered with aluminum foil.

"You want to smoke joints or use the pipe?"

"Let's smoke joints," he said because he knew that Mangini would ask Toni to roll them and he loved to watch the carefully sensual way she rolled up the magic dust into neat tubular containers.

"OK," said Mangini.

And then he asked Toni and she did and Golem watched and, oh, you know . . .

14   With the exhale of his third toke, Golem felt the shell of his body and his brain begin to empty itself of its daily nuisances. His voice tightened and became hardedged and, as the substance of the drug curled up through his head and settled into the crevices and canals of his brain, turning on lights, opening circuits, breathing life into sleeping areas, once again, he began to feel reborn. He took another toke, holding his breath as if he were diving for buried treasure which he had to have in order to pay off the mortgage on Toni's mother's house before Simon Legree foreclosed on the old farm and threw the two women out in the snow. And finally, when he had located the treasure—a chestful of Toni's movements, when he had a handful of leg stretches, raised eyebrows, curling smiles, he let out his air and rose to the surface saying, "This is very pleasant shit, Paulo."

Mangini, occupied with his own descent, simply nodded.

Toni smoked her joint quickly and Golem offered her the remainder of his which he did not need at that Time. She walked over to him, bending to take it, letting Golem see her small, conical breasts as the robe fell away from her body. Golem smiled.

Toni smiled.

Mangini smiled.

Smile and the whole world will be yours.

Put on a happy face.

Smile when your heart is breaking.

Et cetera.

"Listen," said Golem, now that everyone was smiling. "Did I tell you about that Japanese flick that I saw last week?"

Mangini shook his head no.

"It was cheap and small. Actually they're all very weird. You know how small the Japanese are—dig their television sets, a big screen is six inches—and the monsters in these movies are fantastically large, in proportion. About six feet tall. But, you know, they all look alike; they smoke corncob pipes.

Anyway, this one was called Gigantua, the Fire Monster. I was expecting maybe a big cigar, for a change. So. The picture opens with a montage of exploding hydrogen bombs. Right away you start to get worried. I mean, to the average American veteran, this could only mean one thing—they're going to get even. Right? Wrong. The deal is—as we learn from the narrator who went to

USC (you can tell because he pronounces all his *r*'s)—that when the United States exploded their atom bomb, all the prehistoric monsters who had been sleeping for trillions of years in Japan woke up. What an alarm clock!"

Mangini exhaled a toke with a snorting laugh.

"Well, two of these monsters don't like each other . . . people don't get along, why should monsters . . . and they decide to fight to the death for control of the islands. An allegory, you think? Wrong again. Actually, it's a TV commercial. See, one of these monsters breathes fire; this is Gigantua. The other one has very sharp teeth and, also, a protective coating of gas around his entire body. So, it's a fight to the death between halitosis and body odor. I lied to you; it is an allegory.

"So the two monsters decide to fight it out and it looks like they're going to hold the bout in Osaka-by-the-sea. The people of the city are terrified, lock themselves in their bomb shelters, and pray that Coca-Cola will hire Superman to save them. But Coke is already involved in Viet Nam—trying to buy off the Viet Cong —so Pepsi siezes the opportunity and throws up a barricade of empty bottles around the city. For a while, it looks as though the fight is off. Japanese newspapers flash onto the screen. Screaming headlines. MONSTERS TO BYPASS OSAKA, OH HAPPY DAYS, THE CITY IS SAVED, PEACE IN THE PEPSI GENERATION,

"Coke is furious. They hire a band of Cuban exile pilots to bomb the barricade. The defenses are destroyed in the name of free enterprise. Interviewed at his ranch, the President of the United States gulps bourbon and Coke and denies any knowledge of the affair. The UN is called in, but they refuse to help. U Thant explains that they were saving those bottles to pay for the last peacekeeping mission in the Congo.

"Finally, the monsters enter the city.

"A struggle ensues. Buildings are overturned, the subway system is uprooted, the city—which is made of cheap paper —is engulfed in the flames which spew forth from the foul mouth of Gigantua. The fight continues through that night and part of the next day. Then, Gigantua unleashes his secret weapon—a huge five-day deodorant pad with which he smothers the other monster. He belches and the coup de grace is administered. Gigantua roars once, raises his hands above his head, and lumbers back into the Pacific to gargle.

"Panic sets in in Osaka; the monster must be destroyed. He may return. The people run hither and yon through the ashes of their city which they later collect in buckets to sell to monasteries in Viet Nam. The police call a meeting of the top scientists and civil servants in the country. Since there is no army in Japan, the Chief of Police is put in command of the task of destroying the monster. The task is given a code name: Operation Mouthwash.

"First, he starts a program to create an atmosphere of hate for Gigantua. From everywhere, transistor radios blare forth, THE MONSTER MUST BE DESTROYED, YEAH, YEAH, YEAH. It makes the hit parade. Coke counters the Pepsi offensive by offering a million yen reward for the best method of execution, in twenty-five words or less.

"Then, the Chief calls in a renegade squad of ex-Kamikaze pilots, explains the mission, and asks them to volunteer. They refuse. He is stunned and offers them a week's vacation at Coney Island if they will accept. They accept, saying that they'll do anything to get away from the Tokyo beach crowds.

"The men suit up, jump into their American surplus planes, and fly off to meet Gigantua who is recuperating on a kind of iceberg, a rapidly melting iceberg.

"The squad makes several strafing runs, but their Spads are no match for the mighty mouth of Gigantua. He huffs, and he puffs, and he blows three of them out of the air. The planes regroup and, in a moment of heroic glory, the commander orders two of the men to crash into a mountain of snow directly behind the monster. They do and a huge avalanche begins. It starts to fall on the monster. It covers him up to his waist, then to his chest. All the time, the remaining planes are attacking. Shooting rockets, dropping leaflets, throwing Pepsi bottles which contain notes saying BANZAI and DIE MONSTER DOG in three different languages. The snow continues; now it's up to his neck. He roars, tries to breathe fire, but his lungs are frozen. He's out of gas. The snow covers his head. Under this immense weight, the iceberg sinks into the sea. The sun rises. The question is, will the water thaw him out?

"Next week, they're doing *The Iceman Cometh*."

During the telling of the story, the air in the room was clouded with laughter. Mangini lay on the floor, having fallen off his chair in a paroxysm of giggles after the part about the UN saving bottles. Toni was on the couch again, stretched back so that the robe was pulled nearly to the top of her thighs. Golem had been laughing so hard at his own story that his eyes were too misty to digest the smoothness of her legs. Every time another word was spoken, the laughter began anew. Finally, after they were all coughing, Mangini picked himself up off the floor. "The goddamn movie is going to be an anticlimax. You want to smoke some more shit?"

Golem nodded and Toni said she was cool.

"Don't you want any more?"

"No, baby. That's all right. I'm fine." And she smiled that smile again.

That goddamned smile.

Mangini handed Golem another joint, chuckling as he thought of all those bottles stored in the back room of the Security Council.

Golem lit his joint and inhaled deeply. Mangini put a Ravi Shankar on and sat down to groove on the evening raga. They both smoked in silence for a while as Toni watched them. The drone of the music held the three of them, forbidding them to speak, melting the three of them into a single throbbing unit. Golem closed his eyes and felt a curtain of blackness begin to drop over his consciousness; it dropped slowly, a fraction of an inch a second, but steadily. It dropped over his forehead and down his face. As it reached the top of his chest, he shivered in anticipation. His bowels, his groin began to feel hollow. It, THE END, was coming. The curtain descended. It was at the middle of his chest now. If I don't open my eyes now, I'm finished. But he didn't. And now it was at his navel. No. I can't let it get there. Light.

And God Said.

Light.

And Golem opened his eyes and the curtain rolled up as quickly as if it had been a window shade in a haunted house.

"Paulo, have you been doing much reading on Eastern thought . . . aside from the obvious cats, I mean?"

"Some."

"I find it very hard to groove on. I recognize the validity of the mystical experience, of course. Like it would be stupid to dismiss it out of hand. But it is a paranoid/egomania trip. I had one when I was doing speed; I talked to God. In Yiddish, you call it a shmoos, I think. But still, that whole scene is very foreign to me. There's nothing rational about it which is both beautiful and terrifying, if you know what I mean."

"Yeah. Well, they don't separate subject from object. We are all one, etc. That kind of thing."

"That's a very difficult concept to make it with, to live with. The Hasidic bag is something like that. God is in you all the time. I like that concept. But still, it's spirit-stuff. I don't think I could relate to a truly anthropomorphic god, like the God-Men, or an avataric figure like that cat in India, or even like Buddha. Even Christ, for chrissakes! That's not to say that I don't want to. Well, maybe *want* isn't the right word. Because everybody kind of *wants to*. Like you don't want to think of God just as a spirit like ether. Right?"

"Well, I don't know if everybody wants an anthropomorphic god."

"But just about everybody's got one, in so many words. I mean when you promise that you'll stop jerking off if you can get through this particular situation, like if your Father doesn't find out that you stole something from the five and ten, you're not promising this to ether. I really think that Freud had something with the original patricide experience."

"But his scholarship was lousy."

"Screw scholarship. It's the idea that counts. Nobody's going to prove him right or wrong. The idea lives; it governs other people's lives. That's what's important."

"I don't think that's the kind of generalization that you want to apply all the time."

"Of course not."

Toni got up from the couch. Both men watched her move. "Do you want some wine?" They both nodded. And she left the room to get the bottle and three glasses. They were silent until she returned. She poured some in each glass, handing one to Golem

31

and one to Mangini, then went back to the couch with her own, tucking her legs up beneath her as she settled back.

"Thanks."

She smiled again.

Mangini sipped his wine. "From the south of the vine-yard, I would say. The side facing Los Angeles. Wine and grass goes good."

"Sounds like a commercial."

"It is, baby, it is."

"Or an epitaph."

"It is that, too."

"Epitaphs are commercials. And dying words, too. My old man. My father, before he died, said to me, "David, David, I want you to be a good boy."

"Everybody's father says that."

"But not before they die."

"In the movies they do."

"Yeah, in the movies they do. We live in the movies. But the colors aren't as good. My father died of metaphorical cancer. My uncle had the real thing. He was gassed in the First World War."

"Your father?"

"No, my uncle. That was a very bad scene. I used to love to go to his house when I was a kid. We always ate lightly during the day because my aunt made these monstrous chicken dinners with spaghetti—spaghetti because my cousin Bernie had married a beautiful Italian girl from Ohio who was a soprano. Bernie was an opera singer. The whole family sang opera.

"Anyway, we would climb into my grandfather's huge Buick and travel the ten or fifteen minutes to the two-sided brick house—I never could believe that anyone actually lived on the other side—where a parking space was always kept for our arrival —even if one of my cousins had to stand in the street until we came. And I would be the first one out of the car, exchanging the blackness of the Buick for my aunt's dark hug. By the time everyone else left the car, I was waiting for my grandfather—my father was in the army—to open the heavy front door. And, when he did, though never quickly enough, I would run past him into the midst of vocal chaos where the first sound was always a misplaced note from some aria or other.

"Bernie was the only one in the family who sang professionally—I think he sang with the Met for a while—but, like I said, everybody in the house sang, too. Even my uncle, whose off-key, Russian-accented baritone was heard above all, was singing grand opera. Maybe it was a manifestation of some very intense sibling rivalry, but I think that it was mainly done in self-defense. Like nobody would listen to you unless you sang what was on your mind. The house was bursting with *Pagliacci*, Puccini, and Verdi in at least three octaves. And my aunt never missed her high E when she sang that ever popular selection, 'Washa Your Hands, You Bum.' Of course, I stood in the middle of everything, dressed in my Buster Brown suit and singing at the top of my lungs about how I fell down and scraped my knee.

"Anyway, several years later, we came back to my uncle's house because he was dying. There was no singing in the house and the man who had stood by the sink holding up great unnameable fish which he had caught in Sheepshead Bay before my startled eyes—I think that's why I can't stand to go fishing—the man who, though physically dwarfed by his children, had outshouted them all . . . he was lost in the impersonality of a hospital bed and his practically unrecognizable voice came in gasps from the cancerous cavity that had been his chest. That's when my grandfather told me that he had been gassed by the Germans. All I could think of, I remember, was that somebody had turned my uncle into a thin balloon and I stood there waiting for him to fly up to heaven. But, instead, he shrank deeper and deeper into the whiteness around him."

Golem lit his joint and took a deep toke.

"That's beautiful," Toni said, "a real epiphany scene."

"Yes, very groovy, Golem. My family wasn't as colorful but . . ."

Colorful? That is my life you are talking about. Groovy? I am not listening to you. I do not care to trade experiences with you, a death for a death, like a drunk story for a car wreck. My family for your family. I am giving you me. Are you giving me you? What kind of a trade is this? So this is man, nothing but

"TEMPLE ISRAEL"

what he tells of himself. A little story, a little piece, a little being.
I want you to be me. You want me to be you. We are. We are
not. Like so many plucked petals of a flower.

". . . who had a farm on the peninsular which never . . ."

Toni, say something. Make him stop.

". . . grew worms which he used to sell to the local . . ."

I read that poem. You can't put that one over on me. It
was in last week's issue of *Time*, for chrissakes. Make him stop,
Toni. Make it all stop.

". . . so they lynched him."

"They what?"

"They lynched him."

"Fantastic!"

You didn't make him stop.

Toni smiled.

"Wow. Lynched him." (She said that.)

"Yep." (Yep! He said that.)

Golem inhaled again.

14A   Who knows?

But what good is it?

He won't tell.

I suppose not; it would kill it for him.

So what good is it?

III

15   Anna in her bed.
"Is that you, David?"
Anna in her bed. A Jean Seberg of a womanchild drawing the blanket up to her neck as if it were a shield between her
and the rest, her body and that of the universe.

16   Anna had come out of the West, hair straight to the small
of her back, heavy leather sandals on her delicate feet, guitar
fastened by beaded Indian strap, ready to tell the world through
song and story what a schmuck she thought it was. Only, she
didn't know the word schmuck; she didn't learn that until she met
Golem.
Flashback with Anna of the not so frail shoulders but
delicate feet to the meeting of her and Golem. Nothing so Romantic
as checkered tablecloths and dollar-nineteen candle holders of
Chianti. Nor was it Current like coffeehouse love of apple cider

menus written in free verse. Nor Collegiate, like a Mixer where the apple cider was served in paper cups of classic meter. And yet, all three . . . osterized into a don't take candy from a stranger Coincidence.

It was at the circus where Anna had gone alone to consciously recapture the innocence of her childhood and unconsciously, or rather, truthfully, because she loved the aerial acts. Particularly that moment in which the Woman was thrown from the arms of one Man into the hands of the always grandfatherly catcher—a Lautrec vision of the Sistine Chapel. That moment of jump-don't-jump, priest-policeman on window ledge ambivalence that is as characteristic of humanity as is walking erect or talking with a forked tongue. This was the moment, the need for posterization of this moment, which had brought Anna to the circus.

Her life had always rested on this moment of timelessness, even in her great gabled house in the West which faced on a street named for an Indian tribe long vanished. There, the timelessness seeped up through the brickfloored room used by her parents for solar purposes, seeped up through the mortar and infused the two-story house with a constant atmosphere of rainy-dayness as if it were the remnants of a curse left by that Indian tribe when they retreated into the land, back into the earth. A timelessness which one had to push aside in order to walk from room to room. One was always a stranger in this house.

Anna's father had been an ophthalmologist and now he collected stamps, pasting each stamp into a large book with a sigh as if it were a message from another place that he would not see, a fragment from another book that he would not read.

Her mother knitted a lot.

Without vocation, there was no purpose in the house. Without order or authority, there were no real relationships. So much freedom existed and so little interdependence that the members of the household were fatigued by the responsibility of being both free in attitude—engaged one moment, indifferent the next—and in physical function. A sense of drift existed in the soul as well as in the wood and brick. And to Anna, the last of her parents' four children to be at home, this drift in her body fought with her natural antibodies of purpose. The battle waged for years and, like the paradox of whether or not God, being omnipotent and omniscient, could make an object too heavy for himself to lift, it was never resolved. A stalemate occurred and Anna remained a creature of precariousness.

Anna lived at home until she was nineteen, spending her first year of college at the local branch of the state university because she felt herself not yet able to move away from home. Finally, toward the end of that year, when she had had enough of her Emily Dickinson gazings through rain-spattered windows at the trafficless street below, when she had realized that the only way for her to survive was to be, she decided to Become. She let her hair grow, walked through alleys, bought a cracked Stella guitar from a pawnshop and began to finger the protest songs of a decade during which plastic was considered a luxury. She accumulated the uniforms and accessories of a Becomer and, when she felt that she had Become, she went downstairs to the sunroom.

"Daddy, can I talk to you?"

"Don't you want to watch television?" he asked as he put a new Congolese issue in its place.

"No. I want to talk to you."

Frightened by this sudden demand on their attention, her father closed his book and her mother put down her knitting needles. Anna had rehearsed her speech many times in front of her bathroom mirror, trimming a sentence here, adding an exclamation point there . . . and so she began, ready to meet all opposition with the key phrase, "I'm not a little girl any more."

"Well," she said, "I'm not a little girl any more; I'm nineteen years old and I think it's time I moved away from home."

"Ummm," her father said.

Her mother said nothing.

"Now let me finish," she said. "I've decided that I want to go away to college next year. I don't know where yet . . . but I still have time to apply."

"We'll lose you, too," her mother said.

Cue.

"Mother, I'm not a little girl any more."

"You're nineteen years old," her father said.

She looked at him, stunned for a moment, not believing

that he was capable of saying something like that and yet knowing that this was the kind of moment that all little girls were supposed to have. It was very definitely a blow below the belt. "Yes," she said, like a chorus.

"I don't think it's a bad idea," he said.

"Really, George?"

"After all, she's not a little girl any more . . ."

"I'm nineteen."

"We'll be all alone in this big house."

"You can fill it up with sweaters and socks."

Anna laughed in spite of herself and her father looked at her conspiratorily. And winked.

From that day forward, the mailman delivered a college catalogue almost every day. Anna would get the mail first, searching for the manila envelope which might contain her destiny or, at least, her destination. Finding it, she stripped the container from its contents, always being careful not to damage the stamps, which she placed on her father's desk in the sunroom like daily installments on a long-term loan, and ran up to her room to read the Rules and Regulations, look for interesting names among the Faculty, and devise imaginary curricula for herself.

She filled out every application, forcing herself to write her last name first (doing that incorrectly, she thought, was certain to keep her from being admitted), trying to squeeze the name of her city into the always insufficient space alloted by the stingy formsmaker, doing the same with the names of the schools she had attended since the ninth grade (as only two lines were allotted for this purpose, she worried that her three schools—the third one on an imaginary line—might not fit the criteria established by the Admissions Board—hmmm, this one went to three schools instead of two. Maybe she's irresponsible. Think we can use her anyway? What's her last name begin with? R. We only got eleven R's; we could use her to round out the number), and being careful to avoid making marks in the APPLICANT: DO NOT WRITE IN THIS SPACE—FOR OFFICE USE ONLY column which ran down one side of the application as if it were the tag on a mattress.

Several of the applications demanded a brief biographical

sketch with an indication of the applicant's interests and ambitions so she spent one night writing two-hundred-word essays on the life of A. M. Reitzler.

I was born in Costa Verna, California, a suburb of Los Angeles. My father is a retired ophthalmologist and my mother is a housewife. I was educated in the Costa Verna school system up until the tenth grade, at which time I entered the Winchester Country Day School. I was graduated from Winchester with Honors in History and then I attended the Costa Verna branch of the University of California.

At Winchester, I was active on the school newspaper and the literary magazine, as well as participating in the Debate and Dramatic Societies. At Costa Verna, I belonged to Le Cercle Français and the History Club in which my special interest was the Industrial Revolution.

My parents and I attend the First Methodist Church in Costa Verna and during my high school years, I was a member of the church youth group, eventually holding the office of Corresponding Secretary and, later, Vice-President for Programming.

I enjoy water sports and boating, in general. I play the guitar and have performed at local restaurants. I read a great deal and my favorite authors are Ernest Hemingway and J. D. Salinger. I have written some poetry myself and have published it in the Winchester literary magazine and also in *Thrust*, the literary publication of the Costa Verna branch of the University of California.

After I finish college, I would like to go on to graduate school and then become a teacher either at the university level or to work with younger children who are gifted but are culturally deprived.

She worried that she had begun too many sentences with *I* and *my*. But, after all, it was her life. Her life, in two hundred words. Well, all they need to know to let her into college.

Anna was accepted by four out of the five schools to which she actually mailed applications and, of these, after two weeks of listing all the advantages and disadvantages of each, she finally chose the University of North Carolina, perhaps because the geographic temperament seemed most suited to her own. North Carolina was a southern state—with all the stereotyped identifications which that term implies—and, yet, it was reputed to be a *progressive* southern state, a sort of moral and climatic transitional zone.

Anna's parents took her to the airport without too many tears and she waved from the seat near the window as the plane taxied away from the Indians. She did not come home again for two years.

17   On the eve of Anna's twenty-first birthday, she made love with a man for the first time. Actually, it was not a man, but a poetry-reading boy of twenty-one and a half who used his book of poems as a buffer between his desire and his fear. It was his first time, too.

18   On the morning of Anna's twenty-first birthday, she flushed her recriminations down the toilet along with the other debris of her childhood and, without waking the sleeping poet, dressed and wrote FUCK YOU on the bathroom mirror with her Petulant Peach lipstick. Two weeks later, she met Golem at the circus.

19   "Want some Cracker Jacks?"

She turned, missing the tiger's leap upon the horse, missing the opportunity to catch her breath as the trainer's whip snapped in the air, but hearing the snap and the thousand other caught breaths as she turned to face the stranger that J. Edgar Hoover had warned her about.

"Want some Cracker Jacks?"

He was holding the box at an angle of offering, looking into her face, a tall boy with a look of what John O'Hara might have called studied unkemptness. But who knows what evil lurks deep within the heart of a Cracker Jack box? Not evil, but a prize—made in Japan undoubtedly, the revenge of the yellow peril —but a prize, nevertheless. Having already celebrated her official maturity, there was little in a box of candy to frighten her. But as soon as she had lifted her hand to accept the offer, she knew that she would have to play the scene out. The opposite was true, as well. She was, in a sense, trapped.

"Thanks."

And she cupped her hand so that he might pour a few in.

He didn't say anything more until the dog act came on.

"I can't stand dog acts. Want some more Cracker Jacks?"

"Thank you."

"You can have the prize."

"Oh, no. I couldn't take that away from you. It's good luck."

"That's OK; I made you miss the tiger jumping on the horse and now I'm making you miss the dog act. It's the least I can do."

They smiled at each other and he handed her the little packet which contained the raison d'être of Cracker Jacks.

"Shall I open it now?"

"No. Save it."

"All right."

"I'm Golem. I've seen you around the campus, as they say, as they say . . ."

She opened her eyes at that double cliché.

". . . but I don't know your name."

"Anna. Anna Reitzler."

"Hi."

They shook hands, laughed, and turned back to watch a large bear waltz into the center ring.

"You know, it's strange how some of the most menacing of animals or, at least, some of the biggest of them, don't look dangerous at all. Look at that bear, for instance. You wouldn't associate him with death the same way you would the tiger or a lion. Same's true with the elephant. Yet they're a hell of a lot more powerful. Maybe that's the point. These animals seem aghast at their own size and we, as tiny humans, recognize that. What do you think of that, Anna Reitzler?"

"Don't forget, these are circus animals. They probably behave differently in Africa."

"Yeah, I guess you're right. They're out of their milieu, as Lamarck would say. Want some peanuts?"

"OK."

Golem signaled the candy butcher who was holding small stapled brown bags of peanuts in one hand and whistling birds on a thin stick in the other. The boy came to the end of their row.

"How many?"

"One."

The boy handed a bag to the man at the end of the row and it was passed hand to hand to Golem who passed a fifty-cent piece hand to hand to the boy who passed a quarter hand to hand to Golem who, with a sense of history, put the quarter into his pocket and ripped open the bag. He cracked a shell neatly and offered the two nuts to Anna who picked them out with her long nails and placed them both in her mouth.

20   They laughed about how they met. They laughed after the circus was over and Anna balanced the tiny plastic horse— her prize—on her extended nipple as she leaned against Golem in his narrow bed.

"Did we really meet at the circus?"

"Yes," said Golem, leaping off the bed and standing naked in the middle of the room with an invisible microphone held up to his mouth. "And now, ladies and gentlemen, I'd like you to meet our lucky couple. HUSBAND & WIFE presents—drummm rolll, start the Wedding March, Harry—David and Anna Golem! Ah, here they are now. Turn around, folks; just look into the camera with the red light on."

Golem grabbed for Anna's hand and pulled her up next to him. "Face the camera," he whispered into her ear. She did. "Now, tell us, Anna. How did you meet your HUSBAND?"

"Well," she said, eyelids and fingers aflutter in imitation, "we met at the, um, circus."

"The circus! How 'bout that, folks! How 'bout a hand for that grand old American institution, the circus, where our lucky Golems met?"

APPLAUSE. APPLAUSE. APPLAUSE.

"Yes, we met at the circus, just as the tiger was jumping onto the horse. David offered me some Cracker Jacks."

"Isn't that Romantic? How 'bout a big hand for the Cracker Jacks, folks? Even though they're not one of our sponsors, I think they deserve a big hand."

APPLAUSE. APPLAUSE. APPLAUSE.

"And what did you do after he offered you the Cracker Jacks? Did you take the candy from the stranger? Heh, heh, heh."

"Yes."

"Well, it's a good thing you did. Otherwise, you might not be here today. Right, folks?"

RIGHT. RIGHT. RIGHT.

"And then what did you do, after the Cracker Jacks, I mean?"

"Well, then we watched the circus until the dog act came on. Then he offered me some more Cracker Jacks."

"Did you take those, too?"

"Yep."

"Isn't that sweet? Then you were engaged. Did he give you the prize?"

"Yep."

"How 'bout that, folks?"

PRIZE. PRIZE. PRIZE.

"And then what did you do, go to some Romantic Italian restaurant?"

"No. We went to his place and fucked."

"What?"

"We went to his place and fucked."

"Fucked?"

"Fucked. Aren't you allowed to say that on the air?"

"Well, how 'bout that, folks?"

FUCK. FUCK. FUCK.

21   They laughed a lot about how they met. Anna wrote imaginary letters home which began Dear Mom, I met the cutest boy at the circus the other day. He offered me some Cracker Jacks and the next thing I knew, we were in love. Isn't that marvelous! Sincerely, Anna.

And Golem called his mother. Hello, Ma? Listen, I met this girl at the circus the other night. Is she Jewish? I don't know.

The circus was all right. No, I didn't eat too much candy. As a matter of fact, I gave her my Cracker Jacks. When? When the tiger jumped on the horse. No, the horse wasn't hurt. It was just an act.

They told their friends.

"Oh, we met at the circus, you know . . ."

22   They stopped laughing two months later when Golem came home from a seminar to find Anna tearstained and surrounded on the bed by the crumpled contents of two Kleenex boxes.

"Oh no," he said as he dropped his books on the desk and tried to think of something reasonable to say.

"Yes," she said and she cried.

"Are you sure?"

"Sure? How can you ask me that? I feel it."

"But it's only a couple of months that we've been . . . how could you feel it already?"

"I feel it!"

"Didn't you take your pills?"

"Sometimes I forget."

"Why didn't you tell me?"

"I don't know."

"Why the hell didn't you tell me?"

"I don't know."

"But I don't understand it. You can't be sure about it."

"Shit, David. I went to the doctor last week. It happened the first week."

"The first week?"

"Maybe even the first night."

"Christ! Why didn't you say something?"

"I don't know."

She knew, but she cried some more.

Golem's body seemed to fall and he came to sit beside her on the bed, moving the Kleenex away. He put his arms around her. "It's all right, baby. I always wanted to marry someone I met at the circus."

She relaxed into his arms. "Do you mean that, David?"

Hating herself for sounding like a television show but knowing no other way to get the, after all, necessary assurances. "You won't make me have an operation?"

"No. I mean it."

He hugged her and lifted her face and did the right thing by wiping away her tears with his long fingers. Then, he kissed her. "Well, I guess the engagement is over. Where do we get married?"

"Why not here?"

"No. I'm not getting married in secret by some rickety JP between parking tickets. We've got to do it right."

"David, I don't want to have a big fuss."

"OK. It doesn't have to be big. How about a small wedding, maybe at your folks' house?"

"Do we have to?"

"I don't want it to look as though we did something wrong or bad or whatever."

"Will we tell about . . .?"

"No, of course not. We'll keep that a secret."

"Won't it show?"

"Not really. Not if we get married right away."

"Well, who's going to call first?"

"I think you should."

"Really?"

"Yes."

"All right."

23 This, with Golem hovering over her, trying to hear through the outside of the telephone, Anna repeating words to him in parenthetical whispers.

"Mother? How are you? And Daddy? Oh. (His back is bothering him.) Yes, I know I haven't written for a long time. Well, I miss you too. But I called because I have some good news. No, school is fine. What? The fifth, graduation is the fifth and I'm sure my finals will be over by the second or third. I'll be home before then anyway. (She wants to know why.) Well, that's part of the news. I mean, that is the news. You remember that I wrote you about David? David Golem. Well, maybe it got lost in the mail. But I'm sure I wrote you about him. (I can't stand to lie to her like this.) We've been engaged for two months. (She didn't say anything . . . she's holding her breath.) I said we've been engaged for two months. (Engaged?) Yes, engaged. And now we want to get married. (Married?) Yes, married. (So soon?) Two months is a long time, Mother. (She's calling Daddy to the extension.) Hello, Daddy. I'm fine. School's fine. How's your back? (It's better. Mother's telling him. He isn't saying anything. She finished telling him. Neither of them are saying anything.) Well, aren't you going to congratulate me, at least? (Daddy says, you're not in any "trouble" are you?) Unh, no, Daddy. We just want to get married. Yes, I love him. Yes, he loves me. (Are you sure you know what you're doing?) Yes, I'm sure. (When?) Next month. (Where?) We thought a small wedding at home would be nice. (Mother says there's not time enough to prepare.) We'll get married during the spring vacation. It will be enough time. I'll send you a guest list this week and you can have simple invitations printed up. Go to Markels for them. The simplest they have. (They want to know who should perform the ceremony.) A judge. (Why a judge?) Because David is Jewish. (Silence again.) OK? (Daddy says OK, Mother says nothing.) Well . . . (Daddy wants to know how we'll support ourselves.) David has a grant and I'll get a part-time job, if necessary. We'll work it out. (They want to know if you're with me now.) He's studying at the library. (They send their regards.) You still haven't congratulated me. (Congratulations.) OK, I'll write you all the details tonight. Good-bye. (Daddy says, you sure you're not in any "trouble.") Oh, Daddy. Please. (He apologizes.) I'll write you tonight. Bye. (Bye.)"

Anna waited until they hung up before she pressed the button on the phone. The dial tone came back. She gave the phone to Golem and kissed him. "Your turn."

"Now?"

"Now."

"Let me get a cigarette, first."

She handed him the package.

24   This, while Anna rested her head in his lap, running her fingers inside his shirt and tickling his nipples.

"Hi, Mom? How are you feeling? Good. Listen, uh, remember I wrote you about meeting Anna at the circus? (Take it easy.) She's fine. School's OK. Still there. I've been doing some work on it. Listen, remember Anna? We've been going together for two months now and, well, we've kind of decided to get . . . yeah, Married. Yes, I know what I am doing. I'm not a kid any more. She's a very nice girl. Would I marry a not nice girl? No, she's not Jewish. Look, I don't think that really matters. It's my life, anyway. Next month. In California, at her house. A judge. Thanks. I'll write you about the details and stuff. Don't worry. We'll manage. And stop crying."

"What did she say?"

"She said she'd be there."

25   This, while Anna was lying on top of him (so as not to hurt the baby) and into his ear.

"I love you, David."

"Me, too," he whispered.

I've done it, she thought.

She's done it, he thought.

26   Anna went home a week and half before the wedding. The first night, she and her parents sat in the sunroom to discuss the Future. They agreed that there would be one and that it would be interesting. On the second day, Anna went to visit the judge to request that he omit any specific reference to God in the service. He assured her that there would be none, shaking his head slightly and saying, "I understand."

On the third day, she went with her father to the florist —choosing lilies of the valley for the women and carnations for the men. On the fourth day, she visited old single friends in the afternoon and her married friends in the evening. On the fifth day, she went over the menu with the caterer, substituting shrimp cocktail and turkey à la king for the tomato aspic and sweet and sour meatballs that her mother had selected. On the sixth day, she rented sixty-seven bridge chairs and confirmed the band.

On the seventh day, she rested.

And, on the eighth day, like a moel, Golem flew into town with his mother.

Anna picked them up at the airport, meeting his mother's so-this-is-the-girl stare with a hi-mom-to-be hug. In the forty-five minutes it took to drive from the airport to her home, Anna told her life story—an expanded version of her two-hundred-word essay spiced with Yiddish words which she had gotten from a book titled *How to Speak Yiddish for Fun and Profit* which was hidden in the secret drawer of her desk—and ended it as she pulled up the emergency brake to lock the car into her driveway. Golem carried the bags into the house and then it was his turn.

Autobiographies and introductions over with, the new family sat down to a get-acquainted dinner. The seating of five people, regular people, was awkward enough at the Reitzlers' long dining table. Anna was cognizant of the difficulties—our side against your side—involved and so she arranged the seating with Golem on one side (because he could take it), her parents at the head and foot (because they belonged there), and herself and David's mother on the other side (because that would break up the team structure and because she found it impossible to call her either Mom or Mrs. Golem and figured that when she did want to address her, sitting next to her would make it easier than catching her eye across the table).

Beatrice Golem, a small tailored woman in her fifties who had had her hair newly blued for this occasion, kept the conversation moving as if the future of her son and the arrival of dessert depended upon it.

"So, you're in ophthalmology, Dr. Reitzler?"

Just a slice of it, for representative purposes.

"Was. Was. And, please, call me George. Doctor is a little formal for a Stamp Collector."

Everyone chuckled.

"Well, George. My brother—he should rest in peace—was an Eye Ear Nose and Throat Man. David's uncle. One of the best in Brooklyn. All of the politicians were his patients."

"That's a good field."

"Yes, you get to cover a wide range of cases. Nothing major, of course. Mostly colds and styes and earaches and like that. But a very good business. I tell you, George, my brother used to say—and he was right—people have absolutely no respect for the nose any more. None whatsoever."

"Even Freud left it out," said Golem.

"Some people have theirs fixed," said Anna.

"George, remember when you treated Mayor Hendrix for . . ."

"Mother, do we have to talk about that at the dinner table?"

"Don't get upset, Anna. I was just . . ."

"The girl's nervous, Helen. After all, it isn't every day that she gets married."

"I hope not," said Golem, dutifully.

Everyone chuckled though no one knew who Helen was.

"Do you ever have winter here, George?"

"Of course, Beatrice. When I was a boy . . ."

"Call me Bea. All my friends do."

"Well, Bea, I can remember some pretty bad snows. Must admit that the climate is getting milder, though. Or maybe it's just my age."

"Where are the snows of yesteryear?" asked Golem.

"They just don't make them the way they used to," answered Anna.

"Everything's made out of plastic these days," agreed Beatrice.

"No respect . . ."

"George, tell them about . . ."

Enough of that, right?

R   .

After dinner, Golem and Anna drove his mother to her hotel and helped her settle down in front of the color television set. Then they went off to the movies to see a revival of *Divorce, Italian Style*.

27   The night before the wedding, Anna sat on her mother's bed and listened to what it was like to be married. Golem took his mother to see *Divorce, Italian Style* and then smoked a half a pack of cigarettes before falling asleep.

28   "I do."

"I do."

A kiss.

49

It was over. Golem went into the bathroom to vomit while Anna stepped outside for a breath, a very deep breath of air.

29   Golem made her leave the reception at ten o'clock. They stood on the landing of the staircase from which she had made her entrance to the marriage.

"But it's our wedding, David. I don't want to leave yet. I'm having such a good time. Aren't you having a good time?"

"Yeah, I'm having a good time. But it's late; we've got a long way to drive. I've got to drive. You can sleep in the car."

"Oh, David. I don't want to leave yet. Besides, I think I'm getting a little drunk."

"Oh, great! For chrissakes, what a time to get drunk."

"Well, it's our wedding. What's wrong with that?"

"It's dumb as hell."

"Don't you call me dumb!"

"Don't raise your voice. You want everyone to hear us? How will that sound?"

"I don't care how it sounds. Don't call me names."

"All right, I apologize. Let's go, huh? Do you understand that we have a long way to drive?"

"We could stay in town tonight."

"I don't want to."

"Why not?"

"Because I want to get this honeymoon started."

She made him wait an hour before she met him on the landing again. He put the bags in the car he had rented and they slipped out the door after saying good-bye to their families.

They drove up the coast; Anna trying to sleep against the window while the vibrations of the car entered her body through her ear and made her brain tingle like the beginnings of a sore throat, Golem steering into the night as if the car were a pair of shears he was using to cut the fabric of his destiny. Finally, he could drive no more and stopped at a small motel. She handed him the Marriage License in case he needed it to register and he stuck it into his back pocket.

In their room, Golem put three quarters into the Magic Fingers Machine at Anna's insistence and the bed shook them to sleep; they were too tired to make love.

For the next week, they played newlyweds. For Anna, a day was simply a day, a period of time to be dealt with in the least painful manner, but for Golem, it was a challenge. Each one had to be unique; he had to make his mark on it. And so they argued about what time to get up, what time to go, what time to come, where to go (she wanted to lie on the beach, he wanted to tour the town), where to eat (she wanted simple food, he wanted specialties of the region), and, again, When. Always When. Now. Later. When. And at night, they made love to the sound of the waves breaking against the rocks (which they could hear because Golem had opened the windows, despite Anna's protests—and he not telling her that he wanted it open for the sound, only telling her that he could not sleep in a stuffy room—that the cold air was good for growth) with Anna always on top, warning Golem to be careful, not to push too deep inside her lest he accidentally touch it. And he wanted to, but he held back. And then they ran through the catalogue of goodnights which they had accumulated (Good Night. Good Night. I'll see you in the morning. I'll see you in the morning. Have sweet dreams. Have sweet dreams. Sleep tight. Sleep tight. Sleep well. Sleep well. I love you. I love you.) as if it were a litany or some magical incantation necessary to the safety of their marriage, indeed, to their very lives—no joke. . . . Anna had told him once that if he didn't say I'll see you in the morning to her, she doubted that she would . . . see what routine does to you, folks. He laughed but said it anyway, not being one to pass up a Pascalian wager when he saw one.

30   Are you ready for those calendar pages being whipped up up and out of camera range by the winds of Time? Shall I sing you *September Song* the way Boris Karloff used to on the old Kate Smith show? And we'll all cry together.

31   Because.
At one o'clock in the morning—the morning on which Golem was to deliver a paper called "On Recent Trends in the Depiction of Literary Lifestyle"—during the fourth month of their marriage and in the midst of their thirty-second sexual act—according to the total in Anna's notebook, the same one in which she listed the dates of all her menstrual periods since she was fifteen

years old (one could imagine the headings CURSES, under which was a list of dates, and FUCKS, under which were neat rows of four number-one-like marks connected by a dash to indicate a fifth, can't resist, fuck)—the being within Anna Golem surrendered.

"David!"

"What is it?"

"Stop!"

"What's the matter? Am I hurting you?"

"Something is happening."

"Are you coming?"

"NO." And then a gasp. "David!"

"Am I hurting you?"

"Something is happening."

"What is it, for chrissakes?"

"I don't know. It hurts." Another gasp.

"Do you want me to come out?"

"Yes."

He withdraws. She holds his shoulders. Pushes her face into his neck. Her stomach forces his inward.

"Is it better?"

"No."

She moves off him. Puts a hand on her stomach. Takes his hand and puts it on her stomach.

"Is he kicking?"

Another gasp.

"Should I call the doctor?"

Another gasp.

"I'll call him."

Another gasp.

Standing by the telephone, shivering without his clothes, moisture leaking from his penis, he receives the order to bring her to the hospital. Disaster is always without dignity.

32   In the car, cutting the fabric of destiny. $3.98 a yard.

Golem, his hair uncombed, an Irish knit turtleneck sweater in the famous Man of Aran pattern under a tweed jacket and over a pair of tobacco corduroys, hands gripping the steering wheel, knuckles white from not understanding—"Are you OK?"

Anna, wearing sunglasses so as not to recognize herself, huddled in a cloth coat with the hood up, bunched against the door, window shaking in her brain, gloved hands on her stomach to hold it together, small rivulets of perhaps blood beginning to discolor her black tights, would it all eventually fall into her shoes she wondered—"Hurry."

Like on television. Hesitating but not stopping at the red lights. Will a policeman see them, force them over to the curb, ask for driver's license, registration, saying, "You know why I stopped you, Buddy?"

Know before whom thou standest.

"Look, officer . . ."

He doesn't look. He is not allowed to look. Only to see.

The infant dies. The mother dies. Golem gets a ticket for going fifty in a thirty-five mile zone at one-thirty in the morning with no other cars save that of the peace officer in—here's that word again—Sight. A hearing is held. Nobody listens. The officer is acquitted; he later becomes vice-president of the Patrolmen's Benevolent Association. Golem collects the insurance and runs to Rio where he works in a diamond mine for seven years and, when he has regained his strength, returns to the United States. And, in the night, kills the peace officer and his family of seven after waking them from a deep sleep—a sleep into which they had escaped after a family quarrel centering around the right of the eldest daughter to read a book by Henry Miller or is it to be able to stay out past one o'clock on Saturday night so that she could get in an hour of heavy petting with her boyfriend, the lead guitarist with the Tradewinds, after the pep rally at the gym—shoots each one in the groin, in their respective genitalia and then in the face so that they won't suffer too much and, before departing for his rendezvous with a hostage, probably a clerk from the local supermarket, female of course, whom he will use as a shield against the promises of Priests and Police Captains who say they'll go easy on him (the Judge and God) if he surrenders, never knowing or even caring that what he wants is a Rabbi—not wearing space shoes or double-breasted cufflinks—to step right up and say, "Golem, stop behaving like a goy," he leaves a receipt on the table in the livingroom, the end table which protects the prom and confirmation and first communion and graduation and decoration for heroism above and beyond the call of necessity under a circle of heavy shatterproof glass.

Or else.

The infant, while the officer is writing down the registration number, comes out of Mom like toothpaste and the peace officer has to cut the umbilical cord with his Swiss Army Officer's Knife (the one with seventy-nine proven uses, just write in, folks, if you've found a new one and we'll send you on an all expense paid trip for two to all the Swiss Army installations in the Universe)—for which he receives not a decoration but a good solid ten dollar a week raise and they all make the *Daily News* so that the piano player can chuckle over their story at breakfast before he sends out his eighty-five bottles of liquor—who addresses those packages, my friend . . . why you do, of course—and then, two years later, the *Mirror,* sandwiched in between a story about a man who ate two automobiles and lived to tell the tale while remaining ding-proof for the rest of his life, though he did, on occasion, rust while drinking seltzer, and another about an amateur sword dancer (Maria Norville, aged 23, a student at Wisteria College in Wisteria, Mich.) who, while performing on the Harold Cornwall Amateur Hour, let go of her sword and it flew through the air, decapitating the Floor Manager and the Scenic Designer. She apologized publicly. (Said MC Cornwall, "Of course, I'm sorry . . . but the show's ratings have dropped in recent weeks; now it looks like some more heads will be rolling around here pretty soon." Said 22-year-old Gary Garth, leader of the Ozones, a rock 'n' roll group which provided musical accompaniment for the charming coed, "We amateurs get awfully competitive—and someone always gets hurt in the end." Said Lester Wist, of the tap-dancing team of Wist and Muse, who had known the girl for some time, "She was always a cut-up. And she fed on praise. When those people started applauding— APPLAUSE APPLAUSE APPLAUSE— she just lost control of herself." Said an impartial observer, "I'm not taking any more of their bull.")

Like on television?

Except, there are no policemen at one-thirty in the morning.

Not in this life, anyway.

So they get there, Golem choosing the Emergency Entrance as it provides a more dramatic appearance. He parks behind an ambulance of the same make and year that carried John Kennedy's body away from the deerhunt in Texas and helps his dripping wife into the building.

The chairs along the wall are filled with white and colored faces, each one having one thing in common; somewhere on their bodies, a wound is bleeding into layers of real or imagined gauze— and each one is different only by the location of that wound. They are all tattooed, Marines, Waiters, Unemployed, Factory Workers, Beer Drinkers—only Beer Drinkers brawl, others fight or, at least, struggle. All will be in the papers tomorrow under the headline category Disturbers of the Peace. Everyone does his share, like contributing to the United Fund or the Community Chest— "I want to help keep this town a nice place to live in," says Hezekiah Jones, 39-year-old itinerant human being. "I want to be able to raise my kids here. I don't want them sitting in Emergency Rooms."

There are no middle-class faces in Emergency Rooms. Not unless they fell out of tree houses which, as everyone knows, are unsafe to begin with, or are rushed here for unexpected appendectomies which, as everyone knows, are needless anyway, or are driven here by secretly gleeful sons in the middle of long-awaited heart attacks which, as everyone knows, are the result of building too few tree houses and having too many appendectomies. Consequently, the Nurse On Duty is quite surprised to see the Family Golem.

"Can I help you?" she asks, not believing that she can, thinking that perhaps they came in the wrong door and should have turned into the second driveway instead of into the first. Kids nowadays just don't read signs. Everybody's in too much of a hurry. That's what makes horse races.

"My wife . . . uh . . . Doctor Benjamin told us to come right away. My wife is pregnant and she is having trouble. Pains, bleeding, please."

"Your name?"

"Golem. I'm David. This is my wife, Anna."

I'm Buster Brown; I live in a shoe.

The N.O.D. nods hello and checks her list, finds what she is looking for, rings a small bell which brings a colored male orderly dressed in green nylon or plastic.

"Jimmy, take Mrs. Golem up to 310 West and get her settled. If you'll wait here for a moment, Mr. Golem, you can fill out these forms and then join your wife. Doctor Benjamin will be here momentarily."

"He isn't here yet? But this is an Emergency!"

"Don't get upset, Mr. Golem. It's nothing we can't handle; that's what hospitals are for, you know. Doctor Benjamin called to say that he was having a little car trouble but that he would be here momentarily. Jimmy . . ."

Jimmy comes to Anna who looks at Golem who kisses her on the cheek and says, "Don't worry. I'll be right up, honey. Everything will be all right."

"David, I'm afraid."

"Go with Jimmy, honey. It'll be OK."

What is going on here?

She goes.

He stays.

The N.O.D. pulls out her forms and rolls them into a typewriter, straightening the edges with moistened fingertips. "Name?"

"Mine or my wife's?"

"The patient's."

"Anna Golem."

"No Middle Initial?"

"R."

"Anna R. Golem."   "Female."   "Caucasian."   "Age?"

"22 or 23. I don't remember right now."

"We'll say 22. It really doesn't matter."

"All right. I can tell you later, though."

"All right, if you remember it."

"OK."

"Address?"   "Phone?"

"Apartment 4A. University Heights."   "929-6421."

"Is that your permanent address?"

"Well, it's where we live."

"Do you get your mail there?"

"Yes."

"Then it's your permanent address."

"Oh."

"Her Occupation?"

"None."

"Housewife?"

"Yes."

"Nearest Relative?"

"Me."

"You are?"

"I am."

"No, I mean your name. Your Full Name."

"Oh. David Alan Golem."

"One L or two?"

"One. Both with one."

"Same address?"

"Yes. And phone, too."

"Your occupation?"

"Student."

"At the University?"

"Yes."

"Your Nearest Relative?"

"Her."

"Parent or Guardian?"

"What?"

"Do you have a Parent or Guardian?"

"Yes."

"Can I have his/her Name and Address?"

"Beatrice Golem. 2273 Ocean Avenue. Brooklyn, New York."

"Is that a Mother or a Sister?"

"A Mother. My Mother."

"Her Parent or Guardian?"

"Dr. George Reitzler, Father. 22 Hopi Lane. Costa Verna, California."

"Did you meet in school?"

"Yes. Is that for the form?"

"No. Let's see . . . I can get the other information about the case when Doctor Benjamin comes in. So, I guess you can go up. Oh, one other thing. Religion?"

HESITATION.

The sky opens up. Thunder gets ready to crack. Lightning gets ready to strike. The finger is on the button. KNOW BEFORE WHOM THOU STANDEST. The suspense is killing you, right? What'll it be? A bold, forthright declaration, a stutter, a running of the two words together into a single unintelligible phrase of assimilationistic proportions—JEWS WHO GO TO NO SYNAGOGUES HAVE FACES WHICH CHANGE ALL THE TIME [1]—people who go no places have no faces—reductio ad commono, for the Green Giants in the crowd, of course—well? What will it be? Come on, Schmuck, don't be a Baby, be a Man—sell out? (Thank you for that one, O Spirit of American Humanity.) This is the turning point, folks. Whatever happens, happens here. Or does it? Do you ever know what's humping you in the night? [2] And it does matter, friends. But, don't forget . . . it's only a paper moon. It can change. Place your bets, this is where the action starts. ETC.

"I'm

Hit that chord. Play it again, Sam.

Jewish."

"And your wife?"

(Thought you'd get off the hook, eh? Well, you don't get off that easily. Who do you think you are anyway?)

"She's

Here comes the finale, folks.

Jewish, too."

Good evening, friennnnnnds. Clever? Just don't say cute. After all, you were waiting, weren't you?

"All right. You can go up, now."

[1] *Op. cit.*

[2] *Ibid.* (Don't you believe it, Charley.)

58

"Thank you."

"You're absolved."

"What?"

"I didn't say anything, Mr. Golem."

"But I heard you say, you're . . ."

"It must have been your imagination, sir."

"All that?"

"I beg your pardon?"

"Lady, you're absolved."

"What was that, Mr. Golem?"

"Nothing. I just belched. Excuse me."

"Of course. We're used to that around here. Hospitals are like that, you know. All that pain and people tend to forget themselves. Go right up. Take the elevator to the left."

The hospital was white, of course. Though the walls were painted green.

33   What can one say about an elevator? Oh, yeah, lots of things, perhaps. Like, say, there's no thirteenth floor. Or my stomach is falling. Or I can't hear anything. But, what do these things have to do with existence?

Everything, my friend.

That's the problem.

Press the button and shut up.

Say, did you hear the one about the automatic elevator that . . .

Yeah, I heard it. And besides, my stomach is falling.

Well, I'll tell it anyway.

Everything; that's the problem.

34   Outside her room, Golem drank cups of coffee like Fred MacMurray. Inside, legs tenting the white sheet, wrist band identifying her for hospital personnel around her wrist, surrounded by nurses who moved as though they were constantly breaking Ritz crackers, doctors who wore stethoscopes around their necks as if to say, "Fuck you, buddy; I'm a Dr. and if you get smart with me, I'll listen in on your body (see below for continued discussion of the mind-body problem and a possible new approach to organic synthesis . . . what this country needs is a good five cent syn)"—she labored.

Worked like hell.

Worked like a bitch.

Worked like a dog.

They're professionals, he said to himself. They'll take care of her.

"Help me," she cried.

"We're going to take her in now, Mr. Golem."

They were wheeling her out of her room. She was surrounded by figures, personnel. He reached for her hand and mumbled that everything would be all right. She cried, not knowing who was hurting her hand, who else was hurting her. The doctor stayed with him as her bed was wheeled through the swinging doors and into a place where he was not allowed. He had a sudden vision of the swinging doors on a movie saloon; they always led to the back lot.

"Will she be all right, Doctor?"

"I think so, Mr. Golem. It's all premature, but that isn't uncommon. I know it's hard for you, but try not to upset yourself more than is necessary. We'll take care of her."

What is necessary?

"What about the baby?"

"I can't answer that, yet. I really can't say, yet."

"Is there a chance?"

"Of course there's a chance. I'd say it was on the positive side, but I don't want to give you any false hope, Mr. Golem. It is very early, very premature."

Maturity, maturity. All life long they stick you with that shit about maturity and this is the only time it really counts. Really counts.

"I know."

"She's six or seven months pregnant?"

Don't you know? You better not get her mixed up with anybody else. Don't you recognize her? Look at the band on her wrist, for chrissakes.

"Six, I believe."

"It's difficult. At seven, they have a pretty good chance.

60

It's harder to say at six. Did you know, Mr. Golem, that fifty percent of the married couples lose their first child? I know that's not much comfort to you, but sometimes it helps to know what the statistics are, makes you feel a little less lonely, I suppose. My wife and I lost our first child."

Who was the doctor on that case?

Golem saw the doctor's face begin to melt; the features dribbled together. 50%? Oh, yeah? How do I know he isn't making that up just to make me feel better? He doesn't want to be bothered with my sorrow. How do I know he lost his first kid? Maybe he's making that up, too. Getting in there with the Personal Touch. He's a Professional. Anything to keep that shiny stethoscope from being spotted with patients' tears.

"Please try."

Isn't that feeble? But isn't that all?

"We'll do our best."

And what about that?

The doctor touched his arm and Golem felt the limb grow cold. He suggested that he sit down. It would be a while. Did he want to go home? No. Of course, he could stay. Will keep you informed. We'll tell you as soon as anything develops, happens. We'll send a nurse out as soon as we know anything definite.

A message from Garcia.

What has God wrought, asked S. Morse, the inventor of the medium.

35   Did you ever hear the joke about the old beggar?

The one who crossed the street?

No. Not that one.

Tell it. Maybe I haven't heard your version.

There was once an old beggar, a schnorrer who wandered from shtetle to shtetle like a homeless dog, a poor beast with only the clothes on his back and newspapers in his shoes to keep out the cold, looking and begging for a piece of bread, a place to lay down his weary head.

One night, during a rainstorm such as had never been seen in the countryside, he sought refuge in an abandoned barn. He was disgusted with his miserable life and with himself. Though not a religious man, for who is nowadays, he had no one else to turn to. So he raised up his hands to heaven as he had seen the rabbis do, and cried out: "How long, O God, how long am I going to suffer like this?"

By strange coincidence, another schnorrer happened to have picked out this very same barn to lie down in and he was up in the hayloft asleep. The first beggar's cry woke him up and, for a joke, he called down in his deepest, most religious voice: "Seven years."

The first beggar, whose name was Adam by chance, thought that God himself had answered him. He had heard that this often happened and, not being one to pass up an opportunity for receiving anything, whether it be a bowl of cold borscht with a dollop of sour cream floating on top or the answer to his life, he fell to his knees, blessed the Holy One and asked: "And what will it be like, O Mighty God, after the seven years of misery are over with?"

"You'll get used to it."
I heard it.
Who hasn't?
But I didn't remember it.
Who has?

36   God, if you get us through this, if she will be all right and if the child will be safe—I want both, I don't want to compromise or negotiate with you, you're supposed to be above that kind of thing—if you will make everything all right, if you will show us a little of that Mercy you're so proud of, I promise that I'll never jerk off, I mean masturbate, no, jerk off—what am I hiding from you?—again. Never again. You understand that?

"Is that what's bothering you?"

37   "Mr. Golem?"
"Yes, I'm Golem."
"Your wife is going to be all right."
"And the baby?"
"I'm sorry."
You're absolved, lady.

38   You bastard.

39   In the morning, his skin smelling of damp wool, his nails oranged by cigarettes, Golem stands beside and a little behind the doctor as the latter tells Anna. They're Professionals.

She does not look healthy. Her eyes do not want to open. She is exhausted; one works very hard to deliver what is expected of one. Her head is buried in the pillow, but it is not a resting place for her. The unnatural inclination of the mechanical bed makes her body look even more used, like the discarded wrappings of a gift. How can we expect women to bear children? Ah, but you can't judge a book by its presumed contents; appearances are deceiving, my friend. You should know that, but you forget. Her skin is the color of a manila envelope. Is everyone that color in Manila? Or only the dead?

"Mrs. Golem . . ."

Her eyes open a little more. She knows what he is going to say. She knows because he is there; because the baby isn't there sucking at her small breasts surrounded by the smell of get-well flowers and extravagantly congratulatory champagne. What did they send you if you failed? Did they send a wreath? Or did they consider it unworthwhile; after all, it didn't live very long, or even at all, one supposes because one never knows nor really cares to know. All this while more tears than she had ever seen in her life are getting ready.

"I'm afraid that I haven't very good news."

All news is bad news.

No news is good news.

How do you do this delicately? How do you explain a death so that it becomes acceptable, not in the social sense, but in the existential sense? Think man, we're all rational beings. Dig the mind which separates man from matter. We can get over anything —save life, of course. He seems to be hoping that I will nod my head in understanding or begin to cry so that he won't have to say it out loud. You have to say it. Don't you understand that it isn't official until you say it? That's what you get paid for, to make those kinds of judgments. It's a well-paid job, a solid position. Say it!

"The baby didn't live."

The baby. Why not *your* baby? Or was it not mine? Was I just a resting place for it, just a bank or a parking lot in front of the shopping center?

The tears came. The old body takes over when real trouble comes. Remember that for later. She had never seen so many tears before. The doctor had, of course; he was, after all, a Professional which means that he knows that they all give up after a while and cry (Ain't seen one yet that didn't, my boy.). She Cries. The doctor steps away with a few words of encouragement, leaving his place to Golem, the Husband, an amateur, an amateur in a fiercely competitive world. She needs rest, he says. Try to get her to rest. And Golem comes to hold her hand again, saying very little. He does not want to find his signature on the document two years hence.

She Cries. Moans. Beats her Breast.

He holds her hand, dies inside, knocks his head against the green wall that smells white.

Why is everything white in here? Maybe because it's easier to see the dirt. Don't want to miss a Speck, do you?

"I love you," he says, meaning it but still trying to make it better.

So what, she cries still more.

It will stop. There is no alternative. One cannot cry forever.

40   After her rest, he brings her coffee and ice cream. He wants to get a coloring book, but he knows this will be bad. This is not the time for childlike ingratiation. We are all grownups here. Finally. He watches her face, phrasing his sentences carefully to avoid causing more tears. The sorrow he cannot take away no matter how large his wheelbarrow is, but he does not want to cause any more.

She is a bundle of upset. There is no other feeling. Horror. Horror. No why's at this point; no how's. Only the Horror of having failed, having lost.

He talks about a vacation, after she rests, of course. And she agrees, not caring, knowing that you cannot vacation from this, play tennis as if it never happened, swim in the lake as if you were oh I wish I were a kid again, and knowing that she must try. So Brave. We're all soldiers. Civilized.

At the end of Visiting Hours, a nurse walks through the halls tinkling a dinner bell as if she were leading a procession of lepers and the doors of the cubicles open to reveal the Visitors saying their last goodnights. Soon, the floor will be silent except for an occasional gasp, a demanding buzzer which, though it might mean an impending death is treated as though it were a request for a glass of water, and the constant sound of breaking Ritz crackers. The patients will be left with their glass straws and their deaths.

Anna had something more to see her through the night. Golem will stay for a while longer, dozing in the large plasticovered chair at the foot of the bed; but he will leave after she falls asleep. This is not what she will use as a quilt against the December of her grief. It is the subtle agreement which passed between them as he sat on her bed, holding a glass of ginger ale so that she could draw it up into her body through the glass straw—the subtle agreement that it is, after all, his fault.

You're absolved, lady.

41   She rested at home for two weeks and every day Golem brought her something. Some days it was wild flowers or flowers he had picked from some professor's garden. Other days it was cookies or ice cream sodas or doughnuts. Food and Flora; no Fauna allowed in this house, mamma. She could not stand this little game; he pretending that he was bringing home trophies of his daily hunt, gifts for the savage's bride. And, of course, they both knew it was to keep her Happy, to get her involved with small pleasantries to take her Mind off the Big Disaster. Other people live with the problem—50% in fact—he told her. Why didn't they show that on television? Why didn't somebody write a handbook on how to get along with catastrophe, or were they still too busy with neurosis? Ah, but that would be giving away the secret. The Old Secret of Life. Never mind that, win friends and influence people, live with a neurotic and like it, meditate on a single sound, chase your headache away FOREVER, assume the Lotus Position

or, better still, the famed Peacock Pose which—according to THE
YOGA SYSTEM OF HEALTH AND RELIEF FROM TEN-
SION (the great middle-class slayer, the American plague, a
cancerous preoccupation with TtEeNnSsIiOnNn)—"has a good
effect on the expelling action of the colon, and is very beneficial
for obesity, piles, constipation. It also develops the chest." (Man,
said he to her as he read the book, those Indians are worried
about constipation and chest development while their minds are
rotting away from malnutrition. She nodded, of course.) Or go
to the synagogue; receive God, trust in Him, the Lord Giveth and
the Lord Taketh A-way so the Lord is an Indian Giver—see,
everything comes full circle, circumferencing her, circumlocuting
her. Going to the synagogue is fine for Friday nights, but how do
you wash dishes on Wednesday afternoon? Use Bold, Cheer?
What's the difference; it's all powder. OK, there is no secret.
You survive, that's all. You want to survive, you survive. You
laugh when something is amusing; forget about the death of the
kid, George told a joke, for chrissakes. "I want to take a vacation,"
she said one evening over the gingerbread crumbs that remained
from her husband's gift.

"A vacation?" he asked.

"Maybe if we can get away together to the mountains or
someplace like that for a week or so, I'll feel better."

"Maybe you're right. It's very gray around here; we need
some color. The mountain air would be good for you. Do you
think you're strong enough?"

"I'm strong enough."

"Have you rested enough?"

All of us are ignorant at times.

"I've rested enough. I want to get away."

"OK. It's a good idea."

She knew it was a good idea. She had seen it on television that afternoon when a wife whose mother died in an automobile accident was taken to the mountains by her understanding
husband. They thought it would work. Or, at least, the writers
thought it would work. Everybody needs writers which is why we
have them. They give us our ideas. Our lives.

"Can we go soon?"

"Well, I guess we could get away at the beginning of next week. Is that soon enough?"

"All right. It'll do."

"I'll make some reservations tomorrow."

"Do we have to stay in a motel? Could we camp out?"

"Camp out?"

"Yes, in the woods."

"Are you strong enough for that?"

"Yes."

"Should you check with the doctor?"

"David, I'm healthy."

"OK, OK. I just don't want to push you. I'll make the arrangements and we'll camp out. I haven't done that since I was a . . ."

A slip of the tongue, that's all. No wonder the tongue is shaped like a dagger, no wonder they used to call it speaking with a forked tongue, no wonder. 'Cause the tongue is connected to the head and we all know, or do we, who's humping in there. Prong.

"Boy scout."

"We can borrow sleeping bags from Cohen."

"Does he have sleeping bags?"

"I think so; he told me that he camped out a lot."

"I can't see him in the woods. He couldn't see the forest for the trees."

A small chuckle would be in order here, but not too loud, lest you wake them.

"Ask him tomorrow."

"OK, I will."

And she reminded herself not to forget to watch that television show tomorrow to find out how that woman made out in the mountains. Maybe the Old Secret of Life *is* between the Bold and the Cheer. Old sneaky Mad Ave and their subtle methods—subliminal soul from Sears Roebuck and all the rest.

42   The mountain trip was all downhill.

He failed to start the fire with one match.

She failed to bake the biscuits without burning the bread.

Out there with the moon peering like a voyeur on the

cover of a hot book over the tops of the insolent pine trees, surrounded by the sounds of enough fauna to fill a two-record set,
amidst the aroma of more herbs than were to be found in Horatio's
(poor Horatio, he gets it from all sides) philosophy, zipped tight,
good-night, snug as a bug in a bear rug, together in one kapok-
filled, flannelette-lined waterproof sleeping bag that smelled of
Japanese paper and mildewed wool, they failed to make the old
earth move, tremble, or even vibrate except where Golem shifted
his body—Female Still Superior—to get off a fucking pine cone
which had fallen from a fucking pine tree.

They tried. Wearing jeans and lumberjack shirts that
itched like hell and joking about Golem's hesitant beard. They
tried. Catching fish in a cold mountain stream that even babbled
and arguing about who would have to clean the prize. They tried.
Sitting by the campfire telling ghost stories to scare each other
back into real life.

But they had no writers. No plots to compare. Only
remembrances of cigarette and soft drink commercials. Oh yeah,
but who needs writers, man? This is real life, you know. Survival
of the fittest and all that jazz. Fuck your poetry; get back to
Nature, that's where it's at. Plug into the old electromagnetic
spectrum and do a little dance for Saint Vitus as the current
comes coursing through the old limbs. Implode, baby, implode.
What are you waiting for?

They Tried. They Failed.

Fuck your poetry, man. Who *needs* that shit? All the
pioneers come on at 7:30 in the evening, right after the news.
We're civilized. We can get over anything.

43   Three and a half years later, they had gotten over it. Or,
at least, they didn't talk about it any more. Nor about Golem's
first affair which he revealed in a moment of anger upon discovering that Anna was having an *affaire de tête* with a graduate
student in the French department. Nor about the Christmas tree
which Anna insisted upon their having during their second year.
Nor about the anniversary present that Golem had forgotten to
buy during their third year. Nor about the fight they had on one
Thanksgiving during which Anna had threatened to kill herself
and Golem had calmly walked into the kitchen and returned to the

bedroom where he presented his wife, boy-scout fashion, with a bone-handled, serrated carving knife which she took and threw at him but not with enough accuracy to be serious about it. Nor about the time that Golem punched her in the stomach after she called him a fuckass when he refused to dry the dishes which had been sitting in the sink for three days.

They held their chins up high; they told each other it was love. They made love by making it, created it. They experimented, manipulated . . . talked till three, four, five in the morning, tossing psyches about the livingroom with abandon, always making up at the end, always saying it will be better, always et ceteraing

They did try and it was better. Golem apologized constantly; Anna dried all the dishes. They bought each other gingerbread cookies and a large puzzle to work on on rainy nights and gray Sundays, they even suggested the possibility of another child.

"After I get out of school."

"All right. But when will that be?"

"I'm not sure."

They got over it. They got over everything; that was the trouble.

44   "Cohen, you are a regular *deus ex machina.*"

"Hmmm?"

"Every time I come to the cafeteria to drink a cup of self-pity, you show up."

"Just having morning coffee, David. But if I can be of any help . . ."

"You are, you are. When I see you, I say to myself, there but for fortune go I."

"Glad to oblige. Is your cup running over this morning?"

"Cohen, if I ever write a book, you'll be in it. If I ever write a song, you'll sing it."

"All Graduate Students will hate you."

"To say nothing of disc jockeys."

"How is Anna?"

"Fine."

"Why don't we all go out for dinner some night? I'd ask you over to my place, but it's a mess."

"Cohen, are you hiding a schickse in your apartment?

You are rumored to have more than a passing interest in a certain blond cheerleader."

"We all have our weaknesses, David."

"Yeah. And mine are getting stronger."

45   Their bills are on the table. Golem and Anna face each other across the white formica table that occupies one corner of their kitchen, the breakfast nook corner. Golem sits, hand on the holster of responsibility, behind a growing stack of Monthly Statements. Anna sits, properly contrite but fingering a dagger of diminishing reasons under her skirt.

"Did we drink this much milk last month?"

"Yes."

And you liked *Tom Jones?*

"Eight and a half dollars worth of milk?"

"That includes orange juice, too."

"Oh."

"And sour cream."

"Oh."

"And the whipped cream that you said you were dying to have."

"All right, all right. It just seemed like a lot. It costs a hell of a lot just to keep this house running on a day-to-day basis. And that doesn't include extras."

"I know it."

"Well, I'm not made of money."

"I know it."

"Can you economize a little bit?"

"Then you'll complain about not having enough."

A moment here, friends. Do you remember when you were a kid and you and your friends used to argue about if you were going to get killed, if you were going to get it, which would be the best way? Gun or Knife. Remember that? Nobody ever defined *best*. Which may be the trouble with the world today.

Back to our story.

"Well, I can't afford to keep on like this. We won't be getting any more money for a couple of months. And even that isn't going to be enough. Can't you help out?"

"You want me to go to work?"

"I didn't say that."

"But that's what you meant."

"Well, maybe a part-time job."

"You want me to support you?"

"Look, Anna, lots of wives do that. Shit, I'm not asking you for a hell of a lot. Just to help out a little, that's all."

"I'll take in ironing."

"Come on."

"Or scrub floors."

"Come on."

"Or take in typing. I'll do theses."

"Very funny. Christ, you could get a part-time job in the library or something like that. A couple of afternoons a week. We could use the money."

"You want me to support you."

"No. I want you to help out. Marriage is supposed to be a partnership, you know."

46   They made love by candlelight, using the sweat of their bodies to glue their lives back together. But perspiration evaporates quickly in dry heat. Afterward, they shared a cigarette and an ashtray which rested on Golem's stomach, rising and falling with his speech.

"It might be good for you to have a job, honey. I mean, now that you're not in school, you need some kind of activity. Hanging around the house must be pretty lonely and I know I'm not much company when I'm home in the afternoons."

"Yes."

"Working in the library is easy. And you'll be around people. It might help a lot."

"Maybe."

"If you don't like it, you can quit. I'm not going to force you to stick with it, but I'd like you to give it a try, for both our sakes. You can keep part of the money for yourself. Half, if you want."

"It's not the money."

"I know. But it would be nice, anyway. Will you try it?"

"OK, I'll try it."

"Good. I'll call up for you."

"David?"

"What?"

"You won't be mad at me if it doesn't work out?"

"I won't be mad. But don't give up before you try."

"OK, I'll try."

"Good."

And after the good-nights, the sleep tights, etc., only the smoke remains in the air. During the night, perhaps during a bad dream, Golem rolls over and knocks the ashtray off his night table and onto the floor. In the morning, he apologizes for the mess he's made and Anna vacuums it up as if it were never there.

47   "Sometimes," Golem said as he lowered his glass of beer, "I don't even like her. I love her, but I don't even like her. You understand that, Paulo?"

"Yeah. It happens. People screw you sometimes."

"I love her and I can't stand her. She's driving me crazy."

"Come on."

"I guess I'm getting carried away. I really love her, goddamnit."

48   "Cohen," said Golem, lowering his coffee cup, "I think I have to get out of the academic world. It's becoming unfashionable."

"And do what, David? Go into business, become a captain of industry? You'll never do it, David. You will miss all this free expression."

"The free expression is what's killing me, Cohen."

49   "Anna," said Golem, chewing a piece of steak on the right side of his mouth, "you look tired. Is something bothering you?"

"Nothing unusual."

"Do you want to talk about it?"

"That's all you ever do. Let's talk about it, you say."

"Well, sometimes it helps to talk about what's bothering

you. Don't you think so? I mean, isn't that what the twentieth century is all about?"

"Don't get smart. We don't ever say anything new. We're just like two tape recorders. Go get your Cheer Up Tape Number Three while I thread my Depression Tape Number Seven."

"OK, but how do we know what we feel unless we talk about it?"

PRONG.

The power of speech is what makes us men, or so some would say.

50   Down the long library steps (knowledge is worth the climb) and into the charcoal p.m. where the car waits in the parking lot to be driven back to hamburger meat on the sink, waiting for someone to sponge up its juices. If it were left there for another hour, would all the blood run out into the sink and down the drain and into the sewers? It was a Friday; Golem would be napping now with his hand in his crotch. There would be door-slamming, television entrances, and, finally, the six-thirty news and the daily report of catastrophes . . .

> **A Milk Strike in the Midwest**
> **Jetliner Crashes in Ohio**
> **Man Kills 13 in Arizona**
> **76 Americans Die in Hill Assault**
> **"Come and get me," says Leo Held.**
> **"I'm not taking any more of their bull," he says.**
> **"I wanted to get known," says Benjamin Smith, "just wanted to get myself a name."**
> **Born To Raise Hell, says Richard Speck.**
> **God knows what, said Charles Whitman.**
> **I'm innocent, says Lee Harvey Oswald.**
> **I'm innocent, says Jack Ruby.**
> **We're innocent, says our President.**
> **I WANNA BE LOVED BY YOU, sang Helen Kane, also known as Betty Boop, before she died of cancer in Queens.**
> **"A great many mistakes have been made," said President Lyndon Baines Johnson. "There are a good many days when we get a**
> **C-minus**
> **instead of an**
> **A-plus."**

. . . which Golem collects for future reference, perhaps to use in his thesis.

At this moment, Cohen leaves the English department and, as he has probably been planning to do for at least a week, catches up with Anna as she takes the last step.

"Hello," he says.

"Hi," she says.

"How about a beer?" he asks.

"Love to, but I've got to make dinner," she answers.

"Just one won't hurt," he offers.

"I guess not," she admits.

Ah, that fatal glass of beer, the first step on the road to degradation. The oldtimers were right, folks. For that one beer leads to another and another until, quick as a camera can pan, Anna and Cohen are undressing in his apartment, lying on his bed, making their love

perhaps at the same moment that Golem is dreaming the American Dream (if I could kill my wife and get away with it, I'd be in the movies), or awakening and finding his hand stuck to his crotch, going to the bathroom to wash

as Cohen drives himself into Anna's body, as Anna says Yes, Yes and all the other things that women say to disguise the sound of their own heartbeats

perhaps taking a perfunctory shit, expelling his waste without thought, not taking the time to enjoy the sensation of departure

as Cohen comes, spurts his little Bar Mitzvah eve epiphany into Anna's body while she thinks of the hamburger blood running into the sink and begins to choke, not allowing herself to be satisfied

as Golem sits by the telephone, dialing the library, the Police Station, the Ubie, the hospital, the gas station

as Cohen says I'm sorry and Anna accepts his apology while hooking her bra: "So am I," Anna says.

"I'll kill her," Golem says.

"I'm sorry, David. I was so depressed after work that I went to the movies."

"Why didn't you call me?"

"I was upset. I should have called. I made a mistake and I'm sorry. Please accept my apology and let me make dinner."

"All right. Christ. I was worried. Did the movie cheer you up?"

"No."

"You want to talk about it?"

"No. I just want to make dinner for you."

"All right. I'm going to catch the end of the news. Let me know when it's ready."

"OK. Call me if anything important happened today."

"I will."

51   Anna in her bed.

"Is that you, David?"

David at the door.

"Yes. Did I wake you?"

"No. I was just going to bed."

"OK. Sorry I'm so late, but we were talking."

IV

52   Have you got *your* ear to the window? Lean down and put it against the third rail—watch out!—and dig the pure electricity of the subway as the train, the Express (Forget the Local for the time being because that's the one you always pass in the station while you're folding your paper or telling yourself what you should have said and you wonder what the hell those people are thinking and how come they took the Local and is their train really moving too.) comes barrelling, rumblling, humblling out of a tunnel that looks like the hall from a dream by Orson Welles and Zooms past the pimp standing by the pistachio nut machine. That's how it feels. Sing London Bridge Is Falling Down fast three times and blink your eyes in time to the tune. Dig the rhythms; the vibrations are everywhere and they're after us, tra la.

53   SlaM, the door.
   "And not a person shall say who is who or what is what and go into the place wherein the new dress put it on and given

them a show put upon thy face the smear and give them the works and *put thy furbush on*" (emphasis added).[3]

"Sorry, honey. I didn't mean to slam it."

"That's all right. Will you be long?"

"No, I'll just wash up and get ready for bed."

"Were you at Paulo's?"

"Yes."

"Are you still high?"

"Just a little. Actually, I'm down. We didn't smoke very much."

54 "So shall ye put your cards on the table and call an ace an ace and a spade a spade and ye shall also say who is who and what is what." [4]

Good Advice.

Golem looked at himself in the mirror on his medicine chest and was relieved to find that he was not a vampire, that, indeed, his reflection did exist. Sometimes, he had noticed that while drinking and catching a glimpse of himself in somebody else's mirror, it seemed as though his face was that metaphorical candle, rapidly melting from ear to ear, and he would throw some cold water on it to stop the flow of features—what would they think when he walked back into the livingroom; would they tell him to get his chin off his chest and go back to work?

He unbuckled his belt and, in doing so, decided that he would no longer wear one, except, perhaps, with his black suit, because they were virtually useless anyway, that is, if your pants fit you. He pulled it through the loops of his pants and hung it on the hook in back of the door and, for a moment (which is long enough if it comes at the right time), it looked like a weapon of Bergmanesque ancestry. He unsnapped his pants, zipped down the fly, and pulled the whole thing, shorts and all, down to his calves and then kicked them down to his ankles—I'll be goddamned if I'm going to sit on my *own* toilet with my pants wrapped around my thighs.

[3] An example of automatic writing from *When Prophecy Fails* by Festinger, Riecken, and Schachter (New York: Harper Torchbooks, 1964).
[4] *Ibid.*

He sat down on the toilet and rested his back against the lid cover. Cold. His head felt as though it didn't want to have anything to do with the rest of his body—which, after all, is the bulk of the problem. His face reddened, he contracted—but not too hard, for some people, or so they say, die that way. Can you imagine having a heart attack on the toilet? Ugh, worse than having one in the midst of a screw, but not too much worse than having one just as you're telling your son what a bum he is. I don't want to think about that yet, he says to himself.

A distraction is needed.

"The plan has never gone astray. We don't *know what the plan is,* but it has never gone astray." [5]

Shall we inventory Golem's medicine chest?

Forget it. Not time, yet.

How 'bout thinking of things a stone's throw away?

OK. Shoot.

Remember, he says to himself as if he were a commercial for an antacid preparation for the brain written by one of those interior monologists who glut the national airways, nowadays, with their hard-hitting, fast-acting, low-punching pitches for their patent medicines, remember when that guy in the bar stole your raincoat which held your sunglasses in one of its slash pockets and you couldn't make up your mind what to do about it because, well, the raincoat was dirty and old and you did want another one and you really didn't want to chance a black eye or a broken nose over a raincoat (you were always a pessimist, you schmuck), but you did want those sunglasses back because they made you look like whoever you were doing at the time and, besides, though that's not the point, they were expensive? Remember that?

Yeah.

Well, you went right to the guy's house and called him out and, very cool-like—hands in pockets, head down, feet kicking at the ground as if you were trying to start your own version of Grauman's Chinese (I wonder if they'll change the name now that the game has changed again), and said:

"Hey man, did you cop my raincoat?"

He was smaller than you and you remember him as the

[5] *Ibid.*

kind of guy you drink with when the busy signal on the telephone makes you feel like an electronic Kafka, so you didn't want to give him more trouble than he already had before he met you.

"Me?" he replied.

"Well, yeah, man. I mean (everybody was slightly, but only slightly, inarticulate in those days) we were together in the bar and then I gave you a lift home and my coat was in the back seat and now it's gone, dig?"

"Are you accusing me of stealing your raincoat?"

"Well, it's not there now. And you were the last guy in my car besides me and I didn't steal it and the doors were locked when I parked."

That covers everything.

"I'm not even your size!"

A change of pace, eh? All right, enough of this reasonable bullshit. I want my coat back.

"Listen, man, if you need the raincoat that bad, you can keep it. But I've got to have my shades back. They're prescription, anyway."

I said, enough. Didn't you hear me?

"I didn't take your *fucking* coat!"

"Don't call my coat a *fucking* coat!"

Wow! Incredible, right? That anyone, and especially you, would say something like that. Sounds like, "Your Mother Wears Army Boots." And so you pushed him, open-handed to the shoulder, as a warning and he reacted as if you had said, "Your Mother Wears Army Boots," and threw a quick punch to your stomach, perhaps gut is more appropriate but we'll settle for stomach, and—for a second or two—you had an option; it was up to you whether to let the wind leave you or to keep it in and you decided, because you're a Man and not a Baby, to keep it in.

Hurrah!

And then you hit him. Really hit him, open-handed, of course, because, although you were a Man, you were certainly not an animal, but hit him hard enough so that both of you would be able to remember the sound your hand made when it connected with his cheek when you went to bed that night and, if you were lucky, for a few nights after that, too. That sound, what was it like? Maybe, like the noise those guys from the Philippines make when they try to catch the broad's feet in between those two wooden poles. It sounded good and your stomach got down off the elevator and your heart gave you a little good-job-well-done pat in the chest and you felt like an adolescent Hemingway.

The guy started to cry, I think. Did I get my raincoat back or what? Yeah, I must have. I ought to tell Cohen about that; he could work that into a nice little short story.

And remember . . .

55   Three more notes from Golem's diary.

1. **When you get some time, write a song about the generation gap. Maybe call it the Generation Gap Blues—sounds like it has good commercial possibilities. Oh, shit on that generation gap crap . . . how's that for anal symmetry?**

2. **Also, think about changing thesis title to "The Splendor of the Perplexed." It has a good ring; find a topic to go with it!**

3. **Sex and Violence**
   Sex and Violence
   Go together like *(love and marriage?)*
   Sis was told by Brother
   You can't have One without the Other

56   . . . when you met Carol or was it Carolyn? Interesting how some parents will add a suffix to their child in order to make certain that it remains theirs and then society goes and exists solely on nicknames. I always wanted to be called Flash. It seemed most inappropriate and, therefore, most fitting. Carol or Carolyn? Call her Carol and be sorry if you offend anyone. Always Apologize In Advance said the Junky Sage to the Boy about to take his first taste. They'll love you for it.

Carol.

Carol used to dance naked at the parties held downstairs in that old house which is now a parking lot; returned to the ground from *whence* it came. Well, not all naked or, that is, not all naked all at once. It was progressive or geometric, perhaps. The first Saturday night, it was in the spring, no rather it was at the end of winter; it was February. The first Saturday night, she took off her blouse while dancing, while a lot of people were dancing like imitation spades to the sound of Bo Diddley who fed their fantasies by singing *I'm a Man*. Well, I declare. Everybody was surprised because, although everybody knew that she would screw for anybody who would come across with the old I Love You bit (makes you wonder who's pimping for who-m, doesn't it?), nobody expected a public scene. Doing It and Doing It in public were different even in those days and in those ways, despite the fact that the whole concept of perspective of the generation was shaped, nay, decided, by the foreshortened way your average teenage couple looked in that easy chair when the lights were suddenly turned on in the paneled, finished basement and everybody found out—and received the message with exactly the same mixture of Child Pride and Adult Shame—that they were Making Out, which, incidentally, is quite different from Making It.

In any case, people didn't get undressed in public mainly because, and Carol's frantic empiricism served to prove the hypothesis, their underwear was never really clean. Carol's bra was OK in front, but in back, where the pieces joined to hook or snap, it had that used, sweat-stained grayish look that sounds like underwear and makes you feel like you're touching, forgive me, bruised fruit. Not at all the way it looks in the Maidenform Dreams; not glossy, but matte and flat like the little pieces of skin and dirt you rub off your ankle while you are drying yourself after a bath. But people danced with her.

I didn't!

No, you didn't.

But people did. And word of the impromptu performance spread through the subculture like salt butter on corn bread and at the next Saturday Night Party, there were close to twice as many people in the audience, everybody hanging around with glasses in one hand and cigarettes in the other and waiting to see if and what she would take off tonight. It was, in fact and in fantasy, the reason for the party. Will she do it, man? Hell, I don't know, why don't you ask her? Me, man! I'm not going to ask her; you ask her. Well, I just think she's a dirty, sick girl. Yeah, but she's got a nice body. I hope she takes it all off tonight because I've got a date for the basketball game Next Saturday Night. Finally, I asked her.

No, you didn't!

Christ, I can't get away with anything.

She did it. At twelve o'clock, with Lightnin' Hopkins singin' the blues, she, like Cinderella, took off her sweater and her skirt and kept on dancing with Richburg (of whom it was said that he would fuck, with Malthusian élan, any girl who could put her legs over his shoulders and we, being somewhat naive, thought that to be a mark of considerable accomplishment). No fancy underwear, just Woolworth White without so much as the day of the week embroidered on the leg. She was smart, wanting it to appear spontaneous; obviously, black or lace would have given her away immediately. But now, she became even more difficult to deal with because underwear that is not sexy or, rather, a girl dancing in unsexy underwear is not a phenomenon without alternatives. But people danced with her and I have to admit that I liked the way her ass jellied under the acetate when she moved to the blues, but the hair which sprung out in coils from the front legs of the pants turned me off.

The Next Saturday, she didn't show up at all and people, that is the people who knew her name, pretended to worry about her. Was she OK? I hear she flipped out, man. The crowd that came in after the basketball game (Let's go over and see that girl dance naked after the game, darling. Do you really want to, Betsy?) was very disappointed and thought about asking for a refund though they had paid nothing.

This was, of course, a test; one which some of us passed. Because the Next Saturday Night she was already down to her bra and panties when I walked in at ten o'clock. Already dancing with Richburg and before twelve, she had nothing on, no decorations, no pasties, no g-string, nothing but hair and flesh and a semi-smile and eyes that seemed to lock onto anybody else's that settled on her body. Dancing in the middle of the other couples—all dressed for this was not an orgy or anything remotely like that, only a display—who did their best, and you could see it by the way they kept their eyes fixed on each other's arms or noses, on anything that could not be connected by common sexual referents, not to look at the way her breasts flopped, etc. And, I must admit that I was surprised. Even I, who had seen the ultimate vision of myself in startling Freak-O-Scope (more about that some other time) had never seen a chick dancing naked at an otherwise ordinary party.

But I danced with her, later.

I danced with her later and I looked, stared at the way her nipples stood still on her jiggling titties, at the way the hair on her, well, what shall I say?—the hang-up of my generation, I suppose, say it's a cunt 'cause I could never stand twat—cunt sprung when she moved her hips in what she certainly thought was a soulful fashion, cruised her body because I'd be damned if I'd let some chick, no matter how twisted, put her body over on me. Her eyes held mine all the time; they would not let go. She wanted to be sure I saw everything because, I guess, that's all she thought she had. Glad to Oblige. Dump your little vanities on Golem; no modesty in him except, of course, when he belches and excuses himself when no one's there to hear him. He's like a tree in the forest, a little analogy in three-quarter time for the Zen idealists in the backroom. Glad to Oblige.

I took her home after the party. It took her longer to get dressed than undressed, having to do a bathroom scene with me following behind with her clothes and then me opening the back door so that we could get out without having to deal with anybody's remarks. At her apartment, we drank a glass of wine on the couch/bed and she asked me if I would stay the night. Imagine, and I hadn't even told her that I liked her! But, I said all right and then she went into the bathroom and when she came out she was wearing a flannel nightgown that Mother Hubbard would, had she done that sort of thing, characterized as demure. I stripped down to my boxer shorts and immediately understood how she felt at the party. She made up the bed and we went to sleep together. We didn't make love; I didn't even want to kiss her. Didn't seem to be any sense in that. And she liked me for that.

Patting yourself on the back?

Well, I suppose so.

Big deal. So you didn't screw the broad.

It was a decision. A moral decision.

Uh-huh. And now what are you doing, cataloging your existential acts?

I suppose so.

Well, Golem my boy, as they say in the South, shit or get off the pot. (How's that for double entendre?)

Golem got up.

The trouble with everything nowadays, he said to the Modigliani nude hung on the wall in front of him—a print which he had stolen during his get-back-at-the-bookstore days—is that, and I know you'll laugh at this, is that no one understands what color mauve is. Sounds simple, but it isn't. Mauve has been eased out of our color catalog; does Crayola make a mauve crayon? Does Sears sell mauve drapes? See. What's next to go? Chartreuse? Probably not because it will always live on at least as a joke. Beige? I wish it would but it fills the middle-class gap between acolor and nocolor. Corporations are beige. Well, give me the good ·old days, the good old mauve days. Wasn't there a historical period called the Mauve Decade or Era or Eon? Make a note, a mental note, of course (don't write on your arm; that's where the numbers and answers go) to find out about that. Research it. It could be a key, a new form of Rosetta (was that a color, too?) Stone or, at least, the first number in the combination like Pearlmutter's theory of Cultural Definition Via Product Brand Name—P.S., remind yourself to write to Dichter to investigate that one . . . one good fictive turn deserves another as long as we're dealing in allusions.

Golem got up, unrolled four wrist twists of yellow toilet paper—just enough, not too much, nothing so embarrassing as, unless it's the aforementioned heart attack, stuffing up the toilet or more frustrating than not having enough paper with which to erase oneself—and used it. Then, with a practiced eye, he repeated his action and, satisfied that he was Come Clean, Sonny . . . I'm Clean—echoecho I'm Innocent, Innocent, Innocent . . . flushed the toilet, noting as he did so that his feces were formless.

"O Shit," he said over the sound of his own disappearing waste.

"What did you say, David?"

"Nothing. I'll be right out."

57   Rather than listen to the water as Golem washes his hands, indulge yourself in this fable by a boy named Mark Vecchiose.

THE HEAD MAN [6]

This guy was born, but he was just a head. So he went to a witch doctor and he said, "I don't want to be just a head." The witch doctor put up his hands and went puff and turned him into a hand.

Then the guy ran around hollering, "I don't want to be a hand!"

There is a Moral to this story:
"You should have quit while you were a head."
Gee, kids say the kraziest things.

58   "Anna."

"What?"

"I'm sorry about before."

"So am I."

One does not want to go to sleep in a bad mood or with a disturbed conscience for the specter of stirring the unconscious to nightmarish proportions for which one is totally unprepared, morally unprepared, strikes fear into the heart of even the bravest of us existentialists. Bad dreams, p-you!

"Will you try?"

"Yes. Will you?"

"Yes."

Golem gets into bed and rolls next to Anna, gives her a kiss on her neck which is the only exposed part of her body. She does not turn over to respond to him, for that would be admitting defeat, but she does not turn away either and so he feels that he can sleep comfortably. Instead, she says, "Who was there?"

"Just Paulo and Toni."

"Did you all turn on?"

"Toni didn't."

"I suppose she doesn't need it."

"What's that supposed to mean?"

"Nothing."

"She's a nice girl; she didn't feel like turning on. Look,

[6] From H. Kohl's "36 Children" as reprinted in *Books,* December 1967.

I don't want to argue. I saw Cohen this morning and he said that Osterman is having a party on Saturday night. He was anxious for us to come. Do you want to go?"

"I don't know. Do you?"

"I don't have anything else planned. I'll check the movies. Maybe we'll catch one and then go out. I'd like to go, but I don't want to stay all night."

"Whatever you want to do is all right."

"OK. But if you'd rather not go or if you'd rather do something else, just let me know."

"All right."

Golem turns over on his right side, shooting his arm up and underneath the pillow as if in atavistic reference to a western movie in which the Hero keeps his hand on his gun while catching forty or fifty winks. He looks at the darkness, selects a going to sleep dream from his vast catalog, a brain book-film that operates like a juke box, chooses a short little number about screwing his wife from behind while she makes love to Toni, and says, just before closing his eyes and getting down to business, says, "You know, sometimes I have the feeling that I think in numbered paragraphs."

59   On Friday night, Golem took his wife to the synagogue. Well, here we go again, it was and it wasn't the synagogue. That is to say, it was a synagogue in the true sense of its being a place where ten men could gather together with something they all, for one night a week, agreed was God. But not in the old world or even closer Lower East Side metaphorical sense of brownbrick on gray street dignified by white sign on which are blue Hebrew markings that set this house apart, sociologically speaking, from other Houses. Instead, it was one room in the Jewish Student Center on the campus; the Jewish Student Center (JSC) being a place where one could, if one could forgive the rabbi who played golf with the Presbyterian minister—can't you see them down on the links telling jokes about . . . what? What do rabbis and Presbyterian ministers have to say to each other that makers or sellers of women's undergarments don't—oh, I know, but *inflection* isn't everything. It may well be much of everything, in the same way that personality is simply the varieties of neurotic manifestations, but you'll not—Romantic that I am—convince me that it's *everything*. Lost the place. A place. A place where one could remember that one was, indeed, Jewish and, what's more, a Jewish Student; heavyweight, that. But the synagogue or, more properly, the synagogue room (one refuses with all good cause to refer to it as does that walnut-grained plastic plaque on its beige door which advises that beyond this door lies neither the Wrath nor the Mercy of God, nor that place in which it is officially deemed permissible to apologize for becoming what one has always wanted to become, nor that place in which one confesses to himself and in the company of others that he is, after all, nothing more than a man, bigger than an ant, yet no less sociable [Be Sociable—Drink Pepsi, say the engraved tones of the bearded announcer. Remember that one? It came before the Pepsi Generation.], but THE CHAPEL. An airport/hospital euphemism with its origins in the same kind of mind that invented the Rest Room to substitute for the Shit House.) which was a module of grace with tiny pews (Those college kids've got short legs, Harvey; we can save dough on the chapel if we build small pews. But, Sam. Is it *functional*? This he wants to know. Dig the juxtaposition; functional and God—the architects of our synagogues are the architects of our sins for there is where one stands agog at one's sins. But, to resume.) and a miniark which held two minitorahs and over which hung the ultimate product of the Industrial Revolution, a fully transistorized Eternal Light—operates on only two flashlight batteries which, folks, are never included. Provide your own electricity, Mac.

Above, and to the right of that aforementioned rectangle of diluted identification, was the traditional mezuzah; container of a small portion of consistent, dependable holiness. Golem feared, however, that were he to open this mezuzah, he would find a small piece of parchment on which was stamped the words, MADE IN JAPAN.

And it was to this room that Golem brought his wife nearly every Friday night. Not because he was a Jewish Student, not because he felt compassion for the rejects of the Jewish Fraternities who made the Student Center into *their* club, substituting mustaches for frat pins, not because he enjoyed the twenty-minute service, a miniservice as he supposed the rabbi described it to his Presbyterian friends who nodded in agreement and added that college kids wouldn't sit still for longer than that—BOOM, and what does Old Nobadaddy think about that? . . . Well, did you ever hear of any man of the cloth, as they say, making a hole in one? Forget it. No; he came because it was the best place for remembering his father. And that was his duty.

His father was a dress salesman, but he was a furrier at heart. Golem remembered him bringing home sample cases and trying out his sales pitch while Golem and his mother played the parts of Department Store Buyers. Max Golem traveled two weeks out of four and, had he ever seen *Death of a Salesman,* he would have said that the play was lousy because what does a writer know about being on the road, what does an intellectual, yet, know about selling $6.75 dresses as if they were hot off the Paris designer's cutting table, and what does a book reader know about the look in a buyer's eye when she tells you that your line is lousy this season? But Max didn't go to the theater; who has time? I like to relax, drink a glass of tea, eat a piece of strudel. Oh, when I was a boy, Second Avenue was already Uptown and then I went to the Yiddish Theater. That was Drama. That was Comedy. Broadway? I can buy the records for less money than a good seat costs. Your mother goes to the theater.

And she did, every Wednesday afternoon.

But your father? He carries sample cases and sells shmatehs as if they were gold. But I made ten thousand last year and don't you forget it.

Golem remembered.

And this little number at $6.75 is sensational. I'm telling you it will walk right out of your store in two days. (It slips off the hanger and falls to the carpet.) See, how hot it is. I can't even hold onto it! Heh, heh, heh.

On his ninth birthday, Golem was taken by his father to the bicycle store. It was a surprise; they walked to the subway, stopping for a charlotte russe and an egg cream, waited at the station, his father impervious to his questions about their destination, took the train, his father characterizing the neighborhoods through which they passed while Golem nervously tried to unbraid the lacquered wicker seat which refused to indulge his humanity because it was aware that after it would come the plastic deluge (but after that, what?), his father propelling him through the rapidly closing train doors that were especially timed to instill the fear of the unexpected end into the stomachs of the citizens of New York, his father leading him up the charcoal staircase that recognized no one's footsteps, his father holding his hand and guiding him through the people who already occupied this street, people whose children had that peculiarly Brooklyn/Bronx mouse look that Walt Disney metaphorized in the foundation of his Fantasyland, his father gesturing at the appetizer store where one could get good figs, at the candy store where one could place a bet, at the movie theater where, if there was time, they might catch the second feature (and where are the Double Features of yesteryear? On television. Thank you.), and———finally, at the window of the bicycle store through which one could see the Schwinns and the Raleighs and the Rudges leaning insolently on their kickstands, their headlamps and their handbrakes defiantly dormant, their smartly steeled spokes caught in a moment of silence.

Here it is, my boy. I give you America, Kellogg's Corn Flakes, GRIT, Kansas, Columbus, Ohio, the Boy Scouts, and Sunday School not to mention twenty-eight flavors of orange roof. Vote. Think. Make It.

"Gee, Dad. The bicycle store!"

"Let's go in."

And so they enter, a bell above the door announces them to a man in a blue suit and clip-on bow tie who comes forward to shake the hand of Max Golem.

"Good afternoon," he says. "Can I help you?"

"We'd like to look at a bicycle."

"For yourself or for the boy?"

"For my son."

The man turns around to show them how the collar of his coat stands away from his neck and leads them through the spokes of the display to the rear of the store where one may browse through the Accessories or purchase a Youthcycle. The man gestures at the Youthcycles and Golem takes a wide shot of them. Not for him, he decides. They are not sleek like the Mancycles in the window, but pudgy and slightly unformed like the feet of an infant. Worse still, they come with appendages, training wheels; the final humiliation—a four-wheeled, two-wheeled Youth-cycle. No, if I cannot have a Mancycle, I will not have a cycle.

And that, my friends, is how empires are made.

I know it's not what you want, but it is America, my boy. . . . His father's eyes say this to him as their glances meet above the woven basket of a husky red number. Golem closes his eyes.

"I think you might find something here," The Man says.

His voice draws Max Golem into the midst of the Youth-cycles which are arranged like covered wagons awaiting an Indian attack, but Golem, the younger, moves away toward the three glass cases which surround the Accessories.

"See something you like, little boy?"

Fuck you, lady.

The woman behind the glass case had wiry blond hair that sprang from the middle of her head as uncomfortably as a stretched-out spring. She wore a colorless sweater and spoke with a deeply forked tongue. Beware of this woman, Golem.

"Uh . . . I don't know."

"We have some nice baskets. Just right for carrying your books in. Like a regular schoolboy."

"Do you have any horns?"

"What?"

"Horns. You know, horns that you squeeze?"

If I can't make a sound, a continuous tone, then at least I can make a noise.

"Oh yes. They're in this case."

And she leaves her position behind the glassed-in baskets to walk to the horns and Golem follows, knowing that his decision has been made and despite of, or, rather, *because of* the lacquered wicker refusing to surrender, he would have neither Mancycle nor Youthcycle but Horn. Take that, America!

1. "What do you think of this one, son?"
2. "A horn? You want a horn?"
3. "But I want to buy you a bicycle."
4. "Look, I can afford it."

5. "Don't you *want* a bicycle?"
6. "Don't come running to me when all the other boys go bicycle riding."
7. "Here's your horn."
8. "Enjoy it."
9. "And this little number at $6.75 is sensational."

60   "Reversal!" said Siggy, smiling as he snapped his fingers smartly. "That's the key to your soul, you spineless bastard."

61   And there is Golem, standing by the too small pew, reciting Hear, O Israel, the Lord Our God, the Lord Is One, while remembering the horn story. What is man that thou art mindful of him? A burlap bag of anecdotes? And here is Golem with his Wife beside him, both trying—like ontogeny recapping phylogeny—to make a place for themselves. Hoo-ha!

62   Back.

The ride back was filled with natural sound. No lush violins, only the rustling of the paper bag as Golem tried to avoid squeezing the bulb of the horn as if it were a boil on his father's weakened neck. No Second Feature, no charlotte russe, and the lacquered wicker was adament.

"Well?"

"Show her!"

Golem opened up the package and extended it to his mother. He was afraid to take out the instrument.

"What is this?"

"It's a horn, Mom."

"The bicycle is being sent?"

"No."

"No?"

"No bicycle. My son would rather have a horn."

"What?"

"You heard me. You see it. This is his birthday present. Write it down in your diary that on his ninth birthday your son would rather have a horn than a bicycle."

Seal it in the book marked Do Not Open Till Xmas and don't ever call *me* alienated.

63   Our God and God of our fathers, accept our rest.
Saturday.

Saturdays were always a mystery to Golem, like Easter Sundays. Except, on the latter, he knew he was getting away with something, sitting in the park, wearing old clothes, purposefully not shaving—why is this day different from all the other days running through his head in waltz time, enveloping his consciousness and licked closed by his ego—displaying his foreignness to those who cathedralized an event which Golem insisted, had to insist, was an impossibility. At base, Golem thought that he probably hated the Christians for bothering him with the problem of whether or not he was responsible for the death of Christ. "I need that," he said to himself, "like I need a hole in the head."

"With all the other crap in my collective unconscious, I have to worry about whether or not I'm responsible for killing some cat who obviously wasn't hip enough, if he existed at all, man ('cause I'm not giving anything away, you understand), to hang around long enough to be the first Pope

(By the way, does the Pope Do It? I dunno, man, that's a European hang-up and we're all Americans here. If the old man is getting some on the side, who cares?)

And you think I'm going to let the Germans off the hook? Forget it!"

That's what he said to himself, yessireebob.

So, Saturdays were a mystery to him because he had not yet decided whether to grow his sideburns into curls, exchange his olive drab for black bright, and sit in a basement studying The Law or to get a haircut, wash his car, and watch the golf match. What does a Jew do on Saturday? Something cultural, perhaps? Another Americanism, incidentally, replacing religion with art. No, it's not bad being a spade on a Saturday night, but being a Jew on a Saturday afternoon in America is like being Lenny Bruce at seven o'clock on a Monday evening in Center City, Iowa, with nobody to talk to except the man wearing a khaki work suit and leather bow tie who sells you a bag of peanuts from behind the counter of the GroSerSta. which he owns and later asks you why all those folks up in New York City are so downright unfriendly.

And you tell him it's because there ain't no coons, nor no commies, nor no poets to shoot on Thursday night. Nothing but people.

It would be safe to say that Golem had an approach-avoidance conflict with regard to Saturdays.

"What are you going to do today, David?"

As if on cue; marvelous.

Golem was sitting in front of the television set, his body wrapped in a white terrycloth bathrobe that represented the epitome of slovenliness to him, his mind wrapped in a dialogue which was taking place between an eleven-year-old boy from the future (who, through some fantastic miscalculation had traveled three billion years back in Time) and his ageless, prehistoric protector who looked like a Tontoesque version of Superman in leopardskin (pillbox hat, no doubt) drag. The kid's name was Buddy because, although the men of the future knew plenty about machines, they still had no imagination when it came to human beings. And the caveman's name was Gog because the program had at least one writer who thought he understood the connection between a man and his language. They were discussing whether it would be better to cause a landslide to stop the Morons from the land beyond the mountains who were running after them for apparently no reason at all, or to simply make a dash for the nearest cave and keep their mouths shut until the Morons passed. Golem was hoping that they'd do the cave bit because he was getting tired of all those existential heroics on the cartoon programs; they were cutting into his own life, not to mention the fact that a whole generation of kids was being brainwashed into believing that one could *really* stop a Moron, the same kids who would reach maturity without knowing or even acknowledging the possible joys of the seventy-cent spread, the same kids who regarded plastic as a fact and looked upon any organic material with suspicion. Cue Wife.

"What are you going to do today, David?"

"I don't know. What time is it?"

"Eleven-thirty."

"What time are we going to the party?"

"Nine-ish."

11:30 from 9 leaves 9½ hours of Saturday. Subtract 1½

hours for eating and going and that leaves 8 hours. Time enough for a whole day.

"Are you going to watch cartoons all day?"

"No. They go off at one."

Which leaves 6½ hours.

"Why don't you wash the car, David?"

See.

"Are you kidding? It snowed last night."

"I forgot."

"Look outside, for chrissakes."

"Don't get angry at me."

"Well, just look outside. What are you going to do today?"

"I have some shopping to do this afternoon."

"Do you want me to go with you?"

"I just have to pick up a few things. You'll be in the way."

"Oh."

"Why don't you do some work?"

"It's Saturday."

"So what? Yesterday was Friday; did you do anything yesterday? You don't have to answer that."

"You're still mad at me for Thursday."

Anna turned and walked out of the livingroom back toward the bedroom. She moved without style, Golem thought, and having a wife without style is like reaching out for silk and coming up with acetate. "All right," he said loudly, "after the cartoons are over, you can drop me off at the library and pick me up before supper."

64   "Aha," said Sigmund as he clapped his hands together as if to introduce his right palm to his left, "and Eureka as well, for deep within the bowels of my very soul, I have discovered the single most important concept, the fundamental key to the proper study of mankind."

"What is it?" they asked, all twelve of them gathered around the dinner table. "Lay it on us, Siggy baby. We are *ready.*"

"Aha," said Sigmund again, for if he had a fault, it was only that he repeated himself. And then he took another pinch of that very groovy snuff he was doing these days. "After all, the best of what you know—my friends—you may not tell to boys."

"What?"

"Are you starting with that Goethe crap again?"

"Come off that Messianic shit, Sigmund."

"Yeah, lay it on us, baby. Give us the Answer."

"We're all adults here."

"Well," he said, inhaling deeply, "I'll tell you where it's ultimately at."

"OK!" they said in chorus, of course.

"Reversal, you schmucks."

Silence.

"What?"

"What kind of crap is that?"

"That doesn't make any sense and besides, you already put us onto that one, man."

"Yes, my children. But you cannot seem to remember it."

65   "Have you got the map?" asked Golem as he drew on his driving gloves.

"I thought you had it."

"No. I gave it to you."

"No, you didn't."

"Yes, I did. I gave it to you last night. It was in my jacket pocket and I took it out after we came back from services."

"You didn't give it to me. Maybe you left it on the dresser."

"Oh, for chrissakes."

He slammed the car door behind him and stamped through the light snow back to the building. If I find that goddamned map on the dresser, he thought, as he threw open the door to their apartment, I am really going to be pissed off at myself. The snow dropped from his feet like, oh you know, when he saw the crumpled napkin on the dresser.

"You found it."

"Yes."

He started the car.

"Was it on the dresser?"

"Yes."

Should they go further? The second yes is like the precipice. It hung in the air like a dance.

"Where . . .

(What? Heads turn immediately.)

. . . does he live?"

Like a slide to home, they were safe for the Time Being.

"Out in the country. Here's the map." He handed her the crumpled napkin and she unfolded it, examined it, trying to understand what was in Cohen's mind as he made those boxes, sensing an ending, a strange kind of finality in the way the lines of the mapped road had sunk into the pebbled surface of the paper, destroying one pattern and forming another.

Golem backed out of the driveway, shifted gears, and turned on the radio. They started.

66   "Take a left here."

"Right."

"How far away are we?"

"About ten minutes, I guess."

"Do you want to share a joint?"

"Sure."

Golem reached into the pocket of his pea-coat and pulled out a flat can, the kind one could call a tin without having the echo of affectation in one's brain chamber, that had once held French candy and now contained six neatly rolled joints and . . . well, to each his own metaphor at this point because we're busy driving. He handed the tin to Anna who opened it and withdrew one of the cigarettes. "Do you want me to hold onto it?"

A list of actions, options, alternatives ran up in Golem's mind like the No Sale sign on a baroque cash register. "That's all right. I'll hold onto it."

"I can put it in my purse."

"I'll just keep it in my coat."

"Don't you trust me?"

BOOM.

Of all the things in the world to say, why say that?

Anna (*speaking into tape recorder*): Well, uh, I guess I said that because it was on my mind.

Doctor: Why was it on your mind?

Anna: Well, uh, I guess it was on my mind because I was thinking about it.

Doctor: It?

Anna: Well, uh, him.

Doctor: Your husband?

Anna: No.

Doctor: No?

Anna: No.

Doctor: Well, uh, who stole the cookies from the cooky jar?

Anna: Cohen.

"Of course I trust you."

Doctor: Did you?

Golem: Trust her?

Doctor: Yes.

Golem: Well, not really.

Doctor: Then why did you say it?

Golem: I wanted to see where everything was going. It was too early to stop it, yet.

Doctor: I don't understand.

Golem: I was in control. I didn't know what the situation was, but I was in control.

Doctor: Do you often feel that way?

Golem: Yeah, and I go to the bathroom a lot, too.

Doctor: I'm sorry . . .

Golem: You guys are awfully primitive sometimes. Look, I knew Anna. I knew that Cohen wanted to sleep with her. Cohen invited us to the party. The point is that sooner or later he was going to force the situation and she was going to react. I wanted to see how she was going to handle herself. It's very simple.

Doctor: I can't tell whether you consider yourself clair-voyant or some sort of divinely appointed judge. I realize that that is rather strong language, but . . .

97

Golem: Look, I'm just me. I'm not making any excuses. That's your job. You make 'em, I'll live with 'em.

"Then why don't you want me to hold the grass?"

"It's just simpler if it's in my coat, that's all. You don't want to lug around your purse, do you?"

"No."

"So, I'm just being nice. Making things more convenient."

"All right."

She gave him back the tin and he put it back into his pocket and winked at himself. Not badly handled, though one often wishes it could be avoided altogether. She suggested that he take another left and he did. Before long, they were both stoned and started down the dirt road that ultimately led to Osterman's party.

67 "After an hour or so in the woods looking for mushrooms, Dad said, 'Well, we can always go and buy some real ones.' " [7]

68 Franz Kline's mother said to him, upon seeing his black and white paintings for the first time at their first showing in New York, "Franz, I might have known you'd find the easy way." [8]

69 But can Picasso *draw?*

Gimme some o' that good old aura vitalis. I don't drink the greasy kid stuff.

"As for man, his days are like grass . . ."

70 Osterman lived on a farm that looked like a rundown hotel in the Catskill mountains. Buildings were everywhere, having been constructed on impulse based on immediate need (Henry, where'll we put the hogs tonight? Don't rightly know, Martha; guess I'll have to throw up a buildin' next to the goat shack. Isn't Amurica wonderful, Henry? Yup.) wtihout awareness of form.

[7] *A Year from Monday,* by John Cage.
[8] *Ibid.*

All of the buildings had that beautifully weathered color that resulted either from the lack of paint or the pioneers' basic disgust for embellishment—that color which has now become the main concern of the Research and Development teams of Amurica's largest Paint and Plastic corporations who are sending out sample chips of Weathered Wood to every fag decorator in the land (Isn't Amurica wonderful, Henry? Yup.).

But the farm, which Osterman had just rented from what he described as a felt-hatted, tobacco-chewing, Chevrolet-owning genuine shit-kicker and hog-caller, was exactly suited to Osterman's personality for, as you can see, he was an utterly hyphenated character.

And how's that for a diagnosis?

Golem often bumped into Osterman in the hallways of the English Dept. which, in itself, was not unusual or even remarkable for Osterman bumped into practically everyone as he ran from place to place, his nervous blond hair flying back over his head, straining to make contact with the hand-painted tie that flew back over his right shoulder. They had common interests and common friends but completely different life styles and they liked to watch each other from a safe distance as if in fear that any real collision/collusion between them might very well, by the sheer force of the resulting electrical gestalt, bring old Atlas to his shuddering knees. Though it is true that they occasionally compared metaphysics over coffee and Boston cream pie in one of the cafeterias.

Golem parked his Saab with its minimum number (the precise figure having remained with the previous owner) of moving parts behind a long row of cars and immediately knew that, if he wanted to leave early, there would be trouble. He had visions of himself walking through the party asking "would the guy who owns the fifty-six blue Pontiac please move it so I can get my car out," which was about the most ignominious manner in which to exit that he could imagine.

Cue Wife.

"Will you be able to get out from here?"

He didn't answer but shifted gears and backed up, secreting the car between two buildings and taking pains to aim it in the direction of the road as if it mattered.

"We'll have trouble wherever we park unless I leave it on the road."

"I don't want to walk."

"OK, we'll have trouble."

Resigned, he shut off the ignition and reached into his pocket for the can of enlightenment. Golem opened it, withdrew one cigarette, closed the can, and put it back into his pocket. In symbolic imitation of a cigar-smoker/brandy-drinker, he licked his lips and passed the joint across them, wetting it so that it would not burn too quickly. Then he untwisted the top end and stuck it into his mouth, allowing it to dangle casually as he searched for a match. Anna produced the fire and applied it to the cigarette; Golem inhaled deeply, as if trying to draw the essence of the fire from the end of the cigarette and through it like a straw and down into' the plumbing system of his body. When he had filled himself, he handed the straw to Anna and watched the paper burn as she pulled its essence toward her. When he could hear his heart beating loudly enough to wake up all his other organs, he let out the smoke that had not remained within him and said, "Thanks for the light."

She nodded you're welcome.

71   "As for man, his days are like grass . . ."

72   They entered. After having sat in the car for ten minutes and smoked a two-hour joint, i.e., one that makes ten minutes seem like two hours and vice-versa—ha, and you tell me that Time is relative and I'll tell you that it ain't no rich uncle and we'll fly around the Maypole together while the white horses in the court-yard of our ocean wait for us to be through. Enough of this shit.

They entered. And the angels sing.

"Hey, Golem."

That would be John for they were in a long hall and John, who was falling over the edge of thirty and taught a course in the Free Experimental College entitled "On the Nature of Things," always stood in the long halls of parties, his body arched like a praying mantis over nineteen-year-old flowers with blond petals and very soft centers who saved contemporary greeting cards and memorized their verses so that they might have something witty to say at parties.

"What's happening, John?"

"Usual shit."

Golem smiled at the flower against the wall who appeared to be delighted by the thought that she would soon be dried and pressed between the pages of John's encyclopedia, put his right palm—the one without the technicolor stigmata—on the small of his wife's small back, and guided her through the hall and into the living LIGHT room where they entered the mosaic that separated this generation from those which came before it. The room was black, illuminated only by the LIGHT energy from a strobe light which flashed on and off with the speed and intensity of Dr. Erlich's magic bullet and which, running at some LIGHT fifteen to twenty frames per second, fragmented the room and its occupants into characters that might have been seen in the dreams of T. LIGHT A. Edison who, as we all know, was a visionary. The pieces were held together only by sound from the audio system (which is LIGHT why it is no longer called a record player) (and, by the way, if you are counting, be advised that this is a real LIGHT movie) which came forth in nearly visible waves of paraphysical proportions, surrounding each dancer with outlines until they seemed like figures that had stepped LIGHT out of Munch's painting—thirty-eight iron filings in search of an electromagnet.

Through this, Golem and his wife walked toward the kitchen LIGHT as they were not yet ready to play catch with their identities. Though that time would surely come.

In the kitchen, around a potbellied stove like farmers from down the road, holding paper cups of martinis, stood the subculture with which we are concerned, the one which created the right to choose and thereby eliminated the need to act. Wallowing in the luxury of their options. Playing on the other hand, speaking out of the other sides of their mouths, brushing their teeth with electrified dialectical toothbrushes. Considering, reassessing, stalling. And where was the man who kept count of their changes, codified their positions, memorized their moves, graphed their souls? Sitting behind some walnut desk writing soap operas? Guess again, my friends, guess again.

Golem enters, turning the pages of his mental notebook, whetting the pencil stub he carried behind his ear, tilting back his hat at a rakish angle so that the sacred PRESS card which was stuck into the band formed an antenna. OK. Shoot. But just the facts.

"Freud is passé."

"Marx is a cliché."

"Didn't you know he was gay?"

Now, a fast pan; one might even say a whip pan:

"Her father's a lush."

"His poetry's mush."

"He thought he was Moses." (*Bullrushes*, get it? Keep awake, for chrissake.)

Zoom in for:

"Life is really getting to be a drag."

"Pain and passion, that's his bag."

"I'd say her tits were starting to sag."

Don't tell me about mixing my media.

"Are you writing any new poetry?"

"I think I'll turn into a junky."

"Man is descended from a what?"

73   dotdotdot dotdot dotdotdot

A poem from Golem's Diary entitled "A Report to My Friends in the Academy."

Don't speak to me of great poets

Who tear their words from Promethean souls.

Instead

Tell me stories of Puerto Ricans

Whose garbage is a national joke

Instead

Tell me stories of black men

Who shine the soul upon their feet

Instead

Tell me stories of red men

Who buy their pride from the bootlegger.

Don't tell me that comparisons,

Analogies, and all the rest are

Odious.

Let me make mine own parables.

dotdotdot dotdot dotdotdot

74   Golem stood at the entrance to the kitchen with his wife. Anna stood there with her husband.

"Want a drink?" he asked.

"We didn't bring anything with us, did we?"

"Oh, I don't think anyone'll mind if we have a glass of wine."

"We should have brought our own."

Golem considered this. To bring one's own. This, essentially, is what makes the difference between a party in a university atmosphere and one given, say, in the real world. If you brought your own, you could get as drunk, as aggressive, as hostile as you pleased for, after all, you were taking your own medicine. But, should you act improperly on the basis of someone else's booze, it was like stuffing up the toilet in your aunt's house. Consequently, he never brought his own.

In a manner of speaking, of course.

"There's Cohen, David."

"Aha!"

"What?"

"I said, Aha."

"That's what I thought you said."

"Shall I take it back? Open my mouth like an organic vacuum cleaner and suck the essence of the statement back into my bowels from whence it came, like a yogi practicing vajroli?"

"You don't have to get angry."

"Shall I take it back?"

"No, let it stand in the corner. We'll pick it up when we leave."

"I'm proud of you, my dear. You are beginning to appreciate the value of the Word."

"Working in the library is good for me."

"Aha."

"Three strikes and you're out, you know."

"I think we can call that a ball, don't you?"

A ball, Anna thought. Very heavy stuff, riddled with psychosexual connotations. Is he onto me or is this just part of the game? A ball means it goes by without being in the right place, an unintentional or, rather, meaningless pitch. Meaningless until you get enough of them to walk, walk as opposed to run. "All right, a ball. One and one."

"Shall we call it an inning and get something to drink? I'd like to give the other side a chance to take the field. In any case, I'm getting tired of this metaphor."

"OK."

Without waving to Cohen who was standing in the midst of a group of undergraduate English majors whose corduroy underwear squeaked when they walked, Golem and Anna went to the counter next to the sink on which, standing like glass calling cards, were the bottles which the guests had brought with them; their own. Golem gestured grandly at the display.

"What would you like?"

"Burgundy?"

Golem picked up a bottle of red wine, examined its label and shook his head. "It's not a very good year."

"Beggars can't be choosers."

"Oh, yes, they can, my dear."

"I'll have it anyway."

"OK, now a glass."

"Just put it in one of those cups."

"You cannot drink wine from a paper cup, for chrissakes, not unless you're a middle-class savage." There were no glasses on the counter. "I'll find you a glass." None in the sink or drain so, with his jacket flying behind him, Golem opened cupboard door after cupboard door in search of a suitable grail (whew!). Finally, he found Osterman's cache of jelly jars qua glasses and took out two which he figured to contain the souls of grapes. He left all the cupboard doors open and returned to pour the red wine into one of the glasses.

"Thank you," Anna said, both thanking him and telling him that he had used enough of somebody else's wine.

"My pleasure," he said and then exchanged the red wine for a bottle of Liebfraumilch, admired the design of the label, silently complimented the owner, and poured a few inches of the white wine into his own glass.

"Golem."

It was the house detective, the floor walker, the police. He was shoplifting and he was caught, seen by an unseen pair of binoculars, caught by the curve of a mirror, collared to be taken into the manager's office where he would stare at the tweedy carpet and plead his Youth. The man, his hands behind him, behind his back and clenched in anticipation, the edges of his mustache raised in delight, would ask him if he knew what he had done. Golem would plead insanity at the trial. I took it in a moment of absence; I didn't realize its value, he would say. You should know better, the judge would say and then he would ask him if that were any way for an Educated Man to behave. No, Golem would admit, shame dripping down his face like a soft-boiled egg. Put him on probation; he's just a smart-assed college kid. Thank you, your honor.

And they are all honorable men.

Caught with the bottle in his hands. A question here: does he pour out a bit more in a defiantly casual gesture or does he put the bottle down immediately? What would you do? But, of course, you brought your own so you may do whatever you like. Forgive the intrusion.

Golem turns toward the articulation of his name, bottle still in hand. It is Osterman. We get a close-up of Osterman's eyes, a close-up of the label on the bottle, a close-up of Golem's eyes, and then we go back to an establishing shot. That's the treatment.

"Glad to see you helping yourself," says Osterman with honesty.

Golem nods the bottle at Osterman, pours another inch into his glass, and then puts the container back in place on the counter.

"Thanks. Nice party."

"Just a lot of people. They make good background music for my own fantasies."

"Right."

"Is this your wife?"

"Yeah. Excuse me. Anna, this is Phil Osterman. Phil, Anna."

They shake hands and say hi simultaneously and then laugh.

"What are you doing?" Osterman asked.

"Grass," said Golem with an angelic smile.

"I've got some beautiful hash in the study. You want a taste?"

"Sure."

"I think I've had enough," Anna said, thinking that were she to smoke too much more, it would provide too handy an excuse for her actions.

"Have a taste with us," Osterman urged.

"I better not."

"My wife," said Golem as he peered inside Anna's frontal lobes and perceived the shadow of her doubt, "usually knows when she's had enough. Why don't you say hello to Cohen while Phil and I take a little trip."

Golem felt a shiver of uncomfortable certainty. Was he pushing her or himself? Control, yes. But control whom?

"All right," she said.

"All right," Golem said.

"All right," Osterman said.

And then they all laughed again, for it was the obligatory scene, and Golem and Osterman left Anna in the kitchen and walked through the rambling farmhouse and out the side door into the Night.

"Nice place you've got. Where's the study?"

"I'm fixing up one of these outbuildings. Watch the mush over here. That'll be a garden, eventually."

"A regular country squire."

"As my mother would say."

They walked through the yard, each shaking off his own symptoms of paranoia as the ground alternately crunched and slopped beneath their feet. When they reached a small building about a hundred yards behind the main house, Osterman stopped.

"I'm going to string lights from here to the house."

"You really need them."

Then they walked up a thin gravel path and climbed four rotting steps which Osterman promised he would repair or replace. On the porch, Osterman rummaged through his pockets for a key and, finding a single one in his rear pocket, held it up and turned to Golem. "Can you light a match? I haven't put the lights out here yet."

The question caught Golem by surprise as he was considering the possibility of the moon coming loose from the epoxy which held it to the sky, but he responded fairly quickly, considering.

"Sure." And he lit one so that Osterman could stick the key into the rusty padlock.

They went inside and it was dark.

"No lights here, either?"

"No electricity, but dig this."

Golem stood in the doorway and listened to Osterman bump into things as he moved to illuminate the scene. Suddenly, a small light flared in what Golem recognized as a kerosene lantern. The light grew larger, making Osterman, who stood above it, look like your uncle's impression of Bela Lugosi.

"Have a seat."

Said the spider to the fly.

Osterman lit another lantern. Golem sat down in a canvas butterfly chair and saw that the building was actually being decorated in the conscious style of a study/library. He panned his eyes slowly, picking out book titles at random, until Osterman came from behind a large desk and handed him a meerschaum pipe capped with a small piece of aluminum foil on which rested a nugget of hashish. Golem accepted the pipe, lit a match, and placed the fire against the hash. He drew the thin and pleasant-tasting smoke into himself. He held his breath and passed the pipe to Osterman, who sat down in a director's chair opposite Golem. One could hear the crickets and, when they hesitated, the sound made by Osterman as he pulled the drug into his body.

When Golem finally exhaled, some thirty-six magical hours later, he felt like God blowing the kiss of soul into the air.

75   Mind if we step inside his mind?

Only as a preface to the inventory of his medicine chest, of course.

So.

Say, the world is below, receding from me as if it were at the wrong, long end of a collapsible telescope. And I am a kite, an orange kite supporting a trail of baby blue ribbons. Shall I try to patch up my string which is beginning to fray and stop this flight, come on back down to earth? How does one do that? Connect my mind to my mouth and start talking? Perhaps. But about what? About how my heart beats like a small propeller, caught in a stroboscopic moment in Time? About how I am being born, breaking my full-grown self out of a giant egg which, immediately upon recognition, dissolves into a light bulb?

Nah.

Down there, everything is a cartoon. Everybody has blue hair and, if the print job is bad, you can see the spaces between their pores. But me too. I'm Superman, flying up up and away with a clenched fist ready to right the wrongs of a thousand Denmarks. Ah, getting carried away. No. I am God, sitting on a white cloud, hoping I will fall through. The sin of confusion gets you every time and back to earth we go, now Mr. Bluster, now Dagwood, my cowlick slowly dissolving into a pair of horns. Hey! Hold on! I want to see that one again. Horns.

Too late.

Come back, vision, come back . . . Do I want to come back? Isn't this where insanity is, not knowing whether or not one wants to come back?

Turn off my lightbulb, grab the switch! The air is filled with one hundred million pieces of polyurethane, white and floating like plastic snow, but without organic form. They make drifts through which, when I walk, I leave no footprints.

How do you breathe? I'm forgetting how to do it. Take one in, let one out. Isn't that right? Hell, I don't know. There's terror in not knowing that. Terror that surpasses anything I've seen on the screen, mine or yours. Forget how to breathe and you forget how to live. Die.

Death, umm, that's a heavy concept hohoho. Wait a minute; I don't want to think about it, I want to be it. I want to cast off and see what it's really like out there. But, am I ready yet?

Pinch yourself . . . come on, that's a cliché. Pinch yourself; how else will you know that you exist? I think therefore I am. The brain is responsible for growth, why not for decay? What new virus is forming in my head? I think, therefore I am. Screw that. I fuck, therefore I am. Ah, what do *you* know?

Every sound is exaggerated in volume, but not echoed. Every sound becomes itself and then immediately becomes connected to an image. Man is a living, breathing, walking, talking metaphor of insanity. Or for what? Something else? As I talk, I think, I read, no, *I am* the Sunday comics.

Ten-pound weights hang from my ears like earrings. Shall I pull them off? What will come with them? My head or just my ears?

There's Death again, the old bastard. Not Death as perceived in that moment just before your car crashes into another and you feel as though you are seeing a film of yourself, not that romantic life-flashing-before-you that we accept as Television Death. But Real Death; your body crumbling to ashes, every organ coming to a dead halt as if the night watchman had just pulled down the Main Switch in the factory, everything you are turning to electroidal dust.

76   "Are you OK?"

"Huh?"

"I said are you OK?"

"Yes, I'm fine."

"I thought something was wrong. I haven't heard from you since . . ."

"Since?"

"Since."

"Since we screwed, you mean?"

"I wouldn't put it that way, Anna."

77   But we're not down low enough yet. This is only the subconscious, that iceberg-like configuration of subtle meanings and motives which sticks its pointed tip up and into the ego space, the space identified only by a placard which reads RESERVED FOR and then an underline on which you may, as the Mystery Guest, sign in with a self-conscious flourish, intrudes into that space up there at the top of the head not like a pebble in your shoe whose abrasions you may decide to suffer or relieve, but like a splinter in your palm; the problem being whether to admit the possibility of infection by waiting a week while softening up your skin in basins of hot water and allowing it to—what?—disintegrate or to perform the ritual of exorcism with a sewing needle sterilized in the gas flame. Will it be a gun or a knife? And, one might add, a hit or a miss?

Not down low enough? Roll up the chart on the wall and let's have another one with smaller letters; I'll not have anyone question the quality, the holiness of my vision.

Just what is it you see down there, Mr. Golem?

Well, it's like this. See, you've got this Space, sort of an undefined Space 'cept for the fact that it is black (if one can say that a Space is Black) and that on top of it sits that iceberg thing. Well, you can't really call it an iceberg any more 'cause down here, it looks like a clear plastic funnel with the wide end being the end that sits over this undefined Black Space. Are you with me so far?

Gotcha.

OK, inside this Space are these creatures.

Creatures?

Yeah. Creatures in the sense of their being mostly hybrid forms of insects and animals like that sort of almost-spider or near-octopus that wakes you up at four o'clock in the morning before he swallows you whole. Remember him? And they're all dayglo colored, breathing different hues of fire, expelling a variety of multicolored liquids, floating around down there, living, fighting, and dying as if you were seeing a microcosmic, Walt Disneyish view of bedlam, of society, and, naturally, of your own personality. See. Think of it as a tropical fish aquarium of the mind, with each species bearing a sign that very clearly, all too clearly, identifies itself. And down there at the bottom, kind of holding things together as it undulates along the gravel is . . .

What?

Just about the slimiest, most pop-eyed, savage-mouthed, split-tongued, hungriest, evilest-looking creature that ever crawled its torturous way across the pockmarked face of this universe.

THE SNAKE.

Oh, come on, Mr. Golem. Isn't that sort of symbolism just a little *too* heavy, just a little *too* obvious?

Eve didn't think so.

And that's why you hate her?

Hate's a very long word.

Tell me, Mr. Golem, what's it like down there?

It's very hard to breathe.

You described the subconscious as being a funnel. Any particular reason for that?

Sure. How else are those creatures going to get all the way from the bottom of the Tank up to the top? But the opening is very small and during the day we keep a pretty tight watch on it.

So, you suggest that in our sleep, we are, you might say, caught off guard and those creatures of yours tend to come up the funnel and into the conscious. Is that right?

Pretty much so.

Well, that's interesting, but not a terribly original description of the supposed workings of the mind. Why should that upset you?

Have you ever fallen through that little opening in broad daylight?

78 Osterman took the pipe from his mouth and handed it to Golem who, wrapping his fingers around the white bowl in an effort to sense the origins of the carved material, found that he could not discern the difference between the feel of the meerschaum and that of a synthetic imitation, that the white light of technological mysticism had fallen upon the object and, through the heat of its presence, had obliterated all perceptible differences. How does one tell where the soul of a thing is or whether, in fact, it has one? Is growth the qualifying factor? Plastic doesn't grow and so it has no soul. But neither do rocks grow from pebbles to boulders. Or do they?

Here, in his hands, was a composite of the world. Plastic stem, meerschaum bowl, aluminum foil, hashish.

"I think," he said, "and I have been thinking these days about a hell of a lot of things, one of which is what might happen if I was wrong, I think that I've had enough."

79   "I know."

"I don't exactly know what to say. I've been doing a great deal of thinking about this whole thing."

"Is that so?"

"Look, Anna, you don't have to be mad at me. I'm very concerned about you. In fact, I think that I may . . ."

"Love me?"

"Yes."

"Thank you."

"Oh, come on, Anna! You don't have to hate me. All we did was make love."

"I don't hate you, Cohen. In fact, I've been thinking about moving in with you."

"Leaving David?"

"Yes."

"Why?"

"I don't know."

80   "Are you sure?" Osterman asked as he allowed the smoke to escape from behind his clenched teeth.

"Yeah."

"OK, let's go back to the party."

81   It was very cold outside, but the glue behind the moon had not come loose and Golem was thankful for that. With Osterman at his side, he stopped halfway between the study and the main house and lifted his hands above his head in what he knew was a grandiose gesture but one which he, at this moment, permitted himself. "If you stand very still for a moment or two and close your eyes, you can feel yourself being pulled at one end by the Earth and at the other end by the Sky."

"Which one do you think'll win?"

"Neither, I'm afraid."

"I don't want to be caught in the middle," said Osterman, who had the ability to hone a conversation down to its last possible nuance. "Let's go inside."

"That may be a cop-out."

"It may be, but I'll take the chance."

82   They came in through the back door and the first, in fact the only, thing that Golem saw was his wife and Cohen standing in the middle of the room. I'll give them a few minutes to get straightened out before I go over, he thought to himself, keeping his thoughts to himself. But he could not sever the connection which bound him to the situation. He took a few steps, determined steps toward a group of people whose faces were frighteningly familiar, but he found himself unable to continue. If they would only turn the motor off, he thought, then we wouldn't have to have the confrontation so early in the party. He was certain now that Cohen had come through and he was beginning to worry about Anna's response. Not because he loved her, but simply because he did not want another disappointment. Or did he? Golem, you schmuck, he said to himself in a whisper, you've got to make up your mind.

"What are you going to be when you grow up?"

"Gee, Dad, I want to be a cowboy."

"What are you going to do when you get out of high school?"

"I'll go to college."

"What'll you do when you graduate?"

"I guess I'll go into the Peace Corps."

"What are you going to be when you grow up?"

"An older me."

But how many of us can say that?

"How's it going, Cohen?"

He was there now, making a trio in the middle of the room. The last problem remaining was whether or not they knew why he was there and, if so, what he would do. He had never played this scene out before, but he was fairly certain that Cohen hadn't either. And so he gave himself the edge and decided to move slowly.

"All right, David. Good to see you. I was just asking Anna where you were."

Aha, telltale reflections of those muddy puddles of guilt already forming about the eyes. Watch the corners of the mouth for sudden movements.

"I was outside with Osterman."

"He has a nice place."

"Yes."

"Was the stuff good, David?"

"Yeah, baby. It's OK, but I'm pretty tired. What about having a dance and then splitting in a little while?"

"We just got here."

"I know, but I'm really tired."

"Are you having a bad trip?"

"No, my trip is fine. The train arrived exactly on schedule, the man punched my ticket, and I've settled back into the plushy seat and rested my head on the clean napkin. The scenery is groovy, but the noise is vibrating in my ears."

"Why don't you lie down?"

"If you want, Golem, I can drive you home."

"Thank you, Cohen, for that kind offer. But I think that my wife and I will go home together."

"I'm sorry, but David is terribly stubborn when he gets one of these ideas in his head."

"Yeah, yeah. I'm just a stubborn cat."

"No need to apologize. I'll be here if you need me."

"You are a prince, Cohen. A prince."

Golem smiled heavily and took Anna into the livingroom where the LIGHT which now flashed in time with the beat of the music was breaking the ceramic of the quotidian, playing games of chance with the LIGHT gestalt that one accepts both in light and in darkness but which, like colored oil in water, forms and reforms itself too rapidly to LIGHT be identified, categorized when caught in the stroboscopic moment of almost-movement. They went to the center of the room and began to dance LIGHT, each developing a series of movement patterns which were magnified in intensity and, thereby, in meaning (Every little movement has a meaning all its LIGHT own is what they used to say before they knew that hula-dancing was as significant as handshaking.) as they were framed by LIGHT the light and nonexistent when they were not. (And so electricity doth make existentialists of us all, Horatio.)

Now Golem attacked with a LIGHT Dracula-like image and Anna reacted like an Unwilling Victim. Then she attacked and he withdrew. They moved their hands in front of their LIGHT faces to further obscure the images, but the hands seemed to remain there, immobilized. Now Golem did Super Spade, his neck bent as casually LIGHT as his lower back was rigid. And Anna rolled her eyes and stuck out her breasts in imitation of everybody's hungry black whore.

Genres. LIGHT. That was what the Light was about. No time for explanation, analysis. Just a split second of illumination in which to recapitulate the tradition of a LIGHT movement.

All around them were pieces of things.

And nobody to pick them up.

What this century needs is not an innovator LIGHT, but an integrater. Any takers? Any of you homebodies want to dump the puzzle on a bridge table, mix it up, and spend LIGHT the next three or four years fitting the tiny, odd-shaped pieces of this hyper-realistic landscape together? Somebody's got to color in the LIGHT spaces between the pores or we'll all begin to look like badly screened halftones.

From the back of his head, Golem could hear LIGHT the question forming like some giant wave about to answer the prayer of a lifetime of that great golden-haired Surfer whose disdain for LIGHT the land is nothing more than a complex rationalization for the basic dissonance involved in knowing that no matter how well we walk LIGHT, we were all fish to begin with.

Did

Brrrooom. Smashing against the shore, pulling the sand out by its roots.

Cohen

Brrrooom. Rolling like LIGHT great clouds of thunder against the silent rocks that form a Christ-like barrier between the sea and the road. Say, Mac, think it's LIGHT easy being a rock? How would you like to get slapped in the face eight thousand times a day without being able to turn LIGHT the other cheek? Don't ever put down a rock, my dear friend, cause it takes a lot of punishment just so that you can get LIGHT an even suntan.

Ask

Brrrooom. Biting at the edges of the pier which wraps its arms about the stilted, telephone pole legs in LIGHT an effort to keep itself level for the good folks who are cannibalizing the creatures of this sea in that well-recommended restaurant on LIGHT its back.

You?

115

Brrrooom. Opening its gigantic jaws in a curling imitation of a human smile, setting a trap within which it might peacefully LIGHT devour the adolescent who dares to mock its power.

"What did you say, David?"

"Nothing."

The music stopped and so did the light.

BLACK

"Let's go," he said, reaching for her arm a little too rapidly. She drew back.

"Why don't you take the car and I'll get a ride."

"With who? Cohen?"

"Why not?"

"Because I'm in control tonight; that's why not. C'mon, we're going."

He grabbed her arm and started to pull her out of the center of the room. There was a moment of space in there between the point at which she felt his fingers around her arm and the point at which he would take his first step. She raced over the problem and quickly decided that were she to lose, even were she fated to lose, she would not lose without grace. "Don't pull me," she said. "I'm coming."

83   They were driving down the road again, Golem having maneuvered the small car through a random pattern of unfriendly trees and over a threatening ditch (Can you dig his trying to get the Triple A to tow his car away from the party?) with the style and energy of a man who has just tamed a wild horse and is momentarily satisfied with the feeling of mastery that precedes and, perhaps, indicates the descent into the slavery of sentiment which is certain to follow. Golem stared straight ahead, attempting to substitute concern for the condition of the road for the condition of his being. And Anna? Well, Anna struck an internal pose of serenity. They both swung on their respective trapezes, each waiting for the other to signal the beginning of the act.

High above the center ring, performing death-defying feats of acrobatic precision, traveling through the air beneath the big top with the greatest of ease, risking their lives for your entertainment, without benefit of a safety net . . . we proudly present (drum rollll and horn flourish) The Flying Golems. Ladies and Gentlemen, we ask your complete silence now as the Flying Golems prepare to attempt the most difficult and dangerous maneuver in all of circusdom . . . (drum rolllll and horn flourish) . . . the amazing, incredible, trippppple reverse (Put that in ITALICS, please. Quiet, for chrissakes! Can't you see that there's a show going on here? Oh, sorry; I didn't notice. Guess I had my eyes on the ground.), incredible, trippppple *reverse* flying somersault. QUIET, PLEASE!

And it is. We can hear only the noise the wire makes as it cuts through the air.

She swings, reaching for the ashtray in which to deposit the used portion of her cigarette.

He swings, reaching into his coat for a package of cigarettes, withdrawing one and lighting it.

Balance. Coordination.

They are waiting for the signal; some nearly imperceptible movement that will serve to advise them both that they may begin. Will it be an inaudible word followed by a demanding what? Will it be a swift movement of the car to avoid a pothole in the road, causing her to lean uncomfortably toward him? There are no fair catches in this ball game, if you'll permit the momentary mixing or, better still, cross-breeding of metaphors. The ball comes, you pick it up and run with it. Never mind who passed it to you. What'll it be? Any bets? What would it be for *you?*

Ah.

How convenient.

It's a Stop Sign at the end of the dirt road. A place where one must halt, look out the window, and reshift the gears. And that's about as close to an organic pause as you're going to be able to get out here in corporationville. Be thankful for Stop Signs; at least they don't hang you up with problems of chromatic duration. Small things, perhaps. But be thankful.

"Look," he says, half expecting it to be followed by Listen. Well, it was a beginning.

"What?" she asked, not wanting to play until she fully understood what kind of prize the winner was going to receive.

"I know what's going on."

Lesson One: *The Knowledge Gambit.* The party wishing to precipitate the action asserts that he/she is fully aware of Situation X, but does so indirectly by making a nonspecific assertion of what might be correctly termed "free-floating knowledge," i.e., knowledge that is not tethered to a particular point but which is free-floating in much the same sense as are the frustration, anxiety, and neurosis which seem to be symptomatic of the rather harried and nonspecific times in which we live. This open-ended assertion is expected to draw the other party into revealing (unwittingly, of course) the specifics of Situation X, thus placing him/her on the defense and in a position of great vulnerability.

"What do you mean?"

Lesson Two: *The Ignorance Offense.* Despite its name, this is a strictly defensive technique to be used by the accused party in the hope that, by drawing the accuser into the whirlpool of his/her own projected guilt, a momentarily entropical state, and therefore one which contains the seeds of its own negation, will result, thus reducing the vulnerability of the accused. This is at best, however, a stalling gambit for, as it is said, there is nothing so presumptuous as an Idea which has gotten it into its head that its TIME has come.

"With you and Cohen."

"Oh, Cohen."

Simple variations, of course. To be eventually followed by a conversational form of metastasis, the cure for which some claim to be forgiveness. But forgiveness of whom?

Golem looks both ways and sees no traffic. A pair of headlights approach from the distance to the left, but they have no relevance and so, deciding to get it over with, he shifts into first and they leave the pause.

Golem swings high on his trapeze, placing his feet together as solidly and yet as delicately as an unopened pair of scissors. He looks up at the tip of the Big Top and sees that the wires which hold him up are still there. Down below, he notes, with some existential satisfaction, that the roustabouts have truly removed the net.

"Cohen asked you to sleep with him, didn't he?"

And Anna is off her post, swinging through the air to

meet him, knowing that the audience secretly wishes that she were flying without underwear.

"Tonight?"

"Yes, tonight. He asked you, didn't he?"

"No, he didn't."

"He didn't?"

You mean I'm swinging up here for nothing? You mean that the trick doesn't have to be done? Do you mean that I can take off this faggoty costume?

"But I already have."

Get that fucking net over here, you guys; I lost my goddamned balance!

84   **THE JUDGMENT**
Darkening of The Light. In adversity
It furthers one to be persevering.

One must not unresistingly let himself be swept along by unfavorable circumstances, nor permit his steadfastness to be shaken. He can avoid this by maintaining his inner light, while remaining outwardly yielding and tractable. With this attitude he can overcome even the greatest adversities.

In some situations indeed a man must hide his light, in order to make his will prevail in spite of difficulties in his immediate environment. Perseverance must dwell in inmost consciousness and should not be discernible from without. Only thus is a man able to maintain his Will in the face of difficulties.

Remember Prince Chi!

85   "You What?"

Golem threw his legs out at the pedals of the car and hit the brake as if that were all that stood between himself and his own infinity. The car began to skid, it being a machine and, as such, having no wish to become directly involved in this, or, for that matter, in any other truly human predicament—machines, as you well know, suffer from the inability to reproduce themselves pleasurably (interface is not intercourse, as much as it tries to sound like it)—and Golem grabbed the steering wheel like one of the last Lusty Men and, like Robert Mitchum bringing his last beast to its knees, he brought the car to a rest.

Anna had been thrown against the dashboard and she waited there, her head making no real impression on the vinyl protective covering, hoping that she would be killed. An accident was what she wanted, but there are no accidents of consciousness on Saturday nights. The car stopped, they stopped, and finally, the night itself held its breath as the moon began to peel oh-so-slightly around the edges.

"You What?"

"I slept with him."

"You mean he fucked you?"

"Oh, David . . ."

"Oh David Shit. Did he fuck you or not?"

"Yes."

"Yes, what?"

"Yes. He fucked me."

Anna raised her head and looked at her husband who was staring out of the windshield as if he could not trust himself to face her. It was not that; Golem trusted himself. But he had no need to turn to her, for his vision of her, like a postage stamp upon the night, was quite sufficient, thank you. No need to check to see if the scarlet letter was imprinted upon a human face. The foot that the insurance salesman sticks inside your door when he tells you that you will eventually die, that foot may very well be the foot of a human being but, just as a good cigar may at the same time be a good cigar and a phallic symbol, the door is yours to close.

"Why?"

It sounded as good, as valid as any one of the ten thousand other questions he might ask, statements he might make, gestures he might employ. Who What When Where Why are not capitalized for nothing. And besides, once you've closed the door on that foot, once the initial shriek has been lost in its own meaningless echo, once you've thrown the bolt across the door and pulled up the drawbridge, the knocking amounted only to petty annoyance.

"I don't know. I really don't know."

"Shit, that sounds like bad dialogue."

But it was not an unexpected reply. What is? They're all just as equal, just as pat. This was, of course, the trouble.

What are his options?

Well, right off, first things first, he's got to deal with the Double Standard issue. Right? I mean we are living in a very sophisticated time; one can't allow the freedom to oneself that one denies to others, right? Even the movies are onto that; it is no longer mandatory for the adulterer/adultress to die in a snow-storming automobile crash. Screw it. She's my Wife. Don't give me that sexual revolution-emancipated woman crap. She's my Wife and nobody fucks my Wife.

But, like a little bird sitting on the rounded shoulders of his ego, somebody *did*, Charley.

Get off my back, Iago!

OK, now that he's got a premise, i.e., nobody fucks his Wife, he's got to go on and build the rest of the structure. And all the old Humphrey Bogart movies in the world are still not enough to provide more than a momentary metaphor, and a relatively fleeting one at that. Oh, it's easy enough if you are one who does not consider the matter of Choice. For then you pull out the rifle you use to scare away coon and revenooers and spend the rest of your life on Parchman Farm. But Golem is not a cotton-picker at heart, no matter how deeply he yearns to be middle-class. He can hit her. Throwing his manly fist of vengeance against her feminine cheek of soft betrayal. He can do that. But what does that prove except that rock strikes paper? Perhaps it provides temporary assurances that one's fist is, indeed, manly . . . but we're well beyond the point of temporary assurances. Or he can spit at her, but that is a poor substitute and one which is unquestionably devoid of contemporary relevance—it was OK for Robespierre, but you felt kind of funny when they did it to Nixon.

Backtrack.

Don't accept the premise. Fool yourself into believing that, after all, you're a modern man, you can accept the morality of the image of another man's penis inside the body of your wife. What was that? Christ, even Kant, the least passionate of all, says

121

that the contract of marriage assures each party the exclusive use of each other's genital organs. You can't get much more reasonable than that.

There is no track back there. It's all in front of you.

"When?"

"What?"

"I asked when you did it."

"I don't remember."

"What date?"

"I don't remember. It's not important anyway."

"Yes, it is."

Yes, it is. One must know precisely at what hour the death certificate was signed, at what moment one's soul was being violated, at what second the life of another passed into his own and opened the door which held back all the negative images of immortality. One must know for one must know what one was doing at the time and then one must ask, of course, just exactly what it is that constitutes a state of grace. Yes, it is.

"A few months ago."

"That recent?"

"Well, it wasn't last week."

It is from remarks such as these, uttered in the most frivolously defensive manner, wrapped in a bundle of innocence and tied with a ribbon of charm and carrying a greeting card that reads Meaningless—it is from remarks such as these that real, not metaphysical, deaths result.

To kill is not to be insane. To not kill is not to be sane.

But Golem is not certain that he really has the ability to murder his wife and Cohen. Oh, that's not exactly true. Of course he has the ability, but is the desire genuinely there in the pit of the stomach where it belongs? He doesn't know if he's prepared to go all the way, standing in a police station at four in the morning with blood on his hands and shirt trying to convince the desk sergeant that he is really a Moral Man; calling his mother at two in the afternoon to explain that this nice Jewish boy is now on real trial for his real life not because he married a shickse, but because he truly loved her; begging his lawyer to save his life when he is uncertain whether or not it has any truthful existential value. That's a mighty strong desire, son. Not one that you can manufacture like any old emotion.

Got to watch that college talk. Join the Army. Marines build Men. Who else makes that claim? Sure, but do you ever see His picture swinging on an iron sign outside of a post office? At least, He's got the decency to be a little closed-mouthed about the whole affair. Did He scream when they discovered or uncovered the double helix? Is He worried? Nah. He's not afraid of Plastic.

So what? Can't kill her. Can want to kill her. Will work on that later—certain to come up with something, if not crying then at least—at the very least—vomiting. Do what? Shove her out of the car like a nineteenth-century harlot to wander in the snow until she dies? She'll just stay with someone else and come back for her clothes in the morning. Take her home, lock her in the bathroom, no, the bedroom, until you can figure out who you are, where you are, why you are. Why, boy, she'll be in there for days! You'll have to punch holes in the roof so's she can get enough air to live; women are fragile creatures.

"But I didn't enjoy it."

"What?"

"I didn't 'make it,' you know."

"Are you telling me that Cohen fucked you and you didn't have an orgasm?"

"Yes."

"And that's supposed to make it all right? That's supposed to let me know that as long as you didn't have an orgasm you haven't really exceeded the limits? Is that what you are saying to me?"

"I'm not using it as an excuse."

"Yeah, but it's a pretty strange prescription for healing. I don't think that the pharmacology checks out too well, dear. Dig? What do I care whether or not you made it, just as long as you did it? That's like saying the cut on my jugular vein is two inches long as opposed to four inches long. Am I supposed to be thankful?"

"Can we pick up the pieces of our marriage and start over?"

"Who do you think you are, Doris Day? Well, I'm no Rock Hudson, sweetie."

"What are we going to do?"

"I don't know, for chrissakes."

"Well, we can't sit on this road all night long."

"No, we can't do that unless we want to."

Golem started the car again.

"I don't know what to say," she said.

"Neither do I," he replied.

86

They drove home in silence.

87   Chelm.

Before the sun rose this morning on that despair which is called America, I, rising early to write my fiction, was shocked into a morning that ordinarily smells of awakening magnolias, plastic milk cartons, red clay, and delicate mist but which, today, reeked with the body odor of a dying soul. Jolted from the unconscious to the conscious by the crescendo of radio news reporting the shooting of Senator Robert F. Kennedy by a man who refused to identify himself, a man with no apparent past and an all too horrifying future, a man whose photos on the television screen, to which I later turned, showed me a pair of eyes that said, more clearly and more eloquently than could any human utterance from his dubious accent, "I have done this for you, to you—because of you." And, thus, television does make murderers of us all.

You ask me to write fiction?

88   *Item* from *Time* (March 11, 1966): Is God dead? Of course not, preached Evangelist Billy Graham, 47, to the Atlanta Press Club. As a matter of fact, said the reverend, "I can tell you that God is alive because I talked to him this morning."

89   *Item*: Quotations out of context from two admitted Christs.

"That's your belief, sir."

"I am God. I would like to apply for Social Security."

"That's your belief, sir."

90   Chelm.

At a few moments before five on a morning which would and did smell of awakening magnolias, stirring earth, believing animals, on an early morning which one has set aside for the work of a novel, one is awakened by a crescendo of bedside radio news announcing to the world that America, like some Hogarthian vision of Paul Bunyan, has, once again, been brought to its quaking knees, arms flailing wildly to ward off the danger of the tears which drip in plasmic forms from the Oedipal Eye in the midst of its forehead. One immediately wants to make love, if only to expiate the guilt, but even that is not possible. One watches the cacophony of cheers charge like mad armies to the walls of anguish which surround the horror of the event. One watches the instant video replay of the shooting as if it were, indeed, the sporting match which has prompted our national mania for electronic violence. One watches black men and white men crying on each other's shoulders and, finally, one cries oneself—stopping between tears to note one's reactions on beautifully formed legal pads. We participate in our own destruction.

"We do not know who he is. He does speak and understand English," the Police Chief explains with a tight smile, implying that Los Angeles is not Dallas.

The country is seized in the stone grip of moral entropy and you ask me to write fiction. America, I tell you, is an illusion; an image with a transplanted heart, polyvinyl skin, and a presumptuous complex of electrical wires. An item to be purchased in a Hobby Shop and to be constructed with the aid of airplane glue. And, oh, yes, an image with a soul that attempts to cover the stink of its own decay with gallons, no, reservoirs, of aerosoled, sweet-smelling confections of undefined morality and self-amazement.

You ask me to write fiction in America and I reply that this is an impossible task for America is fiction; it has become a metaphor for itself.

And, worst of all, America, with its ugly whore's ass upon the toilet of destiny, finds itself eternally constipated.

91   Sirhan Sirhan.
        Jerusalem, Jordan.
        Nobody likes the Jews.

92   Around the corner from the hospital, by the light of the
police flares and beneath the huge, illuminated cross on the roof,
some people argue heatedly about the significance and meaning of
life and death.

        And do they know that a terrible repression will follow
because a man who had beauty was a victim of their own schizophrenia?

        And do they know that one must, at some time, opt for
Life rather than Meaning?

        No FBI, no Secret Service, no CIA, no LAPD and,
finally, no Security—whatever the initials stamped on its package
—can make that choice.

93   Shem.
        And Golem, the American that he is, sits on his toilet to
decide the fate of his universe.

94   Chelm. Again.
        And now you know even my work habits, for, this morn-
ing, it was not necessary to metaphorize the odor of death. It was
in the air, to be seen as if the smog from LA and that from New
York had finally joined forces above the remainder of the country
and America became, like Odessa, Texas, a mirage beneath a cloud
of black smoke. This morning, at first through the radio and then
confirmed by the television, one discovered or rediscovered that
our self-valued concern for justice and immortality was indeed
rather arbitrary, though by no means irrelevant.

        Robert Kennedy had died as one no longer saw his face
on the screen; already, one saw only an image of his face on the
screen; film on film.

        The President told us that we, as a nation, were guiltless.
He appointed a commission of clergymen, congressmen, com-
municationsmen to explain, explore the phrenology of our national
schizophrenia, and he was most confident that this pseudo-psy-

chological task force would bring in a favorable report on the Patient.

The television set apologized profusely, simpering like a wistful white liberal caught suggesting—through a slip of the tongue, of course—that Nig, uh, Negroes are not all bad people. It apologized in the morning, in advance (as the Junky said to do) of the Prime Time Programming which, tonight, included *Cimmaron Strip* and the 1961 American film entitled *Portrait of a Mobster.*

One looks at the newspaper photo captioned "MOMENTS AFTER SHOOTING—Sen. Robert F. Kennedy lies gravely wounded on the floor. . . ." He is looking up in pain and disbelief at a man who wipes away his blood with a white handkerchief. But there are just enough spaces between the dots of this halftone to present an entirely different impression. It is as if Kennedy, with a strangely halo-ic cast about his face, is seeing his Death for the first and last time and he is awed by its prospect; before his opened and soundless lips, there seems—and one says "seems" for one knows or, at least, willingly defines one's own reality—to be a puff of heavy, white, atmospheric smoke, the kind of Sunday School smoke that all humans would, whether readily or not, identify as their archetypal vision of Soul.

It began at approximately 12:15 a.m., Pacific time (one cannot avoid the irony, nor, in fact, should one) and, by 1:44 a.m. —again Pacific time but of another day— he was empty or emptied. It is said that it takes forty days for the Soul to complete Its filling of the caverns of the human organism and, in this case— whether because the puncture was small or the shell elastic—It had all leaked out in slightly more than one day. At the moment that the photo was taken, the ultimate record made, it appears that Kennedy is wondering, with a profound sense of innocence, where It is going. For one knows that he, too, believes in the Law of the Conservation of Energy and that it is indeed that—a Law. One hopes or, perhaps, wants to hope (the addition of a verb does not necessarily challenge the existential position of that which we now call a Sentence) that his belief is not a delusion.

And the President assures us that we are guiltless, that we are not responsible. To look into the picture of his eyes on

127

the television screen is to know as certainly as one knows that dandruff on his collar is from his head, for he is not the kind of man who offers to let you rest your flaked scalp on the shoulders of his silk suit, that the Wave of Repression—with which one, like our Surfer of before, has always danced a *pas de deux* of love and fear, of now and then, of life and death—is certain to flood the nation. And to flood it silently, with all the exquisite finesse of concept and execution that we attribute and/or recognize in those few seconds of air time to which we award our Clio for Best Commercial of the Year or, putting it in other, cruder, words, those few seconds which represent the Most Palatable Evil of the Year.

One cannot help wondering what it was for a human being to live in Germany as the Nazis absorbed the power. One cannot help believing in the saintliness of Genet. We stand on a perilously poetic mountain in Time. And we must ask ourselves whether or not we shall become the new Nazis and, even more important, whether or not the fiction which we have nurtured, yea, the fiction which we have allowed to flourish in the fertile soil of our fruited plain, that fiction of the "Good German" which, like a tapeworm of morality, can only grow tired of toying with its host organism and, eventually, devour it . . . us, whether or not that fiction will become fact. He who seizes power in order to promote an unjust cause, a cause that leads to the erosion of human consciousness and, eventually, to what must surely be irreversible dehumanization—that man, whether he be Devil or Deluded (and, in reality, it makes little difference which, for it is immoral and, in fact, irrelevant to argue the degrees of Evil), that man, at least, still retains the possibility of grace within the container of his freedom; he, at least, may opt to repent. But for those who, whether through carelessness or confusion, allow that power to be taken, there is a double curse: the surrender of both Consciousness and Choice (and here, if only for a moment because we speak of the mass, we separate or, rather, distinguish) leads to naught but the possibility of unearned mercy. And there are some Courts in which and some Offenses for which one *cannot* enter a plea of *nolo contendere*.

Perhaps we'd best be getting about the business of confessing.

Or is that, too, un-American?

95   Shem. Again. Or Still.

You will recall that Golem's immediate concern is how to deal with and what significance to impart to the phenomenon of Anna's infidelity. As we return to our story, we find Anna in the bedroom, stretched in a conveniently Christ-like position across their bed and calmly—so calmly that even she is surprised by it—considering the possibilities of approach and response contained within the next several, critical hours. However, let us leave her for a moment for she, at least, is in a comfortable position. Let us return to Golem who, besides being *a* hero for our time and *the* hero of this novel, is also the eponymous character of this little screenplay. Let us return to him for we left him in a rather awkward and undignified position; sitting on the toilet, his creased pants and used underwear collapsed like inflatable chain about his ankles, considering that old devil, that old Trickster, that wonderful human being whose quiet manner and quick charm and subtle intelligence bring warmth and good cheer to millions of American shut-ins. Here he is folks, your dear friend and mine—let's give him a big hand now, let him really feel welcome, let him know how much you love him . . .

APPLAUSE. APPLAUSE. APPLAUSE.

(You remember that, eh?

Well, it wasn't so difficult.

It was a long way back.

Yes, but it was in caps there, too.

Eyewitnesses to the crime reported that the accused was heard to mutter mysteriously under his breath as he ran back into the night. Prof. I. Amnon, thirty-two-year-old Chairman of the two-man Department of Philosophy and Fun at the prestigious State U., said, "He muttered mysteriously under his breath and you know how difficult communication is in these days, even in normal ways [wake up!] and so I cannot be positive but it sounded as though, as he ran back into the night, he said or, rather, muttered mysteriously as I previously described the phenomenon [GET BACK—PULL THE STRING; THE WIND IS CARRYING IT AWAY, FOR CHRIST'S SAKE!]—uh, oh, yes.

Forgive my digression. What he seemed to say was, and I quote, 'Guttenberg, Gottenberg!' However, I cannot be certain as not only am I unfamiliar with the specific term, but also it sounds kind of like a foreign language, don't it?"

"We do not know who he is. He does speak and understand English."

Well, back to our show.)

you love him . . .

APPLAUSE. APPLAUSE. APPLAUSE.

And here he is, a man who needs no introduction, whose smiling eyes and ingratiating mouth speak most eloquently for themselves————The Appearance-Reality Problem.

Thank you, folks. Hands over head like a Champ. The way Joe Louis used to do it, the way Joe Palooka—not cause he dint have 'no style mothafuck, but jes cause der wasn't no room enough in dat itty-bitty old frame—never could.

Amen.

Just a moment here to catch your breath or your death.

Go! (Watch the spaces, will you? And don't step on the cracks either, for that matter.)

Well, where we were was just at that point where our Golem was not, no, indeed, not contemplating the philosophical ramifications of his potential to, uh, pass air? No, that's not where we were. See, you got this guy . . .

Golem, on the toilet, taking a crap, trying to decide.

96   Shall we inventory the contents of Golem's medicine chest?

Now?

I've promised.

Not promised. Teased. And now we're just getting to the good part. All that heavy stuff about Shit and Decisions and Sex and Stuff.

Yes, but now's the time.

C'mon. I won't stand for it. I'm not taking any more of their (your) bull.

Ha ha. Got you hooked. That's power, see. You stay in your place and I'll stay in mine. Except yours is defined by your chair and mine is defined by the contents of your head. Everybody and their cousin is looking around in nook and cranny, turning over every stone and rotting log, searching for some definition of reality. And you, my friend, are mine. So sit tight and shut up.

Shit, shit, shit!

Shuddup, you faggot.

I will not; I will not. I'm not your slave. What do you think this is, some new genre? The Novel of Cruelty? The Novel of Fact? What's the fashionable word these days?

Fuck you.

(Which is all that's left to say.)

97 Commenting on the manufacturing of napalm for use in the Vietnamese War, Mr. H. R. Doan, the President of Dow Chemical Company (which also manufactures such other symptoms of American Life as Saran Wrap, etc.), defended his corporate position thusly. "We believe in the general policies of the government. If history should later judge Lyndon Johnson as a mass murderer or another Hitler (get this!), then we too would gladly stand trial for having believed our country was moral" (Context and Emphasis Added).

"This guy," said one Security Analyst to another over the remains of their breakfast conference in one of the Street's more exclusive luncheonettes, "is a man of principle."

"He's got the courage of his convictions, all right. I'll say that."

"That's what makes the difference between a Winner and a Loser. That's how you get your seat on the Big Exchange in the Sky, as the Boss would say."

"Well, you've got to admit that the Boss has gotten a little philosophical as he's advanced in years."

"True, true. But he's still a tough cookie in my book."

"Well, if you've got faith in this thing, we can pick up a few thousand shares for the house portfolio."

"I've got faith."

And then their voices trailed off, the volume having been turned down while they collected their papers and had a friendly little argument about whose turn it was to leave a tip.

OK.

The Medicine Chest or Cabinet is situated, at its bottom point, some 1½ feet from the top of the bathroom sink molding and, at its top edge, some 2 feet from the ceiling, give or take a few inches. Above it, say five inches, is a white and otherwise undistinguished object of the type known as "lighting fixture." (Don't those cats know that light moves, baby? Look, just keep quiet and let me tell the story.) It is constructed of somewhat thin, though not intolerant, sheet metal and edged in chromium. It has a mirrored door which opens with the aid of a single bar-type hinge and containing or limiting rod arrangement. All in all, fairly simple and therefore ingenious and, therefore, deceiving.

The most deceiving part of the Medicine Chest is its door which, as stated above, is mirrorized. If you look at it, you can see yourself—whether you need a shave, if you have any new blemishes, or how well you parted your hair . . . that kind of thing. However, if you do not look at it, you will not see yourself there. Mirrors, you understand, are rather temporary substitutes for reality in a society as complex as ours.

Normally, Golem stands in front of it to see if his face has melted or if he parted his hair correctly or if he shaved well or if he washed that last vestige of toothpaste from the corners of his mouth. And, normally, when he opens it, his purpose is to withdraw or replace some implement of his vanity unless, of course, he wants to take out one of the bromidic concoctions which he secrets there. But on a day like today, when your soul aches because it was accidentally jammed in the door which separates the Two Rooms (appearance-reality, mind-body, take your pick of dualisms), when you entertain serious doubts about the night reaching its natural end, when you not only forget on which side of the world the sun will come up but begin to consider the possibility of its—Old Sol is, I suppose, obligatory here—having been putting mankind on for centuries and that those things which we call eclipses are really warning signals of the possibility of reversal (even the Sun wants to be loved and not taken for granted) . . . well, buddy, not even doctors recommend aspirin for a headache like that.

And so, reaching up from his place on the toilet, Golem opens the mirrored door and, like Luther discovering the Protestant Reformation as he took his after-coffee crap, Golem finds that his cabinet needs a cleaning out. For, as if part of the sound effects for that old radio program, the amber bottles, the poly pill containers that look like they have been manufactured on a plastic sausage machine, the packets of spansules and capsules—QUICK ACTING—DELAYED RELEASE—TAKE ONE A DAY FOR FAST RELIEF OF EVERY BODILY ILL KNOWN TO MAN—the apothecary jars of the intellect come tumbling out, their labels clearly visible:

CONSCIOUSNESS
CHOICE
COMMUNICATION
GENERATION GAP
CHARISMA
KUDOS
ALIENATION
DIALOGUE
CATALOG
ANGST
ORGASM
FAITH
BEING
CHAMELEON
OWL—MASK
WHITE WHALE
L—ASPARAGENASE
LOVE
PEACE
SURVIVAL
POWER
CORRUPTION
ESTABLISHMENT

— —

— —

— —

———

— —

———

RESPON
SIBILITY
&
KONKRETE POETRY
!
.

And yet, none of these preparations, however highly recommended by your professional local druggist, will chase away Golem's headache of the Soul with any degree of permanence, nor will they have any significant effect on the alleviation of his constipation/diarrhea.

"What can I do?" asks Golem of his reflection.

It is a simple problem, one's wife being unfaithful. One remains, attempting to draw a pair of venetian blinds over the screen on which one can see too clearly the scene that took place between Cohen and Anna. But what if she's pregnant? Then he has to play the obligatory bastard son scene and he wants none of that. To leave?

This is what he wants to do. Wants almost as badly as the desire necessary to shoot both Cohen and his wife. But, like that moment, that purely cinematic moment in the silverscreened version of *Who's Afraid of Virginia Woolf?* during which George, knowing that his wife is upstairs making some kind of love with his own "historical inevitability," cannot choose his action, is caught between the need to enter the room (passion) and the need *not* to enter the room (reason), can only manage a small cry of what might be, finally, reduced to an expression of bewilderment at his predicament, Golem knows not whether to flush the toilet—hoping that it will clog neither itself nor his gestures—and come into the bedroom to make love with his wife, hard love, hard enough to erase the chalk dust of Cohen's touch from her body and his mind, knows not whether he should vomit and start again or swear off masturbating for at least a month as self-punishment, repentance, etc. Knows not period.

Taste and See that God is Good.

Blessed are the Pure in Heart for they shall See God.

No Man hath Seen God.

And so, he says to himself . . .

99   **THE IMAGE**

The light has sunk into the earth:
The image of DARKENING OF THE LIGHT.
Thus does the superior man live with the great mass:
He veils his light, yet still shines.

In a time of darkness it is essential to be cautious and reserved. One should not needlessly awaken overwhelming enmity by inconsiderate behavior. In such times, one ought not to fall in with the practice of others; neither should one drag them censoriously into the light. In social intercourse one should not try to be all-knowing. One should let many things pass, without being duped.

100   *Item* from the *Atlanta News-Times* (Georgia):

SEARCH FOR DJ-RAPIST
CONTINUES
Believed To Have Left State

Police in Odessa, Ga., are continuing their search for a former WOGA disc jockey who is alleged to have sexually assaulted the station's sixteen-year-old Music Librarian, three nights ago.

The girl, whose name has not been released by local authorities, is said to have identified her attacker as Davey Allen, a disc jockey at the station. Chief of Police Charles J. Coleman suggested that the name of the sought man is "probably phoney" as "disc jockeys often use an assumed name on the air."

As the two-day-long search has not turned up any signs as to the whereabouts of the accused rapist, Coleman said that "he has probably left that state. I think he was from New York and we are checking on that."

Asked if he would contact other law enforcement agencies for assistance in the case, Coleman replied, "If necessary. But, don't you worry, boys. We'll get him."

Police are also investigating the possible connection between "Allen" and an obscene note which was found nailed to the door of the Collier-Southeast Insurance Company office in Odessa. No charges have been made in that case.

However, Harmon Collier, president of the

firm, ascribed the note to "the work of a malicious vandal with a warped mentality" and added that the author was probably "a commie."

The contents of the note were not released.

101   And so, he says to himself, "All this fancy existential shit is getting me nowhere. I ought to get off the toilet and do something."

Which he did. Leaving the bathroom and entering the bedroom, answering Anna's questioning eyes by putting on his coat and her finally spoken where are you going with a slamming of the front door. He got into the car and drove it through the Night, leaving Anna on the bed, faced with the problem of whether or not to lock the front door.

102   In the morning, Anna opened the locked front door and found a yellow sheet of blue-lined legal size paper taped to the face of it, just beneath the nameplate. She took it down, recognized it as a note from Golem, and brought it into the kitchen where her teakettle was whistling. The note was put on the plastic table while she made herself a small breakfast and then, as she took her first sip of coffee, she read.

WHEREAS, I, David Alan Golem, have been Betrayed by both my Wife and my Close Friend, and,

WHEREAS, It seems to me to be no longer possible to keep up the reality of appearances or the appearances of reality, and,

WHEREAS, It seems to me to be impossible to distinguish between the Absolute and the Relative, and,

WHEREAS, It seems highly unlikely that I could or should love you now, and,

WHEREAS, It seems highly unlikely that You could or do love me now, and,

WHEREAS, It doesn't seem possible to me that I'll ever be able to look you in the face without seeing Cohen's Prick in your Cunt,

THEREFORE, for all of these reasons and for all of those implied by those listed herein, I am splitting the scene.

David Alan Golem

P.S. I'll call you in a few days, perhaps.

136

Anna read the proclamation twice, trying to decide if Golem had gone mad or if he was simply indulging himself. And then she cried because it did not matter; it only mattered that he was gone and she was left with nothing but a guitar around her neck again.

Had she dried her tears in time to read the evening paper from front page to back as was Golem's custom, she would have found, under the heading PERSONALS, tucked in between the search for missing heirs and the confirmation of a secret rendezvous, the following notice:

I, David Alan Golem, refuse to be responsible for any and all debts and/or obligations not incurred by myself alone from this day forward.

But she had not dried them. Her eyes were wet while she tried to reach Cohen but found him to be in class; they were wet when she called Golem's mother and asked if he were there, trying to make the question sound as innocent as possible while still admitting that, "Well, yes, we had a fight" . . . her eyes were still wet when the airplane landed in California and, from her window seat, she could see the words "my poor baby" hung on the lips of her father like a nude painting of a woman on the wall behind the wood and leather bar of a homosexual pub.

THE SECOND BOOK

"For, lo. He that formeth the mountains, and createth the wind, and declareth unto man what is his thought . . ." (*Amos 4:13*).

I

103   In this solemn hour consecrated to our beloved dead, we ponder over the flight of time, the frailty and uncertainty of human life. We ask ourselves: What are we? What is our life? To what purpose our wisdom and knowledge? Wherein is our strength, our power, our fame? Alas, man seems born to trouble, and his years are few and full of travail.

O Lord, what is man, that Thou art mindful of him?
And the son of man that Thou considerest him?

Yet Thou hast made him but little less than divine.
And hast crowned him with glory and honor.

Golem at the door, watching the congregation seat itself, the sound which it makes to accomplish this task of relocation of the body being at least equal to if not greater than that which it makes when confessing to that list of all the real and/or imagined sins existing in this universe. Rabbi Lowe, looking up from his podium to await the final crossing of knees, straightening of jackets, seizes the moment and, before there can occur another rustle, announces, "We read in unison on page 223."

O Lord, as we recall all our departed and the blessings they bequeathed unto us, we pray Thee to keep their souls united with ours in the bond of life. May our faith, like theirs, be strong, our devotion to the Torah unfaltering, our love for Zion constant, and our concern for Israel and humanity unceasing. For as we identify ourselves with the lives, hopes, and traditions of an eternal people, we, ourselves, take on the aspect of eternity. May we so live that when our years draw to a close we, too, shall be remembered for good and for blessing.
Amen.

As the congregation begins to read, Golem is led by the shammes down the carpeted aisle toward the pew where his mother will be sitting, tightly girdled and wearing a black suit of some satiny material, or, perhaps, she has been daring this year and has selected purple.

Father of mercy, in whose hands are the souls of the living and the dead, may Thy consolation cheer us as we remember our beloved and honored kinsfolk who have gone to their eternal rest. May we be loyal to the memory of all our brethren, who in every generation sacrificed their lives to sanctify Thy name. We beseech Thee, O Lord, grant us strength to be faithful to their charge while the breath of life is within us. May their souls repose in the land of the living, beholding Thy glory and delighting in Thy goodness.

As the two men walk, the sound of their footsteps is absorbed by the strip of burgundy carpet which runs between each of the three sections of pews and the sound of their entrance is covered by the voice of the congregation.

O good and beneficent God, turn this day in loving kindness and tender mercy to the prayers of those who serve Thee and plead wholeheartedly before thee. Verily we know that our strength is frail, and that Thou hast made our days as handbreaths. Help us, O God of our salvation, to bear ourselves faithfully and blamelessly during the years of our pilgrimage. Strengthen us with steadfast faith in Thee and Thy Torah. Let Thy grace be with us, that we may rear our children to keep Thy commandments and to fulfill Thy will all the days of their life.

They pass rows of families who have used this day to exhibit a single Jewish face to the world, to temporize their petty crimes and, by their appearance—though not through any special action for, after all, even the dry-goods merchant considers himself to be Chosen—to signify their willingness to accept redemption. It is enough to be there, they say. Let each man pray in his own way, they say. But no organ music, only a simple choir; the organ sounds too goyish, as if to say not that their sense of tradition is offended but that, by some strange form of neologization, the Ears of God might be. What does God care about the construction of the inanimate instrument that produces the sound? It is the sound He cares about. If that. For haven't they already described Him as such a weak Supreme Being that He's willing to forgive if only you'll show your face in the door? To be Jewish is to suffer, they say. And certainly that is the truth. But to be Jewish is also to be supremely arrogant, for what other test do we have for Right in this world if it is not the test of suffering? This they do not say for it would not sit well on country club shoulders. To be a Jew is to be human is what they should say for to be human means simply to exclude no possibilities whether they be most favorable or most catastrophic.

It is said that Jesus died for the sins of mankind; that he died so that mankind might be afforded salvation. And what of the six million Jews who died on the crosses of our technology? Did they die to keep the world safe for democracy? Because God had indigestion that morning? To provide a statistical excuse for what politicians, with varying and regional degrees of indignation, like to refer to as the need to safeguard human rights? One does not know any more what that phrase means: human rights. No. The Jews who were murdered by the Nazis died to show the world that it, too, could perish in an instant should it desire an hour to discuss the possible values, however temporary, to be sure, of Evil. If it can be said that Christ died in the cause of personal salvation and that six million Jews died in the cause of the necessity to recognize and suppress Evil, what, then, can be said of these Jews, these lambs of God, destined to be sacrificed on the altar of absolute justice, these families who occupy the synagogue? What, then, can be said of Golem?

That they are a state of being?

Give us sustenance and let us not be in the need of the gifts of others. Remove from us care and sorrow, distress and fear, shame and contempt. O God, take us not hence in the midst of our days. Let us complete in peace the number of our years. And when our end draws nigh and we depart this world, be Thou with us, and may our souls be bound up in the bond of life with the souls of the righteous who are ever with Thee.
Amen and Amen.

"Let us turn to page . . ."

The rabbi's thin eyes fall on Golem as he nears his mother's row. They do not know each other and yet, they are the same. The rabbi sees him only as a stranger in the congregation, for the rabbi himself has come here only recently from a minor pulpit in Des Moines, Iowa, a place wherein one might not expect to find a Jew. Perhaps, thinks the rabbi, he is another boy home from college for the High Holy Days. Perhaps he enjoyed the luxury of sleeping late this morning and must now face the ire of his parents.

Golem does not look up at the pulpit. He knows what is there and has always known it. And it is possible that today he shall use that knowledge, but to plan it so far in advance would be to defeat its purpose and to mock its intent.

He reaches the row, and the shammes, book in hand, gestures for him to enter. Faces turn toward him.

DISSOLVE TO:

II

Hello?"

"This is the long distance operator. I have a person-to-person call for Miss Toni Croft."

"OK."

"Is this she?"

"Yes, I'm her."

"Thank you. Go ahead, sir."

"Toni?"

"Yes?"

"This is Dave. Golem."

"Oh, hi. Where are you?"

"I'm at the airport, in a phone booth with my legs cramped up under the stool and forty-five cents spread out and falling off this tiny counter."

"What are you doing there?"

"It's a long story. Is Paulo there?"

"No."

"Well, listen. Anna and I are splitting. I don't want to go into the details now, but I'm going to New York for a little while."

"Why? What happened, baby?"

"I'll tell you later. The thing is, I want you to come with me."

"   ?   "

"Did you hear me?"

"Yes."

"Well, will you?"

"You want me to leave here and go with you?"

"Yes."

"Why?"

"Why? What do you mean why? Because I love you, I need you. I thought you loved me."

"I do. But not in that way."

"Not in that way?"

"You know what I mean."

"But we made love. Doesn't that mean something?"

"Sure it does."

"Well, what?"

"It means that we loved each other enough to make love."

"And that's all?"

"What else is there?"

"Yeah. Well, OK, baby. I don't want to go into that now. I'll be talking to you."

"Dave . . ."

"What?"

"Take care of yourself. I care about you."

"Yeah. Thanks a lot."

My milkman cares about me, too, he thought as he hung up the phone.

105   Drinking a prepackaged bloody mary, he looked out of the cabin window and thought about Dickey's poem, the one that started with the stewardess falling or being sucked out of the airplane and continued with her floating down, undressing as she

146

went, to the heartland of America, and ended . . . how did it end? He could not remember exactly, now. And it made no difference for the end is in the beginning, in the thought at the beginning and it is the trip from one pole to the other that is the interesting part. What would he do if his Emergency Exit suddenly sensed an emergency and opened and he felt himself being pulled out of the plane? Gulp down his drink and holler Geronimo, whistle a tune like the High and the Mighty, do every comic routine he could think of as he floated to his extinction? What do people think of as they jump off bridges and buildings? Certainly not the weather. But, perhaps, the Time. Counting the exact number of moments remaining in their lives and, perhaps, wishing that there were a convenient projectionist who could throw the switch to run the film in reverse. A second chance.

It was not that he was considering suicide (because he knew that that act would be as absurd as any other), but only that he was considering Death.

"Can I get you a drink, sir?" the stewardess had asked him. He looked into her eyes and wanted to ask her if she would, once and for all, tell him whether or not the myths about steward-esses and nurses and any/all other public women were true or if they were manufactured by men as a gleefully defensive reaction.

"Amazing," he said to the man next to him, a very execu-tive type who rested his open attaché case on his knees and leafed through onionskin copies while alternately grunting and smiling, "how the people and cars and things down there really do look like ants or toys, isn't it?"

"Hmmm?" The man looked up from his papers, surprised at the liberty which Golem had taken.

"I said," said Golem, turning to him, "that everything looks awfully small down there, doesn't it?"

The man looked at him, still not believing that he had been asked a question which was not immediately relevant to his onionskin copies and then, after accepting the possibility, wondered at the strangely trite nature of the intrusion. Of course, he thought, rather securely, everything looks small down there because we're up here. Yes, was what he said. And then, not meaning to be brusque, added, "Kind of gives you a different perspective."

"Right. Imagine if we were down there."

Golem and the man looked at each other and then Golem, not wishing to involve this anonymous figure in his own passion, simply smiled and turned again to the window. The man thought for a moment and then returned to the contents of his case. Perhaps he was en route to some more significant encounter.

106   As the plane taxis to its place before the terminal, it passes the planes marked *Flying Tiger Lines*; immediately, Golem thinks of Burma, John Wayne, Nordoff and Hall, *et al*. How could such a concept exist today? He wonders. But they are flying under an assumed name. No silken scarf over leather shoulder, no glasses thrown into the fireplace. Only Air Freight.

107   "Hello, Mom?"

"Who is this?"

"David."

"Who?"

"David."

"My son?"

"Yes."

"My son is calling me? Where are you?"

"In Newark."

"What are you doing in New Jersey? You should be home with your wife."

"Did she call?"

"Yes, she called."

"What'd she say?"

"A fight. You had a fight and for that you run away to New Jersey?"

"Look, I'm not in New Jersey, I'm at the airport and it was more than just a fight."

"You didn't hurt her, did you?"

"What?"

"Did you hit her? God forbid, a son of mine should beat his wife."

"No, no. I didn't hit her. Look, I don't want to go into it on the phone. I'm gonna be in New York for a little while so do you mind if I stay at home?"

"Home? What home? Your home is with your wife. You can't come running to momma like a little boy. Get right back on that airplane and go to your home. You should be ashamed of yourself for spending the money you need for food on airplane tickets.

"I can't come home?"

"No."

"Not to my own house?"

"This is my house; you have your own."

"Thanks a lot."

"Go back."

"Yeah."

"You're crazy."

"Yeah."

"Call me up when you get home."

"Yeah."

"Have a good trip and don't forget to call me."

"Yeah."

"And David . . ."

"Yeah?"

"Make it a signal call. Ask for yourself."

108   Golem pulled his address book out of his jacket pocket. A handy, concise, leatherbound list of friends and acquaintances. As he read the names on his list, he pictured the faces of their owners or, rather, loaners. On whom could he impose? Bernie Abrams, Billy Zettle? No, one was in New Hampshire and the other, well, the other had sent him a wish you were here view of Tangiers and he had not replied to it. A girl would be best, of course, in many ways. But how many Susans, Lauras, Amys could be trusted with his little package of sorrows waiting in the baggage room next to the attaché case of copies? Not a one, surely, because they were all girls with whom Golem had made some kind of love and whom he had objectivized out of his life. Just as he had done with Anna, he supposed. Meet her, make her, and then, like a deranged Pygmalion, smash the resultant figure until it is clay once again.

Lane.

Except Lane. Very dramatic. And, indeed, she was; Golem thought of her as one of those dangerously good women who fleet across the pages of great literature like nymphletic symbols of all womanhood, but one who is so rarely encountered in real life. Lane Barnum fit into that compartment in Golem's mind which also carried the burdens of Brett Hadley, Nicole Diver, etc. It was so conveniently melodramatic that Golem was certain Lane would approve. Staten Island Ferry, Empire State Building—ah, Golem felt his soul returning to him as he dialed her number.

109   "I'm sorry, she's not in."

"Well, do you know how she can be reached?"

"Who is this, please?"

"This is Dave Golem. An old friend; it's important that I reach her."

"Uh, she's working."

"Where?"

"I don't think I can give you that information."

"Look, are you her roommate?"

"No, just a friend."

"OK. Well, I'm an old and close friend and I'm at the airport surrounded by myths of every shape and size and it's very important, I can't stress that enough, that I reach her right away. I absolve you of all responsibility; just give me her number at work."

"Well . . ."

"Please."

"All right, but I shouldn't do this," she giggled.

110   "Just a moment, please. I'll see if she's in, Mr. Golem."

"Thank you."

Hanging on the line. It was a good expression, a solid proleterian metaphor. For there he stood, his change exhausted, hoping that she was neither in conference nor out with a client nor any of those foolish things. She had to be sitting at her desk, approving a fab new layout for some fab groovy new product which would turn on the millions. Lane was an Art Director, i.e., she directed art at the synapses of the masses and she had a little rubber stamp fitted to the end of her pencil with which she affixed her LB of approval, content, resignation, or whatever. The stamp said it all for her.

"Hello?"

"Lane?"

"Yes?"

"This is Golem."

"Golem!"

"Hello."

He sensed, though he could not hear for she would not be so gauche as that, that she caught her breath and whispered to herself, "It's him."

"Hi."

"I'm in Newark. I'm in trouble. I need your help."

"OK, do you want to come to the office?"

"No, it's not like that. Can I stay with you for a couple of days?"

"What about Anna?"

"That's the trouble."

"Oh."

"Look, it's not kid stuff. You can trust me on that, Lane."

"OK, you've still got my address?"

"Yes. Still."

"That's nice to know. I'll be home around seven and I'll call the doorman and tell him to let you in. Will you be there soon?"

"Yeah. I'll leave the airport after I hang up."

"OK, baby. I'll see you later, then."

"Thanks Lane."

"You sure you don't want to come over here?"

"I'm sure. Thanks again."

"OK, baby."

Golem wasn't sure at all when he hung up. In fact, he was sure that he did want to go right over to her office, throw himself into her arms, cry on her shoulder. Christ! Get your fucking suitcase and get on the damned bus and stop acting like a twenty-seven-year-old kid. Act your age.

111   There is a story told that in 1961, a yogi in New Delhi had himself buried alive for nine days in order to meditate on the problems of world peace, both physical and spiritual. And when his vigil was over and he was excavated, he is reported to have announced, "Things are not so bad as they seem."

Another yogi, whether out of a sense of transcendental competition or simple dissatisfaction, went the first holy man one better. He had himself interred for forty days—a significant allusion, one would suspect—and, when he was removed from the soil, he was dead.

It may all be a question of Time, but you know one thing for certain—the days of the flagpole sitter are no more.

112   At last count, sometime during the fourteenth century, there were known to be some three hundred and one million, six hundred and fifty-five thousand, seven hundred and twenty-two Angels in the universe. However, it is also a well-known fact that every Jew is attended by no less than eleven thousand Guardian Angels.

Draw your own conclusions.

113   Golem's bladder and bowels were as dry as any record day in Needles, California; his eyes were like musical staffs consisting of the five hundred and twenty-five lines of the television picture on which, like the notes of an unfinished symphony, danced the words that he had read in every magazine that rested in Lane's magazine rack. He had been waiting for Lane for nearly five hours and he had done everything there was to do in her small apartment, including the self-consciously guilty search through her lingerie drawer and the long look for any telltale signs of maleness (of which he found none, for Lane was as appreciative of her loneliness as Golem was destructive about his own), but no matter what he did, he could not erase the colored-chalk image of Anna-Cohen which clung to his mind as if it had been drawn with irreversibly charged magnetic particles. He considered beating his head against the wall to loosen the particles or, at least, to disturb their Brownian movement, but he knew well enough that mechanical action was no match for electricity—unless it meant pulling out the plug and Golem didn't even know where the socket was.

Outside, the city went on as if Golem did not exist, as if there were no such animal. Its pavement, unrolling for miles like a vast gray ribbon of despair from a spool which was sunk deep in the water off the southern coast of Florida, was crowded with women who looked, touched, tasted, shone like wax fruit under fluorescent light and men who kept four extra shirts in their bottom desk drawer, locked in that drawer, for there lay the secret of their success, their unfailing ability to look freshly showered and, therefore, intimidating to any who sought their favor. This, of course, was the "better section," the Upper East Side which wallowed in its self-created reputation as home base for the Single and the Screwing of all sexes, ages, etc. Golem was disappointed that Lane still lived here, still felt the need to be surrounded by her inferiors, people who considered impulse a virtue and, consequently, were compulsive about their seemingly spontaneous actions. But he could understand her need to live surrounded by some form of competition, however boring.

Outside the window was an Irish Pub, an English Pub, an Italian Restaurant, a Chinese Restaurant, a Mexican Restaurant, a Jewish Delicatessen, a German Bakery, a French Laundry, an Oriental Rug Dealer, and an American Coffee Shoppe—as if the residents of the street had gotten together in a kind of peculiar town meeting and said, Here, Here we will make our America, our microcosm, Here we will plant our flag of ethnic coexistence, Here we will light the fire under our melting pot. Of course, there were no Spanish movie theaters Here, nor were there any black "Soul Food Inns"—but there were plenty of maids, porters, delivery boys.

Let them eat cake, she said, and she was, after all, correct. Who wants to eat bread? One is forced to eat bread, one is surrounded by bread. It is cake that the people want; that's why they loot the appliance store and carry off portable color television sets instead of breaking into the branch bank. It's all the same dough, but one has a sugared icing while the other has nothing to speak for it but its crust.

Outside, the city continued to and fro, speaking of Michaelangelo. Except in this time, they said he was a fairy. Outside, the city continued with Freud on its lips and Jung in its heart, wearing a mask of Brillo pads designed in Hollywood by Mr. Shirley, the faggiest, trailer-campiest male hairdresser of them all. Outside, New York, that is this part of New York which had a heart of steel in a rib cage of glass, not that other part of New York which existed on the perimeter as a kind of handy joke (You're from Brooklyn? The Bronx, Queens, the Island?—conjuring up simplified archetypal images of egg creams, kosher pickles, shopping centers, and what have you), this part of New York never forgave itself for being a part of America (though it proudly boasted that it was an island, it knew very well that it was merely a peninsula) and constantly worked to cosmetize its face with the features, fashions, foods of other lands.

The trouble with New York, thought Golem behind the window in Lane's hermetically sealed apartment, is that every time you think you're being introduced to an Italian count, you find out that his name is Arnold Schwartzman.

And then the buzzer rang.

Which meant that Lane was home and it would all begin. Golem cleaned the apartment of the debris of his boredom, put a record on the intricate but miniaturized system, and had just enough time to pour two glasses of chilled white wine before he heard her key inserting itself into the evening.

114 He opened the door and she stepped in. They hugged. It was all hellos, babys, kisses, marvelous. And then, step back, let me look at you, it's been such a long time. They came into the area used as the livingroom and faced off like two angry French deputies before a duel.

Golem didn't know how he looked to her; the same, he hoped or imagined. But she had changed. All Paraphernalia-ed up, hair blond as before but looking now as though it had been plugged into an electric guitar, no longer smooth and balletically long. And her face. She had grown older and harder in that peculiar way that New York girls do and her complexion had changed from corn-fed American to wax fruit-cosmopolitan. Lane had lost. Or looked as though she had lost. Looked as though she were not a Lane Barnum (or P. T. as her friends probably called her), but an Elaine Birnbaum (as her enemies rumored her to be—and from the Bronx, yet) with style. Which, in fact, was exactly what she was. However, it had never been so painfully obvious before.

115 Let them eat cake, she said.

Are we in danger, we ask, of overextending our images?

116   A Fable Break. While Golem and Lane readjust, restructure, let's take a break for a fable which could easily be attributable to that old devil, Mad King Ludwig of Bavaria.

It seems that a very wise and benevolent king learned that almost all the crops in the world had suddenly been infected by a cancerous and fatal disease and that to eat them, to partake of them, would cause instant and permanent insanity. And so he said, "We'll take a few of the good crops—the ones that have not yet been tainted—and we'll build a castle, a magnificent castle around them." When he had done this, he said to his counselors, "Bring me a man with insight and understanding."

And so they brought him an artist.

The king and the artist shared a pot of tea in the royal chambers and became acquainted. When the king felt certain of his man, he set forth this proposition to the artist.

"You alone will live in this castle and eat only of the good crops. But to repay me, you must spend the remainder of your life traveling from kingdom to kingdom, from town to town, from village to village, from soul to soul—saying 'Always remember, you are all mad.' "

117   He looked to her a little heavier, a little harder—particularly around the nose and eyes—in need of a shave, perhaps even a change of skin, like somebody had uncorked the valve for a few moments, just enough to wrinkle up his extremities and leave an oddly shaped depression in his chest, as if he had sent his head from North Carolina to New York by Greyhound bus wrapped in brown paper, tied with shredding cord, and marked DELIVER TO OCCUPANT.

118   "That bad?"

119   They came together in the livingroom and hugged each other, Lane pushing her electrified head into one of Golem's sagging shoulders. Neither knew what to do with the glasses they held and, finally, after a moment, Golem touched her on the back and they separated. "I'm glad to see you," he said.

"Thank you for coming to me, Dave."

They smiled.

"Let me get out of these clothes and (with a lifted eyebrow) into something comfortable like a pair of jeans and we'll make dinner. You can tell me about everything. Or would you rather go out for dinner? I didn't think so. Sit down; I'll only be a minute."

Lane took off her shoes and started for the small bedroom as Golem sat down on the couch again, trying to pretend he had not sat there all day and, too, hoping that Lane would notice nothing out of place in her bedroom. He didn't want to come on as a brassiere-smelling pervert. He drank his wine slowly, not knowing whether or not to begin the conversation or, even, how.

"Did you have a good flight?"

A good flight? When was that? Oh, yes. The airplane. "Not bad, I guess. Very quiet. The airport's crowded. It's hard to get a cab in the city. But your doorman was very nice."

"That about wraps it up, I guess."

"Yup."

"Get your thing, yet?"

"Ph.D.?"

"Yeah."

"Not yet. Maybe someday."

He heard zippers, buttons, snaps. He had to admit to himself, at least, that he wanted to sleep with her and didn't care whether his desire grew out of his wife's rejection or out of some more "legitimate," more "genuine" source. He looked at his watch and realized that he had missed the news this day. If you are the news . . . no use in continuing that line for it only ends up in the contemplation of the whorls, etc., of your fingerprints.

"How did you get my number?"

"What?"

"How did you get my number at the office?"

Oh. I called here and convinced a friend of yours that I deserved it."

"That must have been Valerie. You'll meet her; she's OK."

Lane came out of the bedroom wearing a green turtleneck sweater and too-tight blue jeans which ended in wide bells, making her bare feet look like fleshy clappers. "Now. Dinner. What would you like?"

"Listen," he said, half rising and then deciding against it, "anything's OK. Like hamburgers or anything like that."

"No, no. We're in the Big City now. We do things right here. We'll have fondue."

"It sounds like a lot of trouble."

"It isn't. Come into the kitchen with me while I fix it up."

She stretched out her hand and he grasped it, rising, following closely behind her to the kitchen, tapping her on the shoulder and, when she turned around, kissing her lightly. She smiled at him, a smile that, like Toni's, seemed to come from somewhere deep inside that beautifully flat stomach.

120   "Don't smile at me like that."

"Whatever do you mean?"

"I mean just that. Don't you give me that sassy smile when I ask you a serious question."

"Why, Harmon, I can hardly take your question seriously."

"Why not?"

"Well, here we are, having dessert, and out of nowhere you ask me if I love you. You ought to know better, Harmon Collier. Of course, I love you. Silly."

"Then why did you smile at me?"

"Harmon, I was thinking of just how much I love you. That's why I smiled."

"If you loved me so much why did you flirt with all the boys at the club?"

"Now, Harmon. I didn't flirt with *all* the boys."

"You flirted with Vern Packer."

"I flirted with Vern Packer."

"Why?"

"Good heavens, Harmon. Vern Packer is an old man and you couldn't possibly think that I would prefer him to big strong you, could you?"

"How the hell do I know?"

"I'm telling you. I was just being sociable, like your wife is supposed to be. Now you eat your dessert and don't think another thought about it."

"All right, JoAnna."

"You'd think I was some kind of wicked woman, a Jezebel."

"Well, you sure have got a mean streak in you."

JoAnna smiled and blew him a soft kiss across their candlelit table. It never reached him, though he pretended it did.

121   Golem leaned on the entrance to the tiny kitchen and watched Lane as she opened the plastic packages with a frightening kind of grace. He got bowls at her direction, found plates, cups, made the coffee at her command. He poured more wine for himself and for her. He kept out of her way, not wanting to break her stride, and yet he longed for any excuse to touch her, any part of her, even her elbow, just to assure himself a connection with another body. He mixed sour cream and white horseradish and chives with a wooden spoon, watching the consistency of the mixture change with his movements—though it had its own natural end, to sour, it relied upon him for immediate direction. He could make it soft or force it, against its will if necessary, to be lumpy and self-defeating. He helped Lane choose the kinds of pickles and peppers that they would eat and she used him to slice and butter the long bread before she wrapped it in aluminum and put it into the oven. The oil and spice mixture bubbled on the stove while they set the small table with textured placemats of a red weave and orange napkins from another country. White plates, stainless steel silverware. Wine glasses. Still no talking about The Problem. A few tentative approaches, but they were lost in the cries of the sauces that he beat with his wooden spoon. Lane kept him occupied with what Lamarck would call the First Principle—nourishment.

And, after Golem had poured the oil into the fondue pot, had struck a match to light the artificial fire in the canned heat can, after they had brought all of the elements of the meal to the table and Lane had turned off all the wrong lights and turned on all the right lights, they sat down to dinner.

Golem speared a piece of meat on the end of his long

fork and, feeling or pretending to feel like the end product of a long assembly line of evolutionary merchandise getting back to its original components, stuck the meat into the cooking pot and told himself that he was back in the tribe. The meat sizzled at first and then quieted until Lane put in a piece for herself.

"So?"

"So."

Lane unwrapped the aluminum and offered a piece of the bread to Golem who ripped it off the loaf. He put salad in her wooden bowl and then into his own. Then he busied himself with the dressing.

"Well," he said as he poured the oil and vinegar together over the greens, "it's a fairly long story. But then, it always is."

"I'd like to hear it all if you'd like to tell it to me or if you need to tell it to me, but why don't you start at the end and save me a lot of punctuating facial expressions."

"The end? It hasn't ended; it just started."

"Don't argue with me, Dave. That's not why you came."

"You're right. Do you want some of this sauce?"

"Yes."

He passed the small bowl of sweet and sour sauce to her and said, "Anna slept with another guy."

"Oh?"

"Yeah. A friend of mine."

She put some of the sauce on her plate and gave him back the bowl.

"Once, or has she been doing it for a while?"

"What's the difference?"

"Come on, David. How many times did you cheat on your wife?"

"That doesn't matter. My doing it doesn't make any of it right. It'll all immoral, isn't it? Isn't it?"

"But she didn't leave you. Your meat is probably done."

He pulled the fork out of the fire and dipped the hot meat into the sour cream sauce that he had made. He held the fork in front of him like a pointer. "Maybe it's less important to her than it is to me."

"It's all the same. You know that."

He ate the meat.

"So what am I supposed to do, go back?"

"You're supposed to do what you think is right, whatever you *have* to do. But, like the man said, you pays you money and you takes you choice."

"Very funny."

"We're all adults here, Dave."

"She did it once that I know of. Only once, I guess."

"Then it's your fault."

"Don't give me that feminine logic, please. Spare me that."

"Who do you think you are, Christ?"

"No, no. I'm not coming on to you as suffering—even though I sure as hell am. Don't underestimate me! I've considered nearly everything. Believe me, this is the first time I've ever run away from a situation."

"You didn't come here for a pat on the back, did you? You'll get no sympathy from me, Dave, you know that. I'll love you; I'll always love you. But don't expect me to fuck you for medicinal purposes."

"I was afraid you'd get to that."

"It's unavoidable, isn't it? We might as well have it in the open. Put another piece of meat in the pot."

122   "Y'all come and see us, Leffy."

The man left with his two cigars and his change, passing through the door after having read seven magazines, having examined the contents of five paperback novels with titles that were two-word combinations on the limited variables of Lust and Sin, and having delivered the final insult of an unequivocally false invitation to visit him. Does his wife know that he gets a bulge in his pants every time he comes into the store, Lefkowitz wondered as he came out from behind the dirty now but once extravagantly tiled counter to lock the door and pull down the shade which had the word CLOSED stenciled on its charcoal surface. Better she shouldn't know. Of course, she knows. Probably she found in the back of one of his drawers a card with a dirty saying on it one day and then she knew that he was just as dirty as everybody else on the block. Filth. Filth everywhere you look. Not an honest man to be found. If God should come down to this earth today and say find me an honest man and I will save the world, Lefkowitz would have to tell him to go back upstairs and make one.

Lefkowitz, the only Marranoe in Odessa, locked his door and pulled down his shade. CLOSED. Then he picked three nudist magazines out of the old wooden racks which stood against the wall opposite the counter. Then he went to the revolving wire stand which held the paperbacks and picked out one entitled *A Blaze of Passion* and, with his library in his hands, turned off the lights in the store and walked up the short flight of stairs to his small but clean apartment.

Go back upstairs and make one!

God should ask Lefkowitz? He laughed to himself, at himself, as he lowered himself onto his bed and turned on the reading light.

I wonder, he asked himself, if Spinoza played with himself, too. The lens grinder taking a break from his philosophy with a dirty book. God forbid! But who is he to forbid if he can't even make himself an honest man, if he has to ask Lefkowitz what's going on?

123   He did.

And it sizzled again, though less violently now that the oil had been exposed to meat, proving that one *can* become immune to everything.

"Well, sure I'd like to make love with you, Lane. And to tell you the truth, I don't know whether I want to, uh, screw for sympathy—one good one deserves another—or not. And I don't care, which, I suppose, makes me fantastically insensitive. But you brought it up."

"We'll let it hang in the air because we're eventually going to do it, I know it's my decision and I've already made it, but I'm not going to let you . . ."

"Get away with anything?"

"Right."

"OK."

124   "Don't you OK me, Betty Sue. Now you come home when I tell you to, you hear?"

"Yes, Momma."

Between them stretched a telephone line which started at the ear of Betty Sue's mother who sat at her Early American (Sears Roebuck Early American) Telephone Desk with her flip-open-to-the-touch-telephone-number-pad in front of her and her present behind her and ended at the ear of Betty Sue who, having just had what she considered to be an orgasm, not the Big O, you understand (which, like the Big C, is too much a part of the heart of the U.S.A. to be anything but abbreviated), but a little, lower-case orgasm, was lying naked on the bed of her best friend, Melinda Nash, when she got the call to come home.

Melinda let her hand rest on Betty Sue's breast while the conversation continued, occasionally tickling and pinching the nipple that was still wet from when she had sucked on it, and Betty Sue gasped a few times during the phone conversation, enough times to give her mother more than second thoughts about the real nature of her daughter's frequent visits to the Nash house. Was Betty Sue meeting some boy over there? Were they necking or, worse, petting? Relax, Mom, it's just us girls having a little fun, paying our dirty dues, pressing tit to tit, clit to clit, and wondering what it's like to have a man's thingy in there. Just that teenage stuff.

125   *Memory is the sperm of History.*

Remember that.

Look, I'm playing along with you. But do you have to keep interrupting the good parts?"

Coitus interruptus.

Beg Pardon?

Coitus interruptus. It's an interrupted world we live in. I'm only playing along, making it easier for you.

Yeah, but you're skipping all the good parts.

Ah, what's a verb now and then?

126   They ate for two and a half hours, smoked a joint in twenty minutes, and made love in an hour and a half.

The meal was highly ritualized; one piece of meat cooked at a time, then dipped in one of the sauces or, if you were bold, in perhaps a combination of sauces. Salad and bread were eaten while the meat was being cooked. The meal contained all the elements of life. One had to fight the impulse to cook two pieces of meat at once, to use a slice of bread to mop up the sauces, to remain dignified in the most fundamental of conditions. The longer it went on, naturally, the more difficult it was to restrain oneself, the more difficult to reconcile the reality (New York apartment, wine on the table) with the image (an H. Bosch glutton under a tree with sticky fingers and a stomach over which one could not see, let alone bend), the more difficult to know which one was the reality and which one was the image.

The grass was quiet, New York grass given to Lane by a friend instead of flowers. Presumably, a considered gesture of sophistication. They smoked it quietly, listening to a record of love, Lane and Golem on the couch (once again he was pinned, no, strapped, to the couch) holding together rather than each other. It made them pleasant though Golem had been hesitant to smoke it, fearing that the existential nature of the drug, the feeling of ultimateness which it delivered in so beautifully casual a manner (the way a matador lifts his hat to a woman of much grace in the stands) might magnify his other feelings, expanding the molecules of his despair under an acetylene heat until they simply blew the cover off that hollow iceberg inside his head. It was not, however, very visual grass and so Golem was able, if only for a few hours, to soften the edges of the cartoon of Anna and Cohen which flashed through his corrugated mind like an endless and, therefore, redundant loop of film.

They went into the bedroom to make love, but it was not love that they made. It was a kind of archetypal revenge; one might say that, though all the words were in the right places, the inflection was all wrong.

They explored the insides of each other's mouths tentatively at first as if their tongues were like two wrestlers moving around the ring, gauging their strengths and weaknesses as if the match were not merely a brutalized form of entertainment, as if the end had not been predetermined by the closing of a Locker

Room Door. They explored as if the long walk from the Locker Room to the Ring really mattered. Then they realized, with some degree of shame perhaps, that the fight had been fixed all along.

And when they realized this—who knows whether that moment came as Golem ran his hand down from the back of Lane's neck, beginning gently and ending roughly at or, rather, within the division between her buttocks or if it was during some other movement which required a sustained presence—they did not stop, but pushed further, as if believing that one could exorcise an undesirable emotion by forbidding its frustration—the paradox hiding within the alliteration—and soon Golem was sucking the evil juices of all women from the womb of this one and Lane was using her teeth instead of her tongue, trying to fly in the face of all that we know about ambivalence.

Golem felt his breath become sacred to him as he moved his lips across Lane's slim thigh, resting for a moment. Each inhale, each exhale, was wholly, indeed, holy significant. It was not simply the excitement of sex, not the flush of an energized physical system, but the heavy atmosphere of deep passion clogging his lungs and filling his body as if all the morning mists had been stuffed into his shell like a goose on the way to pâté. He ran his lips across her thigh, feeling the soft hair there, and bathed himself in each of the tiny craters of sensitivity that Lane's teeth made on the surface of his sex. Then he pushed himself up against her tighter still for, if she would have some, she would have all. He reached for the back of her throat and sucked at her thigh, then turned his head again to nourish both his hate and his love at the seat of her juices. They pulled at the life from each other.

After a few moments he moved his body around, withdrawing from her mouth, and dropped it slowly over the surface of her own meat, leaving one arm with flexed muscles between her legs, hand in the Great Divide, and replaced his penis with his tongue. She pulled at it, sucking it away from its roots in his mind and then he withdrew it again, opening his mouth wide so that she might fuck him with her own tongue.

They clung to each other, trying to make their bodies fit together like the two halves of the mold for humanity and, finally, softly at first, almost like knocking at her gates with a gloved hand, but then fiercely, like the locked-out husband that he was, he drove himself into her body, wishing that his sex were a prick, a prong, a sword, an avenger, anything but simple muscle. She gasped, whimpered perhaps OGod, and then sighed as he gripped her shoulders and pulled her down toward him until her legs were bent and he could feel her knees at his ribs. She contracted her insides and he expanded his. All those little animals sounds that we think of as passion's anthropomorphic representatives were there.

Take that, you cunt, he shouted to himself as he began to feel a telephone ring at the base of his prick. Take this fuck to be your. . . . Take this sperm, all that I have to give you that I cannot explain or take away. Kill it, if you must, but don't prevent its entrance, don't deny it its brief moment of grace. Let it live and die, but let it come into its own world.

And she began to Come, capital C, capital O, capital FUCK GOOD TIME FEELING NOW, clawing at his back with fake fingernails that snapped, crackled, popped as she did.

"Ohohoh, fuck me, David. Fuck me, baby."

"I'm fucking you, fucking you."

Words!

He moved his hand under her ass and pulled it apart, lifting her off the bed as she began to shriek as though she had seen the ghost of her own possibilities. He could not help himself, he heard the gutteral sounds coming from his own throat and their brutalness took him by surprise. He was not prepared to be out of control. And there it was, his number was ringing, the line was open, and the Operator was impatient with her Person to Person, Station to Station, Call. Leave a Message. He's in Now. This is Him. This is He. This is She. Come, you motherfucker, Come! Don't think you can elude me; I won't tolerate it. I WILL FUCK HER.

She came, shrieked, cried, creamed all over the place until her limbs moved up and down in a fever of epileptic passion. She came slightly before he did and then he tensed, held his breath to prolong the immediate moment of Lifedeath, to deepen it, pressed himself hard against her tough cunt and spurted his Memory, his History, into her body. They were engulfed by a giant white ball

165

—round and yet amorphous—of white energy, black light, existential stroboscopic humanity. They had fucked, Mother!

And he did not move again, nor did she, until he had melted inside of her.

127   Satisfied now?

Pant. Pant. Pant.

What was that?

Well, at least they made it.

Remember that. Memory is the sperm of History.

Aha! You've already said that.

I know what I've said and what I haven't said. Can you say the same?

Ah, what's the big deal anyway? They all look alike in the dark. One hole's as good as another. Put a flag over her head and fuck for old glory.

If that's your belief sir, then that is your reality. Are you prepared to stick with that kind of tattoo?

What do you mean?

Only that you're a faggot. Of sorts.

You've said that before.

Read on.

128   The smells of his mother's house. No one was home when he called in the late morning and he reckoned that she had gone to spend the day shopping or, perhaps, reaching for an early suntan with an aluminum reflector on the boardwalk at Coney Island, seated in a plastic chaise longue in the long row of old people who spend their days in pursuit of the magical powers—who knows whether restorative or simply fresh air and sunshine never hurt anybody and besides what else have I got to do, watch television? ("Ask not for whom the television tolls."—N. M.)—of the sun, two hours on the boardwalk, then Nathan's for lunch, then back to the boardwalk—maybe a little fishing if you were a man, a little knitting if you were a woman and, when the parlors were open, a little keno in the late afternoon. Retirement. Withdrawal. Wait in the Sun for Death. It was either the boardwalk or Useless City where people who used to be put in Old Age Homes by their im-

patient children were now labeled Senior Citizens and shipped out to die on the plains of Arizona—and everyone knew that no Jewish people ever retired to one of those geriatric concentration camps.

The smells of his mother's house. Would live with him forever. He caught a cab near Lane's—she had gone to work and left him a note asking him to pick up a few things for dinner signed (love) Lane—and then took the subway to Brooklyn, amusing himself by studying the faces involved in the measurement and appreciation of the daily catastrophes as reported in the *Daily News* and bemoaned the passing of the lacquered wicker seat and its replacement by one of molded plastic—molded to what? To some Ultimate Shape, form of perfect human body? What did the architects of the subway, the industrial designers of the transit—read movement—authority know about the evolutionary process that had not yet been revealed to the layman? Certainly the seat was not molded to fit Golem's body nor, as far as he could see in the car, did it assume the shape of any other passenger. Were the seats made for travelers of the future? Or were they just seats, made in a design and a dimension which would most conveniently correspond to the requirements of the most economical plastic machine? Who knew that, the CIA? The Mafia? Ultimates overtake us before we can define them and our search becomes our goal which, in itself, is not unadmirable though certainly neurotic —problem is, nobody's willing to say what we're looking for except the easy way, the comfortable way, the American way, the Way. So much time spent in looking for the Way tends to place the emphasis on efficiency, economy, et cetera. Maybe it's on the Moon. Maybe it's under the Ocean. Let's get there before anyone else plants their tent peg in the middle of the big boulder we call the Way. Meantime, we got nothin' but molded plastic seats on the subway and a lot of people who look like wax fruit and so are afraid to go out in the sunshine lest they melt. And now you know the reason for Smog, which is packaged in huge plastic containers by a team of former Nazi scientists now ensconced in an underground hideout somewhere in Utah and sold by the CIA to the Mafia for distribution to our Major Urban Areas. And you think you got a conspiracy theory?

The smells of his mother's house. Were completely real.

All made from real, organic—as much as possible in these days of AstroTurf and assorted other Second Comings—substances which had their own smells, not hypodermically injected, like food coloring, to make them more attractive to your Average American Consumer (AAC). We make so little use of our noses, though we worry about them a great deal. Perhaps it's because we, unique among animals, stand up straight and so do not need, nor even want, to sniff our way, like newts, home. Nor do we have to search for food or sniff out danger. We use them to breathe but, should we get a cold, we can always use our mouths. The nose, the sense of smell. It seems to be a natural point at which to begin the process of dehumanization. What we don't use, we eventually lose —an aphoristic summation of the lack of an organic regenerative facility in man. Are the legs next to go? To be replaced by an utter dependence upon that invention which started it all, the wheel? And you're concerned about robots?

Smells of chicken fat and chopped liver, linoleum and real leather, dish towels that were not disposable but required their own cleansing process—some say that our Gross National Garbage is greater than the Gross National Product of many other countries and if you'll listen, I won't do that joke about the Moon being made of garbage; not unless you force it. Smells of tribal cooking, not fondue fashion, but the real stuff, meat, potatoes, carrots, all cooked in one pot not as stew but as supper. Smells of life, not of disinfectant, smells of living, not of pretending. No air conditioning; only a fan to move the air around a little bit—man *in,* not against, nature. Odors. Old-fashioned odors, not even aromas. Insist on being fancifully poetic, or disguising the sound of defecation by flushing the toilet, insist on that and one must say that, as Golem opened the door to his mother's house with a key he had not used nor thought he would have to use since the days when he temporarily dropped malteds in favor of malts, he was greeted by a sonata of odors.

It was not a large apartment, but it had that kind of depth and comfort that one associates with a large chair upholstered in genuine though shabby velvet. They had lived there for as long as Golem could remember, for the building was not one of those new Lefrakian complexes that social scientists liked to excuse by referring to them as "living machines," but was an old, solid, plain brick apartment house which, if it had been in another section of the city, might have been called a tenement. One could look out the window in the bathroom and see a Kosher Butcher next door to a Supermarket Under Construction and one could wonder what was going on in the mind of the Kosher Butcher because one knew very well what was going on (PROFIT, progress) in the mind of the Supermarket which is to say only that some people, no matter how many sidewalk museums and culture restaurants they are willing to finance, underwrite, overkill, will never be forgiven. From the livingroom, if you parted the heavy draperies which ran across the entire wall as if to suggest that if there was not then there should have been a picture window in the place, you could see through the smallish window the courtyard and playground and babysitting area and Refuse Removal Area (as it might now be called, though Golem knew it better as the place where the garbage cans were kept on wooden platforms).

On the stove in the kitchen were two large pots, both on burners turned to WARM. Golem lifted their covers and, taking a spoon from the red rubber drawer-organizer (?), tasted the chicken soup in one and the simmering pot roast in the other. If his mother was a cliché, it was all right with him. He dropped the spoon into the sink, not playing detective, not caring whether or not his mother would notice that it was out of place, knowing, in fact, that she would, and turned to face the diningroom, which was little more than four walls surrounding a table, a good wooden table on which was spread a shawl that his grandmother had brought with her when she left Russia. He turned and, for a moment, like a stroboscopic series of film cuts, it, the past, came back to him. FLASH. He and his parents around the table. FLASH. His parents arguing about . . . what? No matter. We're discussing, not arguing, they always said. FLASH. A birthday party, his birthday party which ended with his being spanked by his father because he could not control himself long enough to reach the bathroom, slightly staining his new brown Buster Brown suit. It's the principle, his father said. FLASH. The Principle. In big, block letters. FLASH. His father bringing him home with his horn. Horn. FLASH. Remember the sound of that horn? He

could never hear another one without remembering the look of disbelief on his father's face. FLASH. Father's face. FLASH. His father hitting him with a sloppy right cross to the jaw, not hard, but hard enough to knock him down. Why? Because the look he made when he found that he couldn't go roller skating reminded his father of the look in that Buyer's Eye? What's the difference? FLASH. Falling down. His father apologizing. Golem saying, what, you bastard? Something like that and having it accepted as an exchange between men. If you take the liberty to hit, I take the liberty to curse. He should have used a better expression. Opportunity's gone. FLASH. Father's where? Table filled with food. Relatives. Relations. Friends. Mother in Black and Sorrow. His uncle, the Eye Ear Nose & Throat Man. Good Man, perhaps. Father's where? Dead? Had Golem killed him, finally? Had he wished so hard that God had, for once, listened? Possible? Or do we all bear the guilt of our fathers' deaths? What's the difference? There's no safety in numbers. The end is in the thought at the beginning. FLASH. Bar Mitzvah. FLASH. The furniture of my life, the couches on which I rested my principles, the chairs on which I sat with my ideologies, the tables at which I ingested my experiences. The furniture of my life. FLASH.   FLASH.
  Gone now.
  Or, rather, exchanged, traded in for a totalitarian bedroom suite which turned out to be a Factory Irregular or, even worse, a Factory Regular—nothing that a new coat of paint can't fix up in a minute, sonny. A marriage bought at Discount City is not a marriage, but a walnut-veneer, chromium-plated piece of plywood. And plywood, being a combination of the cheapest in all of us, has little soul of its own; it is a contradiction in substances and, for that reason probably, is the only building material capable of giving plastic a run for its money on the mile-long track of middle-class desires and working-class ambitions. But don't bet on it, not to Win, at any rate. Golem had, marching up to the two-dollar window, money in hand and a look on his face that bespoke the whispered-in-the-ear recommendations of a checkered tout who could spot a mark a furlong or two away, plunking down the bread before the Betting Window through which he had hoped to see the

rest of his life but which he found to be opaqued and stippled like the glass door to a shower, laying his capital on the line to Win on the horse named Love out of Male and Female, wearing the colors of—the mauve and beige silks of the famous No Choice Stables, located in the pleasant surroundings of rolling-with-the-punches Arcadia. And the animal had come out of the starting gate as if the trumpet were the race itself, finishing a poor second and Second is the worst failure of all. Good enough to contend, but not good enough to succeed. Holy Entropic Frustration!

Gone now.

Put the bedroom set in storage with the rest of the old furniture or donate it to the Good Will store, hoping that it will not contaminate another life but knowing that bad conscience, unlike bedbugs, can't be chased out of a mattress. Burn the whole thing. The funeral pyre of his marriage. Not bad, he said to himself, I'll remember that one.

The Splendor of the Perplexed was the title of his thesis.

A knock on the door.

What?

A knock on the door. Life's like that.

Golem is shaken by the sound. It demands his attention even more than a telephone ring. It is not possible to avoid a knock on the door unless you hide in the bathroom and hold your breath, hoping that you won't sneeze, breathing through straws in the marsh as the posse gathers on the bank in search of the escaped Moses. A knock on the door is a knock on the door. Go and answer it.

He did.

"Who is it?"

"Who is there?"

"I'm inside. Who is knocking?"

"Are you a strange man?"

"No, no. This is David Golem on the inside."

"David! This is Mrs. Gold."

"Oh, hello, Mrs. Gold."

"Hello to you, too."

"OK."

"David?"

"What?"

"Are you all right?"

"Sure. Why?"

"Are you locked in or something?"

"No."

"Then can you open the door for me?"

"Oh. Sure."

Answering the knock and opening the door were not necessarily the same and he had not considered the possibility of facing another person on such tenuous grounds. However, like the horse of a different color, he had little choice. So he opened the door to reveal Mrs. Gold, a gnomish woman in her sixties, a board-walk-sitter whose feet were stuck like tree stumps into black velvet covered shoes of uncertain style. A flowered housedress covered her drying body, a body that looked as though it had been bathed in astringent and then, quite suddenly, heated until everything that had been pulled together had fallen apart all over again. The omni-present and obligatory gray cardigan was over her shoulders and a paper cup was in her hand.

"I came to borrow a cup of matzoh meal. What are you doing home from school?"

"Uh . . . just a quick vacation."

"A vacation? School isn't a vacation?"

"Well, actually, I was doing some research, too."

"Your library isn't big enough?"

"Not quite. Come in."

She stepped in and accused him.

"Where's your mother?"

"I don't know. I mean, I just got in and she wasn't here. Maybe on the boardwalk?"

"Not today. Didn't you look outside and see that it wasn't sunny? It's going to snow."

He hadn't noticed, he had to admit. The weather wasn't exactly uppermost in his mind, though the same can't be said for the climate, of the Times, of course.

"Did you say you wanted some matzoh meal?"

"Want, need, what's the difference? You know where it is?"

"Uh, not exactly."

"I'll get it."

Mrs. Gold shuffled past Golem and on into the kitchen; he followed behind her, a stranger in his own house. She opened a cupboard and looked up at it defiantly and then at him. Pausing.

"I'll get it for you."

He towered over her, being nearly two times her height, and extracted the box of matzoh meal from its position between the dark and the light brown powdered sugar. He swung it down and started to fill her extended cup.

"So how's your family?"

The matzoh meal hung in the air between the box and the cup. Many a slip. He had now been indicted as well as accused. Undoubtedly he would shortly be judged and unquestionably convicted. What would the sentence be?

"Uh, fine."

"So why didn't you bring your wife with you to research?"

"She's working, you know. She's working."

"A wife who works, a husband who vacations. To be a scholar is not a bad business."

"Well, it has its own rewards, you know."

"That's enough!"

"What?"

"That's enough. You're overflowing the cup."

And. Sure enough. He was. A little pile of matzoh meal was beginning to take shape on the floor. Building a mountain out of matzoh meal.

III

129   "You look so lonely, David."

"Hmmm?"

"I said you look so lonely."

"Oh. Yeah. Well, listen, Valerie, I'm just kind of down. Don't let me spoil the evening for you. OK?"

"OK. I'll cheer you up."

"Thanks."

She giggled.

A lot. Giggled, that is. Lane had a dinner conference with an out-of-town client and she had suggested that he go out with Valerie for the evening.

"I'll just watch TV or read a book."

"You'll die of boredom. Go out. I'll call up Valerie and you two can have some fun. She giggles a lot, but she's a nice girl."

"I don't want to. Really."

"Do it."

"You sound like my mother."

"Well, I suppose I feel responsible for you."

"I can take care of myself."

"I'll fix it up and call you back in an hour."

They were sitting in an Italian restaurant disguised as an Italian grocery store in what was now called the West Village. It was a place to which Golem often went when he was in New York because, although it was not particularly chic, it was dependable and one could never be certain that a patron from the neighborhood would not pick up a mandolin and begin to serenade either the woman at his own table or any other woman. And the songs were not for sale. Golem was eating prosciutto and melon, wrapping the thinly sliced ham neatly around each piece of fruit, and Valerie sucked the insides from a dish of baked clams. Golem began to get the feeling that Valerie was a girl of a thousand noises, but no single, enduring tones.

Thursday night was Valerie's Guru Night. On Monday, she went to the Movies, Tuesday to the Theater, Wednesday to play Bridge with a group of girls from her office (she worked as a secretary in a talent agency—Girls! Romance, Career Importance! Meet Glamorous Personalities! Contacts Galore with Exciting World of Show Business!! $75.00 per week . . . typing and dictation skills required—that specialized in representing Emerging Celebrities), Thursday to her Swami on the Lower East Side (read East Village), Friday to the currrently fashionable discothèque . . . whether she had a date or not. . . . Saturday she swung and on Sunday she suffered by staying home. This she had told to Golem after her first glass of wine and he immediately knew that she was going to spice up her conversation with a lot of words like alienation, existential, and, the Big Daddy of them all, COMMUNICATION. All the things which he had so recently and so painfully cleaned off the glass shelves of his own Medicine Chest.

She had agreed to babysit with Golem on the condition that he accompany her on her pilgrimage to Seventh Street where her consultations with Swami Bhodvahdblahdista were held. And he, not believing that anyone in the modern world would either have the courage or the lunacy to call himself by a name like that, had accepted the challenge. Valerie had further intrigued him by casually dropping the statement that, not only was Bhodvahdblahdista a genuine guru, but he was also the "semi-official spiritual adviser to the Emerging Celebrities at our agency." A mystic with social standing.

"Should I tell you a joke?"

"A joke?"

"Yes, to cheer you up."

"Oh, no. You don't have to do anything so blatant as that. I'll be OK; I'm just feeling sorry for myself."

"Maybe the Swami can help you."

"Maybe. But I don't think I can afford it."

"Don't be silly," she said, smacking her lips after pulling a clam from its shell and swallowing it whole, "he wouldn't charge you anything for a consultation like that. Besides, you're with me and I'm a regular."

"It's not the money I'm worried about."

"Huh?"

"Nothing." He was being too hard on her. She was just a girl who giggled. So he refilled her glass with wine and leaned toward her. "Listen, Valerie, I'm sorry. I promise to be a good boy."

She giggled again.

130 "Do I detect a note of sadness in your escort's face?"

"Huh?"

"Yes. Oh, I hope that the Wise One can show him the Way out of the Forest of Shadows."

What the hell was that?

What it was, you see, was a shaven-headed young man of something like twenty-two who was wrapped in a robe of saffron-colored acetate and who stood at the painted door to Bhodvahdblahdista's GHQ.

Golem was worried that he was being too obvious. And the second thing, that flowery sentence which followed the "huh" of Golem's contraction, was the transformation which Valerie had achieved as they reached the door. Between the time that they had left the world of Italian Restaurants and had entered the cosmos of the New Consciousness, Valerie had metamorphosed from a giggling secretary into an apprentice saint, complete with a little body of mystically metaphorical goodies like Forest of Shadows and, what was surely to come, Sea of Loneliness.

"If he can be helped on his journey, the Master will help him, for his face shows the lines of an honest but poor traveler."

How's that for a snap judgment?

Sound the gong. The door is swung open from there and the two novices enter the old store, probably once a delicatessen, which now houses the guru and his retinue. The anteroom is carpeted in Oriental, the furniture is low and ornately carved, and, from a brass bowl on a table, Golem picks up a business card which reads

SWAMI BHODVAHDBLAHDISTA
"the storefront swami"
Proud to Be in America to Make You Happy
109 E. Seventh Street   New York City

and, when he turns it over, he finds

THE SPIRITUAL MESSAGE
"Don't Worry, be happy."
"I am the Divine Beloved
Who loves you more than you
can ever love yourself."
"I and God are One and so
are You."

and expected to find, was disappointed *not* to find, the lines, "Hi Ho, Hey Hey, Chew Your Little Troubles Away." But then, Valerie had told him that the Swami was strongly and unshakably opposed to the use of drugs or, indeed, to any kind of "artificial" method of approaching Nervenda, though he did approve of fasting. Waste not, Want not as Ben Franklin might have said, the old head (who else *but* a head could have discovered electricity?).

The room was thick with the odor of smoking incense, a substance which Golem disliked on principle as he held it responsible for the development of air conditioning and other allied aerosol innovations of corporationalism, plasticism, and the general fear/distrust of reality syndrome which had manifested itself in the current, well-known Beige Plague.

177

Black Power.

White Supremacy.

Green Power.

Beige Plague.

Golem longed for a fan, an unembellished paper fan with which he might destroy the fume-clusters of fear-gas rising, emanating, from the hulk of society which packs a pair of pearl-handled, hair-triggered Portable Environments. High Noon time; paper covers rock. Dig the shootout.

Also, he did not like the smell and there's nothing un-American about that. Shit, no!

Good Golly, exclaimed the Golem. Here I am in the midst of all this heavy transcendental ecumenicism and I left my Love Beads behind, stuffed into that bureau drawer along with my Capt. Midnight Secret Cataclysmic Universal Cosmic Organismic Apocalyptic Lever Ring (and Archimedes thought he was a heavy thinker!), my imitation Genuine Made In Japan/Hong Kong Mandrake the Magician's Mysterious Magical Wand, and the forty-two hundred tops torn from the boxes of the Breakfast of Champions/Luncheon of Failures that I have eaten in my dreams! Caught like a eunuch in a room full of pederasts!!!   !

He put the card into his jacket pocket, stretched out his long arm, and gently, but definitely, no mistake about it, pinched Valerie on the ass. She jumped.

"Oh!"

And turned around.

"Did You Do That?"

Golem looked at his hand which he had not brought back into place and he smiled and nodded. Valeries stared at him, trying to forget that she was a secretary, trying to find it "in her heart" to forgive him for this apparent travesty.

"Why?"

That was about as fer as she could go.

"Just wanted to blur the line between the Sacred and the Profane. Sorry, it was an impulse."

She would accept that as profound foolishness. And she did.

"You have to learn how to control yourself. That's what you're lacking, you know . . . self-control."

"I guess you're right," he said. "It has always been a problem of mine."

131   The Swami, looking like an Eastern version of the Wizard of Oz, sat on a group of silken pillows and animal skins which covered a raised platform that Golem guessed had been constructed of plywood. He wore robes of saffron and magenta and his head was shaved and polished so that it shone in the faggy-mysterioso lighting of the Meditation Room. In front of him, on the carpeted floor, legs crossed in various approximations of floral positions, were the supplicants. In the back of the room stood the disciples of his Order, arms crossed like a group of religious sergeants-at-arms. The air in the room was so heavy with the odor of perfume manufactured by starving natives in a state-owned incense factory that Golem had to loosen his tie and open the top button on his shirt. Forget Mace, he thought, incense is what the Police Force really needs.

Valerie led him to a place next to a couple who wore identical American Indian costumes (Twinsies!) and they both sat down on the floor, completing what Golem assumed would be called the, ahem, Holy Circle. Golem thought he saw the Swami smile a bit and incline his head toward Valerie. Maybe he was fucking her on the side. Bhodvahdetcetera, you old reprobate! Self-control, self-control.

No one spoke. Everyone seemed to be waiting for some kind of sign or maybe it was just twenty minutes after the hour and everybody was listening to the beating of angelic wings as the little devils overflew the GHQ, but Golem had not worn his watch and he could not bring himself to be so vulgar as to lean over to the Brave on his right and do a say, fella, you got the Time bit. Why sure, the fella would say, bringing up his wrist to show off the new beaded flexible watchband with the Plains Indian (as opposed to Woods Indian) motif which he had made for himself in a resurgence of cottage-craft spirit—why sure, it's Time. Big hand point to Sun, little hand point to Babbling Brook. Deer run through Forest of Loneliness. Fish swim deep in Sea of Shadows. Ugh. Huuuummmp.

Screw that sign language. What's the numbers, baby?

Somebody at the extreme right end of the circle coughed

and all the other components looked at him. He hung his head in shame. Golem looked at him, inspecting his character. He was a small man who would have liked to have been thought of as wiry, and he wore a blue business suit. His hair was short and his face slightly red. Jewish, Golem guessed, and probably from the Bronx. A continual failure, lived with his mother, is a closet-accountant, and coughs during Meditation Hour.

"Man was never meant to fly, but he who does finds strange things in the air."

What?

Golem snapped his head around to look at the Swami, for certainly it had been he who had spoken. The voice was deep in tone, but whisper-like in texture. A slight lisp? The Big Cat was about to lay down the lick, sock it to 'em, tell it like it is/was/ evermore will 'be, put on his parable dress and dance the answer jitterbug, honey. Do me. I'm ready for the Way. Lay on me how Man is such a groovy cat. Tell me why I'm Happy.

"Is there any among you who questions the sanctity of Happiness?"

You got to be out of you head to raise you hand in this room. Golem looked around him. Nobody had moved.

"My children, we come together to Meditate on the Joy of Being, on the Holiness of Cosmic Generality, on the Sanctity of the True Belief in the Blessedness of Our Way."

Just like all corrupt politicians, this cat talked in capitals and his clauses came in threes. Three of a kind, says the dealer. You're bluffing, says the player. But the dealer is Dealing.

"Isn't he marvelous?"

"What?"

Golem turned his head and found Valerie whispering into his ear.

"Isn't he marvelous?"

"Well, his material is a little dated, but his delivery isn't too bad. I doubt if he'll ever make the Sullivan show."

Valerie looked at him in a manner . . . well, in a manner that must have resembled the looks on the faces of those guys who drove the spikes into Christ's hands. And Golem knew that if he was going to take this girl to bed tonight, the only move that would save the evening, he was either going to have to apologize for *his* Being, or he was going to have to go all the way and knock her off her feet with the aesthetic spectacle of his egomania. Being, there's that awful word again, a man of essentially good conscience, he chose the latter course of action. And raised his hand.

The Swami was a little surprised, but he wasn't a Swami for nothing and so he acknowledged the possibility of Golem. "Yes, my son."

Golem did not rise . . . to the occasion, yes, but to his feet, no.

"I am only a humble guest in your palace of wisdom, O Swami, but I would like to know—in twenty-five words or less —the nut of your Spiritual Message."

The room gasped, the disciples took one step forward, but the Swami held up his hand and smiled. Cool. He figured that Golem had gotten off his best shot.

"Your language is somewhat Foreign to my Ears, but then, I am Foreign to your Shores. (Get that!) The Spiritual Message which I carry to Those Who Would Find the Way to Eternal JOY is uncomplicated and Truthfully Holy. And it may be brief. It is only that we must Be Happy. Love."

"Kind of smile and the world smiles with you?"

"What?"

"That's just a line from an old song, your grace."

"I do not understand."

Wee-u! The Swami, like a man with a heavy approach-avoidance conflict playing Russian Roulette, was in Trouble.

"Well, what it breaks down to, I suppose, is that I figure that you, and this is no metaphorical circumlocution, believe me, well, you're just full of shit, man."

WhizBANG!

That did it.

The Meditation Freaks were on their feet, the Disciples moved from the back of the room like Storm Troopers in Drag, Valeries screamed and the incense was cut off by the cry of Get Him. Only Golem and the Swami remained seated.

"And what's more, Swami, you are a fucking fascist of joy."

The Swami stood up, hands in front of him, giving

181

Golem one last chance to See the Light. Loudly, at the top of his now creaking, definitely lisping voice, he shouted, "Who says so?"

"I do. Me. One."

And then everybody was human again, picking Golem up off the Oriental rug which had just been the object of their inner fantasies, slapping him with what were joyful hands, calling him Pig, Intellectual, Westerner, Egoist, and throwing him—together with Valerie, for she was considered responsible for his intrusion—out of GHQ and onto the cold stone sidewalk of Seventh Street—out the door as if they were being thrown out of a swinging-door saloon in a cheap Italian Western.

Golem laughed and Valerie cried.

"I'm sorry, Valerie, for getting you thrown out like this."

OOOOOhh———! Do you realize that I can never come back here again? How can I show my face in the office? Everybody in town will know. I'll be ruined. Ruined."

"Oh, I don't know."

"Is that so? You think you're pretty smart, don't you?"

"Look, this guy isn't going to last long. He's not good enough. You ought to consider yourself lucky to have gotten out before you had to confess to yourself that you were being silly.'

"Silly!"

"Yes, just silly. Come on, I'll take you home."

And then he picked her up, threw her over his shoulder and, with her legs and arms flailing wildly, they walked down Seventh Street until he hailed a taxi.

Not literally, of course.

132   Her apartment was small and Golem didn't want to spend much time there. It was decorated in Pop/Oriental fashion and while he allowed her to choose the records, he would not allow her to burn incense. Why not, she had asked. Beige Plague, he had muttered and then said, a little more audibly, that it bothered his already troubled sinuses.

"Would you like a drink?"

"Sure."

In a moment, he was handed a small glass of nearly clear liquid which he tasted cautiously. "Pernod?"

Valerie nodded and sat down next to him on the couch, which was a mattress on the floor covered by a bolt of cloth printed in such a design as to announce its pretensions to tapestry-dom. The girl was full of affectations, a personification of the spirit of New Syncretism.

Who to speak, what to play? The man is responsible, thought Golem, and so he made the opening move. By putting an arm around the girl who, though, or probably *because,* she was eclectic, was not inexperienced, responded by leaning as deeply into his body as their positions allowed. No more words were necessary. Golem kissed her once and then she was off, running her hands along his face, through his hair, over his thighs—while he concentrated his attack upon her mouth and his thoughts on not spilling the Pernod which, by now, had turned milky.

133   Slow zoom into glass of milky liquid to indicate (1) elapsed time, (2) a formal transition, (3) symbolic evocation of mood in pictographic terms, and (4) preparation for change of geographic locale.

134   In the bedroom, under a tacked-to-the-wall canopy of more quasi-tapestries and against a nest of plastic pillows with large numbers painted on their slippery surfaces, Golem undresses Valerie with one hand while maintaining his balance on the bed with the other. When she is nude, he sees nothing out of the ordinary, kisses her body perfunctorily and, with a single hand gesture, indicates that she should undress him. She does.

Golem begins to make love to her or, rather, to massage the appropriate nerve endings, zones of excitation, etc. It is a passionless process for him, but one that he knows well from simple experience. It is a lie, he thinks, that all men want to sleep with all women. Desire is not the issue, Duty is. Women make us feel as though we are not Men unless we act like animals. Curious. Then they fault us for being the object of their needs. Curious.

But he senses a tenseness in her body, though she holds him, moves against him, uses her fingernails like a rake through the short hairs of his body, he feels that there is a knot of something unspoken inside her. Some unexpressed negative or positive that would eventually impede if not, indeed, preclude her climax and Golem, being nothing if not generous, throws his good hand into the Love Machine and asks her, "What's the trouble, baby?"

She seems surprised and answers with a "huh" and so he repeats himself.

"Oh, nothing."

"I can feel that something is bothering you."

"You can?"

"Yes."

"Gee, you're terribly sensitive."

He blushes, but plunges in again, his heart waving like a banner of good intent on the end of his prick.

"Well, it's really nothing."

"What is it? Haven't you ever made it before?"

"Oh, sure. But sometimes it's hard."

"It's hard for everybody most of the time."

"I know that."

"So?"

"The thing is . . . I'm kind of embarrassed to say it."

To how many others has she been embarrassed to say it?

"Hey, go ahead. We can't be much more open than we are now."

"Ummm. See, I like to Do It in a certain way."

FLASH. Golem was off on a tour of fifty-seven varieties, positions, inflections, motivations—all means to ejaculation. What's your perversion, baby? And wouldn't that make a great television show? We'll get a panel of established, recognized perverts, Charley. And then we'll have a bunch of housewives and mailmen and decent people come on the show—maybe even a Guest Big Star once in a while. The panel'll try to guess the guest's secret perversion. I don't know if it'll go in the European Market, Frankie. Are you kidding, Charley? The Japanese'll eat it up.

"How do you like to Do It?"

"Have you ever read the Kama Sutra? Don't laugh at me."

Golem reneges on the sound, but the smile has already been played and he can't take it back without raising the ante past an affordable point. The Kama Sutra, the sex manual of the

184

sophisticated sixties. Do It like they used to Do It. And you tell me that there's no tradition any more? I tell you that there's too much. Which is the same, the very same thing.

"Uh, no. I haven't read that yet, but I'm planning to as I understand that it received favorable notices in the *Times*. Also, *Time* liked it. *Life*, too. It's on my Summer Reading List."

"Don't be silly."

"I'm sorry. I realize that this is serious stuff."

"Are you being ironic with me?"

Hooha! Are you being ironic with me? How do you answer that without being ironic.

"Me, ironic? Certainly not."

"I'll trust you. Anyway, there's, uh, a position in there that really turns me on."

"Oh, yeah?"

"It's called yabyum."

"Can't we just fuck?"

"Don't be vulgar. If you don't want to Do It that way, it's all right with me."

"No, no. We'll Do It That Way. Show me."

"I will when we get to It. I just wanted to know if it would be OK with you."

"It's fine with me. Really fine. I'm always anxious to try a new experience."

And now, not only does he have to be Responsible for everything else, but he also has to consider a sweeping and artificial change of style at the moment when he should be thinking of nothing besides that which he feels. You can't even fuck any more. Yabyum. It sounds like an Oriental baby food.

"David," Valerie giggled, "I think I love you."

Thanks.

135   Sitting in Toffenetti's with a club sandwich in front of him and too much behind him, Golem is trying to decide what to do with the remainder of his day. He has little money and does not look forward to the ultimate boredom of poverty, but he has enough for one excursion of complete irresponsibility. Where shall he spend it, that's the question.

"Is everything all right?"

"What?"

Golem looks up to see a woman in a uniform looking down at him.

"Is everything all right? Would you like some dessert?"

"Oh."

It's the waitress, blondined and frilled, with a MISS HODGE nameplate above, very far above, her breast.

"Everything's fine. Are you Miss Hodge?"

"Yes."

"I'm Golem."

MISS HODGE, not knowing whether he is some out-of-town nut, a kid trying to get smart, or a CIA man fulfilling her wildest dreams by recruiting her to spy on the commie kitchen help, does not know what to say.

"I have a message for you, Miss Hodge."

"A message?"

"Yes. A message."

"What is it?"

"Will we be overheard?"

MISS HODGE leans into him across the table. Looks around twice and sees nothing but the usual enemy agents.

"Go ahead."

"Go to Queens Plaza, tonight at 8. Use my name. Follow the usual procedure. How's the cheesecake?"

"What?"

"Queens Plaza, my name, cheesecake."

"Is that the password?"

"Shh. Just bring me a piece of cheesecake."

"Yessir."

She leaves in a breeze of cheap organdy and expensive self-doubt, even bewilderment.

Golem laughs.

He has struck again.

136   Follow Golem on a hand-held tour of New York: one day.

First, up to the Frick where one can pretend that one is a noble Roman, reclining in the solarium, bathed in organ music.

Imagining himself playing polo in what was now a room for meeting pretty girls, bumping into people with leather-covered cameras draped over their resigned shoulders. Wandering through the great halls as if he were on a treadmill placed in front of a perspective drawing with a never-ending vanishing point. Moving *toward,* but never *to,* the horizon. Surrounded by Hollywood echoes, the kind that reproduce the entire word rather than only the last syllable.

Out into the street again. Slush at the curbs. Step over it, never through it, the current of its decay running faster than even his own. Browns and grays, few whites. The city does not recognize white, except at night when the snow is allowed to fall with impunity. A blizzard in New York is like a blizzard nowhere else; the snow falls in strange vectors of force, leaning around buildings to get at the street as if around the trunks of banyan trees. Snow does not come to the city without a struggle, for its very presence represents an immediate challenge to Man the Toolmaker, Man the Designer, Man the Builder, who has thrown up his structures of form and function like so many towers of Babel, not to reach the heavens, but to deny them access to the ground. Skyscrapers. So much in so little a name. Buildings that serve as irritants to Nature, pressing up, pricking into the underbelly of the Cosmos as if to say, we build, therefore we exist. But even the city, with its simple and yet conspiratorial ethos of steel, must lose its battle with the organic and be defeated by the slight movement of a snowflake. Romantic? Perhaps.

But look at Central Park, a monument to inevitability, covered with snow and serving as a playground for two children in red parkas who roll themselves into snowmen while their mother, in black, watches them from a nearby hillock. Run that scene in slow motion.

Golem walks through the park, wishing it were spring and knowing that it was, knowing that the ducks had been sent to Miami for the winter, knowing that a city caught in a battle with Nature is a helpless creature that belongs to any who can walk over it without fear of damp socks.

Like some mythic hunter, Golem stalks the city. What I need, he decides, is some sin. A whore? No, that fits the definition too clearly, too impersonally. Cloudy sin, something on the borderline between the reality and the image, something that has potential, a situation which, like a waterfall, is primarily—or, at least, at its source—composed of what we might call sinetic energy. Something that contains a test.

A movie on Forty-second Street, sitting in the balcony as if he were a hustler or leaning insolently and indolently up against the door to the men's room while men who might wear straw boaters and seersucker suits wink their bulging red eyes at him? No, that's false—either get a blow job next to a urinal or don't; no real test, there.

A taxi dance palace? Moving with fleshy women in spangled red dresses who were born thirty years too early/late and never should have continued their image past the Depression, waltzing between ranks of soldiers and sailors on quick leave who, despite their eyes which advise, indeed, remind, that one can and does murder easily, are only eighteen years old? A country that hires eighteen-year-olds to do its killing for it is a country with an unholy respect for the present and a frightening disregard for the future. A country of Spartans, encouraging its young killers to "let off a little steam" by building barracks with resident whores. A man needs a woman, they say. All a man needs is a good vision and a strong right wrist—if that's all he wants. Killfuck. To some, it's the same. For those with neon hearts, one gas is as good as another. No dancing.

Golem reaches into his pocket for his address book and finds the entry that he wants. Smiling now, tensing himself for the possibilities implicit in the situation he has chosen, he walks down to Thirty-ninth Street, turns right, and—in the midst of a block of upper-level factories filled with small men making small ideas large reasons for living—sees the boldly painted sign that he was looking for.

MODEL CITY
BEAUTIFUL GIRLS—NO WAITING

Inside the gray building is another sign, this one of cardboard, on which an arrow points to the direction of MODEL CITY, one flight up, all roads lead to Rome. The stairs are worn. The walls are worn. Whose feet, whose hands, whose breath, whose dreams? Golem goes up the flight and finds an unpainted, plywood door with another MODEL CITY marker on its otherwise faceless surface. Knock? No, just go in.

"Hello."

A small desk surrounded by green partitions. Sandwiched between the glass which covers it and the wood which bears it is a montage of postcard colored photos of big-breasted, wrinkle-assed women posing in high-heeled shoes and wearing no clothing, but all smiling as if their mouths-for-the-day were glued on in the morning and removed, one hoped, in the evening. Behind the desk is a man whose head is shaped like an almond and is so thin that Golem is certain he might often be mistaken for some kind of animated tomahawk.

"Hello."

"Can I help you?"

"Well, I read your ad and I wanted to try that body painting."

That body painting.

"Are you a member of Model City?"

"Well, I'm a citizen, but not a member."

"The kid's a joker, a regular joker. OK. A couple of the girls are out for, uh, lunch so you can have either Grace or Marie unless you want to wait for Lena or Carmen."

"What do they look like?"

The man points out each of the women between the glass and Golem, as hard as he trys, cannot distinguish one from the other. And he does not want to wait.

"They all look pretty good. I'll take Grace."

"Grace!"

The man hollers through the partition.

"Grace! I've got a session for you."

"How much is it?"

"Six bucks for half an hour plus three bucks membership or, ha, citizenship fee."

"Nine altogether."

"Right."

Golem hands the man a ten-dollar bill and receives in exchange four quarters and a card which reads Member in Good

Standing of the MODEL CITY Art Studio Club. Show This Card Whenever You Have the URGE to Create or Capture a Thing of BEAUTY.

"Just fill your name in there. It's a one-time fee. You want to be on our mailing list?"

"I'm just passing through."

The moment he said it, besides feeling like an absurd Western hero, he knew it was true. He would make plans to leave soon.

"Salesman?"

"Nope."

"Mind if I ask what you do? Don't mean to be nosey, but we take a personal interest in our customers."

"I'm a writer."

"Oh yeah? Famous?"

"Not yet."

"Say, maybe you can write about us and that'll make you famous. No kidding."

"OK."

"Just don't use any dirty words."

Both men laughed at the secret they now shared, neither fully realizing its implications. And then Grace walked into the partitioned cubicle. She was short and perhaps stolid, long brown hair trapped in a pony tail of sorts, black high-heeled shoes which made her calves bulge uncomfortably, and no other clothing save that defensive smile. Her skin was very white.

"Grace, you got an artist here. The man's a writer. Maybe you can tell him your life story."

"What does he care?"

All three of them laughed and then Golem followed Grace's beckoning index finger and bouncing ass out of the cubicle, through a large room in the center of which was a raised platform on which was—Golem supposed—Marie, her legs spread out in a denial of her own sexuality while a Negro with steel-rimmed glasses and a natural haircut satisfied his revolutionary urges by sketching her body image on a large pad of cheap paper, and into another small room which contained two folding chairs, a raised platform, a box of water-color paints (blue, green, magenta, and black) and, tacked to the unfinished wooden wall, a photograph of a professionally painted body.

Golem took off his coat and jacket, rolled up his sleeves, and mopped the perspiration with the red bandanna he carried in his back pocket. Grace watched him.

"You can call me Dave, if you want."

Grace smiled a little wider and Golem could see that she had stretch marks on her face as well as around her hips. He moved in front of her and examined his surface. A large vaccination mark, a reddish birth mark near her wiry cunt, thick thighs ending at the knee and coming out again at the calves. Work with the blemishes on the canvas. She turned around for him and he saw that she suffered from that familiar dropped-ass malady that afflicts women who begin to age before their time. The ass is always the first to go. Hers was not at all happy about its new position and Golem saw her tense her muscles in what was meant to pass for a reflexive action. Over her shoulder, she looked at him, inspecting the inspector.

"You really a writer?"

"Yeah."

"What are you doing in a place like this?"

He was stuck for an answer; it was a switch for which he was unprepared. Looking for some sin, baby. Mortification of the flesh and all that jazz. Punishing myself. See, I'm an existential masochist at heart. Get that?

"Uh, just thought I'd try the experience."

Weak. Weak.

"Are you gonna write about me?"

"Do you want me to?"

"I don't care."

"Maybe I better start painting."

"OK."

"What color would you like?"

"I like the red, but you don't have it."

"I'll use the magenta."

"That's almost red."

Golem dipped the "artist's brush" into the bell jar which surrounded the watered magenta, wiped the brush on the jar's edge and, hesitating a moment, trying to decide where to begin, and then deciding that one might as well begin at the difficult point—or one of them—drew a circle, rough around the edges and somewhat feathery in general, around Grace's right nipple.

The right nipple of grace.

She tensed her muscles as the brush encircled her.

"Does that tickle?"

"I don't feel anything."

This one was a ball-cutter; give her an opening and she'd plunge the knife of her cuntiness into the heart of your sensitivity faster than Superman changes costumes.

"Doesn't it ever tickle?"

"After it's on, it feels funny."

He drew a circle around her other nipple.

"Do you like to get, uh, painted?"

"It's a living."

He washed out the brush and then dipped it into the green jar, held it in front of him and prepared to fill in the hollows he had made.

"Uh-uh."

"What?"

"Don't do it in there 'cause it hurts when it dries."

"So, you do have rules. Where else does it hurt, here?" He used the green to paint a line from her navel down through her patch of pubic hairs and she jumped away, letting the paint drip on the tips of the hairs.

"Don't get smart, mister."

"Just wanted to find out what your limits are, that's all."

Golem did a terrible job on her. All whorls and swirls of green into magenta into black heavily outlined areas of little meaning. He drew a cartoon of a woman's body on the canvas of the real thing, the real body, the image on top of the reality. And without feeling so much as the slightest tug at his own pants. The body, it turns out, is nothing without the mind—and vice versa.

137   "Lane, I'm getting tired. I ought to split."

"Where'll you go?"

"I don't know."

"Why don't you look for a job and stay in the city."

"Maybe I will."

"Did you talk to your mother?"

"No."

"Call Anna?"

"Not yet."

"Why don't you?"

"I'm not ready to say anything yet."

IV

138   "Hello."

"What were you doing here when I told you to go home?"

"Just visiting."

"Are you home now?"

"No, Mom."

"Go home."

"I can't."

"Where are you?"

"In New York."

"Still?"

"Yes."

"What are you going to do?"

"I don't know."

"Is it that serious?"

"Yes."

"Did you talk to Anna?"

"Not yet."

"Why not?"

"I don't know what to say."

"You can start with hello."

"Hello."

"Hello?"

"This is Dave."

"Oh."

"Is that all you have to say?"

"What should I say?"

"I'm surprised you're home."

"Where'd you think I'd be?"

"Never mind."

"Where are you?"

"In New York."

"Are you going to stay there?"

"Do you want me to?"

"That's up to you."

"Do you want me to come to California?"

"That's up to you."

"What do you want to do?"

"I don't know."

"Maybe it would be better if we didn't see each other for a little while."

"Maybe. David?"

"What?"

"I'm sorry."

"Yeah."

"I really am sorry."

"What can I say?"

"I don't know."

140 *Item*: A piece of white paper later discovered between the pages of an old issue of *Life* magazine in Lane's bedroom. Headed "A List of Possibilities" and containing:

1. **Stay in NY—Get Job—Move Out**
2. **Drop Out of School & Travel a While**
3. **Rtrn to School—Live Alone—MOVE FROM APT.**
4. **Stay with Lane? Marriage?**
5. **Anna—How Forget?**
6. **What Else?**

141 "Hi, it's Dave."

"Hi."

"I'm not interrupting anything, am I?"

"Nothing important, just going over some layouts. What's up?"

"I just had to call you, you know. I'm going to look for a job, I guess. Got any ideas?"

"Try Faust Manufacturing. I heard this morning that they're looking for a guy."

"I don't want to be a shipping clerk."

"Take my word for it; this is an interesting deal. Let them surprise you."

"OK, I'll call them. If I don't get there today, I'll try to make it on Monday. What's their address?"

"Four-fifty Park. Talk to Jack Moritz; he's an old friend of mine. Use my name."

"What do they make?"

"You'll see."

"Come on."

"Just trust me. Call them."

"OK, OK. I'll give it a try. Will you be home early?"

"Yes, and I'll bring stuff for supper."

"Let me take you out."

"Where, to Nedick's?"

"Very funny. I'll wait for you."

"OK."

"Lane?"

"Hmm?"

"Would you be interested in, uh, marrying me?"

"What?"

"Do you want to marry me? I realize that it's not a good time to propose, but. . . ."

"David."

"What?"

"I love you. But I can't marry you now because you're not free. It wouldn't be fair to anyone."

"I suppose you're right. How about next week?"

"Ask me again next week."

"Hey, Lane."

"Hmmm?"

"I love you. I really love you. See you later."

"I love you too. Have a nice day."

"You too."

142   "So what did she say?"

"She said it was up to me."

"What are you going to do?"

"I don't know."

"David, I don't understand this. What kind of fight breaks up a marriage? What can be so important?"

"Mom, take my word for it. It's important."

"I think you should call her and apologize for running away."

"Oh, yeah?"

"I'll give you money. Have her come to the city and you can both stay with me."

"And you'll fix up everything."

143   "Anna's not home; she's out shopping."

"Oh."

"Is this David?"

"Yes."

"What's going on with you two?"

"Nothing."

"Anna told me about it."

"Oh."

"David. We're both men. I know how you feel."

"You do?"

"But you can overcome it. You can forgive her."

"I can do anything."

"Will you?"

197

"I don't know."

144   "Do you love me?"
"I don't know. Do you love me?"
"I don't know."
"So?"
"But we can try."
"Try what? To fall in love?"
"You're very pessimistic."
"No. I'm only Golem."
"I need you, David."
Thanks.

145   Golem felt as though it had been he, rather than the phone, which had been dialed. Indeed, like a public utility company caught in the concussions of a proxy fight. Everybody wants a piece of me in exchange for the advice they give, he thought, and yet I can't possibly be that desirable. Even if I am, the decisions still have to be made by me because the data, however philosophically arid you make believe they are, refuse to be contracted, compacted into neat and tidy figures of doubt with binary resolutions. A computer says yes or no; only a man can say maybe. What's that crap about the more you learn, the older you get, the less you know? Why? Because the brain cells decay or because the old solutions, largely binary, on/off solutions, don't seem to quite fit the characteristics of the new problems? What's the scenario on that? Turn it over to the think tank (remember when it was called a drunk tank?) and let them wargame it, label it, simulfuck it, ladder it, light it up on an electronic display board and move the pieces of play by remote control. All you get is an identification of the variables, making them more and more discrete, perhaps. All you get is a Yes and a No Strategy. Call it Operations Research if you must, but don't call it Operations. Somebody's still got to be the "top-level decision-maker" and there's only one in each man's life—whether he realizes that or not. PERT me no PERTs, not when the pickle is real. You survive if you want to survive. OK, we got that. Next problem: How To Be Happy.
1. Think positively.

2. Accept your condition.
3. Pretend.
4. Transcend.
5. Et cetera.
6. Forget it.

The chief problem seems to be that, having decided that man can endure anything, that he can find a solution, a viable solution as it is now called, to any problem, stuck with the original premise that one can, if one is essentially aware, choose one's own trip, wrapped in the net of the belief in eventual and inevitable perfectability—one no longer knows whether to compromise for God or the Devil or, even, in whose name the compromise is being made—which may be just what the Old Bastard had in mind when he pulled the rib out of Adam's cage. Think you're groovy, eh? Think you're the ultimate, earth-living, air-breathing, walking-tall, tongue-speaking, thumb-using form, eh? Now, watch this you dumbmotha. SHAZAM!!! WOMAN!! I give you CHOICE, AMBIVALENCE, CONFLICT, EXISTENCE, CONFUSION, DUALITY, and everything that you give to a smart-ass who has everything on his birthday. Here is a 24K gold toothpick; use it and appear ostentatious or put it on your desk and look pretentious. Now let's see how much good your thumb will do you.

And ever since that day, even before the well-known Apple Episode which, in truth, served only to further illuminate the nature of the problem, we've been governed by the Rule of Thumb. Give it back or not. And to whom. Screw that slavery-freedom jazz; the Rule of Thumb is the central metaphor of our Time.

And you don't use your thumb to dial a telephone number.

Look around, look around. "Yonder stands your orphan with his gun." Which is why Golem saves newspaper clippings. So that when the apocalypse comes, he can pull out his scrapbook and shout, "I told you so!" Here's one he found this afternoon under the headline UNAWARE JEWS KILLED, KIESINGER TELLS COURT. Amazing excerpts follow.

West German Chancellor Kurt Georg Keisinger swore in court here (Bonn) Thursday that he never *officially* knew of the Nazi's Jewish exterminations, but came to believe something *"bad"* was happening toward the end of his service as a top official of the Nazi Foreign Ministry.

"I knew Jews were being taken off. In my own house was a Jewish family which was picked up and taken away. . . . I thought they must be put to work somewhere. . . . But in the course of the war I began to have the feeling *that something didn't figure*," the chancellor said.

. . . the chancellor seemed relaxed and even *jocular* through the three hours of testimony. . . .

All emphasis added or, rather, *replaced*.

Pull the petals off the flower, flip a coin, journey to a sage. Isn't it time you made up your mind. From the back of the room comes the Voice of Tradition—Wise Words For Any Situation: DO NOTHING.

I

146   Was saved by the buzzer. Lane was home and, though she had been lined through as an alternative solution, her presence alone worked on the Problem like a furnace on iron. Let it drip, anything, so long as it doesn't run rodlike from my ass to my neck, forcing a posture so artificial that when it is finally removed, there would be no remembrance of what it is to slouch comfortably.

147   I
accuse
refuse
to use
pay my dues
a ruse
I

148   "don't feel like it," he said, holding his glass of brandy in front of him as if the challenge were in the solution contained by the glass balanced between thumb and forefinger, index finger.

"Come on, Dave. You're hanging around the place too much and there'll be some interesting people there for you to meet. Nobody knows you, if you're worried about that."

"I'm not worried about *that*. I know *that*."

"So?"

"I'm just tired, that's all."

"Bullshit, we're going."

"Hell, Lane . . ."

"Roll us a few joints. I told Valerie we'd come by for her around nineish."

"Her, too?"

"She's got a date."

"With what, some Emerging Celebrity who plays a mean oud on the side?"

149   At eleven that night, should you have been taking a short walk to aid your digestion or simply exploring the territory in the hopes of locating a new egg cream mine, you would have found, on the southeast corner of Twenty-seventh Street and Sixth Avenue, a rather strange young man who, with his head held between his hands in front of him and an unusual emptiness atop and between his shoulders, looking much like a caricature inspired by the well-known I've Got the Urban Hamlet Blues, was engaged in a particularly heated conversation with himself. Probably you would have passed by without a second glance, however, for you know that the city is a place of much mystery.

The young man was, of course, our own Golem and he had, finally, grown tired of himself. Tired of being alienated, tired of being supremely moral, tired of being marvelously philosophical in his own way. He was, in fact, getting ready to throw all that whither goest Western civilization shuck overboard, break out the lifeboats, and join up with what the Indians tactfully refer to as Real People or what is generally known as "us common folks." Hooray! Another one saved!

But, if you did pass by, you would have missed this, forgive me, dialogue. So, take a chance. Let's eavesdrop. It went something like this. . . .

Head: So?

Shoulders: Well, I used to have a good head on my shoulders.

Head: Look in the mirror; maybe you'll see your face for a change.

Shoulders: You don't have to insult me.

Head: Look, this is bad enough. Already I feel like a television commercial. Now, I'd like to get back together with you —it hasn't been a bad relationship and I'd hate to see it end this way—but I'm getting tired of this endless shifting through alternatives. I need a rest. At least a week in the mountains.

Shoulders: You didn't have to unplug yourself.

Head: My circuits are dangerously overloaded. Didn't you read the Owner's Manual? I'm doing all the work for you and you just stand there squinting my eyes. I'm through. Either get a job and take me off the case for a while or get somebody else.

Shoulders: What would I do without you?

Head: Think for yourself. Try making up your arms.

Shoulders: Very funny.

Head: It's not funny at all.

Shoulders: Are you giving me an ultimatum?

Head: This is a question?

Sholders: Then you are. Ha!

Head: Ha your ass, buddy.

Shoulders: But we've always had such a good relationship.

Head: This is a crisis. The most I'll give you is a penny to stick in the fuse box.

Shoulders: I need metaphors like I need a hole in the head.

Head: Watch it! You get one more weekend in New York. The air is killing me; my sinuses are clogged. Either get us a job on Monday or get us out of the city or else.

Shoulders: Or else what?

Head: Legal separation with divorce to follow.

Shoulders: I can't live without you.

Head: They all say that.

Shoulders: I haven't got much choice.

Head: That's the point.

Shoulders: All right.

Head: All right what?

Shoulders: I agree.

Head (*turning to face you*): Hey you! You hear that? He agrees. He made a decision for himself. You're a witness.

You: I don't want to get involved.

Head: It's too late for that.

And then, the Head does a strange little dance, batting its eyelids, flapping its ears, pursing its lips, and, finally, pirouetting back onto its place between the Shoulders.

And You Are There.

150   "Why did you leave?"

"I had to get myself together."

"It was very rude."

"I'm sorry, Lane. I really am. I'm causing you a lot of trouble. Everybody, in fact."

"Stop feeling sorry for yourself."

"I already decided to do that. I'm going to try to get a job on Monday and if that doesn't work out, I'm splitting."

"Where will you go?"

"I haven't gotten that far yet."

"Any ideas?"

"Baby, I'm going to tack a map of the U.S.A. up against the wall, motherfucker, and throw a steak knife at it. Where it hits, that's where I'll go. Very romantic, right?"

"Are you good at that?"

"Going?"

"No, knife-throwing."

"I have no aim."

"It'll be exciting."

"Yeah."

"Do it now."

"No. Monday night."

"You'll get a job. Go to Faust."

"I will."

It was eleven o'clock on Saturday morning, they were still in bed, and Golem, who normally watched the television cartoons at that hour, was busy creating his own, frame by frame. He painted in the background by making Saturday morning love to Lane.

151   Sunday.

The New York Times.

Brunch Out.

A walk in the park.

Trying to pretend he wasn't preoccupied.

A visit to a gallery.

Supper in a chili parlor.

The Ed Sullivan Show.

Trying to pretend he wasn't preoccupied.

They made love again, he trying to pretend that he wasn't preoccupied, she trying to involve them both. His orgasm was small and somewhat timid, the necessary result of aforesaid preoccupation. Hers was bold, even defiant, I will be fucked. She knew that it might be the last time and she would not let him go easily; she held him between her legs until she felt him turning within himself, knowing that it was starting to hurt him. She did not want to be forgotten. Then she let go and he rolled off, falling asleep with his head on her breast. She held him that way for many hours, knowing that he must leave and hating herself for knowing so much and still maintaining a posture of ignorance.

152   Golem pushed button 16 and the last little rectangle on the Plexiglas row of small signs above the elevator door was illuminated. FAUST MFG., INC. Everybody else goes down, thought Golem, I go up.

They had an entire floor and though Golem expected to leave the elevator and enter a world of gray floors and pillared rows filled with manufacturing equipment of some kind, he knew that he wouldn't find a factory on Park Avenue. This must be their Executive Offices. He adjusted his tie, brushed some hairs off his shoulders, wiped his eyes. He had gotten through the weekend and this was his last day. The elevator stopped at 14 and Golem worried—another delay? The doors opened to reveal a thin man with a thick mustache who held a black briefcase by a pair of gold-colored handles.

"Going up?"

Golem nodded.

"Well, I'm going down, but it's only two floors so I'll come along for the ride." He entered and leaned against the wall, whistling some imaginary tune. The doors closed.

"Going to see Faust?" he asked, breaking his own musical interlude.

"Yes."

"What do they do up there?"

"I don't know."

"Oh."

The elevator stopped and the doors opened. As Golem stepped out of the cubicle, he thought he heard the thin/thick man whisper Good Luck, but, when he turned around, the doors were closed.

153   Golem saw the tightly wound young blond at the French Provincial desk which was placed at the end of a long beige-walled hall, nearly like the proverbial light at the end of the tunnel. He stood there and he knew that, whatever Faust was or was not, it was not for him. There'd be no job here for him. He turned to face the elevator again and saw the four lines of gold lettering on the wall.

FAUST
New York
Washington
Paris

He pushed the elevator button.

"Can I help you?" The blond called to him, her voice bouncing off the terrazzo floor.

"Made a mistake," he replied. "Got off at the wrong floor," he pleaded. He stared at the aluminum-colored doors, wishing that he believed in psychokinetic energy. Open, he said to himself. Open, for chrissakes, I've got to get out of here.

154   The knife, bone-handled and serrated-edged, whistled an unrecognizable tune as it cut through the air, as it separated the space between Golem and the map. It carried a heavy burden but it was a streamlined object. It was a good throw, from the living-room into the bedroom; it would reach the map. Golem would be spared the humiliation of a second chance. If one insists on playing with romantic notions, one must, at least, have a correct sense of style. He had tried to aim at the west coast, but shuddered at the possibility of his missing California and ending up in an Arizona waterhole and so compensated by shifting his body slightly to the right. Lot more population over there on the right. Eyes, don't fail me now. There's a lot riding on this one, sweet baby. Come . . .

> Whistle

> Thwack

. . . on, It was In.

Missed California by miles, inches really, maybe a foot or more. Some state in the lower right-hand corner. Christ. The South again? Golem walked slowly up to the map, wishing that he had his hands over his eyes and that somebody would be there to shout SURPRISE. The knife stuck out, quivering a bit, and Golem, unlike Macbeth, had no need for doubt. Or, rather, no more room. It was in Georgia. Somewhat below Atlanta. He withdrew it, carefully. A small slit ran through a dot which was next to the word Odessa.

> Odessa.

> Odessa, Georgia.

> Are you kidding?

155 Lefkowitz, making change for a ten, felt a sudden pain in his right temple. Is this it? he asked himself as he pulled nine singles out of the cash register. Betty Sue bit her tongue. Ouch, she said, right in the middle of geometry class and everybody turned to look at her. JoAnna Collier jumped out of bed with a bad dream. She had allowed her husband to make love to her last night and that always resulted in her being awakened by bad dreams. Harmon Collier, her husband, stubbed his toe.

So much for cross-cutting.

156 "I'm leaving."
"Didn't you get the job?"
"I didn't try."
"Why not?"
"I couldn't."
"Oh."
"I love you."
"But you're leaving."
"I have to."

"All right. I understand. I love you."

"Thanks, Lane."

"Where are you going?"

"Odessa, Georgia."

"In Russia?"

"No, no. In Georgia. U.S.A."

"Oh. Odessa, Georgia."

"Right."

"Golem?"

"What?"

"Are you kidding?"

157   Indeed, he was not.

Lying on his bed in his room at the Georgian Manor (manner)—a five-story brick building with a columned, rocking-chair-crowded veranda which served as greater Odessa's only hotel, a masonry container of anachronisms which lived alongside the droppings of progress (Lions, Rotary, Jaycees)—watching the Waco Bros. who looked small and spangly on the television screen, listening to them singing I Wouldn't Have Shot My Wife, Mr. PoliceMan, But She Hid the Keys to My Chevrolet So's I Couldn't Go Messin' 'Round with My Sweetheart Tonight and Nobody But Nobody Goes Messin' 'Round with My Chevrolet— a kind of banjo hymn to a folk crime, trying to figure out why or how he could grant certain freedoms to himself that he was unwilling or incapable of granting to others. Shit. What he means is, how come he can go fucking around on his wife, but won't allow her to do it? Was he cheating himself and placing the blame on her? What's the difference? I must be a goddamned moral narcissist—something's wrong with that phrase, maybe it should be a Jewish narcissist.

He got out of bed and found a piece of paper and a pencil.

I Am, he wrote,
A.   Self-indulgent
B.   Loving of Self-pity
C.   Self-centered
D.   Right

E. Wrong
WATCH OUT!

Then he went back to bed. We are all people, he thought, am I *more* people? More equal? Obviously.

Well, I'm here, he said to the Waco Bros. who had never wanted more than a comfortable pair of boots and matching Cadillacs. I'm here. Bet you couldn't do that.

"Pleeze, Mr. PoliceMan, I know I should be sorry,
But what can you do with a woman who ain't
Got no respect for your very own private property?"
Well, maybe they could.

158   When he awoke, it was Tuesday afternoon and the television set was still on. He left it on while he showered and shaved, knowing that there was something final in the loneliness of having your conversation space occupied by a television set. I am by myself, he thought. And I don't know if I can handle it, but I'll find out. He turned off the set before he left the room to explore his new country.

159   Anna was in the livingroom, wishing he would call.
Lane was in the office, wishing he would call.
Mrs. Golem was in the kitchen, wishing he would call.
Golem was in a telephone booth, wishing he could call.
Someone.

Instead, he found himself a small furnished apartment in a series of one-story buildings across from the War Memorial Park, a row of brick and glass that served notice on the surrounding countryside that Odessa, however small it was in size, was big enough in spirit and American enough in outlook to keep up with the times. It was within walking distance of the two main streets which constituted the shopping area of the town and so he walked to WOGA, the only non-country-and-western radio station, applied for a job, and cut an audition tape. He was promised a job within the month.

THE THIRD BOOK

"Who would not fear Thee, O King of the nations? For it befitteth Thee . . ."
(Jeremiah 10:7).

I

160   For the past month—twenty-three days to be exact—
there had been developing on—or, rather, to be exact again,
growing on Golem's right buttock (actually, on the precipice of
that orifice)—a rather large, grotesquely red, and extremely painful
tumor. It cared little whether Golem sat or stood or walked. It had
a life of its own and its primary emanation was pain; it hurt him
constantly, indiscriminately.

Each day it grew larger, almost as if all the medieval
humors of his body were collecting in that single spot, pushing
their way through the channels of his system in an effort to stage
a grand and daring escape from his body. Each day he said to
himself, "Tomorrow, it will burst."

But it did not. It grew; it was taking its time about
opening. It would open when it was ready. Golem began to worry
about the approach of what he had come to call, mentally of course,
B-Day. That day on which this Gordian knot of skin would open

and all the fluids which had been saving themselves up, holding themselves in readiness for this tremendous, bursting expression of cleanliness, would come pouring out of his body, wetting his underwear, and staining the seat of his pants. Would he be alone when that happened? And what would the dry cleaner think of him, a man with bloody pants?

"Christ," he said quietly as he swiveled around on the gray plastic chair which was strategically placed between the two turntables and fed a tape into the mouth of the cartridge machine. "Christ, how I'd like to open this goddamned mike and tell all you little ladies just how it feels to be sitting on top of a potential deluge. How the hell would you like to have that metaphor with your ten o'clock coffee?"

"Odessa Drug Delivers," sang a voice which Golem pictured as belonging to a blonde with a cinnamon roll face and a soft, frekled body.

Golem back-cued a 45 of Sinatra's "Strangers in the Night" on Turntable 1 and put the machine into gear as the pastry-voiced jingle came to its end. He set the pot and flipped the Program Key over to P.

"Take it from me, folks," he said, holding one hand against his ear to check the sound of his own voice, "Odessa Drug Delivers Dependability with a Big D. Good old Harry Morgan, your friendly professional pharmacist, will never do you wrong. I trade there myself. And now, here's another kind of dependability. Vocal dependability. Old Golden Throat himself . . . Frank Sinatra doing 'Strangers in the Night.' " Golem flipped on the turntable switch. "Don't forget, now, you're listening to the Dave Allen Show, the only show on radio that nudges you awake. On big little WOGA, Odessa, Georgia." He cut off the mike and sent Frank Sinatra out over the airwaves and into the waiting ears of fifty-five per cent of Odessa's housewives.

Golem lit a cigarette and took the last drink from his already cold coffee which lay uninvitingly in a white styrofoam cup. Dave Allen. Dave Allen. The name fitted him like a second-hand suit bought on the Lower East Side—big around the shoulders, baggy at the knees, droopy over the shoe tops. He hated it and he loved it; it was like getting teeth. But much better, for one rarely has an opportunity to choose one's own name. We name everything but ourselves, not even Adam had a choice about that. This name, Dave Allen, gave him—if he should want it— entré into that society whose hands were unstained by the stigmata of chicken soup, to whom schmaltz was a good description, and not a pejorative one, of Mantovani's music. And yet, the pain of assimilation was very real. Funny that it should bother him; it was simply a matter of a professional name, a stage name essentially. He couldn't conceive of himself saying, "OK, gang! This is The Golem here on the nightline bringing you the best in sound for miles around!" And so he had chosen Dave Allen; it had more zing, more pizazz, as they say in the business. But it frightened him and he wondered if he hadn't lost something, if only for a short time.

He looked up at the large crystalless clock on the wall in front of him and noted, not without relief, that he had only ten more minutes of show to do. The six-to-ten shift wasn't bad; it would have been easy for him had he not agreed to take on the top forty spot every night from eight to midnight. Still, it was better than working a straight eight and it left him plenty of time to brood in his apartment, talk to Lefkowitz, or go over to Chelm (the next town over) to watch a couple of skin-flicks. Except, of course, on Tuesdays, Thursdays, and Saturdays, which were JoAnna Days.

JoAnna Days. It sounded like a special sale at the local supermarket . . . all vegetables marked down for quick sale, come on in and get your roughage, folks. And, maybe, that's what it was.

He had been in Odessa for what, six, seven, eight months, now? He lost track. He felt as though he were losing touch with the surfaces of his existence. He had grown older, that's all. All he had was sex with JoAnna and something akin to philosophy with Lefkowitz. And the last was part of a strange relationship. He remembered how he had stopped into the cigar store to pick up a package of cigarettes and a *Life* one evening before going to work. Lefkowitz had already pulled the shade part way down, but when Golem knocked on the glass, he stopped and the two men stared at each other as if sensing an uncomfortable familiarity. Lefkowitz opened the door for him, the CLOSED shade hanging above them.

"Can I just get some cigarettes and a magazine before you close?"

"It's late, but come in. What kind of cigarettes?"

"Make it Camels."

Lefkowitz went back behind the counter and Golem bent over the magazines.

"I haven't seen you in here before. New in town?"

"Yeah. Work over at WOGA. Maybe you catch my show in the mornings?"

"I don't listen to the radio much. Just the news once in a while. I don't like this screaming they call music. From New York?"

"Uhm. My accent give me away?"

"It's not strong, but I can tell."

"Are you from here?"

"More or less, more or less. What are you doing in Odessa?"

"It's a long story."

It certainly was.

Golem turned around to pick up his cigarettes, his *Life* in his hands.

"Mind if I ask your name?"

"Course not. Golem."

"Golem?"

"Yeah, Dave Golem. I use Dave Allen on the radio, though."

"I'm Lefkowitz."

"Glad to meet you." He extended his hand.

"Are you . . .

(Why is that question such a difficult one for everyone?) . . . Jewish, by any chance?"

"Yeah, as a matter of fact."

Lefkowitz looked as though he did not know precisely what to do with the answer that he had received.

"Aren't you?" Golem asked him, half expecting an answer that might be followed by a secret handshake.

"Yes."

Golem wanted to ask if there were others, but somehow the current scene appeared melodramatic enough. Instead, he said, "That's nice."

"We're the only ones."

"In the whole town?"

"That's right, my boy."

"I don't know what to say."

"Just be careful."

"Really?"

"Just be careful."

"All right."

Golem picked up his cigarettes and put the money in front of Lefkowitz. "Is there a good deli around?"

"Very funny, boychick. Watch your step and come and see me again."

Golem had gone to work that night feeling as though there really were an International Zionist Conspiracy and, worse, he wasn't certain whether he liked that feeling or not. What was it like to be the only Jew in town? And, then, to have another suddenly appear? Like two gunslingers of the old West meeting on the dustblown street of a frontier settlement, each waiting for the other to give some signal of purity? He wondered if Lefkowitz would pray or curse that night. And if they would share Sabbath dinners together, in secret somewhere. Hold clandestine prayer services? It's like being a Christian, for chrissakes. What if they were discovered by the Junior Chamber of Commerce Vigilante Committee, their heads covered by yarmulkes, their shoulders wrapped in fringed talesim, bodies bent in a simple welcoming prayer? Would they be tarred and feathered, run out of town on a rail, or worse, lynched? Nah, that only happened to spades. Not to Jews. Not any more. So what would it mean? Somebody to talk to once in a while? At the very least, he could expect to get a discount at the cigar store . . . when no one was looking, of course.

Golem back-cued the Tijuana Taxi on Turntable 2 and thought about seguing from Sinatra's doo-be-doo-be-doo (do be what?), but he thought better of it. He reached across the console to pick up his Baby Patty Appeal copy and set the neatly typed white sheet, watermarked WOGA, in front of him.

He and Lefkowitz had shared their Sabbath dinners.

Above the store, the table was set in the livingroom and though the meal was sometimes barbequed chicken and hush puppies from a local take-out stand, there were always yarmulkes and full glasses of kosher wine. Golem began to think of himself as a Marrano.

"Why are we pretending?" he had asked one night.

"Pretending what?"

"Pretending to be Jews."

"What?"

"Or not to be Jews. I never felt so Jewish in my life."

"It comes from fear. Suffering . . ."

"Is Jewish. I'm familiar with that line. But why don't you want to be recognized? What's so hard about being Jewish in a town like this?"

"My boy," Lefkowitz replied, putting down a drumstick and wiping his mouth with a paper napkin, "I have lived in this town for practically all of my life. My father, he should rest in peace, before he died, said to me, my son, this is no place for a Jew."

"Where is a place for a Jew?"

"No place."

"So why the wine and Sabbath meal with me and all that?"

"An obligation."

"To whom? Me? The religion? An obligation to bring or to cont'nue suffering is not much of an obligation."

' My boy, to be a Jew means to have no choice. You are born that way or you are not; it is a fact of your existence. Attach another label to yourself and nobody listens. Be a Methodist, a Baptist, and they whisper behind your back, 'He used to be a Jew.' Be a nothing and you are still a Jew. What's the difference?"

"Once a Jew always a Jew. Is that what you're saying?"

"That's right; that's right.."

"It sounds anti-Semitic, for chrissakes."

"Sounds, shmounds. The world is not yours. Did you think it was? It will not leave you alone to be what you want. All you can do is try and get by with what you have, what you are."

"Lefkowitz, you are a pessimist."

"A pessimist? A pessimist, he calls me. And you are what? An optimist, an idealist? This is why you ran away?"

"I didn't run away."

"Excuse me, you made a decision."

"That's right."

"Well, let me tell you something, my boy. You ran away. A man, a mensch, would have stayed and faced up to his problems, struggled with them, let them kill him if necessary. But not you, you ran away to start a new life for yourself. Let me tell you something, Mr. Big Shot Existentialist, there are no new lives. All you get is a change of scenery every once in a while and me, I like the fresh air and the country."

"You're starting to sound like my mother."

"Then you should have listened to her."

After dinner, they would take a walk through the quiet town. The two men, one tall, young, angular . . . the other old, short, stooped, would walk through the sidewalks of night arguing philosophy, politics, religion, punctuating their remarks with humorous insults. But Lefkowitz who, despite his physical stature or, perhaps, because of it, carried his ideas in a most regal manner, would never surrender and Golem began to feel like a man in a hurry to lock up his medicine chest.

It was on one of those Friday night walks—or tours, as Lefkowitz often called them—that Golem told his new confident about Anna and Cohen.

"The whole world is cheating, why should your wife be any different? Because she's your wife?"

"Yes."

"But you cheated on her, didn't you?"

"Yes, but it doesn't change my feelings."

"Why should it? Do you think hers are changed? Feelings are feelings, but they are not lives. You don't live only by them, do you? Anyway, the whole thing is your fault."

"Why? Because I'm Jewish?"

"Don't be a schmuck. It's your fault because you're a man and you're responsible. Still, you don't understand that?"

"It isn't fair, though."

"What are you, a five-year-old who makes in his pants?

217

Fair? Who cares if it's fair? Everybody who comes into my store to read the dirty, filthy books that I sell is cheating. But still, I sell the books. I even read them myself. Listen, Mister Optimist. There is no Fair and there is no Justice. Go back to your wife."

"I can't."

"Why not?"

"Don't you understand, Lefkowitz? I'm caught between what is traditionally considered the role of the man and what one feels *should* be the role of the man."

"Should?"

"Yes. I'll stay with that; I have to. Should."

"Why should it be different?"

"Because the old way wasn't right. It presumed too many irrelevant things and didn't take enough others into account."

They were back in the store, now. It was closed, of course, and they sat on the two woven plastic chairs at the end of the counter drinking sodas, surrounded by the comic book colors of the contents of this otherwise dark container. *True Confessions* everywhere and not a drop of blood.

"Also, I don't want to hold such a narrow view of women. I like women and I don't want to think of them as objects."

"Somebody's got to be the boss."

"Why can't you share the responsibility?"

"Responsibility isn't shared."

"How about God? Does he take all of the blame?"

"No."

"So why should a husband?"

"Look, either be a husband or don't be a husband. But you can't be both."

"Which is what I want, I suppose."

"Stop being so righteously human."

"How about just human?"

"Listen, my boy," Lefkowitz said, withdrawing a wrinkled and dirty handkerchief from his back pocket, "you think you got troubles? You got your whole life ahead of you." He blew his nose for effect. "Someday, I'll tell you the story of Lefkowitz, then you'll see how lucky you are. Here I am, an old Jew, no family, alone in a place of strangers where soon I will die, vanish. Will I be remembered? And how will I be remembered? You think I am a Marrano, a secret Jew, that I believe nobody knows what I am? Believe me, when you hear some meshugenah redneck Christian say to you that he just bought a new Chevrolet and that he Jewed the salesman down in price, that's trouble. I know they call me 'the Old Jew' when they sit in Ransom's Cafe. I know plenty. So what? What should I do about it? A man must keep quiet sometimes. A place without Jews is no place at all."

"I thought you told me that this was no place for a Jew."

"So what?"

"Well, what do you think you are, a direct representative of God?"

"Here, I am."

"Lefkowitz, I'm surprised at you."

"I am the conscience of this town, whether they know it or not."

"Is that what a Jew is?"

Lefkowitz blew his nose again.

Sinatra started to fade and Golem opened the Program Key for his mike.

"Folks," he said, reading across the page, "I'd like to get serious for a moment, now. I'd like to take some time out of this program to remind all of you good citizens out there about big little WOGA's Baby Patty Appeal. Now, as y'all know (it was actually typed that way and Golem blinked at the contraction), Baby Patty Steadman has been stricken with a very rare type of blood disease. This darlin' little girl has been stricken with a disease so rare that it cannot be properly treated at Odessa's fine Memorial Hospital. Lord knows, the good doctors have tried, but they just don't have the right equipment. But, that disease can be treated up in the hospital in Atlanta. If Baby Patty can get to Atlanta in time, there's a good chance, a real good chance, that the fine doctors up there can lick this disease. But if she doesn't get there very soon, this beautiful little girl may not live to blow out the candles on her fourth birthday cake.

"The trouble is, folks, that big city hospitals cost an awful lot of money. Now most of us here in Odessa know Baby Patty's daddy, Vern Steadman. Vern has been delivering milk for Odessa

Dairy for eleven years now and, though he is a good, hardworking, honest, Christian man, he is just not financially able to keep Baby Patty in Atlanta for the necessary amount of time. And that's why big little WOGA is sponsoring the Baby Patty Appeal.

"Here is a chance for all the real community-minded, kind citizens of Odessa to pull together and stand behind Vern. We want everybody, just everybody in Odessa, to donate something, no matter how small, even if it's only a dollar, so that Baby Patty can take that cure up in Atlanta. It's a tall order, cause we need a total of eight thousand dollars to do it.

"Now, I know that sounds like a lot of money to most of us. And it sure is. But if we all chip in, if we all give our fair share, we ought to be able to reach that goal without too much trouble. Don't forget that this isn't one of those fancy national charities, but a drive to help one of our own. And the good folks of Odessa have already donated five thousand dollars to keep this precious child alive.

"Won't you give Baby Patty Steadman a chance to grow up?

"Send in your donations to big little WOGA, one-thirteen Main Street right here in Odessa, Georgia.

"We thank you and Baby Patty thanks you."

The Tijuana Taxi came in like a sudden burst of antiseptic spray.

Golem cut off his mike. Billions for blood, he thought, but not one cent, not one red cent for my red boil. The good folks of Odessa ought to send everybody under ten off to Atlanta to have their blood replaced and their brains washed clean. Everybody in this town needs an interior bath. Golem wondered how the townspeople who hadn't given to "the cause" were able to face ol' Vern each day. How did they drink their milk? And how did Steadman feel, coming to the door with a milk bill in one hand, a tin cup in the other? Poor schmuck. This whole thing must have been his wife's idea. Golem secretly hoped that the Baby Patty Appeal would not reach its eight grand goal. Then he would see if some charitable citizens would kick in the rest or if the town would just let the kid die in peace. And what if eight thousand wasn't enough? Steadman could never beg again. Or could he? Where does the responsibility end once it begins? Tune in next week, folks, etc.

For spite, he ground his buttocks into the plastic, hoping that the boil would surrender. But it did not happen.

Golem took the Baby Patty copy, folded it in quarters, and stuffed it into his right rear pocket; it would be his shield and, at the same time, it would absorb his curse. Blood for blood. He took off the Sinatra record and cued up his theme, which was an old cut of Big Noise from Winnetka. (Ah, Winnetka, a magical name . . . perhaps from Kansas or Iowa or one of those states where everyone was somehow more American than anywhere else. He could remember standing in his neighborhood record store, cramped in a hot booth which held a record player instead of a telephone, listening to the Big Noise and dreaming about cheerleaders, young girls who bobbed for apples, legions of blond-headed, thin-legged, freckle-bodied beauties.)

Herb Alpert, he thought. Herbie Alpert, a nice Jewish boy who made good as a Mexican. And here I am, David Alan Golem, B.A., M.A., almost D. of Ph., genial host of the Dave Allen Show, the housewives' heart throb of Big Little Odessa, G.A., population nineteen thousand Fiberglas insulated souls—in Greater Odessa, as the Chamber of Commerce so pridefully called it. What in hell prompted them to name this place Odessa? Had they some secret memory traces of pogroms to come? His mother got a good laugh out of that, or was it a cry? He could remember when he told her, when he called her collect to tell her about being the Morning Man. "Your father, he should only rest in peace," she had said, "would drop dead. Oi, if he knew that he had come all the way to Brooklyn from Odessa, the real Odessa in horrible Russia, only to have his son take a job as a record spinner in Odessa. In Georgia, yet? What's the matter, my boy, you wanted to see the world? Bensonhurst wasn't far enough away for you? And what's the matter with Long Island?"

"But it's a good job, Mom."

"A record spinner? A Jewish boy should be a disc jockey? If your father, he should rest in peace, knew about this, he would say Kaddish for you."

"Well, it's just for a while, Mom. Just until I get myself sorted out."

"Sorted out? What kind of language is that? Does Anna know where you are?"

"No."

"Why not?"

"I don't know how to call her."

"Put another dime in the telephone."

"All right, Mom."

"All right. All right, I'm tired of this shenanigan business, David. Call me up when you decide to be my son."

"Excuse me, your three minutes are up."

"Thank you."

Click. Humm.

Click Humm, he thought. Click Humm. It's catchy; it's got a good beat. Play a few bars and I'll fake the rest. Sounds like a tune of the times. "I am," Golem said into the dead mike, "going out of my mind. And I do not like it one bit."

Click Humm. "How do you like that, ladies?"

"Talking to yourself again, Allen? Those little lady listeners must really be getting you down." It was Harland, the young copywriter, who leaned into the studio as he spoke.

"It's your damned Baby Patty crap that's flipping me out. How the hell do you sleep nights and write that kind of scum?" That was a bad move; he recognized it immediately. Harland would never understand what he meant. He thought that his words were the only thing standing between Baby Patty and Eternity. Little did he know.

"What kind of a remark is that?" Harland stepped all the way into the studio now, a flush of color coming to his ordinarily transparent face.

Golem cut him off with a wave and flicked up the mike key. The red ON AIR light brought any potential action to a halt. The magic of radio, he thought, has just saved me from a possible punch in the nose. Thank you, Mr. Marconi, *et al*. He faded down the record and spoke into the microphone.

"Well, that's it for this morning, ladies. Time to get back to the household chores on this Thrilling Thursday." Golem shoved an ID tape into the machine while he talked. "Tune in tomorrow for more of the same on the Dave Allen Show and have your first cup of Fantastic Friday coffee with me." He faded up the theme for a moment, using his wrist action as a sensing meter, and then brought it down again. "Stay tuned for the Early Report. News as it happens on Big Little WOGA." He switched on the cartridge machine and cut off his mike. The station identified itself and he swiveled around painfully to find that Harland was gone.

Replaced by Warren, the News Director and Sales Manager, a professional country boy with a twang in his walk, who came into the studio bearing a handful of sheets torn from the teletype. He exchanged places with Golem after a thin nod.

The two men rarely spoke to one another, Warren being permanently suspicious of anyone who was born above the Maryland line, the lower Maryland line. In fact, Golem had once decided in the privacy of his apartment that if it came to a choice between being "enslaved" by the Commies or the Yankees, Warren would choose the Commies every time. Even if they *were* Godless atheists. Better Red than Blue was his slogan. Not unlike the pinch-faced, tight-assed young girl that Golem had tried to pick up at the Saturday Night Block Dance—a local event which took place on a wooden-platformed parking lot illuminated by the headlights of old Chevrolets and pickup trucks covered with the dust of too little rain, bumperstickers aglow with mottoes of praise for the man who promised, should he be elected President, to turn the country over to the police for a couple of years to straighten things out. That girl, her breasts leading a not-so-secret life under her J. C. Penney peasant blouse while she danced the clog with farmhands and factory workers who met once a week to listen to the old-timey, mountain-winey music with a moral that was played by a local country and western band, to talk about crop prices and weekly wages, to compare costs of living, to exchange their visions of America (first off, we got to run out every damn nigger, student, and pseudo-intellectual in sight), that girl, in the midst of a scene which reminded Golem of a solidly American small-town version of Hitler's Nuremburg spectacles, had brushed him off with an "I don't go messin' 'round with Yankees." Obviously, Lincoln had failed to win the hearts and minds of the people.

Golem picked up a handful of records and brought them down to the small room marked Music Lib. He dumped them into a bin marked TO BE FILED. Betty Sue, a teenager about whom Humbert Humbert might rhapsodize at the drop of a bobby sock, would come in later that night and fit the records into their respective cubbyholes. After her work was finished, Betty Sue would often sit in the studio where Golem did his top forty show, sit quietly while the ON AIR light was on, but foam at the mouth as soon as it was turned off. Every time he looked at her, Golem had visions of a T. Williams/E. Caldwell shotgun-wedding, child-bride adventure. Yeah, as we noted before, he dug the Youth.

He limped back into the air conditioned corridor; he was getting to hate this air conditioning—though it was necessary here unless you were doing a white-suit-circular-ceiling-fan bit. Every day, the constantly circulating air beat against his skin, flagellating his eyelids until he could barely open them. He was being exhausted by this cleanliness.

161   In the parking lot, Golem found his old green bought-for-a-hundred-dollars Plymouth and got in carefully. He drove through the downtown area leaning on his left side. Still, he could not avoid the knobby plastic seat covers which pressed against his boil as if in warning.

162   Dear Anna,
I have tried to call you several times, but for some reason, I always seem to lose my voice after I give the operator your Area Code. Still, I must, somehow, communicate with you. Consequently, I have decided to write you this long letter in order to

163   "We have learned that when a man's time arrives to leave the world, on that fearful day the four quarters of the world arraign him, and punishments come up from all four, and the four elements fall into disrepute, each clamoring to depart to its own side. Whereupon a herald goes out and proclaims, and the proclamation is heard in two hundred and seventy worlds. If the man merit it, he is joyously welcomed by all the worlds, but if not, woe to the man and his portion!

"We have learned that upon the herald's proclamation, a flame issues from the North, going through the "stream of fire" (Daniel 7:10), and splitting up to pass into the four quarters of the world, there to consume the souls of sinners. After which it leaves and shoots up and down till it settles between the wings of a black cock, which then flaps its wings and crows at the threshold of the gate. First it cries out: 'For behold, the day cometh, it burneth as a furnace . . .' (Malachi 3:19). The second time it cries: 'For, lo, He that formeth the mountains, and createth the wind, and declareth unto man what is his thought' (Amos 4:13); this is the time that a man's deeds bear witness against him and he admits them as his. The third time, they come to deprive him of his soul, and the cock calls: 'Who would not fear Thee, O King of the nations? For it befitteth Thee' (Jeremiah 10:7)." [9]

164 "For man shall not see Me and live" (Exodus 33:20).

165 JoAnna, a girl of thirty who had not been transformed into a woman by marriage, lived in the split-level section of Odessa. Her husband, a home-town football hero, sold insurance every day of the week from a Holiday Inn modern office which was directly across the street from the radio station. Golem could see him come to work every morning, walking up from Ransom's where he had breakfast with the aldermen who all wore food-spotted suits of little shape and no color, and, though the man was not aware of his existence, Golem always waved to him. Since he was screwing his wife three mornings a week, he felt that was the least he could do.

Harmon Collier, that was his name. Harmon Collier was going places was what they said in Ransom's, the Algonquin of Odessa. Course, he's got to watch his wife, now; she's a restless filly is what they said down at Ransom's, and most of them knew. She's a nag, thought Golem. In more ways than one. Harmon Collier better go places. He was already very close to being the village cuckold.

Golem left his car a block away from the Collier ranch house and limped down the partly completed sidewalk, the only residential sidewalk in Odessa built since the end of the Civil War. He turned into the two-car driveway and went to the screen door at the side of the house. "Da-Da!" he said as he opened the door. (JoAnna had told him once that she liked to be surprised, though

[9] *Zohar: The Book of Splendor*. Basic readings from the Kabbalah. Edited by Gershom G. Scholem (New York: Schocken Books, 1963).

there was no doubt in his mind that she always knew the exact moment of his arrival.)

"Why, David Allen! You startled me."

This she said without turning from the sink where she was rinsing out a coffee cup.

"Yeah," said Golem, unconvinced. "You didn't know I was coming. Right?"

JoAnna turned slowly and gave Golem that disjointed smile which was her specialty (all the boys at Ransom's tried, without success, to imitate it)—right corner up, left corner down, lips parted slightly—how did she do it so perfectly? Maybe she practiced every morning while she brushed her long blond hair with those hundred sacrificial strokes. That smile which always made him shiver in anticipation of the words he knew would follow. "Why, I almost forgot. Today is Thursday, isn't it?"

JoAnna was the first ball-cutter he had ever slept with.

She insisted on playing this game with him and, though he hated it, it was a bit exciting and so he allowed it to continue without comment. Probably, she would not understand any comment he might make, unless it was particularly descriptive. Women, he thought, only women can make love with you one night, suck the life out of your body in the evening and forget your name the next morning. That's because they're so sensitive, of course.

"Right. Thursday. Fucking Day." It came out of his mouth accidentally, but he did not regret it and made no effort to retrieve the statement.

"Why, David! You use such vulgar language."

And then she came to him, putting her hands on his shoulders and hiking up one hip in an unconscious parody of every Beverly Garland that ever walked across the screen of a B-movie. "But I love it."

But I love it, she said.

Golem thought he would cry. How could anyone talk like that in real life? Poor old Harmon; she probably felt his biceps and told him what a big strong boy he was. Among other things, JoAnna was a transvestite, a drag in drag.

Golem screwed this creature with vengeance, letting his semen flow into her body with contempt, each droplet the carrier of another portion of his hate and disgust. She was therapy for him, he told himself. But what changes he had to go through, what games he had to play in order to reach that point. How she used him, how she tried to destroy his potency . . . first with words like these and finally with medications that threw up barriers against his passion, never allowing it, knowingly or not, to penetrate her viscera. For Golem, the frustration was complete and, in a sense, exquisite. She was, after all, impregnable.

"Would you like some coffee?"

"No. Let's get on with it."

"David! The way you talk!" And this she whispered, being purposefully wicked, "Anybody else would think you didn't enjoy making love to little ol' me."

Golem retreated; he winked. "Now, you know that's not true."

She tossed her hair and chuckled. Then she stood up on her tiptoes and brushed her lips across his. That was the only kiss he was allowed during these sessions. Like a whore, you can fuck her, but you can't kiss her. To JoAnna, kissing was something sacred and, as she had explained to him once, very seriously, making love to a person who was married really wasn't adulterous as long as there wasn't any kissing involved. JoAnna lived by her own rules.

"My boil hurts like a bitch today, so let's go easy."

JoAnna frowned; she did not like him to come to her with a problem of any kind. It brought reality too close and forced her to treat him, to consider him, as something more than an object. No doubt she resented this imposition on her "free days," as she called them. "Don't worry, David. I won't hurt you."

Golem understood what she meant and he made that famous James Dean-like movement with his hand to signify that the moment had passed. She turned and walked to the bedroom. He followed her with his head lowered as if being led by an invisible chain which ran around his neck and up through her anus to a point of connection on her vestigial remain.

In the bedroom, colored a soft but not a pastel blue and containing a queen-sized four-poster bed canopied with white ruffles.

(Golem tried to imagine Harmon going to sleep in this bed. Did he wear blue silk pajamas or did he sleep in his underwear? Probably in his underwear. But did he wear jockey shorts or boxers? Probably jockey shorts which folded down at the waistband under the pressure of too many businessman's lunches, jockey shorts which he wore because he had always worn them in college and because he thought that they made him look younger than he was. Maybe next year, if he netted twenty grand, he would buy himself a package of boxer shorts—three in assorted colors (beige, white, and blue). In the meantime, he sprawled under the canopy which he detested, and his wife reposed— reposed, did you get that?—reposed in a lace negligee. Did he ever think of himself as a slob? Did he ever think that he'd like to get up one Sunday morning, not go to church, but sit around in a pair of blue silk pajamas and a matching robe, with his hair neatly combed, holding a cup of coffee and reading the Atlanta paper while his wife called mother—any mother would do just as long as she's long distance—just the way they do in the telephone company ads? But isn't that what he did?)

JoAnna closed the drapes while Golem stood in the doorway. This was a moment which he disliked. Should he get undressed and get into bed? Or should he go to her, enfold her in his arms like in the movies? He asked himself this question three times a week, but it was always answered by JoAnna's convenient exit to the bathroom where she would change into a purple wrapper and a diaphragm.

He undressed, folding his clothes neatly and placing them on Harmon's valet which stood at the foot of the bed like a sentinal. He put his shoes next to a pair of Harmon's and noted that the latter were at least two sizes larger than his own. Golem wore boxer shorts, blue ones with a snap fly, and he left them on because JoAnna liked to pull them off during one of her precisely controlled moments of passion. And, besides, he liked having her take them off, liked forcing her to make the final, irrevocable move—though he knew it was a gambit originated and directed by her.

The bed had not yet been made and, as Golem sat upon it, he realized that there was something disgusting about fucking a man's wife on the bed which still held the nearly warm impression of his own body. Even the pillow smelled of Harmon's Brylcreem. What would his father say if he saw Golem like this? Probably shake his head slowly and go back to his newspaper. Maybe, much later in the day, he would look at his son and say, very quietly, in his best Yiddish-theater-disappointed-father-voice, "You have disappointed me again, David. When you were nine years old, you stuck a knife into my heart and, every chance you get, you give it another twist. But, still, I am surprised. Perhaps, by now, I should expect it. Congratulations, David, you have caught me by surprise again."

Fuck you, Dad.

Was what he had always wanted to say. But, of course, never did. Perhaps, he had given the knife one twist too many and the old man had died. A coronary was what the hospital had said, but what did they know? Golem knew better. He had given the knife one twist too many. At the funeral, he could not cry. His hands in front of him, hiding an inexplicable erection, he felt as if he were in handcuffs and that he was standing there before the grave waiting to be taken off to some horrible dungeon where all the ungrateful sons were imprisoned in perpetual darkness.

His mother had cried; she had even tried to throw herself into the grave—and would have if she had not thought that her new black dress would have gotten filthy. But he wasn't being fair. It wasn't the thought of the dress that stopped her, it was Uncle Jacob the Rock (Everyone in the family called him that. "Your Uncle Jacob is a Rock," they would say and it was always applicable, for Jacob walked like granite itself and hardly ever spoke a complete sentence.) who put his arms around her and held her back from the edge. Golem had just stood there, unbelieving, hands in front of him, staring at the dirt from the newly dug grave at his feet, dirt that was impatient to be returned to the earth. He hadn't moved—aside from his lips—any part of his body, a body which was now genuinely his own. His lips moved, without voice, over the lines of the Kaddish, affirming his willingness to live in the presence of this final tragedy.

People talked about it afterward.

They said that he must have been overcome with grief.

But, still, the son . . . he should have done something. These young people. His mother didn't understand either. At the house, amid the animate and inanimate debris of sitting Shiva, the flotsam and jetsam of seven concentrated days of formal mourning (You get up in the morning and mourn from noon to night—irresponsible!), she tried to comfort him and was obviously hurt when he moved away from her. She tried to tell him how his father, in the safety of his bedroom, had spoken many times of his love for his son. Golem had known that, of course, but he had wished that those feelings had been expressed not when the old man stood in his underwear, one arm on the dresser for support as he removed his pants with the other, but within the mise-en-scène of some properly decorated confrontation.

Finally, everyone said that it would soon pass.

Not that it would be forgotten.

But it would soon pass, soon pass. Everything passes, sometimes immediately after or even during its occurrence. Even Anna. Perhaps. It was a question that intrigued Golem. Did everything pass or did it simply pass from the front of graspable reality to the back of the mental warehouse where it was put in stock on the shelves which already sagged under the weight of all the other canned goods that had served as roughage for the system and had now passed—ready to be called out and delivered via an electrified conveyor belt at a moment's notice, a simple signal so small that it might have gone unnoticed by the Night Watchman of Consciousness? But that was stupid. Of course it did.

Golem had the peculiar feeling that he was inventing Freud sometimes. Too bad it had been done already. But still, it was art—perhaps without a capital, however.

Anna. Golem had done nothing about her. They were still married; that is, the contract had not been officially terminated. He had no desire to sue for divorce, worry about lawyers, money, or any of the problems associated with the breaking of a legal contract. As far as he was concerned, the marriage was philosophically over. He had not talked to her, nor had he seen her, nor had he mailed her any of those partially written letters that remained on his desk. Had he been in need of some symbolic articulation of ending, he might have said Kaddish with Lefkowitz. His marriage was dead, but he did not want to attend another funeral so quickly. Eventually, he would have to do it, for he could not abandon himself to Odessa much longer. But right now, it was unnecessary. He had failed; wasn't it enough to admit that to himself?

The vision of Anna and Cohen had been boiled, decontaminated, and vacuum sealed. It was now pure. And put back into storage until he required some winter nourishment. It had already served him well.

Where is, he asked himself, the order point of my emotions?

And he would have tried to provide an answer had JoAnna not returned smiling from the bathroom. The smile served to erase the question or, perhaps more appropriately, to turn down its volume for a while, thus avoiding circuit overload. It became background music for this morning's activities. Harry Hip and his Living Strings. I'm going to buy myself some kind of musical instrument, he decided suddenly. Something portable like a pocket trumpet or an ocherina that I can pull out and blow a few riffs on every time I want to change the inner tune.

"JoAnna, do you enjoy our three days a week together?"

(Golem had never asked her that question before and he was genuinely interested in hearing her speak an answer, interested not as a lover, but only as a person. He felt a need for some kind of tangible contact between them, for there seemed to be no real reason for their continued lovemaking.

He always came; it was on his schedule like breakfast or a ten o'clock class, TThS. She was always there and always ready. It was on her schedule like her Wednesday Afternoon Bridge Party. What did she do on those three afternoons after they had fucked? Golem did not know. He could never remember seeing her after noon. Even the first time. She had called him at the station, during his broadcast, and had invited him for coffee. And he had gone, not really knowing why. Perhaps out of boredom, perhaps out of curiosity—to see if disc jockeys really do have all the action they talk about.

He had been surprised at her beauty and at his own good fortune and she had simply said that his voice had enabled her to picture him almost exactly as he was—tall, thin, with wavy brown hair in need of a cut, even his long and narrow hands. Except for the glasses. Those, she said, she did not expect. So he had taken them off. Then she said, "You're Jewish, aren't you?"

He had nodded.

"I've never met a real Jew before."

Golem had sighed and put his glasses back on.

"No. Leave them off. I like you better with them off."

"So you can see my suffering eyes?"

She had not understood and he had dropped the subject, again removing his glasses. After coffee, she had asked him if he wanted to make love and he had said yes because he could not think of anything else to say. That was how their relationship had begun and it had not advanced beyond that point, overtly, that is.)

"Why, David! You know I do." She did not elaborate and came to bed, sitting down, curling her legs under her buttocks and brushing his hair with her fingers. "Sometimes I think you are a very silly boy, David Allen."

"So do I."

And then he moved to her and took her small body in his long arms. They made love slowly, but not too slowly—an hour was allotted and the act had to be accomplished within that time period. She wanted him out of the house by twelve for Harmon, a creature of habit as well as of other things, was always home at twelve twenty-five for his lunch.

When the prelims were over and they were both naked and wet with the heat of their anticipation, she guided him to her opening and he drove himself into her body. Then he seized her face and kissed her roughly on the mouth. She turned, twisted away, and stared at him with rounded eyes, but did not break their fundamental connection.

"Why did you do that?"

"Because my name is Golem. David Golem. Not David Allen. The Golem. Do you get that?"

She said nothing and instead of waiting for her to speak, he pushed himself deeper inside of her. He felt the tip of his organ against the wall of her diaphragm and he pushed harder, trying, like a runner who ends the race by breaking the tape with his

232

body, to push himself through the plastic barrier. She cried out, a long cry of real anguish, but he continued.

"David Golem, goddamnit. David Golem." He paid no heed to her, cared not about her desire, but rushed on until he reached his climax, discharging with fury. Then, just as he pulled out, withdrew from the field of battle, he kissed her again. Now she was crying. Sobbing, in fact. He rose and dressed. By the time he had finished buttoning his shirt, she had regained enough of her composure to muster a defense, a second-strike capability.

"You'll always be David Allen to me, whoever you might think you are. I'll see you on Saturday."

"Fuck you."

He slammed the screen door as he left. But the boil had not been broken.

166   "I didn't dream last night, Lefkowitz."
"What else is new?"
"I broke up with JoAnna Collier."
"You'll find yourself another shickse."

167   "The human has two squelch chambers. Some people have four. It depends. It's their privilege if they want one in the sub-conscious region of the brain. It's a little bit beyond the center point—about one and a half inches from the top of the skull—and it is an aid to the person. For example, if the squelch chamber is charged positively, it will counteract negative engrams—grind them up—by grinding up I mean the faculties of the squelch chamber are such wherein a sound is amplified into itself and the inter-amplifications of sound or engrams as such are squelched; that is, transformed into light, organic light as a secondary outlet that refreshes the brain to a certain degree." [10]

168   "I was in a tape recorder once. There is a world in that machine." [11]

169   "That's not the point."

[10] *The Three Christs of Ypsilanti* by Milton Rokeach.
[11] *Ibid.*

"Calm down, calm down. Take a seat and I'll make you a soda. Why should you be so upset?"

Golem limped back to the plastic chairs. He didn't know why he had come here, except, perhaps, for some temporary kind of safety. Slamming the door on JoAnna or, rather, fucking her the way he had and then slamming the door was the first spontaneous act he had performed in months. He began to feel free and, at the same time, frightened by the implications of this sudden release. Who am I, Zorba? Bullshit! But can't Golem be Zorba? Why not?

"Lefkowitz," he shouted, beating his chest, "I'm free!"

A man in a short-sleeved white shirt and clip-on striped tie turned from the nudist magazine section and stared at him. He was at a disadvantage, however, for Golem could see the bulge in his pants.

"Be quiet."

The man looked from Lefkowitz to Golem as if a ping pong ball were being played between them. "Strange bunch you get in here, Leffy."

"He's in show business. You know the type."

The man agreed, he knew about those kinds of people. He went back to serious consideration of his dirty pictures.

"You have to shout in my store?"

"If I was Greek, you wouldn't care. Or Italian. You'd accept it, for chrissakes."

"You'll scare my customers."

"I'm tired of being small."

"Sit down and stop behaving like a child."

Golem sat down. Hard. Hoping to bust the boil with the impact of his freedom. But the plastic, as previously characterized, refused to help and simply moved out of the way.

Lefkowitz mixed a Doctor Pepper and brought it back to Golem who stirred it again with his index finger before drinking it. "A little too sweet."

"Give it back."

"It's good enough to drink. I'll drink it."

"Don't do me any favors, no more. I'll throw it out."

Lefkowitz reached for the cup but Golem moved away.

"I said I'll drink it. I mean what I say. I say what I mean."

"Overnight you became a man?"

"Overnight." He saluted Lefkowitz and the Dirty Picture Man with his Doctor Pepper. "Say hello to The Golem."

"So hello."

The man turned again. "How d'y'all expect a man to concentrate with this fella carryin' on like a crazy nigger?"

Golem stood up and walked toward the man, not even bothering to measure him. "Did you, sir, refer to me, metaphorically, as a crazy nigger?"

The man, Dirty Pictures in both hands, bulge in his pants, was not exactly in a position of strength. But he was Amurican. "'Pears to me, boy, like you're looking for a bit of trouble. Now this is a nice town, and we got nothin' 'gainst show folk, but we don't want no outside crazy agitators comin' in here to stir things up."

"Mister," said The Golem as he reached the man, "you are a pervert."

The magazine fell out of his hands. "What you say, boy?"

"You are a pervert."

The bulge began to withdraw.

"Who you callin' a pervert?"

"Ah is callin' you a pervert, buddyro."

"Nobody calls me that kinda thing. I'm a hardworkin', clean livin', Christian man. Don't even beat my wife like some fellas 'round here. You got no call to say somethin' like that to me."

Lefkowitz hollered nervously from the back of the store, "Golem, sit down and behave yourself!"

"You are a pervert, sir."

The man's face reddened, became brighter in hue than his proverbial neck, colored with truth or something close. His fists clenched of their own accord. "C'mon outside, boy. I'm goin' to teach you a little lesson in Southern hospitality." He reached for Golem's arm.

But Golem shifted his body and stepped a bit out of range. "And it's not me who's the boy, but you."

That was a particularly bad line. To make up for it, Golem raised the Dixie cup full of Doctor Pepper and crushed ice and poured it over the man's balding head. He screeched, a ridiculous sound, and Golem began to laugh uncontrollably. Lefkowitz ran up from the back of the store, arms waving, eyes popping, "Get out, you crazy bum! Bum, get out of my store, you meshugenah, you lunatic!"

"Look what he did to me, Leffy! You saw it. You're a witness. You saw the whole thing: I was minding my own business. My own business!"

Casually, but forcefully, Golem pushed Lefkowitz, who had attached himself to Golem's back like a hump, aside, and bent to pick up the nudist magazine. He opened it and draped it like a tent over the man's wet head. "You, sir, are a sincere pervert and I wish you well."

He walked out of the store and climbed into his car.

170   The moving wheels of Golem's automobile.

Betty Sue, as she moves from class, swinging her ass.

JoAnna Collier, as she douches away the remains of Golem's visit.

Harmon Collier, as he signs another name on his dotted line.

Beatrice (Mother) Golem, as she prepares a chicken for baking.

Anna (Wife) Golem, as she examines the stamps on the last mail delivery.

Valerie, as she giggles.

Lane, as she stamps her LB on a layout she thinks is tasteless.

Toni Croft, as she moves her soft body out of still another hard bed.

Peter Paul Mangini, as he cultivates another friendship.

Marvin Cohen, as he breaks the point on his red ballpoint pen.

Grace, as she pastes on her smile.

Lefkowitz, as he shakes his first at the empty doorway.

The Dirty Picture Man, as he wipes the Doctor Pepper off his head.

The moving wheels of Golem's automobile.

O,
D. W. Griffith!
What have you done to my generation?

171   Golem ate his lunch in the movie theater in Chelm. It was called the Orpheum and it showed semipornographic movies, most of which looked as though they had been shot and processed that morning in Atlanta and then driven to the theater under a false floor in the trunk of a new Buick.

Golem had come here often in the afternoons that followed JoAnna, wagging their tails in front of them. It seemed a fitting device for maintaining a connection between the two parts of the day. Certainly none of the women in the films possessed the finesse or, even, the simple physical attractiveness of JoAnna, but with their creased thighs and drooping asses, they were spiritual Siamese twins.

Oh, Dick!
It's a big one.
I can't stand it.
Just a bit more.
Oh, Dick!
It's coming.
Please!
There we go!
Oh! Oh!

Not an unusual dialogue, one might say. Except for the fact that it was a simple-minded, dirty parody of the Androcles and the Lion musical comedy. There, on the bed in what passed for a humble log cabin, lay a Caldwellian slattern, complete with tattered bluejeans and a no-button shirt that tied above the belly-button, arms outstretched, legs outstretched, while her city-slickered, cigarette pack caught in rolled T-shirt sleeve, pompadoured, Ace comb in back pocket, souped-up-Chevy-driving stud pulled an immense thorn from her thigh. Yether. While her corncob smoking, Dogpatch parents looked on and murmured endearments of admirable narcissism. Digging the recapitulation of the race, symbolically, of course.

Golem ate his barbeque sandwich.

I don't think, he thought, that I'm going to be able to fuck any more. Now there's an issue you can really settle down on. Nothing more basic than that, no smelling of "neurotics are just people who whine about their problems" fascism. Pure and simple. And yet, was it organic/genetic? Or was the thought itself—getting stuck somewhere in the mental system, the mechanisms of the organism, the gears and wheels, and cams—no, that's a metaphor of a different age, say the cathodes, the electrodes, the volumeters, and the rheostats, did the thought itself contain enough wattage, amperage, power by any other name is still power, to short-circuit the wiring plot? To fuck up the fucking synapses? Is unhappiness a function of electrical impulses? Is chemistry a myth? Is interface a frown? Can a young girl from the wrong side of the tracks find out?

What's the difference? Murphy's Law.

If the system is susceptible, you get cancer. Golem's Law.

He drank his Doctor Pepper and wished he had an erection.

172   So where are all those Guardian Angels now?

On vacation. In the Catskills.

Isn't that just like God? Huh? He waits until you're absolutely, unconditionally finished, through, kaput, before he throws down the lightning and points the finger. No stepping in three miles further back along the dirt continuum to the debacle for Him. No anticlimaxes for the Lord. You get what you deserve. Then he comes swinging down with a big and beautiful, "What'sa matter wit you, baby?"

Well, I ain't been yo' boy, Lord.

That's the certain truth.

And I sure do need you now.

You tellin' me.

So . . .

What?

Well, you the Lord, ain't you?

Sure enough. I am that I am, baby.

Then you should know.

238

I do, I do.

So . . .

What?

So, if you got a little extra time on your great and beautiful hands, I was kinda hoping that you could spare just a few seconds for me and swing down here and . . .

Yes?

Save me.

He drank his Doctor Pepper and wished he had an erection.

173   When Golem got to work that evening, his breath smelled of Doctor Pepper.

"Now here's a super golden oldie going out over the nightime lines for Lem and Lou, Vern and Patti, Jack and Jill, Punch and Judy, Bob and Ray, Ike and Mamie, Dolph and Eva, and all those lovely ladies down at Ransom's famous, old-original, world-renowned good eating place right smack dab here in Odessa. Johnny Cash doing his all-time biggie, 'I'll Walk the Line.' "

Down the Key.

Round the Turntable.

Up the Pot.

Back in the Chair.

Easy on the Boil.

"Who's Bob and Ray?"

"Before your time, sweetie."

Betty Sue sat in front of the console, legs crossed high so that the lace edges of her essential personality were showing.

"You're so funny, Dave."

"Think so?"

"All the kids think you're groovy."

"Oh, yeah?"

"They really envy me."

"No kidding."

The foregoing while he considered her thighs. Rationalize.

"Who likes me better, the guys or the girls?"

"Oh, the girls just love you. I told them that you're so sensitive looking."

"Sensitive looking?"

She giggled.

"Well, you know . . ."

"Sexy?"

He said, surprised at the sound of his own voice. Was that my voice?

She giggled again.

It sure was.

He considered her breasts. He what? True. True, they were small. A young lady's polite titties. Small, yes, but not out of proportion. What father doesn't dream of incest? Or, for that matter, what daughter? Love makes the world go 'round. What is happening to me? He asked himself, pointedly.

"Sexy, huh?" He heard himself respond.

Betty Sue got up, walked to the windows at the front of the studio, the windows through which Golem would wave to Harmon Collier. She took small steps, moving her tight ass quickly. Golem considered her back. FLASH. TEENAGE LOVE SLAVE. Rape! What's that like? The boys on the corner always said it couldn't be done; a woman couldn't be raped unless she was ninety-six years old, stricken with leprosy, and the act was initiated by a deranged garage mechanic wearing oil-stained green chino pants, white sox, and smelling of fourteen days' work in the grease pits. They all Want It. That's the justification for male existence. Ego me no male egos, my friend, for it is rightly said that a good fuck will cure any ill. Was she a virgin, he wondered? Were there any virgins? He had never slept with a virgin. Was it a necessary experience? Betty Sue turned around. Her face was slightly red, but it was becoming and she was smiling. Isn't that sweet? Chance it? Why not? At least, choose a good dialogue.

"Does that mean you'd be . . ."

She blushed.

The Record Ended. Rather abruptly, he thought.

"And now, here's a word from Ralph Walker at Walker Chevrolet." Tape in. Cue up another record before she has a chance to change her sweet little teenage mind and before you scare yourself out of your big grownup one. Ralph Walker socks it to 'em, as the pols say. That is, he tells his townsfolk how much he loves them, respects them, wants to screw them so that he can trade in his own Chevy for a Lincoln. Ralph fades; bring up the record without intro. Back to business.

"Well?"

"Gee!"

Gee! Gee! How can you screw a girl who says Gee in response to your subtle proposition? On the other hand, how can you not? You just don't find those kind every day. He looked up at the clock; not much show left, nobody around, I'll be locking up.

"Have you ever?"

Betty Sue lowered her head, her hair falling around her cheeks—but it was a pose, he could tell.

"Sometimes I fool around a little. But I never really Did It."

In a minute, she would apologize. As long as she could Say It, she would Do It. Golem lit a cigarette, offered the pack to Betty Sue as if she were standing in front of a firing squad. But she shook her head no (fuck, yes—smoke, no . . . the new morality) and then walked toward the console behind which he sat. Ah, as Ike once said, the Youth of America are really something.

Golem smiled, looked through the stack of 45s as nonchalantly as possible, and pulled out "Rhapsody in the Rain," a pimply melody of backseat love. He cued it up and looked straight into Betty Sue's eyes. "I'll dedicate this one to you, if you'd like."

Would I like? O Golly Gee Mister Golem!!!

He did and the deal was made.

"Come on over to my side of the board, Betty Sue."

Christ! He was ashamed of himself for that little gem, but it was too late to retract. Too late for everything. Play out the scene, all the way. Let the odors of sex have their chance to do battle against the perpetual currents of air conditioning. Screw her on the floor, with the mike open and the volume turned all the way up, with the echo chamber on so that the whole town would hear her scream. What a sign-off! This is Davey Allen, letting loose the nightline, saying good night, sleep tight, all right. What was that noise, Debby? Sounded like a scream. Oh, that Davey Allen . . . he's such a clown. That was no scream, lady; that was

241

no joke. That was IT. A first. Big Little WOGA gives you live, in color, a full-strength, clear channel, strong signal first fuck! Brought to you by the good folks down at Honest Ralph Walker's Chevrolet.

Betty Sue, Betty Sue. Oh, what's going to happen to you. Come over to my side of the board, baby, and I'll make you a radio star.

She came and he swung the chair back so that she could move closer to him.

Boil? What boil? This is Lust.

He patted his lap and she lowered herself to him. Ouch, he said to himself, suddenly remembering that he was a human and not an animal.

"Would you like to play a record? Spin a disc?"

"Could I?"

Sure.

"Sure."

Why not? A small form of mustache-twirling bribery, to be sure. She chose one from the stack, but he did not look at it for he did not believe her sensitive enough to make a symbolic choice. Maybe it was just an old favorite of hers. He helped her cue it, feeling like a decadent M-G-M tennis pro and then, his hand on hers on the dials, they segued from "Rhapsody in the Rain" to "Sock It to Me, Baby."

"Every time you kiss me,

It's like a fuck . . ."

The girl had a modicum of poetry in her soul. A modicum. He turned her face toward his and leaned into her. Their lips met with astonishment . . . how do *you* do! It was so abrupt. A kiss without feeling, i.e., romantic feeling, plenty of perversity, though. Plenty of that, all right. Don't you worry about that, nosir. He pushed his tongue at her and she opened her mouth slightly, letting him enter her for the first time. After a few moments of exploration, they separated.

"Do we Do It here?"

Why always in capitals?

"Why not?"

"But the radio . . ."

"The show'll be over in a few minutes. Couple more records and two spots."

"Can't we go somewhere?"

"Where?"

"Your apartment?"

"How would that look?"

She began to play with the buttons on her sweater; she was attempting a strategic withdrawal, uncertain as to what or how she should do.

"Look, if you don't want to . . ."

She looked up quickly. Of course she wanted to. "Please, I do." It would undoubtedly be the highlight of her teenage career. She would tell all the girls in Geometry. Guess what, Billy Jo, Lindy Lou? What? I Did It. You didn't! Yes I did. And with a Man. Oooooooo.

"OK, go over there and get undressed while I finish the show." He gestured to the windows.

"Over there?"

"Umhum."

"Can't I go to the little girl's room or something?"

"Nope. Over there. Where I can see you."

Said the big bad wolf.

She rose and turned toward the windows. As she began to walk away, Golem grabbed her leg, held it tightly, then relaxed his grip and slid his palm up her thigh to her ass. He pinched her, then patted her. "You'll like it," he said. Christ, I feel dirty, he thought. But what's sex without a little dirt?

He finished the program, introducing and cuing his records and spots as he watched Betty Sue undress. I'm making disc jockey history. No, even better, mythology. She stood against the windows without any clothes. A small body, frozen like the frame of a motion picture, caught between girlishness and some-thing close to womanhood. With his console of dials, switches, lights, in front of him, he felt like all the evil scientists that he had ever hoped to be; this was a pure vision. He wished he had a Doctor Pepper. He already had an erection.

She did not move, kept her arms at her sides, no attempt to hide her body now that the final agreement had been made. A stainless steel blond against the darkened windows outlined in aluminum.

This is what I should have been, he thought. I've been wasting my time trying to be a Ph.D. when all I am is a pervert. His feeling of power was so great that it gave him a headache; his temples throbbed with the thoughts of what he would do with this girl *after* he screwed her. What else? Kill her? Plug her into the console and electrocute her? Murder? Absolutely beautiful! Defenestration, decapitation, oh whoa, recapitulation . . . what's going on here?

Christ, I feel dirty.

It's good for a change. Get down there and grovel with the rest of humanity. Fuck like a hippopotamus.

He made his entry in his log book. He turned off the transmitter, but left the console on because they might want some music. He leaned back, lit another cigarette, contemplating his vision.

Betty Sue smiled.

Betty Sue, Betty Sue. Oh, what's going to happen to you?

"It's cold in here, Davey."

"Air conditioning."

"Can I come over there, now?"

Golem smiled.

"Please."

He grinned. She asked. Please, she said. What more could a man want to put him in touch with himself. An appropriate gesture is required; run through the catalog—got it!—extend hand, beckon with crooked index finger. Jesus Christ! She came. She would come.

Walked quickly over the cold, green, evenly spaced squares that were the floor, her body swaying slightly, her breasts-to-be already hard, a self-conscious thrust to her step. Reached the front of the console and extended her hand to meet Golem's. He caught it and pulled her forward, against her balance, against her grain, pulling her into contact with the metal barrier between them. Then he rose from his chair and leaned to kiss her quickly over the lights, the dials. Her breasts rested on the top of the console and Golem ran his hand across their surfaces.

Uhn, she said, against his mouth.

He smiled and broke away, pulling her around the board and into the space which he occupied, his territory.

"Want some music?"

"Whatever you say, Davey."

That's right.

No music. You will be screwed against a background of humming electronic instruments, of radio waves locked up for the night, of air conditioned whispers. Natural Sound.

He stood up and undressed. She closed her eyes until he had finished and, when he was naked, he opened her eyes with his hands, then took her hands and put them around his sex, his hard prick pointing at a place within her. The eyes closed again. Hands on her shoulders, he pushed her to a kneeling position so that his penis brushed against her forehead and then he stabbed it into her mouth. O. Betty Sue. Good for You. Lips open and the taste of a Man; mouth full, pull, baby, pull. I kissed Davey Allen's prick. Really, what's it like? Meat, only sweet. Will you ever be the same?

Come on, Golem. Fuck her and let's get on with it.

He grabbed her nipples and pulled her up from the floor, opened his mouth and sucked in first her lips and then her tongue, ran one hand down the front of her, the other down the back, meeting at her middle space and shaking hands with himself—a little comedy to break up the rape. Fingers raking through the hairs around her space, then palm across the opening until he felt her liquids begin to flow, her tide begin to change. First, the index finger on a quick foray into the area, exploratory; she moaned, but it was not unfamiliar. Then the thumb, pushing up to its base and moving in aborted circles. Uhn, uhn. Her sounds were strong, good sounds; a good woman some day. Then, with the thumb still inside, he pressed her up against the console, pulled her lower half toward him, pulled out his thumb, ran a liquid line up the center of her body as he stepped away, then came back, and, bending at the knees, moved into her, breaking her natural barrier, hearing her scream match the vibrations of the frustrated current, seeing her blood trail down her slim, clean legs, pushing up inside her body, inserting himself between her organs, reaching for her heart. Crying. She was crying. He did not listen.

Still inside, always inside, he shifted and arranged their bodies so that they both lay across the small desk space of the console; he pulled the microphone down to the side of her face and flipped up the Key, turning the Pot to full volume. The two huge speakers in the room sent their own sounds back to them. Reinforced her cries, his demanding breaths of sterile air, the squeaking noises that their bodies made as they rubbed together. All signal, no noise; great ratio. True transmission. A stereophonic screw; a high fidelity fuck.

Good evening Mr. and Mrs. America and all the ships at sea.

Come, Davileh, come. A bite for mother, a bite for father, a bite for Auntie Miriam.

Come, Golem, come. A stroke for mommy, a stroke for daddy, a stroke for Annie.

Oh, Betty Sue. Forgot about you.

Oh. Oh. Oh. Oh. Oh. She said.

"Right, baby. Come on." He said, into the microphone.

Always an audience.

Will it be a hit? Reach the top of the charts? Rising each minute, a red bullet by its side, higher up on the way to stardom, to immortality? A number one seller, a gold record fuck?

You Can't Hurry Love, said the Supremes. Do they know How Sweet It Is? Open the Door and Wade in the Water to hear the Heart's Symphony. Go Ahead and Cry, Cherry Cherry. Let Me in, Cinnamon; I think I'm going Out of My Head.

I Am the Walrus.

I Am The Golem.

I Am,

"Dear Lord, Godamighty, help me please I am being Fucked!" All around the room it rang, bouncing off corners, slipping out of the spaces between the floor tiles, flipping out the dials and the lights and ooh, ooh, Betty Sue, *this* is what's happening to *you* . . .

Golem came shortly after she did. It was not great; it was not what he expected, not a great rush of life dying to get outside of his body. Not what he expected considering the circumstances. It was clouded by anger, by fear, by paranoia, and by a guilt which buzzed behind his right ear like a mad wasp. It was there and it could be recorded, mechanically and electronically, but it would not be remembered. His nerve endings did their job, but did so like an untuned radio at near-full volume.

She was breathing heavily and her eyes were closed. He looked at her closely, probably for the first time. Her complexion was good, a few freckles on the bridge of her nose, two or three small blackheads near her hairline, the pores of her skin were small. What would she look like in, say, ten years? Would she remember him? Of course, nobody ever forgets their first fuck. Up on the mantelpiece it goes, enshrined and placed in an extravagantly decorative container. See it?

"Betty Sue?"

"Umm?"

"Well?"

"Umm?"

"Did you like it?"

She opened her eyes, smiled, and smiled, and smiled.

"I feel so scrunchy, Davey. You're so good. Can we do it again?"

Scrunchy.

He came out quickly, leaving her stranded on the console. Smacked her twice across the face, the smack going through the microphone like static, and she began to cry again. He picked her up and sat her down on Turntable 2, impaling her on the spindle which normally held records in place; he released the catch and the turntable began to move in its circle.

Golem grabbed his clothes and flicked on the ON AIR light, leaving her spinning in the control room and locking all the doors as he left the station, blood and disease dripping down his leg in small but unmistakable rivers of relief. The boil—da-da—had broken.

174   HARMON COLLIER IS A CUCKOLD
To Whom It May Concern
And to You Harmon,
I have been fucking your pretty little wife for something like three months now and I just wanted to leave you this note of appreciation. She's not bad, but she can't kiss. Teach her how when you get some

time. Anyway, while you've been assigning risks, I've been taking them. Now we are brothers.

Davey Allen

(The Golem)

II

175   Golem was on the lam again. On the lam, back in the saddle, home on the range. Car in the parking lot of the airport outside Atlanta. One hundred dollars worth of sheet metal and memory left between two yellow lines; his space. How long before they came to investigate at the request of the attendant—I've got an unidentified vehicle here, Joe . . . run a tracer on it for me, will you? He would be long gone when that happened. They would be after him, though. No doubt about it. If Betty Sue would kiss and tell, she would sure screw and holler. Raperaperape, statutory or not, that's trouble. Will have to, unquestionably, no doubt about it, get the hell out. Poor poet Golem arranging an ending for his scenario; look out Hollywood!

Not even a great lay—perversion doesn't pay.

I'll say.

But what was the initial error? Leaving Anna, leaving Lane, or just leaving? You've been gone too long, Bill Bailey.

But I want to come home, get undressed, jump into bed, and pull the covers up over my head. Where are the counterpanes of yesteryear, to say nothing of the metal soldiers? Gone, gone,

gone. You've done gone and got yo'self *involved*, committed, engaged. And it took a teenage twat to do it. Not war, not color, just a fuck. Look out, motha, 'cause we're going all the way back down the track to the old original organic trip.

Primal.

Was not the color of the airport; not even primary. Beige everywhere. Golem swung through the aluminum doors with his two suitcases in front of him, nothing but flight on his mind. Back to New York, Back to Momma, Back to Lane, Back to Anna, Back. I'll be a man, I'll be a man, he said to himself, basking in the glow of his newly discovered nugget of omnipotence, if it kills me. Think I'll let a bunch of broads run this boy out of town? Nosirreebob, Exclamation Point.

Up at the ticket counter where he rips open his shirt to expose his secret identity to the surrogate chick in uniform. What Time? Which Flight? What Gate? When Arrive? How Much? Why? (How'd that get in there?)

"Have a good trip, Mr. Golem."

"Thank you, sweetie," he said as he twirled the ends of that imaginary, but now worn, mustache. And laughed sinisterly under his bad breath.

Free of suitcases, but not of baggage, Golem surveys the interior of his container. He can Eat, Read, go to the Rest Room, or make a Public Telephone call. There is not a single person in this building who cares which one he does first, second, or at all. Aside, that is, from those who provide the Eat, the Pay Toilet, the Read, and the Pay Phone and their reasons for concern matter not to Golem. Strange; there are some people who care, but their care is dismissed. Can we afford that? I think I'll Call, Eat, Read, and Crap. That way, I can use each one as an excuse for the others.

176   "Hello, Annie?"

"Yes."

"This is your long-lost husband."

"Golem!"

"Right, baby. I'm on the lam and I'm flying into the Big Apple tonight. Meet me at mother's."

"David, you sound crazy."

"I'm ready to talk turkey, baby. Fly to New York tonight and meet me tomorrow."

"Why should I do that?"

"It may be your last chance."

"Are you all right, David?"

"I'm fine. Fit as a fiddle and mean, baby, mean."

"You sound like you're drunk."

"OK, Anna. I'm in Atlanta. I'm not drunk. I'll be in New York in the morning. Meet me there and we'll settle up."

"Settle up what?"

"Our lives. What else? Have you got the money?"

"I guess so. What'll I say to my parents?"

"Tell them I'm desperate. That I'm a desperado. Tell them you're going shopping at Saks."

"David, tomorrow is Yom Kippur."

"Holy Christ!"

That took him off the Bogart rap.

"David?"

"What?"

"Are you sincere?"

"Absolutely. Absolutely sincere. Meet me. Please."

"I don't know why I should."

"Because . . . we've loved each other."

". . . . . . ."

"I know it sounds corny. Look (if I have to, I will), I think I still love you."

"Thanks a bunch."

"Will you be there?"

"Maybe."

"That's not good enough."

"What do you want from me?"

"Say yes."

"All right. I'll come."

"Why?"

"Why?"

"Why?"

"Because I think I still love you."

Click. Humm.

No reason for that phone call. None. Absolutely no

reason. Why involve Anna? Why insist, carrying on like a lunatic, that she come? Still afraid, still holding on, still unwilling to let go? But why let go? Can you ever sleep with her again? That's what you really want to know, isn't it? Have you avenged your, what, honor? Was Betty Sue a human sacrifice to the pridegod of D. Golem? What the hell, you asked her to come and she's coming which means that you can still have her if you want her. Wonder if she's slept with anyone else since? That could be messy. Should have left her alone. Too late now.

Yom Kippur.

I couldn't have picked a better day if I was an astrologist. I'll ask for forgiveness, for mercy, for compassion. I'll ask, it'll be given. Never be afraid to ask; you get what you ask for. Uncomfortable feeling, however, knowing that I can walk into the synagogue and ask for mercy, be forgiven for anything except adultery. A Certified Sinner. Step right up and look into the eyes, the glazed eyes, of one who knows, absolutely knows in advance that he ain't agonna be spending Eternity Up There. How does it feel to be one of the beautiful people? To be excommunicated without trial? You threw away your soul with that first fuck (What was her name: Eve?) and no matter what you do about any of those little sins, no matter how much you whine and plead and promise, you can forget it, brother. I am a Sinner. Don't be silly, this is the Twentieth Century. We're all guilty. Remember the New Morality —who's the wise ass that coined, patented, invented that phrase? This is the Twentieth Century. The century of reaction-formation, of sublimation, of automation. Don't tell me about mankind, this is the Era of Paranoia, the Time of the Ego. Each man his own Messiah.

God is Dead! Long Live the GODS!

Step through the turnstiles of megalomania.

Hitler was limited by his technology. Now Watch!

177   "Piece a pie, please."

"What kind?"

"What kind do you have?"

"Apple, blueberry, cherry, pecan, sweet potato, and cheese".

"Apple, with vanilla ice cream."

Sitting next to travelers and off-duty airport service people at the coffee counter. Nothing like the old train stations; no room for darkness, for what time do you get off, honey, for buddy, can you spare a shoeshine secrets. Everything's in the open in an airport, as it should be. Air everywhere and not a drop to breathe. Lights without switches, floors without footsteps; a space to wait in. Filled with the kind of white noise quiet that you can order from the back page of the *Times* Sports Section or from the middle pages of *Signature*, the magazine of the Diners' Club. Buy your own noise, your own silence, your own piece of peace. And what if you haven't got $9.98 this week? Are you to be forbidden that bit of technological tranquility? Certainly not. We are all civilized here. Charge it, sir. Run my numbered piece of plastic through your machine and send me a statement on which will be computyped PEACE AND QUIET (1), FORGIVENESS (3), SALVATION (2)—the parenthetical figures representing the units of grace, of merchandise rather, purchased by, forwarded to, consumed by the customer. Send me a STATEMENT.

178   Feet under this one.
Feet under that one.
No Feet.
Insert 10¢

(Is it really because you want to find out if you can sleep with her again? Is that why Lane, why JoAnna, why Betty Sue? Why you and Harmon are brothers? Pompous note, that. What are your limits? What's it like to sleep with a wife who's slept with another man? Is there any real difference? Will you cut out that romantic self-pity crap, this is the Twentieth Century.)
For Privacy.
Occupied!

179   "He made me do it, Sheriff."
Poor Betty Sue, crying controllably in the control room, covered by interested parties. Mom in a corner by a speaker knowing it would come to this. Dad, just off the second shift, hands still dirty, head choked with the knowledge, the fact that his daughter had been screwed—and not by him. Poor Betty Sue. What's going to happen to you? And Golem thinks he has problems.

"Take two men and pick him up, Ben."

"Right, Sheriff."

The posse is after the Golem. But he is white, Jewish, middle-class, and on the toilet. They won't get him.

"Now, Betty Sue, honey, tell me again how it happened," says the Sheriff, panting for details.

180   "I have to go."

"I don't understand."

"It may be our last chance."

"Your last chance?"

"That's what he said."

"But do you want another chance?"

"I don't know, but I have to go."

181   Golem boards his flight on its last call, taking a seat behind the wing so that he can see the flames from the engines on the propjet and worry about whether or not they are supposed to be on fire. Read? No, thank you. I'll think this one out. What has *Time* or *Life* got for me? If I'm caught, maybe I'll make their cover. Who knows what's going on in Odessa now? Wonder if they're questioning Lefkowitz, if they've traced the car, if they're going to meet me at the airport in New York? Doubt it. Small town, small people. It'll take a while and I can hire a good lawyer to get me off if it comes to that. Poor Betty Sue. The urgency is, however, refreshingly external as opposed to being the same old self-induced shit. A real problem, like not being able to fuck any more, hoho.

Can't stay at home (home?) tonight. Nor at Lane's. I'll check into the airport motel and go into the city in the morning. They'll be at the synagogue and I can meet them there. Do the prodigal son bit under the best of circumstances, in the best possible atmosphere. I'll confess to everything.

182   "Did you know him?"

"Yes. I knew him."

"What was he like?"

"It's hard to say, exactly."

"Did you ever think he'd . . ."

"Never. That is, not really."

"You mean . . ."

"Well, with him, anything was possible, you know."

"Oh."

183   Are you still with me?

So far.

It's been a long haul.

You're not kidding.

Lots of interruptions.

Right.

I won't apologize, though.

All right. But I'm waiting.

Are you ready?

Of course, I'm ready. That's an asinine question.

Is it?

Of course it is.

We'll see.

184   The countryside is black beneath him. A light here and there, but nothing significant, nothing to match the blue engine flames. The plane moves through the blank as if it were flying against a process screen, making the film appear, as if by magic, three dimensional. Would you care for a cocktail, sir? No, thank you. The seat next to him is empty; he takes the plastic sign out of the compartment in the seat in front of him and places it on the cushion. OCCUPADO.

185   Pause.

It is obvious, now, that Golem is headed for some kind of dramatic confrontation. We're all adults and so we know that. Right? OK. Now, the trick is to keep everyone involved and to somehow move them toward this same moment of necessary action. Right? Right. That's what it's all about.

OK. In order to do this, we're taking the liberty of enclosing a few forms which we'd like you to fill out. The first is rather simple and the others, which you will find at intervals among the next several pages, are a bit more complex. We might as well admit that they are all part of a test which was devised by a team of scientists working together in a secret, bomb-proof mountain hideaway somewhere in the Mojave desert and their intent is to help you maintain the proper perspective with regard to what promises to be a rather difficult situation. Hopefully, they will also tell you a bit about yourself, though we have not bothered to provide an interpretive key in an anticlimactic appendix.

Now, this whole thing may seem like an imposition at first. But please, bear with us.

Go and get yourself a pencil.

Come on.

All right. When TIME is called, fill in the form found below. This is not a gimmick or a cheap trick; it is a necessary part of this theatrical genre. We repeat: This Is Not a Gimmick!

TIME
APPLICATION FOR IDENTIFICATION PURPOSES ONLY

Name:

Address:

City: State: Zip:

Age: Sex:

Marital status: M. S. D. W. Sep.

Religious affiliation:

Occupation:

Approx. annual income:

Children: Number:

Will some one read this book after you have finished it?

Height: Weight: Race:

Hair color: Eye color:

Identifying marks or characteristics:

Do you carry life insurance?

    Amount:

Do you own an automobile?

Do you own a television set?

Do you believe in God?   Which One?

APPLICANT— DO NOT MARK IN THIS SPACE.
FOR DATA BANK USE.
1. A-M N-T U-Z
2. A B C D
3. A B C D
4. A B
5. A B C D E
6. A B
7. A B C
8. A B
9. A B
10. A B C D
11. A B C
12. A B C D E

Now put down your pencil (but keep it handy) and continue.

Thank you.

186   "Sheriff, this is Ben."

"What've you got?"

"Bad news. Our pigeon has flown the coop. He's gone; cleared out a little while ago. Everything's been taken outa here."

"No ideas where he went to?"

"No information here."

"Shit."

"I got one thing, though. I don't know if it's anything much."

"Give it to me."

"Neighbor says he was friends with the Old Jew who owns the cigar store."

"Leffy?"

"Right. Figure he's worth talking to?"

"Why not. Go wake him up."

187   Betty Sue, in an old plaid bathrobe, sat in the kitchen with her mother. Daddy had gone to bed, not knowing what to say and so he said that three or four times and then went to bed knowing that his life had changed without allowing him to get a word in edgewise. Children! That's what they do to you. But mother sat with Betty Sue and they played.

"Can I have a glass of milk, Momma?"

"Sure, dear."

She got up and went to the noisy refrigerator, taking a plastic, no-wax-taste carton of milk from the shelf. She brought it to the counter beneath the blond cabinets and opened its lips. Then she got a big jelly glass down from the glassware section of the cabinets. As she poured the milk, she said, "Now darlin', I know what you've been through and I don't want to make you even more miserable, but there is one thing I'd like to ask you. You don't have to answer if you don't want to, you understand."

"That's all right, Momma. What is it?"

"Did it, uh, feel good?"

Betty Sue didn't answer for a moment or two and the milk hung in the air between the carton and the glass. She smiled to herself and wrapped the bathrobe tighter around that which was definitely now her body.

"Yes."

"Damn!"

188   "One way or round trip?"

"Uh, better make it one way, I guess. I don't know exactly when I'll be coming back."

"All right. If you'll wait just a moment, I'll have this confirmed for you."

"Thank you."

189   ". . . for flying Eastern."

You're welcome, he thought as the plane entered its landing pattern. You are entirely welcome. If we make it down, it all begins again. I can't possibly walk out the door now. Not on Erev Yom Kippur. Suicide is irrelevant, anyway. That's not what I'm here for. There are very few, pitifully (perhaps) few existential suicides—unless one accepts the broadest possible meaning of the term. What is there in Death that is meaningful if it is not simply the absence of Life? The underlying theme of reversal—reversal in the psychopathology of everyday life—forbids that kind of simple resolution, prevents it from being a *valid* form of resolution. Look at me. I started out as a comic villain and I'm being turned into an unwilling tragic hero.

Feeling sorry for yourself again, Golem?

Get off my back, will you!

Tsk, tsk, tsk.

Look, nobody says that any more. So just can it, OK? Save your stinking value judgments for later, for after I figure out what I'm going to do. You owe me that.

I don't owe you anything.

All right, not *owe*. But it's my right, as a human. Like Aristotle said, I make decisions.

You haven't been doing a very good job.

Look, all the facts, all the fantasies, all the clues and all the concepts haven't come in yet, so you don't have any right—

well, I suppose you do have a right, but it wouldn't be a valid judgment because it would be based on a pretty limited sample. So do what you want, but keep off my back.

Don't call us, we'll call you. Is that the idea?

You got it, buddy.

My, my.

Getting faggoty again?

NO SMOKING—FASTEN SEAT BELTS

That's a hell of a trick, using a machine to interrupt our conversation.

I'm not taking any more of your bull.

I've heard that line before.

190   While Golem sleeps, nude, in a room which has been printed rather than constructed, the color static-flecked television set tuned to no particular channel aimed at his head so as to provide some link between his isolation and that of the universe, Anna flies across the country. Knowing only that "some part of her" (though she can identify neither the precise part nor even its general location) loves, or, at least, throws up signals resembling a feeling which she once had and called, named, love, her husband. Anna in the sky with rhinestones that she hopes, via the magic of some kind of alchemic confrontation, will be emotionalized rather than rationalized into the precious gems of reconciliation.

A last chance, he had said, and, perhaps, it was. She had had enough nights of crying, of eye-watering remembrances of things past, things lost, things forgotten. Enough nights of fear that the center of her had escaped. Enough nights of wondering, of self-pity, of self-accusation. Enough nights. She would know; they would settle, he had said. Yes or No. On or Off. She had learned that from her husband. What else had she learned? L'affaire Cohen was practically forgotten—the event lost in a battle between cause and effect. Had she actually done it? There were times when she felt that Golem had manufactured the event as an excuse for his own actions. Or, she would say, he drove me to it. And hope that, if that were not the truth, it would at least be sufficient.

What would the meeting be like? He had been bad to her, they would agree. She had been bad to him, they would agree.

It would be Yom Kippur and they would agree to confess and to forgive. What could he say that would make her love him again? Would please, let's try again be enough? And even if that were enough, would it be so because she genuinely needed him or only because she felt temporarily adrift?

The difference seemed significant, but perhaps it was not. We survive because we want to survive. Do we love because we want to love? Why not? Is it chemistry or is that just another Pascalian wager, a hopeful projection of some discovery in the future which we might use to rationalize our actions in the present? God is Love. God is Dead. Is Love Dead? Has it been replaced by an I'll love you if you love me ideology or is that really a replacement? Is love not just an infatuation strengthened by commitments from both sides, commitments made nearly by accident which, like cheap color 'lithographs of Jesus Christ with eyes that mysteriously follow you about the room, hang on the walls of our mental living-rooms to challenge and inhibit our privacy? Can one be a technological Romantic and, if one can, what could be worse? That love grows after the first encounter is simply an excuse for keeping the promises one makes to oneself about the unacceptability of loneliness. Then love is an escape from loneliness, a technique for making the possibility, no, the inevitability, of death a bit more palatable. Let's grow old together so that I won't have to die alone. Somebody has to hear my last words, feel the heat in my last breath. Man is man because he invented love, which is only another mechanism for disguising his basic neurosis, the fear of death. Reason is another mechanistic excuse, the bride of the Devil, as it were.

If he wants me, Anna thought as she looked out the window, seeing her own reflection cast upon the starred night, I'll probably go back to him. Probably? Well, I have no one else. I can try again for a while, but he must ask. He must make the first move. Perhaps that's what the telephone call was, the first move. The strategies of interpersonal relationships are ridiculous, but what else do we have on which to spend our time, to which to give our meanings, around which to create our respective universes?

191 Lefkowitz thought they were Storm Troopers. The banging on his glass door continued beyond the point at which he could have dismissed it as a part of his dream. "All right, all right," he shouted as he rose from the bed, rubbed his eyes, hurriedly stepped into his pants, and picked up his bedroom slippers. "All right, all right, I'm coming," he shouted at the banging. He threw his magazines under his pillow and rushed to the door which led to the store. From a small desk-table in the hallway, he took a .22 caliber pistol. It was not much, but he had never had any trouble before. Still, this Jew would not be quietly shuffled off to his death, not in America.

192   Mrs. Irving Glazer, 67, widowed, her blue-steeled hair entwined in a mesh of nylon, manufactured static electricity while she slept, dreaming of the young Cuban who had waited on her table the last time she was in Miami with Nat, he should rest in peace, her late husband. In her closet, deep within the camphorous smog of the mothballs hung in a corner, was the chocolate brown suit with fox collar that she would wear to the synagogue tomorrow when she apologized for her dreams.

193   Karen Cohen, 19, home from college for the holy day, finished the letter that she had been writing to her new boyfriend, the Revolutionary Standards Committee Chairman of the Black Student Movement on her campus. She had told him that, even though she was white and middle-class, she believed that Black was Beautiful, and she had implied that she would be willing to spend a weekend with him when she returned to school. She signed the letter Love & Peace, Karen . . . knowing that the emphasis was on the former and that the latter had been misspelled. She thought of his black body and shuddered; we must all make sacrifices for the future, she decided.

194   "I tell you the truth, I wish he was dead," said Milton Gable to his wife as he stood in his underwear at the door to the bathroom.

"Milton, on Erev Yom Kippur?"

"God forgive me, but the man is driving me crazy. Everything I say, he says the opposite. For spite. Just for spite. We used to be friends; now we're partners and enemies."

"That's an old Jewish saying, Milton."

"Helen, I swear to you that that man wants to see the business go bankrupt. He is intent on destroying me."

The business, a small tie manufacturing company, provided Milton Gable with enough time and money to make those kinds of judgments. If it were gone, he would have no excuse for his balding head, his potting stomach, and his endemic constipation. No excuses at all.

195   Beatrice Golem had not heard from her son since she had hung up on him. She had considered saying Kaddish for him, no longer a son of mine, a dead man, but that would be disgraceful. Tonight, she wished he would come home. She had difficulty sleeping, took two capsules from a bottle which described her condition as one of "nerves," and hoped for the best. Why had this happened to her? What had she done to deserve this kind of treatment from her son? Nothing. No one ever does anything. Children are all the same. Ungrateful.

196   Defocus gradually from tight close-up of Golem's closed eyes. Refocus on . . .

Golem and Anna (shot from camera position in back seat) sitting in the front seat of a new, red Buick with black vinyl interior. Golem is driving, going rapidly down a dangerously winding mountain road, mountains on one side, the sea on the other, a Kodakian view of the California coast, all blues and browns. The car is swerving, moving back and forth across the dotted white line as if it were in some deep competition with it.

"Is it me in the car?"

"Well, except for that stretch where you were doing ninety miles an hour, nothing happened," they answered.

The car stops in front of a huge, baroque country club, the road having been a driveway, after all. Anna and I get out, climb a long flight of marble stairs, push past two bronze doors that move at our touch as if they were made of balsa wood. Inside now, we see that the ballroom facing the entrance is crowded with people in costume, dancing in an obvious imitation of a scene from a Fellini movie.

"Say, this must be the masquerade party scene."

Quick as a flash (FLASH), I change from my sweater and blue jeans to a costume. What am I wearing? Another quick change to another costume. Still, I can't see what I'm wearing; I can only see my back.

"My death is imminent."

"Is that so?" they say.

I leave Anna to fend for herself. Walk into another room, this one smaller and filled with people in costumes of the Victorian era. Another masquerade party, I decide, and walk over to a young lady whose breasts are exposed. I pinch one red nipple and look over each of my shoulders, suspiciously. In a far corner, I see a young girl, college age, no costume, sweater and skirt, taking notes. She is from a Creative Writing Course.

Tiring, I leave the room, change back to my sweater and blue jeans, buy a package of cigarettes from a vending machine and find myself back in the car with Anna. Now she is driving and I am sitting in the back. I notice that the steering wheel is located on the right-hand side and catch myself wondering whether or not we are in another country.

No, no, we are stopping at a good old American traffic light. A red traffic light. Suddenly, there are two policemen beside us, the kind of cops you thought were nice to kids who brought their bicycles into the police station on Saturday morning for registration and safety instruction (ride with or against traffic?). One is very nice looking, in a redheaded Irish sort of way; he asks for Anna's license which she shows him after taking it from beneath her blouse. Then he is in the car, sitting next to Anna, and the other one, whose features are undiscernible, opens the door next to her and gestures for her to move over. She does. Anna is trapped in the front seat between two cops and I am alone in the back seat. I rummage through my pockets for some identification, but I have none. I cannot prove myself. The Irish cop hands the license back to Anna, saying, "I see your doctor is Dr. Serofin."

They drive the car away from the light as if they were going there and we do not resist.

He drives the car carefully through what appears to be a small, midwestern city and stops in front of a liquor store.

"Listen, man," I say from my position in the back, "last time we were stopped and went through this with an Officer, everything was OK. Has the law changed?"

Somewhat embarrassed, he turns around to face me and puts on his flashlight. "Let's cut this conversation short."

"Look," I say, "I don't want to get into a whole thing, but after all. . . ."

They are gone. Before I can finish the thought. Replaced by another man; this one is bearded, wearing a blue suede jacket and a yellow bush hat with a zebra band around the base of the crown, and he gets into the back with me, unzips his jacket, and pulls out a gun. I realize that this is going to be a holdup.

The redheaded cop now reappears beside the car; he reaches for his gun, brown with a blue plastic handle, withdraws it from his rubber holster, and tries to cock it, but it is so powerful that he must use both hands.

"Listen, baby," I say, "I don't want you to shoot me."

Again he is embarrassed. His hands blush.

"So it's a holdup. But why us? This isn't my bag. I don't know anything about it. I'm not even famous."

The bearded guy next to me unzips his jacket again and takes out three half-pint bottles of an off-brand bourbon. "You know about these. Your daddy must've bought them."

I don't want to go through the "my daddy doesn't drink" changes, so he leaves the plot.

Right away, I sense that they're going to kill us. It is one of those impossible situations that the movies are so fond of bringing to the hearts and heads of America—desperate hours, petrified forest, key largo, etc. But the redheaded cop says that maybe he'll let us transport them if everything goes smoothly. I see through that; I am not taken in. I know my life is at stake, so I try to think of a way out, a plan of escape. Since I'm supposed to go into the store and give the owner a note explaining why the holdup, I figure to write HELP—WE'RE PRISONERS on the reverse side. But I don't have a pencil and I'm afraid to ask for one.

I'm scared shit. Obviously, they'll kill Anna if I screw up. Then I wake up, trying to think of a plan, maybe turn the car over while I'm driving, except I'm in the back seat. A plan. What

is my art? Keep your cool, I'm going back to sleep. I may get shot.
Anna may get shot.

197   Pick up your pencil again.

TIME

APPLICANT'S PERSONALITY INVENTORY

Below, you will find ten statements describing feelings that
people have about themselves from time to time. Mark each statement
T or F, depending upon how close it comes to describing a feeling you
have or have had about yourself. Do not omit any feelings. T counts
5; F counts 8.

1. I sometimes feel like a secret agent of God.   T F
2. I am sometimes worried about my sexual potency.   T F
3. I am sometimes troubled by my lack of concern for
   others.   T F
4. I am sometimes troubled by my lack of concern for
   myself.   T F
5. I have wished for the death of a close relative, spouse,
   and/or friend.   T F
6. I have wished for the death of a stranger.   T F
7. I have wished for my own death.   T F
8. I don't think that sex is all it's cracked up to be.   T F
9. I have wished to be a person of the opposite sex.   T F
10. I am sometimes troubled by God's inhumanity to man.   T F

TIME

Put down your pencil and begin reading. Keep in mind,
however, that there will be one more interruption of this nature.

198   Golem awoke.

The television set was on. A game show that he had not
seen before, some part of the second season he supposed, or was
this the beginning of the first? He had not been keeping up with the
mass media. He rubbed his eyes and picked up the phone to order
some breakfast. Then he realized that it was Yom Kippur and he
made a quick decision to fast, to deny himself food for this day in
accordance with the traditions of the religion, to purify himself.

Whether he owed it to God or to himself, he was not certain, but he would be hungry today and he would know what his stomach felt like. But someone, some desk clerk, picked up the phone at the other end. Golem stuttered and asked for, what, the Time? The Time. It was 10:07. "Thank you," he said quietly, and then hung up.

He would have to hurry. It would take him an hour and a half to get home. But no one would be home. His mother would be in the synagogue, praying, perhaps, for his return. Good. He would leave his suitcases at the apartment and then walk to the shul. He would surprise her there, maybe provide an instant answer to her prayers. Anna would probably be there also. Waiting. Not knowing what to expect. Who did, nowadays? Who knew what to expect with things the way they were? Lefkowitz didn't expect him. Betty Sue didn't expect him. Nobody expected him. "I don't even expect myself," he said to the Host of the game show, who did not reply. But then, Golem did not expect an answer.

They'll be after me soon, he thought, but they don't know what to expect. Hiphiphooray! It's the revolution of absent expectations!

199   The taxi stopped in front of his mother's building. The street was quieter than usual; some of the stores were closed and relatively few people sat outside on their stoops, few children rode bicycles up and down the sidewalk, the vocalized engines of their minds competing with the shouted testimonies of fear and care which came from the young/new mothers. Normally a street whose inhabitants lived perched on the edge of hysteria as if it were just another step on the staircases or stoops of their lives, it was quiet now because of the holiday. The Jews were in shul. Only the Italians, the Puerto Ricans, the Gentiles, remained to occupy the territory and they seemed a bit fearful, not unlike the way Jews feel on Christian holidays. Perhaps it is a fear that God, whatever his name may be, is somewhere else today.

The sun was out and the sky was as bright as it should be on a holiday. No helicopters in the air carrying a posse from Odessa, no mysterious black sedans parked nearby. Nothing to make one believe that anything was different today. Golem gave the driver, Vincent J. Probiscus, a quarter tip. Vincent thanked him, said haveaniceday, and then turned back to the wheel while Golem pulled his two suitcases out of the back seat. Then the cab drove away and Golem stood on the sidewalk, alone again.

200   They had asked Lefkowitz where he might be and Lefkowitz had asked them why. Some trouble with a girl, they said. What kind of trouble? Just trouble. It must be bad for you to wake me up in the middle of the night. It's bad. He didn't hurt nobody, did he? Now that depends on how you look at it, Leffy, one of them had said and then the three of them laughed and laughed, laughed the way his customers laughed at the dirty pictures, keeping one hand in their pockets. Well, I don't know where he is. C'mon, you old Jew, we know you were a friend of his. Was he a Jew too? We know how you and your kind stick together. Lefkowitz had studied their faces and then looked at his gun which he had put down on the counter. Then he told them that Golem, though that was not the name he had given them, was from a small town in Colorado, the name of which he could not, for the life of him, remember, but thought that it began with an S. They thanked him, apologized, and left.

Today, he sat in one of the chairs at the back of the store. He knew that it was Yom Kippur, but he had never closed on a Jewish holiday and he was afraid to do so now. Two Jews make an argument, trouble. Feh! He got up, put down his Doctor Pepper, and went to the door. He closed it and pulled down the CLOSED shade. Shaded. CLOSED. I won't tolerate fear, he thought, not this kind of fear.

201   "I'm home," he said, but nobody answered. He pushed the door aside and brought his suitcases into the livingroom, snapped on the television set, and sat down on the couch. Lit a cigarette, saw no ashtray, and went into the kitchen to get one. Then came back.

"I'm here," he said.

"And now a message of importance," it said.

But nobody answered.

Maybe I should just wait here. Nah. I'll go. Make everybody happy. I choose to go; I choose to choose. What have I chosen today? It could be life, death, madness, sanity. All my life I have chosen sanity. Has that choice been right, true, good? What did I choose this morning? Abstractions. I chose not to have breakfast; I chose to come. I choose to go.

He called the airport to find out if the flight that he guessed Anna would be on had arrived yet. It was reported in two hours late so she would not be at the synagogue but she would be here when he got back. That's all right. First I'll confess to God and then to my wife. What are my sins? Why bother to catalog them, they're all written down for you to enunciate. After all, it is not man who defines sin, is it? Or is it? What is sin if you do not believe in some kind of eternal punishment? It becomes a "guideline," at most, perhaps, a potential absolute. But what is a potential absolute? Nothing but a fear which we use to avoid certain aspects of life. Destruction of the community? Another possible. So what? If we are all alone, what difference does it make whether we are alone together or separately? Is there really some kind of mystical security to be had in a group existence or is that security available only to the individual on the basis of accepting his own consequences? The individual, then, is the only absolute. Shoddy, perhaps. Unfortunate, perhaps. Melodramatic, perhaps. But unavoidable. Nothing has meaning except for the meaning which we ascribe to it, by naming it. Shoddy, unfortunate, solipsistic, but—still—the operational definition of our times. We are all Adams, all Golems.

Yet, one doesn't choose life. Life is thrust upon one and one may choose to continue or not—but haven't we been through this before?

I choose to go.

Therefore, I rise from my place in front of the television set and go into my mother's bedroom to look for my father's talis. I will wear it for it is a high holy day (and a pretty significant secular day, as well). Would he, wherever his soul may reside, in whomever it may breathe, appreciate this symbolic act if he were alive? We attribute much to those who are dead, much more than would be acceptable during their period of life. Myth. Golem's the name; Myth's the game.

APPLICANT'S MYTH QUOTIENT INDICATOR

Pick up your pencil and mark the appropriate answer.

1. All great novels are about:
  a. Love and Death
  b. God and Man
  c. Current Events of Historical Significance

2. This novel is about:
  a. Love and Death
  b. God and Man
  c. Current Events of Historical Significance
  d. All of the Above
  e. None of the Above

3. Fiction is:
  a. Thinly Disguised Truth
  b. Stranger than Fact
  c. A Lot of Crap

4. An artist is:
  a. Just Like You and Me
  b. A Weird Commie Homosexual Dope Fiend
  c. An Interesting Person and a Warm Human Being
  d. A Mytherfucker

5. Golem's hair is:
  a. Brown
  b. Black
  c. Blue

6. The ending of this novel will be:
  a. Happy
  b. Poignant
  c. Sad but True
  d. None of the Above

7. If I had it to do over again, I would choose:
  a.
  b.
  c.

8. I would like this novel to end:
  a. Soon

b. *Happily*
c. *Poignantly*
d. *Sadly but Truthfully*

TIME

TIME

Well, now, dat Golem, dat brer Golem, he go into his momma's bedroom and what do he find but fear an' hisself. Nothin' else. He see de bed dat his momma and his poppa dey use to sleep in an' he wonder how it was dat dey cl ɔose to make him an' he wonder if maybe de whole ting weren't some kinda funny acciden' like love.

An' he is a little 'fraid 'cause he 'member de time dat he go alookin' tru his poppa's chest an' he come across a set a real, bona fide, genuine Dirty Pitcher Playin' Cards Complete wit Men wit Mustaches just alayin' it into de backsides of a couple a honeys in Mack Sennett smiles an' he 'member dat he was mighty scared when he found 'em. Mighty scared dat his poppa would catch him with dose Dirty Pitcher Playin' Cards and den bof of deɯ would know dat dey bof knew about de fuckin' business.

An what would his momma say?

(Don't tell me there are no spades in this theater.)

Ooo-eee! But she would be mighty upset to learn dat her one good an' only son had found out about de fuckin' business from de Dirty Pitcher Playin' Cards dat her an' her sweet daddy used to look at before dey made a little lovin', just to stir up dem old sweet juices, a course, no serious dirty perversion stuff, a course. A course, a course. Ooo-eee!

Well, now. Dat Golem, dat brer Golem.

Went to the closet where he knew there was a cardboard box that contained some of his father's things. The things, personal effects, that hadn't been stored, or sold, or given away. And he assumed that the talis would be there. He pushed aside his mother's dresses, taking, perhaps, a moment to inhale her aroma, to check it against the aromas of the other women he had known, found the box, and pulled it out of the closet, moving a group of her shoes as he did so. It was not heavy and he picked it up and brought it to the center of the bed where he set it down.

Well, now, Mister Time.

He looked at it before opening it. All that was left of his father. That box, his memory, and that of his mother. Mortal? Ephemeral, for chrissakes. Absolutely temporary. Why such a big fuss?

He opened the box and let the odor of old must, old mist, old Mister Golem escape into the bedroom. Inside, he found two pairs of tan, perforated shoes (laces missing), four wide, hand-painted ties, three books (*The Brothers Karamazov*—Surprise!— *Successful Salesmanship,* and a worn prayer book with no front cover), half a dozen leather wallets which locked as though they had never seen the insides of anybody's back pocket, a gold pocket watch and chain (set at 11:00), a package of sepiaed photographs held together by a rubber band, his own high school yearbook, a— so that's where it was!—bicycle horn, three moth-eaten sweaters, a black leather address book (Any women inside? Did his father have any affairs? What father doesn't?), a smaller box containing three tie clips, one key chain, two silver dollars, four pennies, two and a half pairs of cufflinks, a once silvered but now tarnished pistol, two turtledoves, and a partridge in a pear tree.

What?

A once silvered but now tarnished pistol. Where in hell did he get that? And kept it, yet? What other Jewish man in Brooklyn kept a gun in his home? Golem looked at it closely. Then he took it out of the box, finding it heavy, turning it in his hand, examining its history. Looks like a Mauser or a Luger or something like that. Where in hell would his father get a German gun? He was never in the war. Any war. Ah, my uncle, not Jacob, the other one. Right. Golem remembered the scene now. He had given it to him as a souvenir, a memento, a prize, a treasure taken by one cancered relative in the heat of battle to be given to another and, now, to still another.

"I claim this weapon," Golem said aloud.

Why? Why not? Don't register guns, register Commies. Let old men keep their guns to protect America. No talis, though. No talis inside either box. What could have happened to it; who wore it now? Or was he buried with it, in it? Check into that; an interesting custom. A gun instead of a talis. I won't be taken alive, Father Flotsky. Come on in and get me, warden. I'm not going back to stir. I don't care how sore Betty Sue's little cunt is, I won't do TIME for fucking. Fantasy!

But what if they do come after me?

Shit, I'll get off.

Sure?

Of course.

Better take it. Just in case.

To the synagogue?

Who'll know?

Who do you think?

He won't mind.

How do you know?

Who else would know?

Yeah. All right. What the hell. It'll be dramatic as shit when I show it to Anna. She'll flip, absolutely flip. The rod, the old equalizer, my heater. Stick in the belt, wish I had an under-arm holster. Christ, it's heavy. Pull down my pants and the gun fall out when I get up to pray. What a scene that would be! "Yonder stands your orphan with his gun." And his trousers down around his knees. If I go, I'll take seven of you with me. I'm a deadeye dick shot, eight bars from the NRA and a marine medal for marksmanship. Think it over. Give me a car and a broad and I'll disappear. I'll be an outlaw. Hooha!

Golem turns around, sees by the radio alarm clock on his mother's night table that it is time to go, knows that he has one last chance. Take it or not. Why not take it; afraid that you'll use it? Can't you control yourself? Isn't that what I've been doing? Don't you trust yourself? There's something about a gun, just the metal presence of it that is absolutely irresistible, an awesome sense of potential power, perhaps. Potential energy. Even if you don't use it, you know that you can. A very appropriate act for Yom Kippur; deny oneself not only sustenance, but also the power over sustenance. Take it.

All right.

He does.

"Why do I live my life as though it would be history?" he asks himself as he leaves.

204   Golem walks quickly down the streets of his life toward the synagogue. Not looking, barely thinking, aware only that he is going. He arrives. Stands in front of the building for a few moments and then goes inside where he borrows a yarmulke and a talis and follows the shammes into the room where the congregation is going through the motions of metaphoric confession, down the aisle until he arrives at a row of pews in which his mother is seated. There is an empty space next to her and she is wearing black. Faces turn toward him. He whispers excuse me and legs are pulled back so that he can pass. His mother looks up at the intruder and her eyes open widely in astonishment, she seems about to shout oi gevalt. Golem smiles and reaches her place.

"David!"

"Hello."

"David!"

"Sorry I'm late."

"Shh," somebody says.

Golem leans toward his mother and kisses her on the cheek, feeling her worried skin against his lips. "Good yuntov. We'll talk later."

She does not know what to say, what to do. Her verbal reactions are limited by the atmosphere. She has been given no choice.

"Anna's coming, too."

"You'll be together?"

"Maybe."

"Oi, thank God."

"Shh," somebody says.

Who?

And the service continues. The congregation stands, then sits. Some sway with the rhythms of their prayers, others bend in boredom; some ask, some plead, some command. Each is alone with his unique vision of Godhead. Golem watches them, wishing that he could see inside their heads, to see what images are projected upon their screens. Is it an old man in white robes with a long beard? Is it a word, in boldface, **GOD**, or, perhaps, **NA-TURE?** What is their image and from where does it come? This is the generation before him, two, three generations before him; the people who made the rules for his life, made those rules without knowing who or what Golem was. Know Before Whom Thou Standest. The people who made the rules, even without knowing that they were making them. Society existing, feeding on its own private delusions. Perpetuating itself in public while denying itself in private. Hypocrisy? No. The issue is much larger than that convenience. With what meanings are they content? None, all, some? God gives meaning to their lives, they explain. But who gives meaning to God? Just another circle, just another reversal?

"Please rise . . ."

Our sins. Neatly packaged, listed on three pages. Read aloud. A little box of surprises, gift wrapped by The Man Himself and delivered once a year to earth by a winged messenger. Gift wrapped, satin bowed, contained in a larger cardboard container, brown, air mail, marked PERSONAL * DO NOT OPEN UNTIL YOM KIPPUR. This is what we did wrong this year and, yet, this is what we do wrong every year. It is, after all, just another circle. We insist upon perpetuating all our old meanings, and call that cowardly act necessary for the preservation of our sanity. Oh, change a word here and there, true. But what is a word, if *the* Word means so little? "Thou knowest the mysteries of the universe and the hidden secrets of all living."

Rise. Confess. Beat your breast; polished fingernails against the holiday suit, the gesture a mockery of itself. Forgive us for we have sinned. We have sinned compulsively. We have sinned of our own will. We have sinned knowingly and we have sinned unknowingly. We have sinned through word, through deed, through thought, openly, or secretly. Forgive us; we have been unchaste, we have hardened our hearts, we have had evil inclinations. Forgive us for we have sinned.

Forgive us for we have been human beings. Pardon us, grant us atonement. Save us. Forgive us for the sins of which we are aware as well as for the sins that are unknown to us. Forgive us for we have sinned.

"You've got us coming and going, you Old Bastard,"

muttered Golem. No way out. To be human is to sin. What more do you want? There it is, an entire race of creatures begging for Your forgiveness. Well, I do not beg. I come to You as a Man. You want to forgive, forgive. If not, I will survive. None of that God's Will bullshit for me, brother. No automobile accidents attributed to Fate, no slips in the bathtub that I can blame on You. I am willing to accept Your forgiveness, but I will not beg for it. After all, it is You who created Me, isn't it?

"And for the sin which we have committed before Thee with confusion of mind."

The clincher, right? Leave me no choice and call me sinner.

Golem looked up at the bimah, the platform on which the rabbi and the cantor stood. Behind them, set against the wall, was the Ark, the Ark of the Sacred Covenant. A heavy, ornately carved-scroll decorated cabinet of dark, rich wood, behind whose plush red velvet drape and sliding wooden doors rested, covered in satin, reclined, decorated with silver breastplate and horns (horns?), lurked the fantastic twin Torahs—the absolute, nonstop, motherfucking LAW. The Word. The Answer. The Truth. Arranged so that when the cabinet was opened, the light reflected off its metallic interior and radiated out upon the faces of the congregation as if God were a heavy-handed interior decorator with the presumptions of an electrician. Get the Message? Get the Spirit!

And Golem looked at that cabinet and knew that he had no chance, knew that he was human and that he was doomed. Looked up at that cabinet and saw, carved into the wood, overlaid with 14K gold lacquer, the lamé letters which said, which saith, KNOW BEFORE WHOM THOU STANDEST.

And Golem knew.
And Golem spoke.
"Bullshit!" he said.
"Shh," somebody said.
"David! My God, what's the matter with you?"
The prayer stopped. In midsentence. The congregation turned toward him. God waited.

"What is the meaning of this interruption?" the rabbi demanded to know.

"Are you going crazy?" his mother asked.

"What the hell is going on?" someone said.

"Shh," someone said.

"Get him out of here," someone said.

"I choose," Golem said.

And he opened his jacket, whipped out the pistol, and shouted, and aimed a shot which would have put a neat hole through the O, the Big O, in THOU. Screams! Men ran toward him, but he jumped over pews, pushing old ladies and young children aside. I let go of the conscious, he said to himself as he ran toward the bimah, waving the gun in the air. I choose madness, he said as he leapt up the stairs, gesturing madly at the rabbi and the cantor, who fell back toward the Ark for Holy Protection. Yonder stands your orphan with his gun. Like Billy the Kid, the Sundance Kid, up there above the shouting, chaotic congregation, gun in hand, eyes blazing with the fierce clarity of finality. I see light, he said, as he looked down upon his people. God was waiting. "Now," he shouted like a wild evangelist, "Now, listen to the WORD. LOOK AT ME AND LISTEN TO THE WORD!"

"BANG," he shouted.

Mrs. Irving Glazer.

"BANG. BANG."

Milton Gable.

And with each "bang," the congregation became a chorus. Oh, they cried. Ah, they cried. No, they cried.

"BANG."

Karen Cohen.

"Save yourselves, goddamnit!" Golem shouted above the noise of his own turmoil. "I am the Lord, thy God! BANG." Into the air, at the Eternal Light, bulb, glass, and peace. People under the seats, trembling as if God Himself had come down to earth with the news that the Book was CLOSED. There would be no forgiveness today. "BANG." Again into the air, up toward the ceiling.

CLICK. HUMM.

FINISHED.

He dropped the gun.

Fell to his knees.

They rushed toward him. All of them.
"Look what you've made me do," he cried.
You know the rest.

THE END